THE DAUGHTER

a&b

THE DAUGHTER

LIZ WEBB

Allison & Busby Limited
11 Wardour Mews
London W1F 8AN
allisonandbusby.com

First published in Great Britain by Allison & Busby in 2022.

Copyright © 2022 by Liz Webb

A CIP catalogue record for this book is available from
the British Library.

First Edition

HB ISBN 978-0-7490-2875-6

TPB ISBN 978-0-7490-2880-0

Typeset in 11/16 pt Sabon LT Pro by
Allison & Busby Ltd.

Printed and bound by
CPI Group (UK) Ltd, Croydon, CR0 4YY

For Andy and Archie

And the Lord God commanded the man, saying,
Of every tree of the garden thou mayest freely eat:
But of the tree of the knowledge of good and evil,
thou shalt not eat of it:
for in the day that thou eatest thereof
thou shalt surely die.

Genesis 2:16–17

CHAPTER ONE

Normal people don't eat raw quince. But I sink my teeth into the smooth skin of a fat yellow specimen, and the astringency of the hard pulp floods my mouth, making me grimace. I plucked this one from the tree in Dad's front garden at around 2 a.m. last night, as I followed his stretcher to the ambulance. It's been touch and go, but Dad's stable this morning, dozing in his high, precisely made hospital bed. The view's spectacular up here on the ninth floor of University College Hospital, but Dad's oblivious. I lean my forehead on the big wrap-around corner window and fog it with a wet circle of quince spittle.

'Where's Feynman?' Dad says suddenly.

I plaster on a smile and turn to face him.

'He's at your house,' I say.

'Have you walked him?'

'Yes, I walked him round the block this morning.'

Dad nods.

9

I lift a scratched plastic cup from Dad's untouched lunch tray and position the bendy straw by his mouth.

'Where's Feynman?' Dad repeats.

'He's dead,' I mumble.

'When did he die?'

'Twenty-three years ago.'

Dad nods again.

As I replace the cup on the easy-wipe table over the bed, I glance across at the motionless old man in the bed opposite and the perspiring woman sitting beside him, sheathed in thick woolly tights, despite it being mild for September.

'Where's Feynman?' Dad repeats, yet again.

'Who's Feynman?' I snap.

'Our dog!'

'I've never heard of him.'

With this last exchange, I see panic in Dad's watery eyes. Christ. So what if we've had this same conversation ten times this morning. My brittle, bruised Dad still engages for the fifteen seconds that these conversations take place. Swiping my arm across my face leaves a watery snail's trail of my tears.

Feynman was a gorgeous golden Labrador that my brother Reece and I had when we were growing up. He was named after Dad's hero, the jovial quantum physicist Richard Feynman. Both Feynmans are long dead. Both coincidentally succumbing to kidney failure. Feynman the physicist died in 1988, his final words being that dying was boring. Watching Dad's disintegration over the last six months since I moved in with him, I can only agree wholeheartedly. For me anyway. Given Dad's goldfish mind, he's either completely unaware of his impending death or it comes as a horrible shock daily. I really hope it's the former. Reece, always my opposite, would hope for the latter.

Feynman the dog died in 1996, as a result of canine kidney failure. This was precipitated, according to our bastard of a vet, by 'poor oral hygiene', despite my religious commitment to brushing his drool-coated teeth. After Feynman was peacefully put to sleep by the vet, we held a family funeral in the garden. I wore one of the many black knee-length T-shirts I sported at fourteen as I threw Feynman's favourite (and clearly redundant) teeth-cleaning chew toy into the grave. Reece, dashing in the new designer suit that Mum had recently got him for his eighteenth, threw in a Snoop Dogg album. Dad, his hands plunged into his maroon cardigan's pockets, wept at the wrenching loss of his beloved companion. And my beautiful mum, stunning in a tight black dress, leant on Dad's shoulder for balance, as her vertiginous, red-soled stilettos sank into the grass. It all felt so traumatic at the time – but then I had no idea of the jamboree of hatred and accusations that would, just three weeks later, constitute Mum's funeral.

'How he doing?' calls Woolly Tights woman from the other side of the pristine ward, indicating Dad.

'M-mm,' I grunt, with a shake of my head, hoping that if I don't make eye contact, she'll leave me alone. Just my luck that Dad's bed is opposite the only other bed, on this fully occupied eight-bed ward, to have a visitor.

'Your dad?' she enquires.

'Mmm.'

'Dementia?'

'Mmm.'

'Just like my dad,' she says, gesturing to hers. She speaks in a heavy accent I can't place. Her dad is unresponsive, lying under a non-regulation bedspread of yellow, green and red stripes, which looks garishly out of place alongside the other seven blue-blanketed beds.

How has my vibrant, athletic dad joined this male cloister of reverie?

'Is terrible thing, dementia,' she continues, 'cuts people off.'

'Mmm.'

How many 'mmm's will it take to cut her off?

She'd be horrified if I blurted out that dementia is not in fact all bad. But it does have one dark upside for Dad: he doesn't remember much of the last twenty-three years. He's often time-travelling back to when Mum was still alive, when I collected interesting pebbles, not nervous tics, and when Reece only called Dad deranged for saying Spurs could win the league.

Anyway, Dad's got bigger problems. When the paramedics arrived at his house last night, he was spreadeagled at the bottom of the stairs, barely breathing, his left arm bent under him at an unnatural angle. This morning, I was told that he's snapped his collarbone, but he's so old they'll just let it fuse wonky; also that it's too soon to tell if his present confusion is concussion or just his regular dementia; and worst of all, though nothing to do with the fall, his doctor was surprised that, as his carer, I was unaware of Dad's advanced prostate cancer. It's beyond hope of treatment, but they've put him on morphine as they think he's in considerable pain.

'Nice pear?' enquires Woolly Tights, gesturing at the

12

quince I'm munching. She's got the same pointy nose as her unresponsive dad. They're like Mr Pointy Nose and Miss Pointy Nose in a set of Happy Families cards. I'm not part of a recognisable family set. I've inherited Dad's once-brown hair, but not his original fine features or his tight cyclist's body. I've never looked like either of my parents – not my handsome, wiry dad, nor my beautiful, willowy mum – although the pressure of hiding my shameful secrets this year has jettisoned more than half my body weight, and I'm occasionally disconcerted to catch Mum in my silhouette in a shiny shop window.

'The pear?' Woolly Tights repeats, her little white boots squeaking on the lino as she swivels towards me. 'Is juicy? I get all my fruit at market. To feel before I buy.'

'Mmm,' I respond.

'Got any more?' she asks, still upbeat despite my wall of 'mmm's.

'M-umm,' I say, shaking my head.

I've got four more in my bag, but why make her day even worse. These aren't sweet, juicy pears; these are hard, nasty quinces. Quince is usually only eaten cooked. In gooey pink jam, which no one in their right mind would choose if strawberry, raspberry or any-bloody-berry was available as an alternative. Raw quince is even more disgusting. And this is especially unpalatable as it's early season. But I've been impatiently watching these growing in Dad's front garden over the last six months, desperate for them to ripen as they remind me so much of Mum. She was a terrible cook, but every autumn she would announce 'the crops are in!', theatrically wrap a scarf around her head and make a big pantomime of 'harvesting' our quince with a wicker

13

basket. Then she'd stack them carefully for a few weeks to mellow, constantly checking, like they were fragile treasure, and finally, wearing a ridiculous frilly apron and singing along to the radio, she'd spend hours boiling them with mountains of sugar to make vats of jam.

I've no desire to produce that slimy concoction but to connect with my vibrant, larger-than-life mum I relish eating this quince raw. It makes me feel – here – in this moment: the taut skin splitting under my front teeth; the granular flesh crumbling as it rolls around my mouth like cement in a mixer; the bitter juice stinging my cracked lips and searing my dry throat. I should market this experience as a shortcut to that mindfulness crap.

'Hen,' Dad mumbles as he flails his right hand out, banging the table, spilling the water and sending shrivelled peas in all directions.

'Careful, Dad. No hens here, just me,' I say as I roll the table further down the bed so he doesn't hurt himself.

'Een,' he continues, staring at me intently.

'I don't understand, Dad. What are you saying?' I lean in, inhaling soap and gravy.

'Jen.'

Oh. This is new. I guess my weight loss has confused his poor vision.

'No, Dad, I'm not Mum. I'm Hannah. Han-nah.'

'Sorry,' he rasps.

'It's OK, you don't need to—'

'I'm so sorry, Jen,' he says, reaching for me. I jerk away, unnerved that he's touching me as if I'm Mum. But as a loosened tendril of my hair flicks across my face, I realise it's the longest it's ever been. Mum's length. I had a short brown bob as a child, razored it army-short after Mum's death and then rattled through shaved, permed, green, blue and spiky tiger stripes as I tried to get a grip on my spiralling life with drastic rebranding. But since embracing the course of least resistance, I've got a brown version of Mum's long blonde hair. Combined with my pronounced weight loss, it's clearly working like a Mento sweet dropping into the Diet Coke of Dad's mind, foaming out a splurge of locked-in memories.

'Sorry for what?' I murmur. Flattered that Dad could possibly mistake nervous, twitchy me for my confident, charismatic mum, I momentarily indulge the outlandish idea and my usually hunched stance softens into her loose-limbed ease. Moving like her, whilst simultaneously inhaling the exotic scent of quince coming from my bag, sparks an intense visceral memory of Mum feeding Dad some of her quince jam with one of her little ornate crested spoons. He'd laughed and inadvertently spat some out, making her throw back her head, her long blonde hair flying out and her high-pitched laugh exploding out of her, sounding like a yelping fox. Reece and I had rolled our eyes at her antics, but she'd kept on spooning the jam into our spluttering dad like she was a busty, disapproving matron doling out medicine. Soon all of us were crying with laughter, clutching ourselves and begging her to stop.

I miss her antics. Miss the way she ignited a room. Miss who I used to be around her. Time hasn't healed me. It's just hardened me.

'Aaagh,' cries Dad. His thin lips part, his tiny pupils expand into black counters, and the trace of colour in his cheeks washes away to grey clamminess.

I gently pat his good shoulder, feeling his birdlike frame under his worn striped pyjamas.

'It's OK, Dad, everything's OK.'

He breaks into a broad smile.

Except it isn't a smile.

It's a grimace. His thin skin stretches taut around his open mouth; his yellow teeth bare; his tongue sticks out, pointy and reptilian.

Thoughts of Mum have induced a heart attack.

'Help, please help us,' I shout.

But as I step away, his right arm shoots out and he grabs my upper arm with uncanny force. His ragged fingernails scratch me as he lurches up, spittle dripping down his chin, and as he rises, I'm simultaneously yanked towards him and our foreheads clash. The searing pain makes me lose my footing, and I collapse onto the bed, jarring my elbows. I try to right myself, but Dad's pushing down on me, his nails ripping into my arm.

'Jen,' he pleads.

'Stop it, Dad,' I beg, struggling to stand and twisting to try to loosen his grasp.

'Are you OK?' calls Woolly Tights, rising from her seat in alarm.

'Get help,' I call and she rushes down the ward.

As I stand, I lift Dad with me, forcing my fingers under his, trying not to hurt him, but he scrabbles them back on.

'I'm so sorry, Jen,' he whispers, his lips brushing my ear, his sour breath on my neck. 'I didn't mean to.' He twists his head so I'm eyeball to eyeball with his wide, staring eyes.

'Didn't mean to what?' I cry, still scrabbling to loosen his rigid grip.

'To—'

But before he can say another word, I finally succeed in unlatching all his fingers simultaneously and he collapses onto the bed. I stagger back, struggling for breath and clutching my throbbing arm, blood oozing between my fingers.

'I'm Hannah, Dad,' I sob, 'I'm your daughter. Mum's . . . not here.'

Woolly Tights is shouting in the distance.

Dad's lying motionless across the bed, staring up at the ceiling, as if the last minute never happened.

But it did.

He thought he was talking to Mum and he begged for her forgiveness. That could be forgiveness for anything – for not putting the bins out, an argument, even an affair – but the rigid dam in my mind is cracking and memories are cascading through the crumbling barricades: looking at Dad's scrawny legs, I remember when they were muscular and fast; staring at his mottled gnarled hands, I remember them broad and powerful; and raising my tear-hazed sight to the purple vein snaking across his right temple, I remember it livid and pulsing, at moments of exertion – or anger.

I lean in and whisper the question I have never let myself utter in twenty-three years.

'Dad, did you murder Mum?'

CHAPTER TWO

'Hannah Davidson?' says a sharp voice behind me.

'Yes?' I say, twisting round. It's a slim, middle-aged woman with a blonde bob and that not-there-but-there make-up sheening her face. Woolly Tights must have called her to help me. But she doesn't look like a nurse – with her pencil skirt and her beige silky shirt that seems formal, but is casually sexy in the way it lolls across her chest. Perhaps she's a consultant.

'Thank you, but he's fine now,' I say, trying to slow my breathing.

'Could I have a word, Ms Davidson?' Her eyes flick to Dad lying half off the bed.

'We're OK, honestly,' I say, settling Dad back onto his pillows. How much of that did she see?

'I need to talk to you in private,' she continues, her eyes darting to my bleeding arm. 'Please could you follow me.' Not a question – an order.

'But why?'

She gives a half-smile, like a baby pooing. 'This way,' she says, walking off.

I'm thirty-seven, but feel like a kid called by the headmistress. I pull on my shapeless grey sweatshirt to cover my arm, hitch up my cartoonishly loose jeans and shove my feet into my trainers, not getting the heels fully in, so that I have to shuffle awkwardly after her clicking beige shoes.

I glance back at poor Dad. Why did I suddenly doubt him? He's already asleep on his hill of pillows, looking like a warped version of 'The Princess and the Pea'. Unlike that fragile princess, I have no pea-of-doubt bruising me. Dad's befuddled sorry to 'Mum' momentarily sparked my hungover brain to spiral, but I know Dad's innocent – every cell, every atom, every particle in me thrums with certainty.

Ms Beige-heels has entered the small room by the nurses' station. I clocked it before – a 'bad news' room. Oh God, she is a consultant – with awful news. It's Friday the thirteenth: of course it's happening today. I follow her into the scrupulously tidy little room. She sits down at the desk.

'Take a seat,' she says briskly, gesturing to a grey plastic chair. The door has swung in behind us, but she reaches over and pulls it firmly to engage the latch.

'So, your father is Philip Davidson?'

I nod. This is it. And it's not the dying-lite Dad's been doing recently. This is the full-fat version. Now Dad and his kind brown eyes, his awkward glancing kisses, and the way he dances exuberantly, making castanet motions, will all be burnt in a box. Like Mum. Everything around me is very defined: the screen and keyboard precisely perpendicular; the zigzag of the white anglepoise light; the grooves between the durable grey carpet tiles. This is the final moment before no going back. Five, four, three—

'So, Ms Davidson, in the case of an injury like your father's, when concerns are raised—'

I jerk my head up. 'What?'

Her face is a mask of non-reaction.

'—it is hospital protocol to consider the domestic situation. The paramedics who accompanied your father noted that you seemed' – she checks her notes – 'confused.' Her matt-beige lips part slightly as she tilts her head.

'Me? No.'

'Confused and' – she glances down – 'disorientated.'

'Well, it was the middle of the night, so I guess I was a bit spaced.'

She scribbles in her file with her glossy maroon fountain pen. I shift on my hard seat.

'And it says here you smelt of alcohol?'

'No! Well, I'd had a few drinks earlier.'

She scribbles.

'But that's not illegal.' My voice is too loud.

'And you told the paramedics that you "found" your father at the base of the stairs.'

I cough and thump my chest.

'Would you like some water?'

I nod and she pours me a glass. I gulp it down and take a breath.

'I didn't "find" my father – I found him. At the bottom of the stairs. Where he'd fallen.' Wakey, wakey, Hannah, this is formal, with real consequences.

'It's hospital policy to follow up domestic injuries, if a

20

flag is raised,' she says, arching a stylishly plucked eyebrow, 'in order to rule out elder abuse. I'm sure you understand that protocols must be followed.'

I nod, trying not to look bug-eyed with panic.

'But I'm here to consider both the safety of the patient and the needs of the carer. Could you explain your father's living situation?'

Boy, she's got this 'not engaging' thing down to a tee. But maybe she's right to talk to me. Perhaps my chaos has bled into Dad's real world. Certainly, none of this would have happened if good old Reece had been in charge – and painful though thinking of him is, to combat this beige threat, I try to summon Reece's swagger.

'I live with my dad at the moment,' I say slowly. Since moving back to London, away from my Brighton doctor's prescriptions of antidepressants, my mind spirals at the best of times but under stress like this I'm on a roller coaster. So, remembering Reece teaching me to combat carsickness by focusing on a spot in the distance, I stare at two indents in the grey tiled carpet. 'His health has declined gradually and I'd arranged carers for the last year but he was struggling – remembering stuff, getting about, looking after himself.'

'U-huum,' she says, giving me enough 'time to explain' slash 'rope to hang myself with'.

Reece said he got into Cambridge with eye contact and selling himself, so I look straight at her and fillet my recent life story to present the best cut.

'Dad needed me. So six months ago I gave up my home in Brighton, left my job and moved in full-time to care for him,' I say, blinking past my glaring omissions. 'I know Dad's been avoiding the doctor, but he kept saying

21

everything was OK. I can't believe I didn't know about the prostate cancer.'

'So, talk me through exactly what happened last night.'

'Well, it was all the usual, we went up at the usual time, he had water by the bed, had a commode and he always calls me if he needs anything. I sleep directly above him and keep all the doors open. He's never wandered at night before – I have no idea why he did last night.'

She nods, then I catch her eyes flicking to her watch. She wants to get on. 'Believable detail,' Reece whispered to me as we blamed our dog Feynman for eating the end of the banana cake Dad had just made.

'Dad probably fell over the cat,' I say. 'He's got this ancient cat called Schro, who literally sticks himself to your legs every step you take – I've nearly fallen over him loads of times.'

She half-smiles. Is the beige tide turning?

'I came downstairs to get some water in the middle of the night and found Dad at the bottom of the stairs – I guess I was pretty stressed when the paramedics got there, I thought he was dead.' Reece cried on cue on finding Juliet's dead body in his sixth-form *Romeo and Juliet*, by plucking nose hair. As Ms Beige looks down, I swiftly pincer my nails and rip. Christ.

'Would you like a tissue?' Ms Beige asks with concern as she looks up, handing me a nearby box.

'Thanks.' What's wrong with me, that I'm having to injure myself to evoke emotions I actually feel?

'It can be hard adjusting to the role of carer,' she says. 'You should seek advice from our care team – if your father returns home.'

If?

'I can give you leaflets about the care that's available.'

'Thanks.' The energy has definitely tilted. I'm forms and hassle for her if she stays on the attack. I'll be out of here soon.

'Do you have any family,' she asks, 'siblings?'

'No.' I grip the metal edge of the chair.

'Oh?' she says, tilting her head as frown lines bunch the flaky beige patch of skin between her eyes. Can she check this?

'Oh, yes, sorry,' I say, burping out a strangled laugh, 'I do technically have a brother, as in, I have a brother – but, we're not close.' Understatement of the millennium.

'It's a lot to handle alone. Surely your brother would help out in the circumstances?'

'I'm sure he would.' Ha.

'If your dad returns home, he'll require round-the-clock care. And eventually—' We both pause, solemnly being adults, silently noting the unsaid imminent eventuality. 'I see nobody's taken over power of attorney?' she says, checking her notes. 'The hospital didn't need permission for emergency treatment last night, but there'll be more decisions coming up about' – she does her momentary pause for effect again and I want to cuff the back of her head to knock out the words – 'whether to intervene medically in the future. Given his rapidly declining health, it would be prudent for you and your brother to organise that.'

She passes me a folded leaflet headed 'Power of Attorney' above a photo of a woman smiling down at her aged relative as she passes him a cup of tea, but with a glint in her eye as if to say: 'Sip that tea carefully, cos now I make all your medical and financial decisions and if you choke, I'm letting you snuff it in front of me to get to your cash'.

'You should talk to your brother.'

Haven't seen him in the flesh for fifteen years.

'Your other family.'

Nope.

'And your wider social circle.'

Social what?

'People say "it takes a village to raise a child", but it also takes a village to help people die.'

But what if your dad's the witch who's been ejected from the village?

'You don't have to face this alone, you know. Most people are fundamentally well meaning.'

Are they really! Well lucky-plucky-you to have had a life that lets you state that as a fact.

'Do you have a partner who can help you?'

'Oh yes,' *lie*, 'and friends,' *lie*, 'honestly I'm fine,' *lie*. 'I need to reach out more I guess.' *Ugh*.

She smiles. My words seem to be the right shapes for the holes in her block of expectation.

'And you intend to stay at your father's?'

'Of course.' Where else can I go, after the mess I've made of my life. 'For as long as – he needs me.'

We make eye contact. Fuck these knowing looks. *I'm a child*, I want to scream, *can't you see I'm faking all this adult composure. How are you going along with me?* But the bubble of her spirit level has centred itself. She can tick her box, submit her file and have done with me.

'OK,' she says after a final scribble. 'Given that there've been no prior incidents and you seem to have an awareness of your situation, I won't be escalating as long as there are no further concerns.'

'There won't be. Honestly. This has been a wake-up call for me to seek more help,' I say with fake-humble warmth.

We shake hands.

I hope she's slammed by a speeding lorry as she totters too slowly across the road on those beige heels.

I take the lift down to the hospital shop, where I buy a multipack of breath-disguising extra-strong mints.

CHAPTER THREE

'And up we pop.'

As I walk back to him, Dad's being enthusiastically encouraged out of bed by a young nurse with short black pigtails, whose badge reads 'Valeria'. She's got the covers back and is lifting his legs to the floor.

'We're doing very well, Mr Davidson,' she trills.

I feel I should do something, but I just watch helplessly, like they're enacting a film: Valeria flourishes her hand with the enthusiasm of a Russian inviting their lover for a sleigh ride, but Dad stares beyond her like Dr Zhivago inscrutably assessing the snowy Russian hills. Then they channel hop to Laurel and Hardy: she pulls him up to sitting, the instant she lets go he falls back flailing theatrically, and she makes a 'doh' face; and again: she pulls him up, lets go, he falls back, 'doh'; and again. Final channel hop to a Bergman film: she sighs and looks at the wall, ignoring Dad who has slumped face down on the bed, his skinny nakedness visible through the back of the loosely tied gown, a crusty smear of shit dried on his left thigh. Jesus.

'We'll try again later,' she says brightly, helping him back into bed, then striding off. The white plastic squeaks as I settle into the high-backed patient chair, chewing my extra-strong mints, crumbling the nose-clearing white chalk two at a time. Dad mistaking me for Mum makes me feel like she's hovering inside me, looking at him through me – tutting that he's let himself go, that his hair's too long and straggly and that he needs to shave those uneven white hairs on his chin. Mum adored clothes and preening and she was always buying natty new stuff for Dad and fussing with him. Since her death, I doubt he's bought a single new piece of clothing, he's completely avoided the barber and cut his own hair, and he's never again had one of those professional wet shaves that he used to love.

'All right, Dad?'

He's looking at me, but who is he seeing? His freaky new response to me as if I were Mum was so unnerving. Surely it was just a singular synaptic malfunction? I don't think Dad's ever confused us before, but we've been coexisting in such a blur. I've watched helplessly as he's slipped further and further away from the present these past six interminable months, since I moved back in with him, into what was once our family home. When we were a family. Since he'd only eat small meals like spaghetti rings or cereal, I'd given up serving much else. I tried to get him to walk, but he refused point blank. I tried to get him to the doctor but he said he was fine, never told me about any pain. I'd just gone along with it all, drinking to blank off. I'm a joke, not in any way a fit adult for this responsibility.

I'm so far out of my depth with my lovely, time-travelling, shit-stained, dying dad. I am exhausted by what a pathetic cliché I've become, my anger at Ms Beige being so obviously my own fear and panic reflected outwards. She's right. I do need help. But I don't know anyone in London, haven't done for years.

Except for Reece.

These last six months, I've debated whether to make contact with him again, so he could see Dad before he dies. Perhaps Reece's disdain for Dad might have dulled by now, I thought, as I kidded myself that I could orchestrate a Netflix-worthy deathbed reconciliation. At the very least, I reckoned I would have to get him to the funeral so that we will have stood side by side at both parental incinerations. But I've dithered and avoided and obliterated the thought in alcohol and endless Netflix and Amazon Prime.

Is it finally time to face him?

There is the slight problem that I don't have Reece's phone number, email or address. I've had no way of contacting him for fifteen years. When my curiosity did occasionally get the better of me, I easily discovered what he was doing via Twitter, Instagram, Facebook, the press, or fan sites – because my brother, who I called Reece Davidson for fourteen years, is in fact the actor Ryan Patterson. So far, he hasn't been famous enough for anyone to join the dots. He changed his name by deed poll at university, telling me it was a better stage name, but I knew he wanted to reinvent himself, to throw off any connection with our infamous family. I know his breakfast routine (hot water with lemon, run, green protein juice), his political beliefs (Labour centrist) and the part of his body he likes least (hairy feet), but I don't actually know him any more. He has an ever-expanding Wikipedia page detailing his career. Normally I'm annoyed by the omission of a personal tab – the absence of all those juicy details of cheating, failed marriages, bankruptcy and bizarre crimes – but in Reece's case, I'm relieved.

But then just after I moved in with Dad, I was at the supermarket till, waiting to pay for our cereals and spaghetti rings, when I registered a side panel on the front of the newspaper in the rack before me, with Reece's photo. The poisonous rag was serialising some puff-piece autobiography he'd written about how wonderful it was to be him, calling it 'Solving Me', like he was some fascinating puzzle. I already had a deep loathing for the tabloids after how they treated us, and now Reece was publishing his celeb drivel in the newspaper that had skewered Dad most grotesquely as a murderer. I didn't waste my money and vowed to avoid all media references to him, which wasn't hard as Dad and I descended into our insular domestic routine. But while I could block out the present 'Ryan', I always have the past Reece rolling around my mind, however much I drink.

I grew up alongside him for the first fourteen years of my life in a regular boring family. Then Mum was murdered on Friday 4th October 1996, the day before Reece, four years older than me, was due to leave to take up his place at Cambridge. In the following weeks, Reece and I morphed from emotionally conjoined siblings – to strangers. I knew that my lovely dad had nothing to do with Mum's death. Reece, primed by his already tense relationship with Dad and pumped up by teenage hormones and seismic grief for his beloved mum, had his thoughts fatally skewed by the outlandish press accusations about Dad. He decided that he 'knew' Dad was guilty. Neither of us could prove our certainty. Then, two weeks later, the day after Mum's funeral, Reece left for university. And never came home or spoke to Dad again.

Reece (I can't call him Ryan, cos that's not his name and it makes him sound like an American secret service agent, bodyguard to the President) kept in occasional contact with me as I watched his professional rise: he was in the Cambridge Footlights (the good-looking butt of the jokes of a group of future comedy stars); he did regional theatre (classics, farces, edgy new writing); he worked for a spell at the RSC (with a highly revered Iago in an Othello set on an Israeli army base); he landed a small role in *Emmerdale* (young farmer trying to find a wife), and a sidekick role in an edgy British film that did unexpectedly well on Netflix release (undercover policeman seducing eco-terrorists). His increasing fame had me worried.

Meanwhile, I sleepwalked through four years of barrel-scraping GCSEs and thin-ice-skating A levels, going up three dress sizes as I blanked my grief and Reece's accusations with Tunnock's Teacakes, Wagon Wheels, Pop-Tarts, Yoyos and Iced Gems, burning acrid holes in my clothes by sitting too close to fires as I could never get warm enough, however thick the layer of flesh I encased myself in. I was endlessly tortured on the rack of my family – on one end was my destroyed dad who I knew was innocent, and on the other, my belligerent brother, vehement that Dad was guilty. With one person I loved murdered and the other two people I loved hating each other, it became excruciating to think, to feel, to even function. I was a seriously fucked-up Goldilocks: Mother Bear was dead and Baby Bear hated Daddy Bear – nothing could feel 'just right' ever again.

I applied to the University of Brighton because Mum and Dad had honeymooned there, and I thought I might be able to 'find myself' in a different place. Of course, I couldn't escape being me, but there I did discover that alcohol was an infinitely more efficient brain-wipe than food. Not only did it erase pain, it actively promoted pleasure, albeit with a pesky hangover payback, rendering study laughably pointless and alienating my so-called friends. I dropped out in my first year, but stayed on in Brighton to continue my early morning swims round the pier in the rough sea, revelling in the peace of the freezing, life-threatening buffeting. I topped off the anaesthesia of food, alcohol and dangerous swimming with a busy job single-handedly running a stationery shop in The Lanes called 'Write to Life', living in the low-ceilinged bedsit above, and got into a safe routine: six days a week busy at the shop, drinking slowly in the evenings, one day a week blind drunk. I was efficient and numb. It felt safe, but infinitely fragile. I could not let my pattern be disturbed, except for one day a month when I visited Dad in London in the dusty memory-laden 'house that stood still'. As a tidiness freak, I was appalled, but for Dad to change anything would have been for him to move on without Mum.

'You're looking so well,' Dad would say during my visits, my cheeks flushed from vomiting outside the front door.

'Any news of Reece?' he'd ask coyly as if as a vague

afterthought; but I saw the pathetic hope in his eyes.

'He's good, Dad, just very busy.'

And he would nod, his eyes sparking at the thought of his worthless prodigal son. What an inexplicably dumb parable that is – joy at the return of the deadbeat sibling and ignoring the stay-at-home patsy. But Dad never got to kill the fatted calf for Reece, because he never came home, rigid in his certainty of Dad's guilt. But I knew, riven through me like a message in a stick of Brighton rock, that my lovely dad was innocent.

Reece and I kept up a tenuous link for the first eight years after Mum's death: the odd meet-up (not talking about Dad), the occasional phone call (short with long pauses), texts on birthdays (mine and Mum's, never Dad's) and Christmas presents (his shop-wrapped with a generic message in a generic card). Our meetings got more and more spaced out, with me endlessly analysing the delicate power play between us.

Reece gained a bit of a cult following for his supporting role in the ITV series *Man On*, about a League Two football team with dreams of the Premier League. He was the team physio, playing his charming athletic self: rushing onto the pitch to resuscitate a young player having a cardiac arrest; attending a gay club with a player too scared to come out; helping an older player accept the end of his career and transition into TV punditry. The first series had just aired when I saw him for the very last time, fifteen years ago. Meeting Reece was always hard: with each year I became fatter, sadder and more reclusive, whereas, as if we were on a cosmic see-saw, he become slimmer, happier and more famous.

I hated breaking out of my safe marble-run existence, but Reece 'only had a brief window', so I hunkered down in the train to Victoria and followed Google Maps to Bar Italia in Soho. We sat on high rotating stools at the long thin counter, the walls awash with Italian cycling magazines. His dark brown eyes were bright, his curly brown hair especially long like some Spanish gigolo, and his jeans were rolled up pretentiously with no socks in his loafers, making him look louche and European, and simultaneously like a big kid. I caught my reflection in a mirror – hooded eyes, fleshy cheeks and heavy jowls, my generous flesh encased in taut layers of black lace, my short blue-black hair slicked from my plump face, black lines round my eyes, and dark purple lipstick against my white pallor. I was not the brooding, fascinating outsider I imagined myself to be, but a twitchy fat goth, only too aware of the irony of Reece's childhood name for me being 'the itty bit'. Reece had a double espresso in a little white cup; I had a latte with an extra shot in a tall glass with a tiny handle.

'How's life in Brighton?' he asked after knocking back the espresso in one gulp, trying not to stare at how much extra weight I'd slathered on since our last meet.

'The shop's doing well.'

'You're still there!'

'Yep,' I said, arranging the sugar packets to face the same way, 'I'm the manager now.'

'Hey, if you're happy in the mecca of coloured pencils and Hello Kitty rubbers.'

'Deliriously. And you? Haaappy?'

'I guess. We're waiting to see if we get a second series of *Man On*. Which we should do, given the reviews.'

I straightened up the serviettes in the silver dispenser and girded myself.

'Reece, we have to talk about Dad.'

'No.'

'But he's virtually housebound now.'

He shrugged. 'Appropriate, since he never went to prison for killing Mum.'

'You have zero proof of that,' I hissed, slopping my coffee.

'Lack of evidence doesn't prove innocence. He did it or he drove her to it with his angry outbursts.'

'That's ridiculous. I totally don't recognise your description of him.'

'What is the point of going round and round again? Do you ever feel better after?'

He slid off his stool and I thought he was leaving, but he returned with another espresso.

'Did you like *Man On*?' he asked, as if we were just doing chit-chat.

'Didn't see it,' I lied to annoy him.

'Well, it got four stars in the *Guardian*,' he said petulantly.

'Not five?' I said, in mock horror.

'No one gets five.'

'Then why do they have five?'

'An impossibility to aspire to? Not that you . . .'

'What?'

'Forget it.'

We both sat silently.

'You know, I should have cake!' I announced, swinging violently round to glower at the array of cakes in the body

34

of the old-fashioned counter behind us: gooey cheesecakes, stacked gateaux, stuffed cannoli. 'And if I have a heart attack from overeating, you can resuscitate me, like you did that footballer in the trailer!'

'I could resuscitate you actually, I got proper training from a real physio for authenticity.'

'Could or would?' I said, narrowing my eyes at him.

'Oh whatever,' he snapped, 'I'm trying here.'

'I'm not *not* trying,' I said, shifting my bulk on the ridiculous seat.

'You're just so . . .'

'What?'

'Nothing.'

'Go on. Say it. I'm what?' I lifted my spoon and flicked his knuckle.

'Ow,' he cried, rubbing his hand. 'OK. Self-involved. You're so self-involved. If you looked around outside of yourself for just two seconds and took part in the real world, you'd be so much happier.'

'Real world!' I spat at him. 'That's rich coming from you – Ryan!'

He winced.

'Not only do you have a fake name, but your job is actually faking being other people.'

He sucked in a sharp intake of breath, then reassembled his composure like the *Terminator 2* cop reforming from a silver puddle.

'Don't make a scene,' he said, glancing round. 'I really don't need this. You have no idea the pressure I'm under.'

'Sorry,' I mumbled. We were back in our roles. He was the star, I was the audience, heckling was forbidden. I turned his cup so its handle was in line with my handle and with the metal serviette dispenser.

'You like everything just so, don't you,' he said, 'tidy, tidy, everything the same, God forbid life should move forward.'

He lifted one of my parallel spoons to rap my hand but I pulled away just in time, so he threw the spoon down, messing up my pattern.

And that was it. I was so angry I didn't make contact for a couple of months. Then I left the occasional chirpy message on his answerphone, which didn't get returned; then I sent texts, but they pinged out into the air, unanswered; then his mobile went dead; then my emails bounced back. Finally, I posted an old-fashioned letter, after carefully crafting multiple drafts and weighing up every word. It was returned marked 'Not Known at this Address'. And I finally got it. There was no carefully balanced power play between us. I was the only one endlessly analysing our relationship. He wasn't even thinking of me. He'd moved on. From Mum's death. From Dad, who he blamed for Mum's death. And from me, the last reminder.

I've tried not to check out what he's doing over the years, unless I'm especially drunk, but proof of his existence was easy to access: low-budget film trailers, Christmas lights pressing in Slough, pulling impressive muffins from an oven with other C-listers on *Celebrity MasterChef*, skits for Comic Relief with his more famous comedy friends, and even reading to kids on bloody *Jackanory*. I even know where he is tonight. With that awful synchronicity of thinking of something then seeing it everywhere, I picked up a discarded *Evening Standard* from a visitor's chair as I left the beige inquisitor's office – and there he was in the Culture section: *Solving Me*, which was previously serialised in the paper, is now being forced on the world in book form. He's doing a reading at 9.30 p.m. tonight at Foyles, just down the road from the hospital. So near and yet so far. I skim the newspaper copy, which babbles on about how fabulous Reece is. Then I jolt as I read the final line, a direct quote from Reece: 'Like a beginner solving a Rubik's cube, I've only ever shown one completed layer of myself to the public, but with this book, I'm taking my fans backstage to solve the whole puzzle.' That pretentious, thieving git. I was the one who excelled at solving Rubik's cubes when we were kids, despite being four years younger, and Reece always ridiculed my skill.

'Look at this,' he once said, smiling impishly and holding out a cube with the top layer completed, but covering up the lower mixed sections. 'Done it.'

'But the cube's not complete,' I bleated. 'You have to follow all the steps to solve it.' He laughed and tossed it aside.

Reece was gleeful when he caught me secretly finishing it later. 'You couldn't bear to leave it unfinished, could you? Had to "follow all the steps to solve it",' he joked. 'You're an itty bit crazy.'

I jolt back into the present of the immaculate white ward, registering a hand on my shoulder, which I violently swat away.

'Sorry – didn't mean to scare you,' says Woolly Tights, backing away. 'Is home time.'

She's looking at me as if I'm . . . dangerous. What's wrong with me?

'Oh, OK,' I cough. After three packets of extra-strong mints, my throat's horribly dry.

She turns, but I catch her arm. Her eyes widen in panic. 'Thanks for letting me know,' I falter out.

She nods, frowning, and I let go of her.

'Hi, I'm Hannah. Sorry I've been so quiet.' I feel like my skin is cracking with the effort of basic decency.

'Is OK. Is so hard. I understand,' she says, offering her hand. 'I'm Loreta.'

'Hi, Loreta. I . . . I like all the colour you've got going on over there,' I say, gesturing to the non-regulation multicoloured blanket over her dad.

'Thank you. Is our Lithuanian flag,' she says, 'to remind him of home.'

Of course: the bedspread's one giant flag of mustard yellow, school-skirt green and brick red.

'Nice idea.'

She smiles, and the simple human connection is overwhelming.

'I didn't want to wake you,' she apologises, 'but is eight o'clock, time for home.'

'Oh, gosh, I have to go,' I say, giving Dad a quick kiss and willing him to survive the night.

'Hot date?' she asks.

'No. I'm off to see a film star.'

CHAPTER FOUR

It's been fifteen years, but Tottenham Court Road's still all furniture shops: puffy comfy chairs, sleek minimalist desks, black Balinese chests, formal Regency beds, and huge geometric lights; so many ways to furnish a home, if I had one. Dad's home isn't mine any more – it's a historical exhibit and I'm the scary wax doll propped up amid the detritus of Reece's and my childhood.

I'll just hunker down at the back of his reading and see whether I can face going to him for help. He'll never know I'm there and he wouldn't recognise me anyway: I'm fifteen years older and rougher, he only knows me with short hair, and best of all, I'm inadvertently some kind of 'after' of a slimming magazine's 'before'. But without any of that teeth-jangling grinning the 'after's do, as I don't feel better thinner, just less moored. My drastic weight loss has changed not just my size, but the whole structure of my face and the proportions of my features. I'd already dropped four stone over the last six months in Brighton, with all the stress of my imploding life and my increased drinking, and since being back home I've joined Dad in barely eating and had frequent stomach ache and diarrhoea from the truckloads of fruit I've been gorging on. I've been copying Mum's fruit obsession, but in my own feral way. She loved making a ceremony out of eating it, nibbling on thinly sliced Granny Smiths, sensuously swallowing elegant depulped globules of orange and licking her delicate pink quince jam from her tiny spoons.

I'm far less refined in my fruit annihilation, hoovering up mountains of unwashed, unchopped fruit, but I'm slim for the first time in my life – the perfect disguise.

At a Tesco Metro, I buy a small bottle of vodka. In the next-door chemist's window, I see rows of severed heads topped with multicoloured wigs and buy a blonde one and some large-framed dark glasses. I'm embracing the role of Extra Number Three, a non-speaking part, for which the directions are: 'blend into the crowd and actively don't stand out'. It's a role I've been perfecting for years.

As I reach the intersection of Tottenham Court Road and Oxford Street, rain falls like a sky-sized bath has been upturned. I run on down the road, searching for the familiar doors of Foyles. But as I arrive at the corner where the shop is, I'm in *The Matrix*. It's not there. Literally not there. How is Reece having a reading at a non-existent shop? Looking up and down the street through the sheeting rain, I catch the familiar glowing red letters of the vertical Foyles sign, but further up the road than it should be. The big solid there-for-ever building that I visited as a child has somehow floated up the road. I walk on in a daze and stand in front of not the old heavy doors of my memory, but sleek sliding panes of glass which swish open to present an endless wall-free savannah of books, all surrounding a central glass core. It's a completely new shop. I expect the whole thing to shimmer into a sea of binary code at any moment.

I back out, and look up at the rain-drenched window. And there's Reece, less than a foot away, smiling at me with his famous lopsided smirk. I stumble backwards off the kerb and a car screeches to a halt inches from me. I lurch back onto the pavement, but Reece seems totally unfazed. How can he not even register my existence?

Then a young woman picks him up. He's a life-size cardboard cut-out. As she repositions him, I step closer. After fifteen years, he's the same, but more defined – his brown mischievous eyes, his narrow straight nose, his thick eyebrows and his mop of dark curls. But his smile is crafted into a curious lopsided grin; he never smiled like that as a kid. His body is so languid, like he should be smoking a long cigarette in a Madrid square. He's wearing a soft loose blue suit, slightly over-shortened at the ankle, and a pale pink shirt, the top two buttons undone. He's much taller and broader than Dad, less wiry, but has his dark hair. His real charm comes from Mum, that effortless ease and fluidity – and those intense eyes. But it's his familiar boyish hunch that jolts me – that tiny rounding of his shoulders, that jutting of his chin and pitching forward of his weight – that brings all my memories viscerally alive. In an instant, I'm his little sister again, a 'me' I thought had been totally erased.

It was good to get a dry run at seeing him, given

my slack-jawed amazement. I'm usually shellacked to numbness – but this reminds me that I'm only ever a pigeon-step away from losing it. I step back in through the sliding doors and approach a tall sales assistant wearing a paisley waistcoat.

'Hi, umm, the Reece – Ryan Patterson reading later?' I ask nonchalantly.

'Just join the conga line,' he says, gesturing at a queue of women snaking up the inner glass staircase.

'Oh, OK. Is there a toilet here?'

'Fourth floor.'

I walk up, appalled to be lumped in with all these excited middle-aged fans. Yet of course my body is middle-aged, however childish I feel. I don my long blonde wig, and in the toilet's stark mirror see an ageing version of that Thor actor from the Marvel films – well, him if he had a drink problem, after years in brutal captivity. Christ. I pull up my coat collar, ram on my dark glasses and have a big swig of vodka. I join the end of the queue, behind a grey-haired woman in a purple padded jacket, who is clutching Reece's book to her bosom.

'Exciting, isn't it?' she gushes.

'So is,' I say.

'I've seen him live several times – at recordings of *Man On* at Pinewood.'

'Awesome.'

'Of course, *Muerte* is filmed in Spain with no studio audience. It's filmed, "on film",' she says with awe.

The cherry on the icing of the many-layered cake that is Reece's career is that he's finally got a lead role, playing a bloody detective: Ralph Pennington, in a new BBC series called *Muerte* (Spanish for 'death'; bet those execs took the rest of the day off when they came up with that corker), a light drama about murders in the expat community in Spain. The show's credits have an annoyingly memorable jingle over a montage of Reece prancing about in various clichéd Spanish settings: riding bareback on a palm-treed Spanish beach; dressed as a matador outrunning a bull; disrupting a stage of shocked flamenco dancers. It finishes with a shot of a manila file being stamped 'RESUELTO'. If you were making up a ridiculous comedy version of a language, that's how you'd translate 'solved', but that actually is the Spanish for it.

It's a long hour's wait. I pop back to the loo a couple of times for more vodka. My padded compatriot gets into conversation with other fans and it's so weird hearing about Reece as they know him – his shows, his skits for Comic Relief, his Twitter posts, his girlfriends. They giggle over a celeb questionnaire by him:

Who do you most love?

'My dog, Baxter.'

Not me then? Or Dad?

What trait do you most dislike about yourself?

'Being a perfectionist.'

So not breaking your father's heart . . . pretending you don't have a sister.

If you could change one thing about your life, what would it be?

'How can you improve on perfection?'

Oh, I don't know – you could get back in contact with your estranged family maybe, you arse.

Amongst these adoring fans, I experience how worryingly

43

famous Reece is becoming. He's a real person – writ large. I'm a troll under a bridge.

Finally, we file up the polished wooden stairs into a big industrial-looking loft, with a low ceiling festooned with snaking silver pipes and overlapping electric cables. An elfin girl in a short black tunic is taking tickets.

'Oh, I didn't realise it was ticketed,' I say.

'You're lucky – I've just had a return,' she says. 'This sold out in minutes – Ryan's like Glastonbury!'

I swallow.

My padded friend dashes to a seat at the front while I hunker down at the back, taking a surreptitious swig of vodka. There are images of Reece everywhere with the glossy red background of the book cover: two more cardboard cut-outs, a huge projected image behind the stage, and on two large vertical banners either side of a table piled high with books. Red may be the colour of blood, but Dad would be disgusted by this nod to Arsenal.

There is a palpable, simmering anticipation. Eventually a slightly hunched middle-aged man with tastefully shaved receding hair steps out of a white door to the left and onto the painted pallet stage.

'Hello – if I could have your attention,' he says into his handheld microphone. The festering excitement calms. 'Thank you. I'm Alex Canning, book critic for the *Guardian*, and I'll be interviewing Mr Patterson after he's done a short reading from his book *Solving Me*.'

Cue excited whoop.

'Mr Patterson is well known as an actor but it is a pleasure to introduce to you his fascinating, often funny, and also highly moving autobiography, which has been a revelation to us all. Without further ado, I give you, Ryan Patterson.'

Cue wild applause.

The plain white door opens and out steps Reece.

CHAPTER FIVE

Reece is so crushingly familiar to me. I should be tickling his feet to see if he can last longer than me before laughing. He's wearing his trademark overly turned-up jeans, a crumpled linen jacket and weathered posh shoes, with no socks. He's even slimmer than usual, with model-cheekbones sharpening his beauty. I know that lolloping gait so well. He's entered with a woman with ironed-blonde hair who takes a seat at the book table. He flashes his boyish smile as I sink lower in my seat. Coming here was an astoundingly awful idea.

He raises his hand self-deprecatingly to quell the clapping.

The audience is rapt.

'Hi,' he says coquettishly, giving his strange, brooding half-smile. 'It's a real honour to be here. But I've got to admit, I'm rather nervous.'

Disbelieving sounds from the audience.

'No, really. I've no problem saying other people's words, but reading my own, I feel – naked.'

Suggestive 'oooh's'.

'Well, if you promise to be kind, I'll read an extract, then chat with the lovely Alex here and answer some questions.' Alex blushes as Reece steps to a lectern, opening his book and pulling off a Post-it. The lights dim, except for a cluster of spotlights illuminating him.

'This section is an especially personal moment from when I was eighteen years old.'

What? I thought this was a celeb biog, fan-fodder, a light-hearted behind-the-scenes look at *Muerte*. Not his childhood. Our childhood. I need to get away. But the gap between the back of the seats and the door would make leaving hideously obvious.

'Nothing ventured,' Reece says, repeating his detective's catchphrase.

A titter of laughter, then he starts to read.

'My journey as an actor began long before I ever thought of performing. There is a darker side to my early life, which adds a sad irony to my famous role as a detective. It has always been far too painful to talk about publicly, but now I want to face up to what has led me to where I am today. It was Friday 4th October 1996. I was just eighteen, fresh from taking my A levels, and having just enjoyed a last long easy summer at home. The very next day I was off to take up my place to study Medicine at Cambridge. It was a beautiful crisp autumn day, the last normal day I ever had.'

Normal? But Mum, Dad and Reece were all so weird and tense that afternoon. Mum left without saying goodbye and Reece slammed out a few minutes later. I'm throbbing inside my coat, the inside of my wig is scratchy and sweat is dripping down my face. This troll needs to get back under her bridge, with a big drink.

'That evening, under a vivid orange sunset, I played a boisterous farewell game of five-a-side football with my schoolmates on the astro pitches nestling on the edge of the North Circular, and scored the winning goal. Then we went for a few beers in the Mossy Well Pub in Muswell Hill. That was the last carefree drink I would ever have. I was so in the moment, so simply happy, and so unaware of the tragedy that was about to befall me. I returned home after eleven, tired and jolly.'

Jolly? Reece slammed the door violently, refused dinner and marched upstairs. I'm right back there in our lounge, hearing his feet stomping up the steps, hearing Dad's abrupt 'fine' when I ask if he's OK because he's so monosyllabic, and seeing the uneven ring of dried red wine around the rim of his petrol-coupon glass, that he keeps on refilling.

How can Reece keep reading this? But he does.

'"I'm starving," I said as I entered the lounge where my dad and little sister were watching a gameshow.

"Keep your voice down, son, Mum's having a lie down," laughed my dad.

"There's cheese on toast if you want it," said my sister.'

So I'm in this abomination too. But I made lasagne, from scratch, as we'd been taught that week in home economics – and no one ate it. My snapshot memory is filling out into bits of continuous film, but Reece's words are fudging the print.

'I don't know if it was eating cheese late at night, or some kind of premonition, but I had a terrible night's sleep. The next morning, I was up early, a bit hungover, getting ready for Dad to drive me to Cambridge, when the doorbell rang and I saw two figures through the coloured glass of the front door. I opened it to find a uniformed policewoman and a serious young man in a dark overcoat.

"Could we come in?" the policewoman asked. My sister, my father and I all filed into the front room. "I'm very sorry to say that a body has been found in the woods behind your house," she said. "I don't want to distress you unnecessarily, but we have reason to believe that this may be Jennifer Davidson."

"That's impossible. What reason?" I blurted out.

"A long-strapped purple tasselled handbag, with identification," she replied. Dad let out a slight moan. We all knew it was Mum's. Everything went into slow motion as Dad stumbled back in disbelief. I shouted that they were wrong and that I'd get Mum right now as I ran to her room.

"She's not there," I exclaimed, as I rushed back down. "But that doesn't necessarily mean—"

"Do you have a recent photo of your mother?" asked the man in the dark overcoat.

As my father stood rigid and my sister started to cry, I lifted a framed photo from the mantelpiece. Mum in a green cocktail dress, her long hair piled high, laughing.

"Will this do?" I asked.

The man in the overcoat nodded and left.

We waited together in the front room, Dad telling us that of course it was a mistake, of course it was, Mum was always losing things, and she often stayed the night at a friend's after a party, didn't she? The policewoman watched us fabricating hopes.'

Tears are streaming down my face. I should smash my fist into the red fire-alarm box to stop this. It's all running in my head. That ponytailed policewoman with the cratered pockmark above her left eyebrow is smiling sadly at me. The hands of the little gold carriage clock on the mantelpiece are crawling round. My tongue sears on the tea that Reece makes me.

'But I knew that Mum would never have missed saying goodbye to me – that something awful must have stopped her. And the man in the overcoat returned half an hour later and confirmed the identification. My father had lost his beautiful, clever wife, and my sister and I had lost our beloved mother and best friend. She had plunged a kitchen knife into her chest.'

The audience gasps and Reece pauses theatrically.

I see Dad's face crumpling in as his head drops at the news – then he raises his eyes to Reece, and Reece's swirling agony seems to contract to rock-hard granite as he stares back at Dad.

'I will never know why she did it. She was a rare, complex creature, who must have suffered in silence for so long to reach that point of desperation and leave her loving family bereft. Her death is why I have campaigned on behalf of mental health charities and supported the work of the Samaritans at Comic Relief.'

Suicide? That theory was exploded at the time. Wasn't it? A stranger murdered her. After all your accusations about Dad's guilt, Reece? Now you're saying that Mum killed herself – and that's why you dressed up as a chicken last year on Comic Relief. I should launch myself at you, screaming and clawing.

'I had to make a decision that day. Whether to go under with the excruciating grief, to live always looking back, always submerged in anger and regret. Or to do what Mum would have wanted, to be strong and carry on with my life as a testament to her. Our dog Feynman had died a week before Mum and she said to my sister and me that, yes, it was terribly sad, but what an awful tribute to him, if we moped instead of remembering all the joy he had brought us. She went to the animal shelter the very next day and returned home with a kitten. Mum always refused to look back, always faced forward into the wind, embracing the new. I chose to emulate her. Straight after the funeral, I left home for Cambridge University. And ever since, I have grasped the nettle of life and shook it, just as she did.'

He closes the book.

There is a reverent moment of silence.

I'm sunk in my chair, gripping the sides so hard they should snap.

Then there's a huge wave of applause and people are standing and cheering.

Is this really what he remembers? Or am I remembering wrong? In that last bit, Reece is so obviously talking about me – I'm the one who 'went under with excruciating grief', who 'lived their life looking back, submerged in anger and regret'. I am so searingly humiliated by his remarks about me, that I feel winded.

'Thank you, Ryan, that must have been difficult to read,' says Alex as they take seats facing each other.

'Yes, but it's also a release,' says Reece, relaxing back in his chair. 'I wanted to be open about what underlies who I am now. But also,' he says, frowning, 'I wanted to show anyone who's going through a terrible time, that it is possible to survive, to live through unimaginable pain and live richly and fully. Nothing ventured, nothing gained.'

There is a volley of supportive applause. God, does he think that he is his TV character?

'So why now for your autobiography? You're still a relatively young man,' says Alex, flirtatiously.

'I'm already four years older than my mother was when she died. She was so vibrant and amazing, but never got to look back on her life. I wanted to capture my thoughts on my first forty-odd years, while I could still remember them.'

'Well, we're very glad that you did.'

Applause.

They chat on about Reece's writing process and other such guff. Reece is forty-one, and I'm thirty-seven. I'm fully aware of the numbers, but I suddenly grasp what they mean. In just a few weeks, on the anniversary of Mum's death, I will have lived as long as the entirety of her life. It was so shockingly short. What more would she have done if she'd had time? And Reece has had this huge, life-writ-large experience. What have I been doing?

'So, we've got time for a few audience questions,' says Alex, jogging me back to the room. 'Emma, where are you?'

The elfin girl from the door holds out a mic to the flurry of hands.

'Thank you,' says a slim woman with grey plaits. 'I wanted to ask how you prepare for a role, what's your process?' And on they go. 'How close is the character of Detective Ralph Pennington to you?' 'What role would you love to take on?' 'Who's your favourite leading lady?' 'Would you like to be the next Dr Who?' 'James Bond?'

Reece is funny and considered. The questions are all about his work and I lose focus with the inane drivel.

'And we've just got time for one final question,' I hear Alex say. 'Shall we take one from the back, Emma? Yes, the lady with the long blonde hair?'

I look round to see who she's approaching, but she's looking straight at me. I'm wearing a blonde wig and, inexplicably, I've raised my hand. She pushes the microphone at me and I rise unsteadily to my feet.

'Thank you,' I say.

Reece's eyes widen imperceptibly as they meet mine.

'Hi. BIG fan of your work, "Ryan", but I just wanted to ask you' – I pause and see him swallow – 'while I LOVE your show's mash-up of comedy and murder – some might say it's trite and insensitive. Given her "suicide", what do you think your mother would have made of it?'

Reece has blanched, but he is ever the consummate performer.

'She would've loved it,' he says, jutting out his chin. 'It's frivolous escapism – purely for entertainment. And my mother was always up for excitement.' He flares his eyes fractionally at me then looks round the room. 'Our plots give people the satisfaction of endings which sadly don't often come in real life – as I know, only too well.'

The audience is nodding like he's Gandhi. He swings his gaze back to me and raises one eyebrow.

'Great question, thanks,' he says with finality.

'OK,' says Alex, 'good question to finish on.'

I slump back into my seat.

'Ryan's book can be purchased at the door, and if you'd like your copy signed, do join the queue at the signing table.'

I join my padded friend in the queue, feeling like a beetle who's been trapped in solidified lava for years, but now the volcano is suddenly active again and I'm spewing up, reanimated. I fume in line for the ten minutes it takes to reach the front, watching the effervescing fans flocking to Reece. He glances up occasionally, as if checking the room, but really he's clocking my position in line.

'So fascinating,' says my padded friend. 'That extract explains a certain something about him, doesn't it?'

'He's certainly full of something,' I reply.

'And I didn't know he had a sister? I come from a family of seven,' she prattles on. 'Do you have siblings?'

'No. My brother – died – a long time ago.'

Reece is sitting next to the willowy blonde woman he entered with. She's opening people's copies to an appropriate page for signing, and directing the flow.

Now my padded friend is holding out her book to him.

'Thank you, Ryan,' she says. 'Sorry, can I call you Ryan?'

'You can call me whatever you like,' he laughs.

'Husband-to-be then?'

'Oh, I asked for that, didn't I?' he says as he does his swirling flamboyant signature with his left hand. I remember him practising it in an exercise book on the kitchen table, when he was ten, saying he was going to be famous one day.

And here's 'one day'.

My friend steps away, winking back at me.

Reece gives me a nod.

I hold out my book, glaring at him.

'And who should I make it out to?' he asks with a smirk.

'Desdemona,' I say with heavy emphasis.

He raises an eyebrow fractionally. 'Shakespeare's beautiful heroine. I had to smother that poor woman night after night at the National,' Reece says to the assembled crowd, who laugh nervously as he jokes about murder. 'But what the audience couldn't see was that every night the actress used to stick out her tongue, to try to get me to laugh!' Now the fans relax and guffaw.

'Killed by lies,' I blurt.

'Kill me tomorrow, let me live tonight,' he says quietly, quoting Desdemona, but like it's an order to me. He holds eye contact, there's a fleck of our old connection, and then he slides back into his formal persona. 'OK then . . . Desdemona,' he says as he scribbles in my copy.

That looks like more than just a signature?

'Monsieur, you're really spoiling me,' I say sarcastically. Reece glances up at my reference to the Ferrero Rocher ad we made fun of as children.

'Thank you for supporting my book,' he says as he hands it back to me.

'Great work of fiction,' I say and his eyes narrow.

'Well, thanks for coming,' he says, turning to the next in the queue.

I stay put.

The ironed-blonde smiles with pursed lips. 'Thank you for supporting Ryan today,' she says, 'but we've got so many people waiting, he has to move on.'

Surely that can't be it. After fifteen years!

'Reece?' I say loudly.

The ironed-blonde's eyes widen and she gestures frantically. Paisley Waistcoat is at my arm immediately, pulling at me.

'No, I need to speak to him,' I shout. 'Get off.'

Everyone's looking at me with horror and glee: the desperate fan, unable to prise herself away from her idol. What's she gonna do next? A security guard joins Paisley Waistcoat, each taking an elbow. My padded friend looks to the floor as I'm dragged past her.

Reece doesn't look up.

CHAPTER SIX

I finally understand the phrase 'shaking with anger' as I stride back up Tottenham Court Road, scything through the crowds. Why aren't they all fighting, like in a zombie film, whacking each other's heads off, like I want to.

I reach UCH, but it's past visiting hours, so I sit on the steps, amongst a few defiant smoking patients. I look up at the towering hospital, counting nine floors to where Dad's life is draining away through that big corner window, then pull off my scratchy wig and throw it down.

'Can I?' asks an emaciated bald woman in a wheelchair, attached to a drip and dragging on a cigarette as she indicates the fallen wig.

'If I can have one of those,' I say, gesturing to her cigarette.

She lights one for me and pulls on my discarded blonde hair.

After a deep drag, I open Reece's book. On the inside

page, in his familiar slanted handwriting, he's written *For Hannah. So like our wonderful mother. Let sleeping dogs lie. Ryan. X.* How dare he use that fake name with me! And that's it. No phone number? No tentative olive branch? He's making fun of the inadvertent effect of that stupid wig. How could I have been so crass as to choose a blonde one? Did Reece think I was purposely dressing up as Mum? I know I'm nothing like our beautiful mother. At most, a fairground parody in a bendy mirror. Same age, hair and weight maybe, but Mum was beautiful, spontaneous and charismatic; I'm gawky, seized and reclusive. Reece meant to hurt me in the most painful way he could. To ridicule me for parodying her.

The skeletal bald lady is now wearing my wig at a jaunty angle. She nods down to a plastic bag at her feet, unearthing the top of a bottle with her toe.

'You're a long time dead,' she says, 'bottoms up.' As she raises the bottle wearing my Thor wig, sitting in her wheelchair and silhouetted against the evening sky, she looks like Boadicea rallying her troops. She's clearly dying, but she's magnificent in her refusal to admit defeat. I remember learning Boadicea's speech at school: 'Win the battle or perish, that is what I, a woman, will do.' Boadicea's emaciated arm holds the bottle out to me. I nod and the whisky sears my throat.

'Win or perish,' I proclaim.

'Rock on,' Boadicea laughs.

I flick to Reece's Acknowledgements, beginning: *A huge thank you to my agent Anastasia Rudd for all your advice, patience and inspiration.* I google the website of The Anastasia Rudd Agency, and find a photo of the ironed-blonde from the reading, on a white page with a grey looping typeface and ivy hanging from it. Pretentious bollocks.

I click on the phone link. Straight to answerphone.

'Hello, this is Anastasia Rudd,' says her saccharine voice. 'Please leave a message after the tone, with your name, number, time of call and message.'

'Hello Mssssss Rudd,' I say in a wildly upbeat tone, 'this is a message for your client Ryan Patterson – from his sister, Hannah. We met just now at his book reading; I was the woman dragged out screaming. Please could he call me ASAP.' I rattle off my number and almost hang up, but can't stop myself. 'I hate to sound like I'm in one of his shitty little shows, but if I don't hear back from him within twenty-four hours, I'll bring down a whole world of trouble on him – exposing to the press how he abandoned his family. Byeee.'

Boadicea high-fives me.

I buy a screw-top bottle of cheap red wine and swig it on the tube back to Highgate. I trudge back to Dad's along Muswell Hill Road, which skirts Highgate Woods, where Mum was found. I haven't set foot in there since, always walking along the far side of the opposite pavement, as if the wood could suck me in. But today, I trail my hand along the slatted wooden fence, which bows outwards as if struggling to contain the wood's energy. I'm bouncing the back of my hand along the slatting and when I finally reach the end, I find it's full of splinters – like I have a set of Wolverine's claws.

My bag's pinging away, as both my and Dad's phones announce we are in the 'home zone' of the 'Here then

There' tracking app I set up to monitor Dad, when he could still physically leave the house but couldn't be trusted. I stumble along the short row of houses that back onto the woods and I'm finally back 'home'. Such a normal-looking house: typical Edwardian brick, wooden-framed porch and bay window, with mock wooden Tudor cladding at the top. It's chocolate-boxy normal. But I can only ever see it through the filter of the photograph in the newspaper, shot dramatically from below so it reared up like a house of horror.

I push open the peeling gate and fall up the three steep steps to the tiny front garden to reach my twin, the pointless quince tree, its untended foliage encroaching malevolently over the path. It's early autumn now, so its thin trunk supports a huge bouquet of green leaves and a fat yellow crop. Each beautiful fruit has the lyrical shape of a pear, the exquisite colour of a pale apple, and the aromatic scent of a ripe guava – but also the bitter taste of an astringent floor wipe. Totally pointless and fake. Just like this new Mum-look that Dad and Reece see in me – a pathetic thin veneer of her gorgeousness over my tasteless centre. I brush my fingertips through the dark leaves, then shove my head in and breathe into our bond. Twenty-three shared seasons of pointless budding and flowering, swelling and ripening, shrivelling and rotting to mush.

'You all right, Hannah?' calls a voice to my right. I drag my head out.

It's Dad's neighbour, Mr Roberts, calling from his adjoining front garden. His tall, rangy physique sports one of his many loud Hawaiian shirts.

'Fiiine, Mr Roberts,' I say, realising just how drunk I am.

'Frank,' he laughs. 'I think you're old enough for first names.' I fumble with my keys, trying to jam them into the blurry lock, but they clatter to the ground.

'Sure you're OK?' He's suddenly over the small dividing wall and beside me.

'I'm fiiine,' I say, unable to locate my keys.

'Good. Good. And is your Dad OK? Libbie and I saw an ambulance last night. We tried to call you.' Of course they were curtain twitching even in the dead of night.

'Had a fall. Dad did. Don't know what's gonna happen.'

He peers at me. 'You're not OK, Hannah. Where's your key?' he says putting his hand on my shoulder.

'Dropped somewhere,' I mumble, stepping away from him and falling off the porch step onto the ground.

'Oh dear,' he says. 'Take my hand.'

'I'm fine, Mr Roberts. Home safe. Ha, I said "home" about here.'

'This will always be your home,' he says, reaching for me, but I lie flat out on the path.

'There's no escaping this place. It sucks me back,' I say, spreading my arms and making a huge slurping sound.

'Everything's going to be OK,' he says gently.

'Is it?' I snap, slapping his hand away. He steps in and forces his arms under my armpits and heaves me up, so we are momentarily in an embrace and I feel the power of his still-athletic physique.

'I'm not a child,' I mumble, trying to break free but unable to engage my limbs.

'I know,' he laughs. 'Let's get you in.'

He picks up my keys from somewhere and jiggles them in the lock expertly. The door opens and I fall in with relief, but as I start to close it, he steps his right foot onto the threshold, blocking it.

'You're so like—'

'Not you too – shut up,' I moan, pulling at the door.

'It's not a bad thing,' he says, picking up my bag.

'It's not true,' I say, coughing and spitting on the floor. He frowns and steps into the house. I stumble back and my heel knocks into the base of the stairs so that I thump down heavily, jarring my back.

'Hannah,' he murmurs, leaning in close and stroking my cheek with his calloused fingers. 'I can't possibly leave you alone in this state.'

'Please,' I mumble, trying to twist away from him.

There's a sudden yowl and hissing from Dad's cat, Schro. Mr Roberts straightens up.

'OK, if you're sure,' he says.

I nod.

'Please look after yourself, we're always here for you.' He hands me my bag and keys, and turns away. As he walks through the door, I lurch up and slam it violently, jolting the stained glass. One day a final slam will shatter it. I know how the glass feels.

I lean on the door, eyes closed, breathing heavily.

When I open my eyes, I register a dark figure on the other side. I peer through the wavy coloured glass. It's Mr Roberts. I step back sharply.

Why's he still there?

CHAPTER SEVEN

My hair's being sucked. I bat away squealing fur, then register it's Schro. I'm lying fully clothed on the hall floor, my head's banging and, oh lovely, I've wet myself. I've been here alone all night, yet I feel horribly exposed. I think of Mum seeing me like this and moan aloud, as I drag off my cold wet jeans and sodden knickers and shove them into the washing machine. Then I reach for a dusty packet of kitchen surface wipes and scrape at my clammy skin, leaning into the chemical searing. I numbly wrap a sheet around me and stumble into the lounge, where the dusty carriage clock says 8 a.m.

The lounge looks like a tornado's hit it.

Mum's two large wooden photo-storage desks, untouched for years, have been ransacked, her carefully organised photos and papers strewn everywhere. All her mounted prints that had been leaning against the wall are tipped over. Books are swept off the shelves. Why did I do this?

Mum trained in photography when we were small and in her final years had become very successful – holding exhibitions, publishing glossy books and being in great demand for shoots. Her photos cover every wall of the house, different collections congregated in specific rooms. I hugely resented that her success kept her away from us so much, felt rejected every time she left, but she thrived on it and said we were lucky to have her doing our family snaps. The lounge is a time-lapse view of Reece and me growing up, as her style developed. Firstly, the conceptual shots: Reece and me at five and one, superimposed onto flower stalks. Progressing to moody lighting and oblique angles: there we are at fourteen and ten, looking away from the camera in shade. Finally, the candid-camera natural shots: and there's us lounging on the green sunbeds in the garden, laughing, aged eighteen and fourteen, my eyes closed to the bright sunlight – taken at a barbecue we had with our neighbours just a couple of weeks before Mum died.

Our photographic progression ceased with Mum.

I've always thought the estrangement between Reece and I began with our arguments after Mum's death, but looking at these photos now, I see how different we were all along – him so good-looking, relaxed and photogenic, me so pudgy, awkward and startled. Was I mistaken about our childhood sibling bond?

I try to remember what I was doing last night, but only have a vague memory of creepy Mr Roberts – nothing after that. Was it explosive anger about Reece's lies? Or was I searching for something specific? And if so, what?

Schro is mewing plaintively and as I stroke him, loose fur flies up. Poor old Schro (short for Schrödinger, another of Dad's physics names) was the kitten Mum got for us the day after Feynman died, twenty-three years ago. He's got a shit name, his owners are murdered or dying and he has advanced cancer. He's got an all-white back-boot, like a Dick Whittington swashbuckling cat, but the top of the boot is an ever-swelling mound, a big lump of cancer growing out of the bone. When I took him to the local vet six months ago, she advised putting him down.

'But he's still eating, still purring,' I said in horror.

'Well bring him in, when you know it's time.'

'How will I know when?'

'You'll know,' she said portentously.

But I never 'know' anything; nothing feels instinctual.

I couldn't kill Schro there and then, so I brought him home and now it's six months of sprouting cancer later. Most cats would be dead by twenty-three, but Schro is clinging on gallantly. For Dad I think. Or am I just cruelly forcing him to suffer on?

I follow Schro into the kitchen, which is stuffed with more of Mum's photos – all the way round the top of the walls and on the ceiling are endless small photo canvases from her collection entitled 'Look Closer' – a series of everyday things shot to look terrifying: a pothole looking like a crater, a nipple as a mountain, a kitchen knife as a sword, a grater as a torture instrument and a comb's teeth as prison bars. I remember being dragged along to that launch in some arty gallery. It was catered with food designed to look like anything except food: fingers, books and flowers; all the drinks were dyed to unappetising colours: black, UV purple, highlighter yellow. Dad took Reece and me for a Wimpy on the way home cos we were starving, and we had double cheeseburgers and Knickerbocker Glories in tall glasses.

I rip the top off a silver-and-pink sachet of cat food 'for older cats'. Schro's well past hoovering up the reeking rectangle as it falls from the sachet, but he takes a few mouthfuls. Thank God. I think cats stop eating when they decide they've had enough. So at least it's not time for me to murder him. Yet.

I ring the hospital and am told that Dad had a reasonably comfortable night. I pour hot water onto three heaped spoonfuls of coffee, adding milk that's not off, but teetering, like Dad, and use the concoction to swill down four Nurofen. Soon, I'm oddly cotton-woolled and oiled up. There's more pain later, but right now, I'm Alice-through-the-bloody-looking-glass. My anger with Reece and Boadicea's bravado in the face of death has shifted some tectonic plates in my head and after twenty-three years, I'm going into the woods again. My whole life I have felt two ways of being: stuck and safe; or intrepid but ridiculously fragile – a swollen caterpillar or a frail butterfly.

I feel light-headed as I assume my brittle self.

Our back garden leads directly into the woods via a metal gate in the back wall. Reece and I ran through it to play endless games there, making camps with long, bent-over branches, hiding in the bracken, timing ourselves getting from one end to the other, and competing in physical and mental endurance trials. But Dad padlocked our gate after Mum's death, so I have to enter from the street. The public gates have been replaced during my absence, so this is my first time facing the large green metal sheet with cut-outs of deer and foxes amongst the metallic foliage. I slither round the corner portal.

'It's ancient woodland, mentioned in the Doomsday Book,' Dad would remind Reece and me as we rolled our eyes. But now I feel it. It's so seismically bigger than me, like a wood in a fairy tale, and at this time of year the thick canopy cuts out most of the light. There are trees of so many varieties, heights, angles and states: thick, vertical, dark-trunked trees with high leaves; slimmer, inclining, silvery-grey trees; clumps of holly; sprinklings of saplings; needy anorexic trees desperately fusing together; proud trees uprooted and humiliated with their undersides laid bare; sad old fallen trees past hope; and strange fantastical trees hit by lightning, with mystical seared streaks.

The temperature falls the deeper in I get. I move from the outer ring of pathway towards the centre. Artificially rustic wooden signs direct me to the children's playground, which is very near to where Mum's body was found. But I know the crow-flying shortest route, so I ignore the signs and cut directly into the foliage. I'm breathing deeply, bounding over fallen branches, ducking trailing leaves. I should run a marathon with a hangover like this. But as I cross one of the paths, I vomit into some bracken. A posse of slim women in tight Lycra jog past me, each pushing identical brightly coloured prams with heavily padded geometrical sections and thick wheels. They glance amongst themselves censoriously. Move along ladies, nothing to see, you lot haven't had a drink for nine months.

I wipe my mouth and set off again. Flashes of the brightly coloured play equipment pull me on and suddenly, I've arrived. Lightning struck two hornbeam trees here in the terrible storm of 1987. One tree continued to grow straight up, resolute and refusing to be scared – like good old buccaneering Reece; the other tree split in two, and the sections grew vertically along the ground, as if too scared of risk – like me. It's an odd sight, mystical and threatening – as if a dark force has broken through into our realm.

Mum's body was found right here, lying on the dusty ground between the sundered sections of the split tree.

It's so unnaturally quiet. And cold. Everything is intense and precise – the curling silvery bark, like delicate pencil shavings; the myriad shapes and curves of the leaves; the fine dust floating in the streaks of sunlight. The breeze skims the hairs on my arms and goosebumps flare. A fat squirrel dashes up the vertical tree and freezes, clinging on tight with his bulging thighs. His glassy eyes lock me in a Vulcan mind meld.

Then my mobile rings, and the Spock squirrel bombs off up the tree. It's not a number I recognise. The hospital cos Dad's dead?

'Hello?'

'Hannah?' It's him.

'Oh, hi Reece.'

'No one calls me that any more.'

'Well, I'm not calling you Ryan.'

He breathes in. 'My agent passed on your rather colourful message.'

'Message?' Oh God, I'd forgotten till he says it.

'You don't need to involve Anastasia to reach me, you know,' he says, tersely.

'I didn't have your number.'

'Oh.'

All my bravado from last night has evaporated. I'm back to fearing that if I say the wrong thing, use the wrong tone, I'll be shut out again, deemed unworthy. The cut-off-er of contact always trumps the cuttee. I must be bland and nice.

'I'm sorry.'

'Were you drunk?'

'I-I'd just had a couple.' I wilt under his silent judgement. 'It's been fifteen years.'

'So you decided to confront me in public, dressed up as Mum?'

'No. That was a mistake.' My voice is trembling. 'The stuff you read out, it was all wrong,' I mumble, trying not to cry. I hold the phone away again and mouth *Fuuuuuuck*, silently. An old man passing with a sausage dog looks over in alarm. I make a face at him and he picks up his pace.

'Hannah, are you there?' I take a deep breath as I jam the phone back to my ear. I can't call him on all his bullshit like this, I have to wangle a face-to-face meeting.

'Dad's in hospital,' I say, disgusting myself by using Dad to manipulate him into connection.

'OK,' he says quietly.

'OK?'

'OK, he's in hospital.'

I sit down on my low tree branch and touch Reece's skyward form.

'Is he dying?'

'It's touch and go.' I have to drag Reece into my orbit, I can't do this alone.

'OK.'

'Okaaay?'

'Is that what you wanted to tell me?' He's a master at

polite distance. I should introduce him to Ms Beige.

'Don't you want to see him?'

'No.'

'This could be your last chance.'

'Time has passed, my decision not to see him hasn't.'

'But this is – the end. I've been living at Dad's and there's so much to do,' I gabble. 'So many practical things, like power of attorney. I can't make decisions alone about' – I reach for clichés from hospital dramas – 'prolonging life, resuscitation, turning off life support. Please, Reece, you owe me one meeting surely.'

Silence. Come on, come on, come on.

'OK,' he says finally. 'Tomorrow. Ten o'clock. But I haven't got long. Come to my flat in Chelsea, I'll WhatsApp you the address.'

'Do you know where I am?' I say, rubbing my hand along the silky bark of his tree.

'You said – at Dad's.'

'No, I mean, right now. This precise moment.'

'How would I—'

'I'm at the split tree.'

'What split—oh.'

There's no sound from the phone, but I feel Reece at the other end.

The wood shifts around me.

'I'll see you at ten,' he says eventually.

The phone clicks off.

I'm nearly back to the house when I see a tall figure stepping down from our front path, a hoodie shielding their face. He looks furtively up the street and clocks me. I make myself walk towards him. It's broad daylight, I'm perfectly safe.

'Hannah?' calls a deep voice. How does he know my name? He pulls back his hoodie, revealing blonde hair, and as he smiles, his eyes crinkle at the sides. Oh my God, it's Marcus, the Robertses' son. My sort-of-brother Marcus. Reece and I spent much of our childhoods next door, while Mum was busy at work. Reece and Marcus were the same age and I joined in their games till they grew away from me as teenagers, into their hormonal moody selves. He's hardly recognisable from the teenage Marcus of my memory, with his long-haired surfer good looks. Now, he's got short receding hair and his features have strengthened. But he's still got that same ridiculously good-looking, healthy vibe – like a Diet Coke ad in his jeans and tight T-shirt. And I'd know that smile anywhere.

'Marcus. God, it's been for ever,' I say as I reach him. Although I grew up alongside him, I had quite a crush on Marcus as a teenager and I'm shocked by the jolt of attraction I feel now.

'Long time and all that,' he says, stepping forward and giving me an awkward hug. Dead embers flare inside me.

'Yes, a lot of all that,' I laugh as his muscled arms release me. 'How bizarre to see you – I've just been on the phone with Reece.'

'Cool. God, Hannah – look at you. I mean wow.'

I smile nervously.

'You're so much—are men allowed to comment on weight these days?'

'I guess if the weight is downward!' This attention on my looks feels different from Dad's and Reece's creepy comparisons – like he's really seeing me. 'Who knew there was a thin girl waiting to get out of me all these years!'

'Ah no, you were always pretty,' he says, blushing.

We grin at each other and I feel weirdly light and fizzy.

'The-It-Ty-Bit,' he laughs. In our woodland games, we three were very into Morse code for communicating across distances. 'The-It-Ty-Bit' was a mnemonic we made up for remembering the Morse code for H for Hannah: four short dots.

'Surf Dude,' I respond – which was how we remembered the two long dashes for M for Marcus.

We smirk at each other.

'Did you want something?' I ask eventually.

'What? No.'

'But you were just coming from ours, weren't you?'

'Oh, yeah of course. Came to ask how your dad's doing.'

He's lying. He was coming to see me. His parents must have said I was back. I feel like the fourteen-year-old girl who used to sneak glimpses at his physique as he horsed around with Reece.

'Dad's still really touch and go. I don't know if he'll come home again.'

He frowns sympathetically.

'And if by some miracle he does, this place isn't anywhere near suitable for him.'

'What d'you mean?'

'Well, if, and it's a big if, he does come home, he's going to have mobility problems, and this place is a wreck.'

He frowns again.

'Sorry, I'm just worrying out loud.'

'I could help you,' he blurts out.

'Oh, I wasn't fishing for help.'

'No, that's what I do. I'm a builder slash handyman now – I've got my own company. See.' He gestures to the road, at a small purple van emblazoned with *The Handyman Can – No Job Too Small*. He starts to sing. 'Who can take a sunrise, sprinkle it with dew.'

'Nooo.'

'Cover it with chocolate,' he continues as I laugh, 'and a miracle or two, the handyman can.'

'You didn't,' I say, remembering his mum singing 'The Candy Man Can' to us as she brought out some confectionery treat she'd baked us.

'Hey, people like it – and more to the point, it contains the words "handyman", for all those Google searches.'

'Brilliant.'

'Seriously, I've done it all – ramps, bed moving, accessible showers. It's a big market in North London – all that money keeping people alive for way longer than they should live – oh God, sorry, I didn't mean . . .'

I wave away his embarrassment. 'I was more meaning mending the toilet and such, but I guess I need to think about all that. Are you sure, Marcus? I'd pay the proper rate and everything.'

'My card, milady,' he says, producing a purple business card with a flourish. 'And I'd only charge for materials, you're family.'

But we're not real family, I think, checking out his finger for a wedding ring. Nope.

'Thanks, Marcus.'

He grins.

'Have you heard from Reece lately?' I ask, desperate to keep this conversation going.

'The King Rat,' he says, using the Morse mnemonic for R: short, long, short. 'Nah, took different paths,' he says with a shrug. 'You know how it goes.'

Wow – for the first time ever, Marcus is more interested in me than in Reece.

'Look, I'm sorry to cut and run but I have a job to get to now,' he says abruptly. 'I mean it though about the help.' He touches my arm awkwardly. 'And it was so good to see you.'

'You too,' I say, play-punching him lightly as he passes me.

I'm smiling as I walk up the path to the house. Then I see Schro sitting by the front door. Strange. He hasn't been outside for months, barely able to drag himself from the lounge to the kitchen, so I've kept him in. I must have missed him slipping out this morning?

CHAPTER EIGHT

Loreta seems to be doing handicrafts when I get to the hospital. She's tying little woven-straw creations onto the bottom railing of her dad's bed and today he's conscious and smiling at his daughter.

'I like your – decorations,' I say.

'Traditional Lithuanian Christmas decorations I make with my dad when I was child,' she says, as I realise they're made out of hospital straws.

'But it's not – Christmas?'

She shrugs. 'Dad thinks it is, and is good for dementia, to go along with the patient's thoughts, not yours. So, Happy Christmas! Or *Linksmų Kalėdų*, as we say.'

'Jen,' Dad says as I approach him. 'I'm so sorry.' Not this again. What if Dad gets stuck in a past where I don't exist? What if he loses all his memories, even the early ones – then is he even Dad any more?

'No Dad, I'm Ha—' I freeze as I clock the decorations

opposite and Loreta putting on a jaunty little Christmas hat she's fashioned out of newspaper. I look back at Dad and smile, tilting my head like Mum used to do. What can it hurt to be her for him?

'It's OK, Philip. I'm here. Everything's OK.'

'Do you forgive me, Jen?' he whispers.

'What do you want me to forgive you for?' I whisper.

'You know,' Dad pleads as a tear runs down his cheek. 'You have to forgive me, Jen. You didn't deserve it.'

'I – can't,' I whisper.

He lets out a strangled cry.

Loreta looks over, concerned.

'Please, Dad, please calm down.'

He shrieks at full volume and Loreta rises.

'OK, OK, you're forgiven, all right. I forgive you, Philip.'

Dad falls back on his pillow.

How dare I forgive Dad on Mum's behalf. A belch of putrid hospital-coffee-vomit spasms out of me and down my chest. As I pull my jacket closed to absorb the liquid, I see that my hands are clutched right over my heart, exactly where Mum was stabbed.

I need a massive drink as soon as I get home. I ignore Dad's petrol-coupon tumblers and reach for one of Mum's delicate long-stemmed glasses with its white fleur-de-lis engraving. I grab it with my palm, but then feel Mum's delicate French-tipped fingers wanting to grasp the fine stem through my chewed fingertips. Shifting the glass from my fist to my fingers changes the way I'm holding my arm and I stand taller. I always drink red wine, but tonight it's white for Mum and while I usually gulp it, the thought of Mum's delicate lips on the rim of this very glass as she sipped, makes me sip. Just like at the hospital yesterday, I have the sense of Mum's physicality sliding into me, like smoke into a glass. Dad is disappearing while his heart still beats, yet Mum is re-emerging in me, when hers doesn't. As I lick a stray droplet from the corner of my mouth, I recall Mum's bright red lipsticked lips so clearly that I'm surprised not to see a scarlet smear on my glass.

Looking up, I see that Mum's high kitchen frieze of close-up photos is askew and one's missing. When did that happen? And which picture was it? A cup? A fork? I can't remember. I boost myself up onto the counter, feeling Mum's hands working through mine as I re-align the pictures so they are exactly perpendicular, just how she liked them, and move one photo from the end to fill the gap – it's a photo of a bubble of hot tarmac, close up, looking like a fiery pit.

I top up my glass and carry the bottle upstairs to my bedroom.

Normally I avoid mirrors, but now I take off all my clothes and stand naked in front of the full-length mirror on my wardrobe door, sipping my wine. For the first time I fully comprehend that my body is no longer a deep scaffold supporting a column of flesh – it's a thin, angular skeleton wearing its skin, like Mum's; my breasts now sit on my frame and curve out like hers; my long hair enhances my thinner face to her proportions; and while my skin's dry and flaky, my cheekbones have risen up, my lips are defined and my eyes have lifted from their sunken holes and settled into Mum's ovals. I see myself in the mirror as I simultaneously remember Mum, and the two images overlap and fuse.

If he did kill you, Mum, you must be seething. But you can't seethe, you can't do squat, cos you've got no mind, no form, no essence. You're dead and burnt. As ceased as it's possible to be. I'm a scientist's daughter. I know that seeing Mum in me is just genetics and memories fermented by exhaustion, nothing mystical. But it feels like Mum's been biding her time inside me and has finally risen, a mummy from my crypt.

I shiver and turn away from the mirror. As I sip my wine, I look out over the garden wall at the dark woods. My family lived their whole lives slammed up against these woods. They were my childhood playground, my adolescent world of excitement, and where Mum never returned from. Dad should have moved years ago.

'Your mum's still here,' he would insist. 'That quince tree out front was my gift to her when we moved in – because quince is what Paris really gave to Aphrodite when he judged her to be the most beautiful goddess, not some silly apple. And she adored those woods out back. Her spirit's still there, I'm sure of it. I'll never leave.'

I always thought that was love talking. But was it guilt all along?

The woods encroach on our house, the leaves clogging our drains and guttering, the tall foliage blocking out the light and the roots sucking up water and weakening our foundations. Dad had to put up blackout curtains for me because I was terrified that the tree shadows would drag me out of my bed and suck me down into the ground, where the roots would feed off me. And I thought the quince tree in the front garden was a locking lever, holding our house rooted in place; were it to be pulled up, that chain holding the house fast would finally be loosened and the wood would roll down over the house, smashing the roof in, crumbling the walls, and destroying our family completely. Perhaps like the quince, I've been a locking mechanism all these years and my refusal to suspect Dad has stopped Mum's murderer being exposed?

Well tonight, I'm leaving the blackout curtains wide open, unlocking the mechanism and unleashing the woods.

I pull out a large wooden box from under my bed, that I haven't looked at for years. Mum's old sewing box. The lid's detached and the inside is smothered in a silt of dust, dirt and dead skin cells – her dead skin cells. I lift the warped plastic tray from the top, full of old buttons, browned packets of needles and rusty tins of pins, to reveal a small pile of yellowed flaky newspaper fragments hunched underneath. Despite my confidence in Dad, something made me keep these accusatory press cuttings from the red-top papers. It's time to read them properly.

The first is dated 7th October 1996, with a full-page photo of Dad looking wild-eyed and creepy. The headline, in huge letters, declares 'SLEAZY KILLER'.

Local university professor Philip Davidson, 60, nicknamed 'Sleaze' by his students, is helping police with their enquiries into the brutal stabbing of his much younger glamorous wife, photographer Jennifer Davidson, 37. Her body was discovered at 6.30 a.m. three days ago in North London's Highgate Woods by a dog walker. She died from a single stab wound to the chest, inflicted with a large kitchen knife. The physics professor from King's College London, and author of several popular science books, has been brought in for questioning.

The inside pages are awash with photos of Dad: a work headshot from the university website, college social pictures and multiple furtive shots of Dad scurrying into the police station, trying to avoid the cameras.

Professor Davidson is described by his colleagues as 'a bit of a loner', 'a very private person', and 'stand-offish'. At age 60 he is 23 years senior to his murdered wife. They met when she was a 19-year-old undergraduate at King's studying Philosophy. Students describe Davidson as being 'solicitous of young female undergraduates'. Jennifer dropped out of university to have her first child at 19 and had her second when she was only 23. Neighbour Libbie Roberts described Jennifer as a 'vibrant, sociable young woman', and 'a devoted wife and mother', whereas Philip was 'much quieter' and 'a very private man'. Her husband Frank Roberts talked about the effect of the slaying on the community. 'We are all devastated by this tragedy, everyone's afraid of going into the woods. There will be a meeting tonight at the local church to remember Jen.'

There's Mum and Dad's demure wedding photo, and then one of Mum in some bizarre glamour shot in a long tight-fitting silvery dress.

Detective Chris Manning confirmed that Mr Davidson was helping the police with their fast-moving murder inquiry: 'This is a terrible discovery. We ask anyone who has any information which may be of use to the police to contact the Wood Green Investigation team.'

I lift the next paper in the pile. It's dated 9th October 1996, and this full-page photo is of Dad in a flowing university gown, beside a pentagram chalked onto a tree. The headline reads 'SATANIC RITUAL KILLING'.

Professor Philip Davidson, 60, is still helping police with their enquiries into the satanic murder of his wife Jennifer Davidson, 37. At King's University, the maverick professor taught a class on the 'physics of magic' and earnt considerable royalties from his popular pseudo-science series 'Unreal But Real', and these dark interests are now major leads in the investigation into this brutal slaying.

Highgate Woods, which swarms with bats at night, has long been recognised by those interested in black magic as a focal point of dark energy and it is a gathering place for local witches and Wiccans, often used for satanic rituals and orgies. Photographs taken in the woods at night regularly show unexplained orbs of light. Most sinisterly, there have been many sightings by numerous independent witnesses of an entity, tall and dressed in black robes, gliding silently amongst the trees and seemingly causing the temperature around it to drop sharply. It was thought to be the ghost of a nun who nursed the many plague victims buried in the area, but now residents fear that a recent sighting of this figure may have been Professor Davidson himself, practising his dark arts. Locals have also surmised that Professor Davidson was involved in the recent desecrations of Highgate Cemetery, believed to have been committed by Satanists looking for trophies for their rituals.

There are spooky photos of the wood, the sinister one of our house, and a ridiculous one with groups of parents and children huddled together at the edge of the wood, looking terrified.

The quiet North London suburb of Muswell Hill has been rocked by this shocking murder in what is normally an idyllic area, popular with families. Was Jennifer sacrificed by her own husband in a demonic ritual? Will anyone ever feel safe to go back into the woods again?

It was all tabloid guff. There was zero evidence against Dad and he was never charged. But the papers never withdrew their accusations, so they lingered like stale cigarette breath. Dad took early retirement from his university job, never published again and became a recluse. The papers called him a loner and stand-offish but, though quiet, he had had a richly connected life. He was a born teacher who cared about every student whatever their ability; he was driven to spread his own boyish wonder at science through his teaching and books; and he thrived on the minutiae of college life, organising courses, running committees, genuinely enjoying the old-fashioned college rituals and hierarchy, relied on and admired by his colleagues. To be cut off from all that in one fell swoop left him blinking and lost.

Over the years, whenever I asked how he was doing, he would nod then smile with his mouth, but his eyes were those of an animal that had been run over, its broken body and its useless legs twitching behind it. Pain is pain whatever your age and sex, but there is a particular agony when an older man loses his position, his goals, the respect of his peers – a raw bruising marinated in testosterone. Yet Dad never turned that torturous sting into anger against anyone, never tried to assuage his humiliation with blame and never tried to drown his misery in drink or annihilate it with self-destruction. He just existed through each long, lonely day, ordering stronger and stronger reading glasses online whose prescription he guessed at rather than visit an optician, cooking his repetitive little meals of food purchased in furtive late-night shopping and then online too, and putting the bins out under the cover of darkness.

But was that grief? Or guilt?

Schro limps up to me, mewing faintly. Reece and I used to make fun of him: 'Ooh, what a big fat fatty fat cat,' we would say, rubbing the soft fur on his big white-and-orange belly. Like with me, the weight's rolled off Schro, and while I look scrawny, he's fading away. But I can't put him down yet, not without Dad seeing his only companion for all these years, one more time.

When Dad named him Schrödinger, I thought it might be a Nazi name – my parents had a twisted sense of humour – but it's a physics theory. The day before Mum's murder, Dad was sitting with me in our big square lounge watching me flicking a butterfly on a string for Schro.

As he catapulted himself into the air with increasing abandon, Dad explained the theory of Schrödinger's cat.

'There's this cat,' he said, in his patient teaching voice, 'who's in a box with a radioactive sample, which has a fifty per cent chance of decaying and killing the cat. Until the box is opened, the cat's both alive and dead simultaneously.'

'Durrr,' I said, flicking the butterfly again.

Dad laughed, then shot his hand out at lightning speed and caught Schro mid-air by the scruff of his neck, making his eyes bulge.

'It's OK, it's how mother cats hold their young,' Dad reassured me.

'Put him down Dad,' I laughed.

Well, I think I laughed. But now I re-experience the memory as violent. Memories aren't videos – we re-edit them in hindsight, selecting other takes, creating new ones. I was always sure that that's what Reece had done in re-imagining Dad, rewriting everything about our childhood to make it dark. But is his memory the true one, or is mine?

My family has been held captive by our very own Schrödinger's cat – Dad both did and didn't kill Mum. I Wikipedia'ed Schrödinger's theory recently, and it's a thought experiment in quantum physics, designed by an Austrian (not Nazi) physicist called Erwin Schrödinger. The end of Schrödinger's experiment is explained with a final, incredible, heart-stopping statement: 'observing collapses reality to one answer'. Ah, ha ha – wouldn't it bloody just. The idea that someone might have observed the actual events of that night and be able to tell me the solid, punchable truth.

I could turn off the lights in all the other cinemas in my multiplex brain, close the curtains on all those screens which for so many years have been running the various films of what happened: a stranger murder, suicide, someone we may or may not have known with a secret hatred, or Reece's ugly version starring Dad. If I had just one single reel of film of 'the truth', I could get myself a huge striped bucket of sweet-and-savoury popcorn and a gallon of Diet Coke, ah fuck it real Coke this is a celebration, pick the perfect seat at the centre of the middle row, and play it over and over, certain that I was finally watching *What – Actually – Happened*. Before Dad dies, I have to find that lost reel of film – whoever it stars.

Chris Manning was the detective in charge of the investigation – who gave the various tight-lipped quotes in the press. He was the serious young man in the dark overcoat who visited us that awful morning. He was twenty-six then according to the papers, so he'd still be working now. Perhaps he'd talk to me. I search online – and it's so stupidly easy, one search and there he is in a LinkedIn entry: 'Chris Manning, ex-police detective (1996–2017), available for teaching and research into police techniques for novelists.' God, he was only just a detective when he took on Dad's case, ludicrously young. Why weren't we taken more seriously? Was that why the case wasn't solved? The boy detective would only be forty-nine now. Why doesn't he do detective work, or even security work, any more? Seems an odd career trajectory. The entry was placed two years ago. Before I can talk myself out of it, I send him a private message.

Dear Detective Manning,

This is Hannah Davidson, the daughter of Jennifer Davidson, who was murdered in Highgate Woods in 1996. You were the lead detective on the case. I'm writing because my dad's dying and I wanted to talk about the investigation before it's too late for him. I know it was a long time ago, but I would very grateful if you would get in contact and we could meet.

I look forward to hearing from you.

Yours sincerely,
Hannah Davidson

I feel a familiar wave of dread.

I once gave some old childhood books to a local charity shop. The very next day I bought them back and was flooded with relief when they were all back in place, though I've never looked at them since. I reassure myself that this shimmering warning just beyond my consciousness is just my usual pathological fear of change.

But is it?

CHAPTER NINE

The next morning, I spew out of Sloane Square station with the constrictively suited workforce. I checked Dad was stable and then agonised about what to wear for Reece, having nothing real-worldish. All my stuff's autopilot-comfort, loose and thought-free – 'for the girl who's beyond caring'. I arrived at Dad's six months ago with only the clothes I was wearing and ever since have made do with them and Dad's stuff. Today, I again plumped for my washed Tesco jeans, belted to keep them up, but with Mum's blue shirt with a French label that she left over the back of a chair. I haven't been able to face looking in her wardrobe yet, but that shirt has taunted me these last six months. It's still got a very faint trace of her Chanel No. 5 perfume and I feel creepy wearing it. I can't get my head around fitting into her clothes. She was a lanky 10, I was always a 14 at school and pushed up to an 18 to 20, till this year's impressively effective diet of misery and fruit.

I walk down the Chelsea Road, past skeletal mannequins draped in pastel togas, suspended above bowls of water strewn with decapitated pink gerberas, following my moving dot on Google Maps. Mum loved shopping in these stuck-up shops that I always felt too fat to set foot in, so I always waited outside. My flashing dot and Reece's dot are now overlapping on my phone – I'm amazed they don't repel each other like magnets. There are eight flats in the imposing red-bricked building. I ascend the steps and am buzzed into a pristine marble-floored foyer. My old Brighton bedsit's entrance had a tiny square of dirty curling carpet, strewn with old post and pizza menus. Reece's has a uniformed porter, who's looking at me quizzically. I'm clearly not the right type for this building.

'Ree—Ryan Patterson? He's expecting me,' I announce.

He mumbles down a phone, eyeing me suspiciously, then nods.

'Take the lift to the top floor,' he says.

The lift's all polished wood and mirrors. I think of Reece smearing the glass as he leans one of the many model girlfriends that I've seen him pictured with, onto it, and kisses her. Ugh. I pull a biro from my bag and inscribe my palm with: 'Don't be too much'. I've already got an elastic band round my wrist, to ping if I feel like I'm being too inappropriately me.

The lift opens to a large hallway and Reece is leaning on a door frame opposite.

'Come in, I'll put some coffee on,' he says as he retreats. I follow him down a long corridor. He turns off to a kitchen on his right but gestures me towards the door ahead.

I went to my first ever football match aged eight, with Reece and Dad, and as I rose from the stairwell into the old White Hart Lane, with supporters, music and shouting all around me, I was overwhelmed with the magnitude and intensity of it all. I get that same hit now as I enter this huge, beautiful room. White wooden floors, white walls, discreetly sunken white shelves filled with novels, photos and art in between tall sunken windows with wooden seats. In one corner, a huge silver TV screen faces a right-angled white leather settee with a low transparent table in front, and behind that is a period chaise longue upholstered in red velvet in front of a purple cube covered in magazines. There are gold-stemmed lights with white concertinaed shades dotted all around. In another corner of the vast room, a round smoked-grey table has maroon sculpted-plastic chairs around it and on the wall above is a massive painting of a white plate set on a dark red table against a paler red wall. Everything balances, just right, and yet moves your senses on to the next element designed to match or complement the last. It's so peaceful and yet so alive. I've never been in a room like it.

'Wow,' I shout.

'Yeah, it's OK,' he calls back. 'Espresso all right?'

'Sure.' I hate espresso.

As I turn to look at the wall behind me, my eyes swing along the floor to register a large white fireplace, but my vision is instantly dragged upwards to the massive gash of colour above – a huge framed print – two enormous bright red rectangles on top of each other, the top one smaller than the bottom, on a lighter red background. I recognise the style immediately from an exhibition that Mum dragged Reece and me around. It's a Rothko print. Christ, I haven't thought of that day in years. But now I hear the muted muttering of visitors, smell the polish on the shiny floors and see the huge canvases stretching down the white-walled gallery. Reece and I were comatose with boredom, slumped in front of these massive rectangular splodges of colour that seemed so dull and indistinguishable. But Mum would not be hurried.

'Look at the blurred edges – see how they make the paintings pulsate,' she said. 'It's so – sensuous.'

'Muuum,' Reece moaned with embarrassment. He must have been about fourteen, which would make me ten.

'They're so big,' I whined.

'Yes. So you don't just look at them, you enter them,' Mum said in wonder.

Reece rolled his eyes at me.

'They're landscapes of the soul,' she continued, 'windows into our deepest desires.'

I was equally transfixed, but not by the art – by the intensity of her focus. When we finally dragged her to the coffee shop, we were whooping with relief. Has Reece become pretentiously sophisticated in adulthood? Or is this just in memory of Mum? At least he's chosen a bright upbeat one, not one of the depressing black or maroon monstrosities I remember. Positioned in front of the painting is a single white leather armchair and matching footrest. Does Reece sit here, staring up at this intense print? Why?

'You like this stuff now?' I ask as Reece enters carrying two small white cups of coffee.

'Kinda. It's from—'

'I know,' I say taking the stupidly tiny cup and wincing at the bitter concoction. I am about to turn away when I notice something on the minimalist white mantelpiece, below the massive print: two little grey-framed pictures, a small rectangle and a long rectangle, like a tangential nod to the dimensions of the Rothko above. I step closer and incline my head to avoid the glare of light on the glass.

'Oh my God.'

The long one is a series of photos like in a flip book, showing teenage Reece from the hips up, shirtless, his head thrown back off camera, foregrounding his stunning rope-muscled torso as he arches up in a leap. And I know instantly that these are from Mum's final undeveloped roll of film, from her 'Falling' series, that I've only ever seen in negative form.

'Why?' I ask.

'They're me. Why shouldn't I?' he says, combatively.

My eyes slide across to the smaller framed photo, a single instamatic-camera picture, with its thick white base margin – of Mum, lying on one of our green sunloungers wearing the skimpy red bikini that she got that final summer, smiling up at the photographer, shading her eyes. Her full breasts are pushed up by the revealing top, the top one almost spilling out, and the scanty briefs hug her hips. It was Reece who got an instamatic camera for his eighteenth from the Robertses, just two months before she died.

'You took that?' I ask.

He nods.

'Must be one of the last.'

'The day before – d'you want to sit?' he says, gesturing. In Reece's presence I feel like a kid again. I stride towards the poofy white settee, crouch, and then jump onto it, trying to do one of the standing-start jumps that we used to practise in our endless physical prowess games in the woods. Not having done one for years, I miss the edge of the settee entirely and crash to the floor.

'You all right?' asks Reece, running over. 'What happened?'

'I'm fine,' I say, struggling up. 'I was doing a standing-start jump.'

'Why?'

I shrug.

The edge of his white marshmallow of a sofa has a dark smear from my boot, so I quickly sit down on it. Reece sits on the far side of the right-angle. I realise that I'm tapping my fingers rhythmically on my thigh: *Tee-hee-hee – Oh my God – Tee-hee-hee*: short short short – long long long – short short short. Morse code for SOS, as if I'm trying to signal him across a long distance. All those childhood games we shared in the woods – races, endurance trials, coded messages – now it seems like we were training for war.

'It's really freaky,' he says, peering at me with what can only be called fascinated revulsion, 'you look so like her now.' So, it wasn't just the wig for him.

'I'm just thinner,' I say, crossing my arms.

'Have you been on some extreme diet?'

I haven't seen him for fifteen years and we're discussing diets? God, this weird British ability to keep a conversation going with so many elephants in the room we should both be trampled.

'Oh yeah, I've got a personal trainer and everything,' I say sarcastically.

'So have—oh. Well, you're much thinner.'

'But I was still lovely before?' I say pointedly.

He raises his eyebrows and I feel a spark of our old sarky sparring.

'It just dropped off,' I say to needle him, but also I don't want to get into what really happened.

'Are you still in Brighton?' he asks.

'No, I'm at Dad's – like I said.'

'Oh, I didn't realise you'd actually moved in. Couldn't you sort carers?'

'He's had carers, twice a day for months. You haven't been around.'

Reece sighs.

I ping the elastic on my wrist.

'He was getting worse, so I gave up the shop and my flat.'

'You were still at the same shop?'

'Yes.' I can't believe it: we're having the same conversation we had fifteen years ago. 'It was the right thing to do,' I say, stiffly.

I knew Reece so well once, and being in his presence required no self-aware shift, but now I feel formal and embarrassed. I clamp my hands under my thighs to stop my Morse signalling.

'So you've moved in with him – permanently?'

'Yes. Well, till he . . .'

He brushes an invisible fleck from his white chinos, as if I've just commented on the weather. 'Do you need money?' he asks.

'No! And I'm not leeching off Dad, if that's what you mean.'

'I didn't say you were.'

'Fine, but I'm not.' I stand abruptly, walk over to the window and look through the thinly slatted white blinds. 'Dad's really ill,' I say, trying to find an even keel of connection.

'And?'

I look back at him, but he just stares impassively.

'And – there's stuff to do. All the consent stuff – power of attorney for medical decisions, financial stuff. And you know – "do not resuscitate" when the time comes.'

'Yep, sounds good.'

'What? Not resuscitating?'

'If he's really ill,' he says matter-of-factly.

'Reece, come on.'

'It's really disconcerting that you keep calling me Reece.'

'OK. Ryan, come on.' I walk back, trying to swallow my annoyance. 'So, shall we apply for joint power of attorney? I've got all the forms.'

He makes a face. 'You do it. I'll sign whatever you need.'

'You don't have to. One sibling can do it without informing the other, if the parent signs of course. Although I'm not sure if Dad will be up to it – if not I'll have to look into all the competency stuff.'

'Great, crack away,' he says, with a flourish of his hand.

'It's not tiddlywinks, you know. More like – solving a Rubik's cube?'

He smirks. 'Yeah, yeah, I know that was more your thing. Sorry about nicking it. I bow to your superior mastery,' he says, inclining his head.

'It's complicated but OK, I'll do it.'

Then I catch him glancing at his watch. Oh no, he's not getting off that easily.

'But Dad could still rally, could come home even and the house isn't in a fit state for his needs. I ran into Marcus and he said he'd help—'

Reece's eyes flare. He stands and walks out of the room. Have I been dismissed? I scan his bookshelves: *The 5:2 Diet*, *The Shredded Chef*, *Juice Fasting*, perhaps he's not quite so effortlessly slim; *The Art of Now*, *Mindfulness*, *Anger Management*, ha, this walking-away trick is a typical anger management technique – but it's such a power play, leaving the walked-away-from flailing.

A few moments later he returns with two waters in delicate long-stemmed glasses, places them on the low table and sits down.

'You don't need to involve the bloody Robertses,' he says. 'Use proper, qualified workmen, I'll pay.'

I sit down on the black mark again, but notice my boot has also left a dark smudge on Reece's perfect white floor, so put my foot over that, like I'm playing a private game of Twister. I remember Mum, Reece and me laughing uproariously as Dad read out the colours until we all eventually collapsed on the plastic map of coloured dots.

'Why did you write that stupid book about us?' I say quietly.

'It's not about you,' he says darkly.

'Weeping sister?'

'You were my sister. You did weep.'

I register his use of the past tense, like a slap.

'You're hardly "letting sleeping dogs lie".'

'I had to control the narrative.'

'What?'

'The press had finally connected Ryan Patterson with Reece Davidson.'

'So you decided to help them?'

He looks at me like I'm a silly child. 'They were going to do a big spread about Mum's death, with or without me. Their version would have been lots of scurrilous supposition. My agent Anastasia advised me to write a memoir they could serialise, so they'd have their scoop, but I would control the story.'

'But why didn't you contact me? Or Dad?'

'According to you, Dad's beyond caring. And you and me – weren't in contact.'

Like I chose that? But I can't bring myself to bleat that he dumped me.

'Why say suicide?' I ask instead. 'After everything you said before.'

'You'd prefer I'd written "my dad killed my mum, boo hoo, poor me, son of a murderer".'

'No! That would be libel,' I say, my voice too loud.

'Are you still such a Pollyanna? Dad was a drunk and a bully who ruined Mum's life, then killed her.'

'That's ridiculous. You've just decided that he was a monolithically difficult angry man. It's not what I remember.'

'Well, you're not me.'

'That evening you described – it wasn't like that – it was so tense.'

'It was twenty-three years ago, you're the one not remembering clearly—'

'Low-fat spray cream,' I say, cutting him off.

'What?'

'That he made sure we never ran out of for your hot chocolate after football.'

'So?'

'So, he cared.'

'No, he shouted all the time,' he shouts.

'Sometimes. But he took you to football, taught you cricket bowling, and did football bets with you at the weekends.'

'Ah, so a bit of sports cancels out murdering Mum,' says Reece sarcastically as he takes his glass of water and moves away to the smoky table.

I have to somehow swim up through this thick sheet of ice that Reece's frozen certainty always forces on us – or I will drown under it.

'He thought I was Mum,' I say slowly.

'Who did?'

'Dad, at the hospital yesterday. Talked to me like I was her.'

He jerks and spills some water. 'What did he say?'

'That he was . . .' And now I pause, like he did in his reading, enjoying how annoying he finds it. 'That he was sorry.'

'Oh, finally he's sorry.'

'You think that's what he meant?'

'Of course. Sorry for killing her.'

I shrug.

'Oh Hannah, you're not thinking of digging it all up again?'

Lucky I haven't told him about contacting that detective.

'Are there sleeping dogs to be woken?' I ask. 'Like you inscribed in my book?'

'No, course not, it's just a phrase. I meant don't churn up all your sleeping emotions.'

He's re-interpreting his original meaning. Reece used to do an improv show at the Comedy Store with his famous chums and each week he'd read out some dull text like a shopping list and cleverly imbue it with all sorts of dramatic meaning. Now he's trying to do the reverse and suck the meaning from his portentous scribble.

'Why did you choose that particular extract to read,' I continue, my voice cracking. 'Don't you find it painful?'

'Anastasia said to pre-empt what would most excite interest. I didn't know you'd be there.'

'And of course, it was suitably dramatic for your adoring fans!'

He purses his lips. 'Come on, Hannah. It'll be old news by next week, and we can move on with our lives. I have lots of filming coming up and I need to focus.'

'What about what I need?'

'You need to move on,' he says, checking his watch again. 'I'm sorry, but I've got an appointment.'

'I should be going anyway, lots to do,' I laugh, getting up.

'Once Dad dies,' he says as I approach him, 'maybe you can finally bury all this with him.'

Anger explodes through me like a bomb and I swipe his long-stemmed glass off the smoky table. I thrill at its violent catapulting, the water globules momentarily suspended mid-air as I stride out.

Tearful and adrift in the street outside, I check my phone in case Reece has called me back inside. Of course not, but I freeze as I see that there's an email from Detective Manning.

My finger hovers above the link.

I do want to move forward in life without looking back. But it's like when you try to rename a document on your computer – you can type in the new name, but it won't be accepted if the document is still open. I have to close the document of Mum's death once and for all, whatever the truth, so I can move on.

I open the email.

Dear Ms Davidson,

I received your message via LinkedIn. I remember your mother's case very well and regret that we were unable to bring anyone to justice. I am no longer with the police so can't talk in any official capacity, but would be happy to talk to you as a private citizen.

Yours sincerely,
Chris Manning

Reece would vehemently disapprove of me replying. So, I click the phone number link.

'Hello?' says a deep male voice.

'Detective Manning?'

'It's just Mr now,' he says, sounding clipped and annoyed. 'Who is this?'

'Oh, hi, this is Hannah Davidson. You replied to my message.'

'Ah, yes, Ms Davidson.' He's so abrupt and matter-of-fact.

I think of the young man in the overcoat who lowered his eyes as he confirmed that Mum was dead.

'Could I come to talk to you about Mum's case?'

'There's a consultancy fee of £70 an hour. Would this be acceptable to you?'

'Fine. When might you be free? I mean as soon as is possible.'

'Sure. Tomorrow morning? I'm in Northwood, on the Metropolitan Line – I'll WhatsApp you the address. Is that OK?'

'Great. Thanks.'

As I click off my phone, I notice my biro'ed hand, warning me 'Don't be too much'.

Too late for that.

CHAPTER TEN

How did Schro get out again? He's sitting out on the pavement outside the house, and as I get closer, I realise that the lights are on. Did I leave them on? As I quietly push the front door, I hear the shifting of crockery and catch movement in the gap of the half-closed kitchen door. A thief? These big houses backing onto the woods are so vulnerable and so tempting with the easy pickings of all the old people now living alone in their family homes.

'Who's there?' I shout from the porch.

The noise ceases.

I shift my weight onto the balls of my feet, ready to run. Then out comes Mrs Roberts.

'Ah, Hannah, dear, there you are.'

'Hey, Mrs . . . Libbie.' She's insisted I call her Libbie since I've been back, but it's like thinking in a different language and then translating before speaking – she'll always be Mrs Roberts in my head.

I'm slammed back to when Dad and I were trying to get by in our bleak little routine after Reece left for good. Mrs Roberts kept letting herself in, bringing us meals, tidying up, trying to cheer us up, and it took us months to make clear that we wanted to be left alone. We've had very little contact since I left for uni at eighteen and since I've been back, I've only exchanged pleasantries.

'Come here,' she says as she envelopes my rigid form in a comforting M&S-cashmere hug. I stiffen with the memory of Mr Roberts' Hawaiian-shirted embrace yesterday as he manhandled me into the house. What a grubby mind I have. He was just trying to help. And she was a second mother to me once. My irritation evaporates in my body-memory of her embraces through the years.

As she releases me, she peers into my eyes, giving me her familiar wordless nod.

'Frank said you were having a tricky time of it, I'm so sorry. We thought we should pitch in, so I'm restocking your fridge. It was pretty empty,' she laughs. Given her fastidiousness, this house must be her seventh circle of hell.

'Come on in,' she continues on the way into the kitchen, 'I'll bring the teas in.'

She was Mum's best friend, although in so many ways her opposite: Mum was slim, wild and exuberantly talkative while she's sturdy, plodding and a great listener. Mrs Roberts is greyer now, plumper, and her face is more lined. But then everyone's aged, except for Mum, who is forever young and beautiful.

When we were growing up our houses were more like two buildings for one extended family, with very different timetables set by two very different mothers: home was bunking off school for impetuous trips, wild storytelling sessions with flamboyant costumes and tips for hangover cures; next door was regular homework time, nit-combing and helpful articles for teenagers carefully cut from magazines. It was Mrs Roberts who came with me to buy my first bra, who collected me after a school fight and who quashed my embarrassment when I fainted trying to insert my first tampon. But it was Mum who showed me how to apply liquid eyeliner without smudging, who screamed with me as we watched *The Exorcist* together and who bought me my first alcoholic drink at age thirteen, a thrillingly exotic Bacardi Breezer, purchased during one of our 'girls only' trips without Dad and Reece. The summer before she died, she took me to Wembley Arena to see The Cranberries: intoxicated by the daring of the trip, by the admiring glances at my glamorous Mum and by the thrillingly illicit alcohol, I was enthralled by the diminutive Dolores O'Riordan belting out the song 'Zombie' twice that night. In Mum's last year she would endlessly sing 'Zombie' with me; she would help me to apply the non-permanent red or black hair dye I used at weekends to look like Dolores, that never quite washed out enough for Monday morning school; and just a couple of weeks before she died, Mum gave me a beautiful silver cross identical to the one Dolores often wore, which I dug out last year when Dolores herself died tragically. The cross hangs on the chain round my neck now, nestling next to a small pebble with a hole in it from Brighton beach.

'I miss her too,' says Mrs Roberts as she catches me caressing the cross when she returns. Mrs Roberts is the only person I can really share my pain with now that Dad is fading.

'It's been so long,' I stutter, 'but, especially being back here, I kind of feel her presence.'

She nods. 'I know, me too,' she says gently. 'I feel her so close sometimes – especially in the woods.' She lowers a tray with two mugs of tea and a plate of her famous home-made Florentine biscuits. I used to love these as a child. If I can't have a proper drink yet cos Mrs Roberts would disapprove, at least I can eat. My teeth tingle on the sweet crackling, and the dark chocolate makes me salivate. Mrs Roberts smiles encouragingly as I take a second bite, my pleasure giving her pleasure. I'm lucky to have one of my mums left.

'How's your dad doing?' she asks, catching my frown. 'Oh no, he's not—'

'No, no,' I say, swallowing, and putting the biscuit down surreptitiously as the sweetness is overpowering. 'He had a bad fall, but he got through the night. But at the hospital, they kind of implied,' I say, my voice cracking, 'that I was a bit to blame, that I've endangered Dad.'

I sob as she strokes my hair.

'You're doing all you can,' she says eventually. 'Where there's life there's hope.'

'But he could die any day now. Best-case scenario, he comes home an invalid – and the house isn't in a fit state.'

'Oh well, I can clean up, I love a project,' she says with genuine enthusiasm.

'Actually, I bumped into Marcus yesterday – he said he'd help.'

'He doesn't really work in this area. But I can always find you the number of someone who does.'

'Look at him there with Reece,' I say, motioning to a

large photo canvas lying on its side. Mrs Roberts gets up to right it. It shows Reece and Marcus, leaping through an arc of water from a garden hose, laughing in total abandon, with the sheen of a rainbow in the suspended droplets. It was part of her final exhibition before she died: 'Falling' – endless photos of things mid-air, but with no reference to where they fell from or what they would land on. All the hallways and staircases in the house are full of these photos: a china cup arcing through the sky (Mum broke half of our cups for that shot); Feynman at the height of a leap, twisting to reach his favourite chew toy (so many attempts, even he lost interest in his favourite game); and me dropping backwards from the monkey bars in Highgate Woods (I did it so many times, I lost my grip and broke my elbow). 'It's the moment in between,' Mum would say, 'after something leaves the safety of support, but before it lands and becomes prosaic again – in that moment, it can't be controlled.' I'd always thought of Mum's falling photos as rather dangerous. But now, as I remember swiping Reece's fragile glass off the table and the thrill it gave me, I think perhaps these photos aren't dangerous – maybe they're wild and free, like her.

'Your mum was a brilliant photographer,' says Mrs Roberts. 'Really making a name for herself when . . .' She squeezes my arm. 'Are you having a sort-out?' she asks, motioning to the mess.

'Yeah, last night, I think.'

'Oh, I'm always doing cleaning and sorting at night,' says Mrs Roberts. 'I find it calming.' I think of her spotless modern home. Since moving back in I've gone along with Dad's rigid hatred of change in this dusty, cluttered house.

So, why last night? I get up and restack a pile of unframed prints of Reece – a sports series of him playing football in a singlet, playing beach volleyball bare-chested in jean shorts, and diving off the high board in tight, form-hugging speedos. He had a fleshy abundant physicality back then – so different from his present almost sheared-to-the-bone quality. Must be all that fasting and meditation.

'Philip will pull through,' she says.

'But he's so fragile and confused.'

'Confused?' she asks with concern.

'Today he didn't even recognise me, and before that, he thought I was Mum and wanted my forgiveness. You don't think – that Dad had anything to do with what happened to Mum?'

'Of course not.'

'Do you remember them arguing at all?'

'No. Well . . .' I nod for her to continue. 'Well, your mum came back really late sometimes, what with her busy job, and your dad would be out on the step frantic with worry. There'd be a bit of shouting, but it was nothing – just him worrying about her.' She puts her hand on mine. 'Your parents adored each other. Just because people argue occasionally, doesn't mean anything. Look at Frank and me. We can really go at each other over the most trivial things – doesn't mean we want to kill each other. Sorry, that was—' She stands. 'I'll get some more hot water in the pot.'

Tee-hee-hee – Oh my God – Tee-hee-hee. I tap my lips for SOS while holding my breath, like I used to do as a child, a spell to keep everyone safe. Everyone and everything I could mention while tapping and holding my breath would be safe: my family, everyone we knew, famous people, people in the shops – I would speed-name every category of person I could think of, and just as I desperately needed air I would add the universe, any other universe, matter, antimatter, everything I knew, everything I didn't know, past, present, future . . . and then I would take a huge gulp of air, hoping that the world would not be sucked into a black hole because I had forgotten some loophole that dark forces could use to wreak havoc. I suddenly remember doing it standing at the top of the stairs with Reece once, hearing Mum returning in the early hours and something being smashed in the kitchen. But that was just a one-off argument, wasn't it – the next morning I was stirring my chocolate Ready Brek into a thick paste as usual as Mum bustled around the kitchen and Dad read the paper. But does Reece remember more of this kind of thing because he's older? Can two siblings remember the same childhood differently?

Mrs Roberts returns with the tea.

'Goodness, your hair's getting so long isn't it.'

'I know,' I moan. 'Reece says I look just like Mum now.'

'Oh, have you seen him?' she says hopefully.

'Just a quick chat.'

'I circle the *Radio Times* whenever he's on,' she says with a grin. 'He's so good in that *Muerte* thing, isn't he?'

'Haven't seen it,' I lie.

'Really?' She picks up our remote and flicks to iPlayer. I read the blurb: *Muerte: Detective Ralph Pennington (Ryan Patterson) solves cases and conundrums in the expat community of Torremolinos – 'where beer is cheap and life is cheaper'. Series one, episode one: 'Rocking on Empty'.*

'Ooh, this is a good one, it's got loads of stars in it,' Mrs Roberts says with glee. The show attracts good actors, who probably see it as a jolly out in Torremolinos. 'It's about an ageing rock band,' she gushes, 'holed up in Spain to finish their comeback album.' I clench my fists as the formula kicks in – 1. Short, intriguing scene, 2. Dead-body shot, 3. Implausibly upbeat music over the credits.

The band are lounging round a private villa's pool.

'What the hell are "bells of doom"?' asks the pasty-faced guitarist sarcastically, while the balding lead singer knocks back tequila straight from the bottle.

'Who cares, it rhymes with moon,' slurs the emaciated singer in leather trousers despite the heat.

'You may not need the cash,' snarls the long-haired bandana-sporting drummer, 'but some of us have three lots of alimony to pay.'

'More fool you,' the singer sneers.

Cue drunken fight. Cue cross-fade to the inevitable shot of the singer staring up glassy-eyed, a swordfish stabbed through his chest. Cue the jolly music of the opening credits and the montage of Reece leaping about in Spanish settings.

'Great,' I say, reaching for the remote, 'but I should—'

'Let's just catch a glimpse of Reece.'

The credits end and there he is, all tanned and stylish, questioning the drummer.

'My dad loves your music,' says Reece as Detective Pennington.

'Yeah, we're old, cut it out,' snarls the bandana'ed drummer.

'No, I love rock, and you're legends,' says Reece with sincerity. Reece loathes rock music with a passion.

His beautiful police sidekick pushes through the swing doors, replete with long tanned legs, short shorts and sultry Spanish curls. The guitarist pats her bottom and Reece springs up.

'Nothing ventured,' he quips as he pushes the guitarist into the pool.

His grating catchphrase makes me shoot to my feet, and I grab the remote and snap off the TV.

'Ahhh,' she croons. 'How's he doing?'

I look at her excited face and can't trash him to her.

'He's dealt with all this so differently to me – he doesn't look back—'

'He's right: you should have a haircut, buy some new clothes, and get out and about – focus on yourself.'

'But I'm not earning right now – I don't want to use Dad's money on me.'

'It would be like a salary. You're doing loads for your dad. Not many young people would move back in for a parent. My Marcus is a good boy but I can't see him doing that for me and Frank. You're a really good daughter.'

After she leaves, I dart into the kitchen and glug warm white wine straight from the bottle. Mrs Roberts' admiration is so seismically misplaced. I didn't move in to help Dad. I'm not the good Samaritan everyone thinks I am.

Far from it.

CHAPTER ELEVEN

I breathe more easily as I escape central London the next morning, trundling along in the high-ceilinged Metropolitan Line train. I couldn't eat anything first thing because of my hangover, but I've cleared my head with caffeine and painkillers. I've drawn three hundred pounds on Dad's debit card to cover costs. If I prove Dad innocent, it's money well spent; if he's guilty, it's blood money, so who cares. I get out at Northwood's small nondescript station on the corner of a well-to-do high street – all squeaky-clean commuter belt, big cars, wide roads and fat detached houses with pointless front gardens. Manning lives on 'Links Way' – so presumably near a golf course. He made his money failing to solve crimes like ours, then retired early to relax on the links, enjoying boozy lunches in the clubhouse. Bastard. After a fifteen-minute walk, I arrive at an ugly yellow bungalow with a massive triangle in brickwork surrounding the front door. It has a large metal electric gate and I have to ring the pavement intercom.

'Yes?' says the gruff voice from our call.

'Hannah Davidson, Detective Manning.'

'Mr. I'll release the gate.'

It slides back with a loud mechanical straining, then a clunk. I walk up the crazy paving to the triangular portcullis. The door opens and there he is. Not what I was expecting from his gruff voice. He's younger looking than his forty-nine years. His brown hair is longer and wavier than the short, clipped style I remember. But his eyes are still dark and intense. He's got a shaving cut on his chin. Oh, and he's in a wheelchair. Great, I'm in an episode of *Ironside*, that wheelchair detective programme Dad loved.

'Hannah,' he barks, as he backs his chair up to let me enter. I step in, extending my hand, which he ignores, so I run it through my hair as if that's what I intended all along.

'Come through.'

He rolls towards an open door ahead of us. I follow into a bright square room with dark blue walls, a leather sofa and a leather easy chair. He faces the settee, so I perch there.

'I was shot during a robbery,' he says matter-of-factly. 'I don't explain upfront on the phone as it puts people off, when in fact it has no effect on my capacity.'

'Right,' I say, nodding stupidly. 'That happened to me once.'

'Being shot?'

'No.' God, why have I started this. 'I was internet dating, and just before I was about to meet this bloke I'd been chatting to, umm, he texted to say that he was paralysed from the neck down – and did it make a difference to me.'

111

'And did it?' he says with interest. Jesus, could I get my once-fat foot further into my once-fat mouth.

'I didn't go,' I say quietly, feeling my face flooding bright red with shame.

He nods inscrutably.

I tongue an ulcer inside my cheek.

'Fair enough,' he replies. 'I'm not paraplegic but I assume you only want me for my mind today?'

'Yes, absolutely,' I stammer.

He laughs.

'I've got your money, one hundred and forty pounds, enough for two hours,' I say, holding out my envelope of cash to him. 'But I've got more if we go on.'

'No need to put the money straight on the nightstand,' he laughs.

'Sorry,' I say, dropping it on the glass table. 'I'm weirdly nervous.'

'No, I'm sorry, I always overdo jokes. You're meeting a man you last met when you heard your mother was dead. Weirdly nervous sounds par for the course.'

I feel myself relaxing slightly with this gruff, straightforward man. But I must keep my wits about me.

'I hope I'm not putting you out, seeing you on such short notice.'

'God no, I'm bored rigid. Since this,' he says, nodding to his chair, 'I do a bit of teaching, and advice for writers, but—' He shrugs and assesses me. 'I remember you, from that day.'

I swallow, wrong-footed by this abrupt swerve to the past.

'I remember you, too. You were – very young – for a detective.'

'Yeah,' he snorts, 'youngest ever in my station, golden boy, glittering career, and then . . .' He gestures theatrically to his chair.

'When did . . .?'

'Two years ago. Stuff happens,' he says with a shrug. 'But I don't need to tell you that.'

'No.'

We both smile.

'You, on the other hand, have changed a lot,' he says. 'Though of course now you look like—'

'My mother. Yes, so I keep being told – it's the long hair and the weight loss.'

'I've often thought that criminals on the run should just eat a lot of burgers – easier and cheaper than dodgy surgery.'

I laugh.

'You'd be near the same age she was when—'

'I'm exactly the same as she was when.'

'Is that why you're looking into all this now?'

I shake my head. 'My dad's dying.'

He frowns. 'I'm sorry. He was a decent bloke.'

I'm shocked by this unexpected assessment of Dad. 'You thought that? It's been so hard, not knowing if—'

'—he killed your mother?'

'Yeah.'

'Lots of decent men do kill.'

I swallow. 'And the other reason I'm looking into this now, is that my brother – you remember Reece?'

He nods.

'Well he published an autobiography recently, in which he said that Mum killed herself.'

'Did he indeed. Well, I do know who your brother is. Stuck here, I watch a lot of TV. He plays that tosser of a cop in that Spanish abortion of a show.'

I laugh. I'm so used to hearing Reece talked about reverentially as such a star.

'And of course, I remember him from the interviews. Very' – he searches for the word – 'smooth.'

'Also, and it's probably nothing – but my dad's got dementia and he mixed me up with Mum' – he shrugs as if to say, *of course* – 'and when he thought he was talking to her, he begged me for forgiveness, so, I wanted to ask—'

'If I think he did it.'

I nod.

He manoeuvres his wheelchair to the kitchen area.

'At least you haven't said you're looking for "closure",' he says over his shoulder. 'I can tell you what I remember. But I can't produce a silver bullet,' he adds, filling the kettle.

'I don't have any expectations,' I say as I walk over to lean on the immaculate grey granite countertop. 'My bar is set really low.'

'My second favourite kind of bar,' he says, 'after The Weavers up the road, obviously.'

I smile. 'It's . . . difficult, delving into my old life.'

'I get that. I've pretty much holed up here since my accident. This is my parents' old house – well away from my old life.'

'Ah. It didn't seem very – you.'

He shrugs. 'They died very close together, just before my accident, and left me it. I needed somewhere to lick my wounds.'

'I think that's what I've been doing too. But how much

licking is enough,' I say, and then go bright red at the innuendo.

He smiles and looks away. 'Tea or coffee? I can talk you through the leads we considered.'

'Whatever you're having.'

'Tea, then. And I assure you, we followed every lead.'

'I'm not here for blame. But I was only fourteen at the time and kept out of the loop.'

He prepares the tea in cat-photo mugs and catches me eyeing them.

'My niece made them – I use them as often as I can in the hope that I smash one. Could you?' he says, gesturing at the tray. 'As I'm sure you're aware, the coroner ruled an open verdict. Which is often used for suspected suicides, but when motive and means aren't clear, or where events are too confused for any definitive ruling.'

'But I thought the police had ruled out suicide – and that's why you questioned Dad.'

'Your mum died from a single stab wound with a kitchen knife, at around midnight. A knife with an unusual black oriental-effect handle, not from her kitchen. It penetrated the sternum at an odd angle.' He goes back to the kitchen area and returns holding a knife. 'It was a typical kitchen knife like this, a formidable weapon.' He lifts it in the air. 'Will you be mother?'

'What?'

He registers my horror.

'Sorry, I meant will you pour the tea. Unfortunate turn of phrase.'

I snort.

'It was an odd angle for suicide, from above but with a

sideways turning. Which is physically just about possible to self-inflict,' he says, demonstrating on himself.

'Here, you try,' he says, passing me the knife. 'Lift it really high and then angle it to the side.'

I try but I can't get a proper purchase.

'Now I can show you the angle an assailant would have used. On you. If that's OK?'

'Sure,' I say, passing him the knife.

He lifts it above me, widening his eyes to ask permission. I nod.

'We're both sitting down, but we're parallel,' he says, bringing the knife down slowly. 'You see how the angle is much easier to achieve if another person is holding the knife.'

I lean in slightly to feel the tip pressing into me.

'And to get the right angle,' he says, lifting the knife higher, 'the attacker would need to be taller than the victim, even taller than I am to you. So, it was almost certainly a man, of considerable height and strength – as it would take real force to jam the knife in, shattering a rib and sinking in so deep.'

I wince away from the blade.

'So, murder was much more likely?'

'Yes. But the knife only had your mother's fingerprint on it. And there were no signs of a scuffle, no other injuries, no torn clothing.'

'So, it could have been suicide?'

'Unlikely. I have a photo of the actual knife here, if you—'

I nod.

From a thick manila folder on the couch, he pulls

out a coloured photo of a large kitchen knife against a scale. The thick, shiny black handle has a samurai effect, expensive-looking, heavy, and with the burnished dull metal that properly posh knives have – designed to slice cleanly and smoothly into meat. It's stained with a dark, dried brown substance – Mum's blood. Manning doesn't comment. He passes me another photo – a close-up of the handle dusted with powder, showing a partial print.

'See how the end of the handle seems to have been wiped. The only print, hers, was an odd partial, suggesting either she gripped it very oddly or someone wiped it. There was heavy rain that night, but fingerprints are oil based and usually remain intact. However, from the traces of canine saliva, we know that a dog, most likely that of the dog walker who initially discovered the body, did lick the knife.'

'Stop it.' My chest tightens and my forehead is clammy as I brush my hair away.

'You've gone very white,' he says, looking at me with concern. 'Head between your knees. Now.'

I bend forward and feel my sight folding in with a lurching nausea.

'Breathe,' I hear him calling.

I can feel that boisterous dog nuzzling and licking Mum's blood on the knife impaled in her, and I swipe at my chest and gasp for breath.

A brown paper bag appears in front of me with the top funnelled in his hand.

'Breathe into the bag.'

The crinkly paper inflates and deflates. Like a heart. In. Out.

My breathing slows and as the blackness recedes, I sit back up.

'Slowly,' he says, 'lie down.' I swivel and lie back.

'I'm sorry,' I mumble.

'Most drama this room's seen in years. Since my niece pranced around re-enacting *Truly, Madly, Deeply* after she forced me to watch it recently. Have you eaten?'

'I—'

'So, no. Stay there.' He comes back with chocolate fingers on a plate with cats round the rim. 'Feel free to smash it Greek style after.'

I laugh, munching the fingers, and feel the world righting itself.

'Panic attack,' he says.

'I'm not a panicker.'

'Yeah, yeah.' He sits next to me in companionable silence.

'So, on balance?' I say eventually. 'Murder.'

'Almost certainly.'

'And you never charged Dad,' I say, twisting my head to look at him.

'There was no direct evidence. He was adamant that he was at the house all night. And your brother confirmed it. They alibied each other.'

'Did they?'

'But they both slept for some of that time, so it's hardly rock solid. They both said they woke not knowing that your mum wasn't there in the morning. Your parents didn't sleep in the same room?'

'No – Dad snored, so he usually slept in the spare room, next door.'

I think of her closed bedroom door. How we all had to tiptoe past in the morning because Mum was 'sleeping in'.

'I never saw her that night.'

'But your father and brother both said they thought she was there. Are you doubting them?'

'Nooo.'

'Has your dad ever said anything to make you doubt his story?'

'He refused to talk about it. And now he's got dementia—'

'I'm sorry.'

'As you said, stuff happens.' I sit up slowly. 'Why do you have this file – if you've left the police?'

'It's a copy. It was my first case and I couldn't let it go, always thought I'd think of some new lead. What do you believe?'

'Dad couldn't have done it.'

'And your brother?'

'He's saying suicide in the book.' I don't want to out Reece's real views on Dad.

'To be fair, there were those faint scars on her wrist, from an earlier suicide attempt.'

'What! Which wrist?'

'Her left. Very faint.'

'Jesus.' She always wore a gold watch on her left wrist, but how did I not know this? 'So, what else?' I say, focusing on moving the envelope of money so that it's perpendicular with the table edge.

'We interviewed the dog walker who found her, but he appeared genuinely shocked by his discovery and there was no reason to doubt him. And we interviewed lots of local residents.'

'But you mainly focused on Dad, because of course it's always the husband. That seems very simplistic,' I say, my voice rising.

Manning remains impassive.

'It is statistically likely. But in this case, it was more than stats – it was his unusual behaviour.'

'What d'you mean?'

'Well, he was completely distraught in the first interview, as I might expect. But also aggressive.'

'Aggressive?' I think of my mild-mannered father.

'It didn't seem that suspicious at first. Spouses react in many different ways – monosyllabic grief through to desperate, powerless anger. But I felt he was hiding something from the get-go.'

'Hiding what?'

'Possibly something private or embarrassing. If for instance their marriage was less happy. Or he was gay.'

'What?'

'Highgate Woods is a gay pick-up point – not of the order of Hampstead Heath but there's certainly activity. But there was no evidence pointing in that direction. He claimed that they had a happy, conventional relationship. Though of course, there was the age difference.'

'Meaning?'

'That they got together when she was just nineteen and he was forty-two. So if he liked 'em young, maybe he wanted to move on? But there was no evidence of any affairs . . . of your father's.'

'Mum?' I whisper, knowing the answer.

He nods. 'In his first interview, your father claimed that your mother had lovers, various lovers.'

My eyes are tearing. He points to a box of Kleenex Extra Large on the side table.

'Did you ever suspect anything?' he asks.

I shake my head as I blow my nose.

'Well, you were a child.'

'I was fourteen,' I say petulantly. 'You spoke to these men?'

'He only had one name, a photographer, a Jeremy Leigh. At the photography studio she worked at, but Mr Leigh was seen on CCTV in Norwich that night.'

'But if Dad was guilty, why would he bring up a motive for himself?'

'True. But then he didn't come in the next morning for questioning as arranged. We had to go get him. He'd got himself a lawyer and totally clammed up – like we were interviewing a different man, eerily calm. He claimed that he only really knew for certain about the photographer. Said he was a hiccup in their otherwise happy marriage. Said they led rather separate social lives – but it worked for them. But after years of seeing behind the facades of "happy families", I have ceased to be surprised.'

'Your bar is set pretty low too?'

He nods.

'So, my mum may or may not have had affairs, only one proved, but this Jeremy had an alibi. My parents led socially separate lives. She had tried suicide before. And Dad was strangely tight-lipped. How on earth was that enough for him to be the prime suspect?'

'As I said, husbands are statistically the most likely perpetrator. And shutting down and hiring lawyers to run interference did not inspire confidence. We surmised that your dad had been distraught initially because he'd killed her and was trying to throw blame on real or imagined lovers, and then he clammed up once he'd calmed down so he didn't give himself a motive.'

'But you never charged him?'

'There was no direct evidence – some trace evidence of him on her, but we'd expect that. We couldn't bring a prosecution with no chance of success.'

'And other leads? The whole dark magic angle?'

'Load of codswallop. Just the press trying to sell papers.'

'But it could have been anyone – some lunatic.'

'Theoretically yes. But the murder didn't fit any serial events in the area or across the country. It could have been just an unlucky meeting with someone who never did anything like that again. But that always felt like a cop-out when we had a viable suspect.'

'So, you think he did it?'

'I do.'

Those two words, that in another context are such happy words, fell me.

'I'm sorry. He was hiding something. And if he knew anything, why wouldn't he want the killer caught?'

He touches my hand.

'I get it,' he says gently, 'it's impossible to believe of someone you love. I've had wives presented with clear evidence of their husband's guilt still refusing to accept it and standing by them.'

'You can't unlearn the route,' I say quietly.

'What?'

'That's what Dad said when he was teaching me Morse code – I was writing out all the letters and corresponding dots and dashes and he ripped it up, insisted I learn by sound alone. He said that if I learnt visually, I could never properly decipher aurally, the neural pathways would be too strong.'

'Exactly – our brains won't comprehend information which doesn't fit our original embedded knowledge.'

'But now I do want to look into all this without my preconceptions. So how do I do that?'

'By really listening to other points of view to build a more 3D picture, separate to yours – but it's hard.'

'Is that why you gave up with Dad's case?'

'I didn't give up, even when it wasn't an active case.'

I give a disbelieving frown.

'I'm not lying. I wouldn't, especially not to you. I used to drop in on your dad at random times, with no warning, trying to use "accusation out of the blue" to prompt an inadvertent reveal.'

'And?'

'The last time was on the ten-year anniversary. I remember his exact words. He said "You have to let this go – the scales are balanced."'

'What scales? Of justice?'

'I guess.'

I think of Dad through those years – so thin, so quiet, barely leaving the house. Had he sentenced himself to being a prisoner in his own home because of his guilt?

'But I don't understand. If you were so sure it was Dad, how was I allowed to live with him afterwards? A young girl, living with a murderer.'

'Because we had no evidence, so no right to interfere.'

'That seems astonishing,' I say, standing, my cheeks hot.

'And you had your brother.'

'Reece,' I say with incredulity.

'I know I was ridiculing his TV show earlier, but when your dad was losing it, he was really strong, liaised with us, shielded you as much as he could – he seemed like a rock for you.'

'He fucked off to uni, three weeks later.'

'Our hands were tied. You'd be amazed how many suspects that we're sure are guilty get to go back to their families.'

He keeps manoeuvring his chair to face me as I pace the perimeter of the room then stop abruptly.

'You allowed the papers to print all those wild accusations.'

'We had no control over what the papers printed—'

'Do you know what all that whispering did to Dad – to us as a family.'

He opens his mouth but I cut him off.

'It was all bloody conjecture. You're still suggesting his likely guilt, but you haven't told me a single thing that's solid.' I swipe at the envelope of money and twenty-pound notes fly into the air. 'You killed us all with your accusations and failure.'

'You're still resisting considering his guilt, Hannah,' he says gently.

'Thank you for your time, there's your money,' I say disdainfully, pointing to the notes on the floor.

'You don't need to pay me for today.'

'This was a transaction – information for cash.'

His open face closes in. 'I'm sorry we failed you. Do come back if you want to talk further. And please be careful.'

'Why?' I blurt, childishly.

'Because things don't always lead where you want them to.'

CHAPTER TWELVE

All the carriages are busy on the journey home, so I stand by the toilets, next to a woman smoking out the window. I sip from a quarter-bottle of vodka I got near the station. Intellectually considering Dad's guilt is one thing; accepting it is . . . I'm so wound up that I call Reece for the hell of it, knowing my call will click straight to answerphone. I leave a message designed to infuriate him: 'Hi Reece, just been to see Chris Manning – you remember, the overcoated detective mentioned in your reading. It was . . . interesting.' I hang up.

My phone rings thirty seconds later.

'What do you mean "saw him"?' barks Reece.

'Well, in the sense that I was in his physical presence, opened my eyes and his image was projected onto my retina and inverted upright – so I saw him.'

'What the fuck?' he shouts down the phone.

I move to the other side of the carriage, watching the

woman smoke, and try to let my shoulders settle in the way hers do each time she exhales.

'I told you not to go digging up the past,' he shouts.

'You and Dad alibied each other?' I say evenly.

'What?'

'You alibied each other. You never told me that.'

'So? I alibied you too!'

'And did you know that Mum had tried to kill herself before?' I say, my voice low and hard. 'Is that why you put suicide in your book?'

'Of course I knew – she had a scar on her wrist. How did you not know?'

I gulp a breath. How quickly he takes the upper hand.

'But why would Mum try to kill herself?'

'Because she had to bear living with Dad?'

'Stop it,' I say, kicking the carriage wall, and the smoking woman flinches and chucks her cigarette out the window.

'Sorry—' I attempt, but she walks off.

'It's OK,' says Reece, obviously thinking I'm apologising to him.

'And Mum had an affair,' I continue. 'Perhaps many affairs.' The line seems to have gone dead. 'Did you hear me?'

'Hannah, you're losing it. Leave all this in the past.'

'But it's not in the past for you with your spanking new book, is it. And it's not for Dad.'

'He's totally out of it.'

'No, he seems to be living that time period as if it's happening now. If you're so sure of his guilt, don't you want him to admit it – to pay for it? Did you know about the affairs?'

'She was bored rigid with Dad – it's not surprising.'

'Oh, so now he was a murderer and a bore.'

'You need to stop this, Hannah. It's dangerous to your health.'

'What? If I question anything, it's a sign of my poor mental state.'

'You looked totally unhinged at my reading, then you smashed that glass at my flat, and now all this crap. You're off your pills, aren't you?'

I stay silent.

'So, you are off them. Wow. You're sounding really crazy.'

'I'm crazy if I ask questions?'

'I'm worried for you. You need to see a doctor and get back on the straight and narrow. Everything will look much less bizarre once you're evened out.'

I stab the red disconnect button.

But is he right? How can I use my thoughts to think about whether I'm being rational, if my thoughts are themselves irrational? He's right that I'm not taking my anti-anxiety medication. Haven't since being back at Dad's. Without it, on top of my increased drinking, I do sometimes feel like I'm losing my grip. I've always drunk in the evenings, used alcohol to blank out from thought, but as my stationery shop in Brighton started to go under, I began drinking in the day as well, for courage. And it worked, for a bit: I hit a manic phase, ran huge promotions, got deals with local schools, dressed as favourite book characters to promote creative writing classes. I had a few small surges in profits, but with people buying more and more of their stationery online, the overall angle of the graph of those profits was always downwards.

I stare out the train door window at the rolling countryside zooming past: *da dum, da dum, da dum*. I think of Reece affronted by me hanging up on him just now – going to his beautiful white room, sitting in his stylish white chair, and staring up at his joyous red Rothko poster right now, letting the tension I've caused melt away.

My phone is vibrating in my pocket. Reece trying to make up? Well, he can – but no – it's Chris Manning's number. My chest contracts, but I'm too curious not to pick up.

'Yes?' I say, combatively.

'It's Chris – Manning,' he says gruffly.

'I know – what can I do for you, Detective Manning?'

'I don't like being told what to do.'

'Well, I'm so sorry if I made you feel awkward,' I say sarcastically, 'I—'

'Not you,' he interrupts. 'Don't be ridiculous.'

'What d'you mean then?'

'That brother of yours. I've just had a call from him, saying that you're struggling? Emotionally.' He says the word with distaste.

'What!' I feel instantly threatened by this overlapping of the strands of my life.

'He said you were off your medication and needed help?'

I reach for the lip of the train window, yank it down and gulp the buffeting air.

'Hannah?' I hear him in the distance and drag the phone back to my cold cheek.

'Look, I know I got upset at yours,' I say, 'but I'm really not—'

'Stop it.'

'But—'

'Will you let me get a word in?'

I grip the phone tightly but stay silent.

'Thank you. You seemed eminently sane to me when you were here. If you ask me, he's the one in need of help.'

'Oh. OK. But what makes you trust me and not him?' I ask cautiously.

'Policeman's nose,' he laughs. 'I'm tapping it right now.'

I laugh, relaxing a fraction.

'Thank you. I'm sorry he called you like that.'

'Ah, whatever. You OK?'

'Yeah.'

'Good. I know he's your brother but – fuck him.'

I snort out a longer laugh and he joins in.

'What else did Reece say?'

'He wanted to know what you'd asked me, and I said it was none of his business.'

'Bet he didn't like that.'

'Nope. He ordered me to call him if you got in contact again. Which of course I have no intention of doing. If you do get in contact again, that is.'

'Thanks, I – I would like to be able to call you. I know I got a bit riled earlier.'

'Forget it. Remember I'm a "stuff-happening" survivor myself – I've been there with the anger, the hitting out, the paranoia.'

'You?'

'I know I look suave and sophisticated,' he says with a laugh, 'but inside I'm a helter-skelter of flailing and adjustment. We strugglers need to have each other's backs.'

'Thanks.'

'But Hannah – I've had to accept unpleasant facts, so while I'm not saying your Dad is definitely guilty . . .'

'I know,' I say quietly.

'You be careful – you're clearly a feather ruffler!'

I laugh.

'And call me if you need to, any time. You're not alone.'

'Thank you, Detective.'

'Chris.'

'Thank you, Chris.'

If Reece doesn't want me to look into this, then, however painful, that's exactly what I'm going to do. I google Mum's old photography studio, the one that Detective Manning, Chris, mentioned – the name, in its over-elaborate cursive purple typeface, is imprinted on my memory from seeing it emblazoned on all the endless prints and bags that filled our house: Leigh Photography. And amazingly, it still exists – in Camden, proprietor Jeremy Leigh – the website has the familiar deep-purple typeface: *At Leigh Photography we recognise that we all have our own character and passions – and we will create stunning images to convey your unique story. Our photos will be treasures to enjoy for years to come. We specialise in family, baby, children, and pet photography (adult and couples' intimate photography on request).*

This doesn't sound like the artistic photography that Mum specialised in, but I guess businesses change tack.

Clicking on the tabs, I gather that 'intimate photography' is 'tasteful glamour and nude shots', for which Jeremy promises that he will 'put the subjects at ease and follow the lead and vision of the subject'. I'm amazed that in this era of selfies, people bother shelling out for such staged erotica. But perhaps people just like the showing off. That does sound like Mum.

Given that Jeremy Leigh is the only man that Chris was able to confirm had an affair with Mum, I don't want to risk scaring him off with a direct approach, so I decide to do something that makes my skin crawl.

My call is answered on the second ring.

'Hello, Leigh Photography,' says a smarmy voice.

'Oh hi, yes, I wanted to book a photography session.'

'And what "kind" of photos were you looking for?' he asks, with an odd inflection.

'Oh, just some regular shots, to send to – my mum – in Australia.'

'OK. Well, that would be a hundred pounds per hour and then prices vary according to the print format. I have a cancellation for tomorrow – if that works, three o'clock?'

Not very booked up then.

'Great.'

'And your name?'

'Oh, Desdemona – Clark,' I say, looking at my comfy shoes.

'And do bring a variety of clothes with you, different colours, styles, necklines, so we can – play around with options.'

'Sure.'

'I look forward to seeing you tomorrow, Desdemona.'

'Before you go, could I just ask.'

'Yes?'

'Who will be taking my photo tomorrow?'

'Oh, sorry, that'll be me. Jeremy Leigh.'

CHAPTER THIRTEEN

As I approach the house, the quince tree is silhouetted against the sky, a dark apparition appearing to float malevolently. If Chris's revelation is true, then perhaps Mum didn't adore quince because of Dad's romantic story about Paris and Aphrodite, but for the darker association that she told me about.

We were chopping quince together one autumn. While I loathed the final jam, I loved being part of the yearly ritual of harvesting, ripening, boiling and bottling. Suddenly she scooped up a whole quince and smiled at it.

'Eve's temptation,' she murmured.

'What?' I asked.

'You know. The "forbidden fruit" – from the Garden of Eden.'

'But that was an apple. The Bible says so.'

'No, it just says "the fruit of the tree of knowledge". Apples weren't around in the right region in biblical times – but quince were. So that naughty fruit that destroyed mankind's innocence could well have been the quince.'

'Really?'

'It's totally believable – look at them, so swollen and firm.' She brought hers close and inhaled. 'Mmm, so musky,' she said seductively. Then she sank her teeth into it and grimaced. 'But such a shock when you bite into them raw,' she laughed, spitting the quince into her hand, and flaring her eyes dramatically. 'No wonder Eve felt her innocence had been ruined.'

I'm jolted back to the present when a figure suddenly materialises from behind our quince tree.

'All right, dear?' Mr Roberts asks, his eyes running me up and down.

'Fine,' I say abruptly.

'I was so worried about you. Everything OK? You've been in and out a lot.'

He's watching me?

He reaches out and touches my arm.

'Hello,' calls Mrs Roberts from next door.

He steps back instantly. So, this odd inappropriateness wasn't in my imagination.

'What are you doing, Frank?' she asks. Does she know about his interest in me? 'Invite Hannah in for a cuppa.'

'Oh, no,' I say, but she purses her lips in mock disbelief, with her familiar not-taking-no-for-an-answer look. She was always there for me when Mum was busy. Her pervy husband isn't her fault. 'OK. Thanks.'

'Were you just coming from my house?' I demand of Mr Roberts as we step over the little wall separating our two front gardens.

'Yes, to see how your dad was doing.'

'He'll be home very soon.'

I want Mr Roberts to know I won't be alone, but will Dad ever come home? He slept through the whole of today's visit looking very grey as I watched Loreta knitting across the way. We were like two old ladies waiting for the guillotines to fall.

'Why don't you get on with the garden,' Mrs Roberts says, dismissing her husband. He obeys with resignation as she turns to me. 'Now you settle yourself down in the front room and I'll pop the kettle on.'

I know this house so well. The layout is identical to ours, but there the similarity ends. It's like an alternative reality for our lives – if Mum hadn't died and life had moved on. Our house is all dark walls, heavy velvets and multicoloured throws, surfaces crammed with dusty knick-knacks, endless photographs, and a smell of fustiness and off soup; theirs is all clean lines, empty surfaces, magnolia walls, muted colours, and scented wall plug-ins. This calm, functional house of healthy eating, of working for exams and of little acts of kindness was built on rock. Our vibrant, messy house of pizza for breakfast, of bunking off and of grand gestures has started to feel like a house built on sand.

Above their empty mantelpiece is a large portrait photo of Mr and Mrs Roberts standing either side of a sitting Marcus – an oddly formal photo by Mum, considering that everything else she photographed that last year was unposed, candid camera. In this hyper-formal portrait, the Roberts all face directly forward, backs rigid, looking straight at the camera.

Mrs Roberts bustles in with more bloody tea.

'Your mum took that, a few weeks before she died. I hadn't even taken it out of the bubble wrap when . . . anyway, how are you doing, lovely?' She glances at Mr Roberts who is dragging a large sack of something over to a flower bed.

'It's like I'm underwater.'

She nods.

'I did a bit of a bizarre thing – I saw the original detective.'

'Chris Manning,' she says without a beat.

'You remember him?'

'Of course. He spoke to all of us.'

'He implied that Mum might've had – affairs.'

'Did he!' she says, sounding affronted.

'Did she?'

She looks up to the ceiling. 'Your mum was an amazing woman. Flirtatious yes, but that was just how she was with everyone. I'd never met anyone like her. But then I grew up in Croydon,' she laughs.

'So, you met when they moved in?'

'Yes. Your parents came to look at the house with an estate agent. This big green car pulled up and out she stepped, wearing a short orange dress with tiny beaded tassels and high green shoes, and her long blonde hair shone in the sunlight. She looked up and I was so embarrassed to be curtain twitching, but she gave me this amazing smile.' Mrs Roberts' whole face lights up with that glow I saw Mum ignite in everyone. 'Other people came to look at the house and I kept saying how noisy the street was and how the leaves clogged the gutters, but I thought your parents had passed on it. Then, hey presto, two months later they moved in and she was pregnant.'

'This was '78, when Reece was born.'

'Oh no '77, she lost that first baby.'

'What?'

'She had a miscarriage, very early on.'

'She was pregnant before Reece?' How did I not know this?

'It was tricky. They'd got the house and got married in a hurry cos of the pregnancy, and then – no baby. I felt bad when I got pregnant soon after with Marcus, as I didn't want her to be jealous – but she took it like some sort of challenge – said she and your dad just had to "try harder" – and she was pregnant two months later. We really bonded, being pregnant at the same time, though I was a traditional stay-at-home wife, whereas your mum, even when she was heavily pregnant, wore these super-short little dresses, with boots, heavy mascara and lipstick. But then—'

'What?'

'Well, she had a really difficult birth – three days and nights of pushing, then an emergency caesarean – so she started on the back foot. And it was hard for her being home with a young baby, with her still a kid herself. And then she—'

'Her suicide attempt?' I say, as if it's old news.

She nods.

'Your dad found her just in time, thank God, and after that, he and I encouraged her to go back to university to finish her degree, while I took over having Reece at mine in the day.'

'I'm amazed she went on to have me after that.'

'She'd vowed that she'd never have any more. But then she was feeling a bit adrift from Philip and she was desperate to have another child to feel that connection they'd had after Reece.'

'So, she didn't actually want me?'

'Of course she did. Once you came along. But your dad and I were really careful of her this time. She went straight back to university to do a postgrad degree, and you joined Reece at mine.'

'That seems like a very big favour.'

'Oh no, we were one big happy family. I loved having you both at mine.'

'But do you think she was unfaithful?'

She shrugs. 'I was her best friend, but she kept up with a bitchy little group from university who partied hard. She used to say "there are two 'me's – home me and party me". But partying was just her way of letting off steam. She was very focused, did that course in photography – and then her career really took off and she was in huge demand. It's not wrong for women to want a career. But it's a lie that you can have everything.'

She still hasn't answered my question, but the sound of the back door cuts us off as Mr Roberts enters. I feel awkward under his prurient gaze in front of his wife, so get up.

'Don't leave on my account,' he says.

'I have to get back.'

'Busy lady, like her mum,' says Mrs Roberts, who seems oblivious to the tension between me and her husband.

'Thanks so much for the tea, Mrs . . . Libbie. Sorry.'

She waves my apology away.

'Do you need a lift to the hospital?' Mr Roberts asks with enthusiasm.

'No, I've already been today, Mr Roberts.'

'Frank,' he says awkwardly. 'Let me show you out.'

'No need,' I say, but he follows me to the door.

'I noticed you were having trouble with your lock – I can sort it out if you like? Anything you need doing round the house, I'm pretty handy.'

'It's OK, Marcus said he'd—'

'Oh no, he's very busy. You'll be waiting weeks. Just ask me.' He pats my arm but I slide away.

Back home, I lie on the floor of the lounge, disorientated. I've only ever thought of Mum as the mum I knew: warm, funny, the beating heart of our family. When she wasn't at home, I just missed her horribly, but I never thought of her existing away from us, living her own life.

My eyes are drawn to the bright purple in one of the heaps of strewn books on the floor around me – Mum's university scrapbook. The multi-coloured pages crack as I turn them, tickets, programmes and postcards loosening from the dried-out glue. On the last page, there she is in a formal graduation photo – Jennifer Martin, as she was then – the cloud of golden hair, the fine cheekbones, the porcelain skin and the intense eyes. *The world always at your feet* is scribbled below it. The page is awash with annotations in different handwritings. I scrutinise the scribbled comments and see that three of them have lines connecting to a strip of photobooth pictures on the inside of the back cover: of Mum with three girls labelled as Franny Soames, Mary Stanton and Anne Dangoor. Perhaps this was the bitchy little group that Mrs Roberts mentioned? Would they be able to tell me about Mum's 'party me'?

Franny, the delicate girl with long blonde hair, has

written in neat joined-up writing: *Soul Sister X.*

Mary, the plain girl with a dark bob and chunky features, has scribbled: *Always by your side.*

And Anne, the grinning girl with wispy brown hair, has written in capitals: FRIENDS FOR EVER X.

I try LinkedIn and amongst the King's alumnae from Mum's year, I find the first two. Franny is a dentist in Southampton and Mary is a doctor's receptionist in Putney. I direct message them.

Dear Franny/Mary,

Sorry to contact you out of the blue like this. My name is Hannah Davidson and my mother was Jen Davidson – or Jennifer Martin as you knew her. I'm not sure if you heard about my mum's death in 1996. I wondered whether I could meet you for a chat. My dad is dying and I want to talk about memories of her to him. I look forward to hearing from you.

With all best wishes,
Hannah

Eventually I find Anne on Twitter and follow her. She's a florist in Clapham, single with two children. She does that knee-jerk thing of instantly following me back. I send the same message I sent to Franny and Mary to Anne, by direct message. I wait to see if she'll reply but the DM has disappeared. I check her name again and am disconcerted to find that she's blocked me. It feels so purposely offensive to be blocked by someone I don't even know. As if she has

141

somehow intuited my fundamental worthlessness. I look up Anne's photo in Mum's scrapbook– the smiling brunette in an Alice band – 'FRIENDS FOR EVER x'? What changed?

There are so many photos of Mum in the scrapbook, less formal than the headshot: several at a disco, one of her doing archery, and one at the leavers' assembly with a large group of gowned students throwing their hats into the air. In each photo, Mum seems to be the central focus, as if everyone had arranged themselves around her – their bodies arched towards her, their smiles meant specifically for her, their eyes hanging on her as if she were the centrifugal force in the room.

CHAPTER FOURTEEN

To prepare myself to meet Mum's lover, I shove on my usual scarf-belted jeans and massive grey sweatshirt. My hair is pulled back under a woolly hat of Dad's. I doubt this session will get far, but I might get more out of him by prolonging things, so I need some extra 'looks'. I have to face opening Mum's wardrobe.

Her bedroom is all decked out in the Chinese style that she loved – the painted wooden headboard, the silk-screen wall hangings, red paper lanterns, even a painted Chinese scene on the ceiling. It seemed so exotic to me as a child, but now it looks cheap, tacky and a bit racist. Along the back wall are the black slatted wardrobes that have been closed for twenty-three years. I reach for the little wooden handle, take a breath and pull.

There, in all their rainbow gorgeousness, are her clothes. Dad hasn't moved anything since she died? The stale air inside must contain her exhales from the final time she got dressed. I hold my breath, to avoid breathing any of her in, pull out the first dress I touch and slam the door. It's a full-skirted green dress with tiny pearl buttons down the centre – and there's a huge blow-up photo of Mum wearing it, on the wall behind me. She's spinning round so it swirls out, showing off her slim legs, and her head is thrown back, her hair swinging out, her mouth open in a huge laugh. Perhaps I can use my fleeting likeness to her? I bundle the dress and some high heels into a bag and slip one of Mum's lipsticks into my jeans.

I check my messages on LinkedIn. There's a reply from Franny Soames, who scribbled 'Soul Sister X' in Mum's book.

Dear Ms Davidson,

King's was a very long time ago. Your mother and I were certainly not friends. Please do not contact me again.

Franny Soames

So that's two women who were supposedly close friends of Mum's at university, who want absolutely nothing to do with me. Why not?

At two-thirty, I get the bus down to Camden. Now that I'm about to meet Jeremy, I'm nervous. The dot on my phone takes me down a small side alley, off the high street. I'm not sure what I was expecting, but not this dilapidated shop. Mum's job always seemed so glamorous – so much travel, all the exhibitions, the parties. I peer through the grimy windows at the cheap shelving crowded with empty frames, some fallen flat, others splaying wildly, along with various overexposed pictures of babies and gurning kids. Is this really where Mum worked? I open the door and a little bell tinkles. It's a square room, filled with more photo frames and a print-your-own-photos machine in the centre. A man in his fifties with a small paunch smiles at me.

'Ah, Desdemona, right on time. Jeremy Leigh,' he says, extending his hand. He's a good-looking man for his age, with clear blue eyes and a slightly receding hairline, wearing jeans and an open-necked pale blue shirt.

'Mr Leigh,' I say, shaking his smooth hand, trying not to wince at his touch.

He peers at me. 'You look familiar, have we met?'

'I don't think so.'

'That's an unusual name – Desdemona?'

'My mum was big on Shakespeare.'

'OK, well the studio's downstairs, if you'd like to follow me,' he says, turning away. I watch his buttocks undulating under his jean pockets.

'Did you want to change?' he asks, clearly unimpressed with my look.

'Could we do a few shots first? I'm a bit nervous.'

'Sure, just put your stuff behind the screen.'

His 'studio' is a low-ceilinged room, with a huge roll of white plastic from ceiling to floor, surrounded with cameras and umbrella lights. The screen is a Chinese-style folding one – it's the first thing that does ring true for Mum. I dump my stuff behind it as Jeremy fiddles with the lighting.

'There's some boxes of dressing-up accessories back

145

there,' he calls. 'And a rail of clothing, if any of it appeals to you.' I ignore the garish silky gowns, hats and wigs. I remove my coat, but keep my hat pulled low.

'Come and stand in the centre and I'll do a few test shots,' he says as I emerge.

I wonder if Jeremy photographed Mum here?

I stare at him. *Click.* I turn my shoulder towards him. *Click.* I laugh at the awkward madness of this. *Click.*

'Would you like some music?' he says.

'No, it's—'

A heavy rock beat blares out.

'Could you turn it down a bit?' I shout.

'Oh, sorry,' he says, reducing the volume and focusing his lens on me again.

'Have you worked here long?' I ask disinterestedly.

'Thirty-five years, give or take.'

'Alone?'

'Pretty much. Now shall we lose the hat?' he says, hand extended.

'OK,' I say, sliding it off. He tucks a stray strand of hair behind my ear as I try to breathe slowly. I haven't been touched by a man for years, except for creepy Mr Roberts, and I feel my treacherous body reacting to his closeness.

'Let's loosen you up a bit,' he smirks. 'Turn away from the camera and then look back, to get a more natural look.' I turn and swing back. *Click.* He turns up the music as I straddle a stool awkwardly. *Click.* I sit cross-legged on the floor and look up at him like a child. *Click.*

'Let's try one lying flat out on the floor.'

I lie back. *Click.* He stands over me, one leg on each side of my torso, shooting his camera directly down. *Click.* It is exhilarating being ordered around and so – seen. *Click*. I feel rivulets of excitement trickling through me as I watch myself reflected in his lens.

'Just open your lips a little,' he says, which is easy cos I'm breathing so heavily. There's no one else here. The shop's empty. We're underground, out of earshot. But I feel powerful and unafraid.

'Great,' he says, lowering the camera closer to my face. *Click*. This is Mum's lover. Did she lie here for him? Suddenly this feels incestuous.

'I wonder if this is a great angle for a photo for my mum,' I say abruptly, shuffling out backwards from under his legs.

'Sorry, getting carried away, you're very photogenic – great eyes,' he says, lowering the camera. 'How about a clothes change, and perhaps a lager?'

'Sure,' I say, as I escape behind the screen.

'Try one of the outfits back there,' he calls. 'Photos are all play-acting. You can be whoever you want today, don't be shy.'

I pull on Mum's green dress and her high green shoes. My feet are slightly bigger than hers, but I force them on. I remember Mum's lipstick in my jeans and feel her pouting my lips as I paint on a red gash.

'Lager's here waiting,' Jeremy calls.

Slumped on the top of one of the boxes of accessories, like a discarded mop, is a yellow princess wig. I think of the inadvertent effect of that other wig on Reece at the reading and this time I slide on a Mum wig on purpose. I flick open a couple of the buttons at my chest, step out from behind the screen and swirl around with a huge smile. Jeremy looks at me in horror, his bottle of lager leaping from his grip. I watch it rise, wishing he'd photograph it for Mum's 'Falling' series, as a stream of golden beer shoots out in a sheet, before splashing across the white floor.

I tingle all over with the effect I'm having on him.

'Who the fuck are you?' he demands.

He turns off the rock music and we face each other.

'Who do you think I am?'

He shakes his head at me. 'But you can't be – you're . . .'

'Dead? She is. And she would be a lot older than me by now.' I smile at his slack-jawed horror. 'I'm her daughter. Jen's daughter.'

He's looking at me, but remembering Mum and trying to match us up. I've never before inspired this effect in a man, never felt this electric power. I know how to get men by signalling simple availability for sex, but I've never before provoked this extreme admiration and desire.

'Bloody hell. I knew you looked familiar.' He walks towards me, through the lake of lager, drinking me in. 'That dress! I photographed her in it here.'

'You took that?' Mum looked so utterly happy and free in that photo. She felt like that here? With him? Away from us?

'It's uncanny,' he says. 'How did I not see it before? I mean, you're not exactly the same as her, you're slightly broader, slightly fuller, but still. Blimey O'Reilly.'

I suddenly feel exposed, judged as a less-good version. I start to turn away, but he catches my arm.

'No wait, let me look at you,' he says, holding my wrist tightly.

'I'm not her,' I growl at him, and he drops my arms. 'I'm

a totally different person. I'm going to change.'

I retreat back behind the screen, pull my sweatshirt over the dress and kick off the painful shoes. I pull my jeans on under the dress and wipe my lips on the front of my sweatshirt, leaving a red blotch, then step out again and I see the intensity in his eyes dim. This feeling I know.

'What do you want from me?' he asks.

'Just to talk.'

'God, I'm not your dad, am I?' he blurts, looking appalled.

'Well, thanks for that,' I say sarcastically, 'at least it clears up whether you slept with her.' I pull out a stool. 'No, you met Mum when I was about five, I think.'

'Look, I don't want any trouble,' he says, wiping his hands on his jeans.

'Nor me. I just want to find out about Mum. About her past.'

He frowns.

'I'll still pay you for the hour?'

He wavers but then sits down at the prospect of cash.

'This is seriously weird. I need a smoke,' he says.

'Hey, it's your fire hazard bunker.'

He shrugs, takes a crumpled pack from his table and lights up.

'I'm having another beer. D'you want one?'

God, do I. 'Why not,' I say casually.

He pulls two San Miguels from a little fridge on the floor, flips the tops and hands one to me.

'So, you're Jen's daughter,' he says, leaning back.

'Yep,' I say, taking a large gulp.

'I'm sorry about what happened to her. I was shocked

when I heard about it. And I swear I had nothing to do with it. I was cleared by the police, so if you're here—'

'I know. And I know about your affair. I just want to find out about her – back then.'

He takes a long swig.

'Hey, she was – well you know, she was something else. I mean she was beautiful and all, but it was this' – he splays his hands and his eyes light up – 'this energy she had.' I tense up, inexplicably annoyed at the implication that while I may look like her, I lack her magic ingredient.

'Did you know she was married – had children?' I ask, tersely.

He squirms. 'Yes, but she never really mentioned you. She seemed – unfettered.'

My chest feels tight and I look down.

'I'm sorry,' he mumbles.

'No, I want to hear,' I say, raising my eyes back to him. 'She's dead and my dad's dying. There's no one left to hurt. How did you meet her?'

'Got an email out of the blue. A mass email – saying she was looking for work. She'd just finished some photography course and said she'd do anything, wanted to "learn on the job". I thought I might as well get her in for an interview.' I bet he did. 'Once I met her, well, I had to find her something – took her on as an apprentice.'

'And was this place like this then?' I say, gesturing.

He looks affronted.

'Sorry, but I thought Mum was mostly focused on her projects, rather than spending time working in – a place like this.'

'This is a successful studio,' he says peevishly, 'but yes,

Jen was very driven, had lots of ideas.'

'She worked here, as what – what did she actually do?'

'Well' – he looks shifty – 'she just mucked in. She was good with the glamour stuff, getting people to loosen up. But it was an unpaid position – she helped out if she was around, and in return I taught her and printed her hobby stuff.'

'You mean her projects? But they weren't hobbies.'

'Well, kind of,' he says with a tilt of his head. Oh, I get it now. He didn't actually know Mum that well. He was just some hanger-on, basking in her brilliance. I'm so relieved that this dirty little shop wasn't the setting for her main professional life.

'So, she never had a paid job here?'

'No. She was more – my girlfriend. And just worked here on and off.'

'Well, I imagine she was busy with her proper work,' I insist stiffly. 'She was always on shoots – often overnight,' I gabble, realisation flooding through me as I say the words.

'Well, you know – she stayed over here quite a bit. Sorry.'

I try to mentally recalibrate Mum as a cheater because of her talent. I suppose artists are known for their looser morals?

'How long did you and her . . . ?'

'About five years full on and then whenever. Your dad built her a darkroom at home, and she'd learnt everything I could teach her by then, so it got more casual.'

'Right,' I say flatly. 'She got bored of you.'

He stares at me sulkily. 'Jen had a very low boredom threshold. She always needed the next fix. I was shocked by her death – but not surprised.'

'What. Why?'

'She loved risk.'

'Like this "dalliance" with you?' I say witheringly.

'She didn't follow the norms, in any way. She worked her way through several of my friends. Flaunted it in my face, in fact,' he says bitterly.

'That's upsetting for you, but hardly dangerous behaviour.'

'It was the way she did it. I remember seeing her in the window of the World's End pub and dropping in to sit next to her – and her saying "I'm sorry, but could you leave, I'm trying to get off with that tall guy over there." Just like that, as if we weren't together. I thought, fuck her. And then in she waltzes a couple of days later saying "Oh, that was nothing darling, just letting off steam."'

'Then you broke up?'

He shrugs. 'I let it slide, ignored her other "friends" and just accepted what she was willing to give me.'

I grimace at him and he averts his eyes. But this makes sense. Of course – Mum was just using this pathetic little man.

'So, she was promiscuous and casual with your feelings. But how does that lead to you saying you weren't surprised that she was murdered?'

'It was more than that. Like once we were at a rooftop party in Soho. She was hot and bored and said, "I'm outta here" and she just jumped – literally jumped off the building. We all screamed and rushed to the edge – and there was another building about a foot away below – but did she know that? She laughed and we all applauded.

But it really unnerved me. It was like she was one of those bloody falling pictures of hers.'

'A-ha! Exactly,' I say, pouncing on this proof. 'Her "Falling" photos – so you do know about her art.' Mum may have cheated, but this grubby little man can't just take away her worth as an artist. 'She had all those exhibitions, published books . . .' I tail off as he raises his eyebrows at me. 'She did,' I insist. 'I know she did. I went to the exhibitions, I saw the books, the press . . .'

He shakes his head and I slam my bottle at the wall in frustration, beer spraying over his equipment.

'She did,' I shout.

'Calm the fuck down,' he says. 'I'm just telling you what I know.'

'Well, I know that she was a very successful photographer,' I say petulantly. 'Like the "Falling" series you just admitted to knowing about – that was really big.'

'Yes, but—'

'It's really sexist to deny a woman's career like that, you know.'

He raises his hands in defence and smirks. 'Hey, chill, OK. You don't understand.'

'What don't I understand?'

'Your dad shelled out for all those exhibitions – they cost thousands.'

'My dad?'

'Yeah, he paid for the galleries, the prints, to get the catalogues printed professionally. OK, she did sell a couple of prints, but it nowhere near covered the costs. He even paid for publicists, not that they could get much traction on what were, essentially, vanity projects.'

'Vanity projects?' I say weakly.

He looks at me with pity.

I stand and walk to the other side of the studio, breathing deeply. So Mum wasn't just cheating. She was – ordinary?

'That "Falling" series was pretty cool,' he admits. 'Very her. It all started with Evel Knievel, over there.' He gestures to a large blown-up photo on the wall of the studio, of Knievel astride his motorbike, suspended in the air as he jumped over a line of buses. 'She loved how he was endlessly flinging himself through the air with abandon, and all that nonsense he talked about living life in the moment. She made us watch all these endless videos of him and was always pausing them at the height of his leap and shouting "freeeeeeeee". That's how she got the idea of photographing stuff mid-air.'

'Right. And that "Falling" show was her break into the big time, serious interest from international galleries, her agent said.'

He's pointing his finger at his own chest. 'I told her what she wanted to hear.'

This two-bit narcissist is what she meant by her agent? The film of Mum's whole glamorous life, that's been running in my head for years, is unspooling.

'Your dad would always fund another show, to keep her delusion going.'

I sit down, ashamed by my ignorance, my gullibility. But I can't waste time on that. I have to follow up on her death.

'Did you tell the police about all these other blokes you claim she was with?'

'She was with them. I'm not lying about anything. But no, I just told them I'd been in Norwich all week – which they confirmed.'

'But why not be totally honest with the police? If you had nothing to hide.'

'Look, it really freaked me out. Her dying – and all that black magic stuff in the papers. I didn't want to get involved in whatever creepy shenanigans had got her killed.'

I feel defeated but when I glance back, he's looking furtive.

'What?' I demand.

'Nothing.'

'No, come on.'

'OK, well, I couldn't have helped her – cos I didn't hear the message till it was too late.'

'What message?'

'She left a phone message for me the day she died.'

'What?'

'I didn't get it straight away – I was with my mum and I'd left my phone at hers and gone to the cinema.'

'But what was the message?'

'She was in a right state. Gabbling. Saying I had to phone her straight back cos something really bad had happened.'

'What exactly did she say?' I snap and he jerks his head up. 'Word for word.'

'All right – umm: "Hi it's me. Where are you. Something really bad's happened, you need to call me straight back."' He frowns, grasping for the memory. 'Umm, "I've really fucked up – really gone too far, I can't talk my way out of this." Oh and, yeah, that's right – "He'll never forgive me."'

'He'll never forgive me? Who won't?'

He shrugs. 'Then it finished with lots of "call me, call me" at the end.'

'And did you?'

He shakes his head, looking sheepish. 'When I rang back next morning, it went straight to voicemail. I left a message saying we could hook up when I got back – but of course, by then, it was already too late.'

'But why didn't you ring back that night?' I ask desperately.

'Ah, come on. I hadn't seen her much for the last couple of years. She was such a bloody handful when she was like that and I couldn't face it.'

I stare at him in disbelief. 'What time did she call you that night – exactly?'

'It was late afternoon, half five-ish.'

'And you've really got no idea what she meant?'

'No, but something'd really freaked her out. She never got upset – not properly.'

'What does that mean?'

'Well, she got hysterical and hyper all the time, but it was an act, to manipulate people – I was onto it but I was mostly happy to play along. But that was the only time that she sounded genuinely scared.'

I could throttle this self-important tosser, but I keep going.

'Did you ever consider that she might have killed herself?'

'Jen! Nah. Not in a million years. She lived her life, didn't dwell.'

156

'Did she ever say that Dad knew about you – or any of these other "lovers"?'

He sighs. 'I'm sorry, but she didn't talk about any of you. All I knew was that your dad was paying to maintain this "career" of hers. I thought he must be a bit of a sap, but hey, that was up to him.' He glances at me. 'Sorry.'

I stare at this ageing Lothario and realise he's being honest, and this is all I'm going to get. I mumble my thanks and offer to pay, expecting he'll refuse. But he lets me pay the full hundred pounds. What a gent.

I stumble out of the shop and back towards the tube. I have to talk to someone, but obviously can't ring Reece. I consider Marcus, but I don't want to mess up whatever that is. And Mrs Roberts told me to move forward, not backward. There's only one option.

'Hi,' Chris says warmly; he must have saved my number to know it's me.

'I'm sorry to ring you.'

'But I specifically said you should ring me.'

'I know, but you were probably just being nice.'

'I'm pretty unpleasant. Hence, don't do pleasantries.'

'Hence?'

'It's a word.'

'Yeah – at finishing school! But thanks for talking. I couldn't think who to call, but you know what I'm up to and I guess you've already seen a chink of my intense side.'

'There's more?' he says in mock horror.

'You've no idea.'

He laughs. 'So, what's up?'

'I talked to Jeremy – and you were right about Mum's affair with him and with lots of others, if he's to be believed. Which I think he is. And he said that Mum's career was pretty much a lie, a vanity project paid for by Dad. It all gives Dad clear motive.'

'Or it confirms that your dad knew the true her and accepted her?'

'I guess. It's like I didn't know her, or him, at all.'

'You did. They just had other sides. But I get you feel discombobulated.'

'God, you're a thesaurus today,' I laugh.

'Look, if you dig, you'll find new things, not all palatable – but it doesn't mean your memories of your parents aren't also true.'

'I guess. Thanks.' I pause. 'And Jeremy had a call from her that afternoon. Saying she'd really fucked up and that some "he" would never forgive her.'

'And you think that was your dad.'

'I don't know,' I whine. 'God, I'm sorry I called to moan.'

'Are you?'

'No,' I laugh, 'thanks.'

'Remember, every bit of new information is part of the answer. Call whenever. I still want to solve this. Not as much as you of course, but I do.'

'OK, I will.'

I get on the Tube still frustrated by the 'what if'. If Jeremy had picked up Mum's message that night . . . but what's the point in being angry with this sad man. The way he tells it, he was manipulated and used by Mum. He didn't call her back cos he was sick of her using him.

That wasn't new information to me. I'd watched Mum manipulate people before: a teacher who let me do Mandarin GCSE even though my grades were too low; a sports coach who picked Reece for every game despite rotating everyone else; and endless handymen who fell over themselves doing additional unpaid jobs. It had seemed like a pretty harmless power.

Then.

CHAPTER FIFTEEN

'Oh my God,' I exclaim when I see Loreta's dad, as I arrive for my late afternoon visit. He's conducting, his face suffused with radiant joy. I've never seen him this animated.

'Is wonderful,' Loreta says, looking like an excited child as she watches him. But suddenly his arms drop and his face blanks.

'Oh. Sorry,' I say.

'Hang on.' She presses play on the old Walkman attached to cheap headphones perched on his head, and he lights up immediately.

'It's The Beatles,' she explains, 'he used to listen to them on Radio Luxembourg in the sixties. The music is taking him right back to his youth.' She's right: he's reanimated by this sensory catalyst.

'That's amazing,' I say.

She nods enthusiastically, eyeing my clothes as I realise that I'm wearing my jeans, Mum's full-skirted dress, then my sweatshirt and coat – like some punky student.

'It's a good day for both of us. Your dad's up, too,' Loreta says, gesturing across the aisle. Dad's sitting in the high-backed patient chair. He looks so frail, but at least he's out of bed. Poor Dad – how much did he know about Mum's sordid extracurricular activities? He certainly knew she wasn't the professional success I believed in, cos he paid for the illusion. But that shows what a good liar he was. I had no idea whatsoever that Mum's whole career was – 'curated'. What else has he lied about?

'Dad, how are you doing?'

'Hello, Hannah,' Dad says as I approach. He's here with me in the present, at last. Thank God.

'I think it's time,' he says, looking at me with filmy, hopeless eyes. Oh no, he's too present.

'For what, Dad?'

'What's the point any more?' He shifts and winces. Him being in the present enough to recognise me should feel great – but it means that he recognises the bleakness of his situation.

'You're OK, Dad,' I say, as I stroke his hand.

He groans. 'It's too much. The pain. I've had enough,' he cries.

'Everything OK here?' asks Valeria.

'Good, all good,' says Dad with a broad smile. He was clearly talking about wanting to die ten seconds ago and now he's fine – for strangers.

'He's in pain,' I confide to her.

'We've put him on a slow morphine drip,' she whispers, pointing to a timed contraption on a wheeled stand attached to a cannula in his hand. 'I'll increase it slightly to make him more comfortable.'

'Thanks.'

What an odd job these medics have, relentlessly applying all their years of training and focus trying to keep someone alive, when it's clearly a race they can't win – what a strange purgatory they must travel through before finally being forced to give up – or perhaps actively withdrawing help – or even helping facilitate an easier death? Has Dad reached the point the vet talked about for Schro, when he said 'You'll know when'?

'I saw Reece,' I blurt out, desperate to distract him.

Dad's face flicks alight, so I double down.

'He said to say hello. He's doing well, and he said he's thinking of you,' I gabble as Dad smiles and nods.

'Yes, he's been visiting me at the house recently.'

'Yeah, sure.' What harm can it do, to confirm this comforting fantasy for him. 'That's right. And he'll come to visit you here soon.'

Dad's pained body sags with relief – is this at the influx of the morphine or the thought of the prodigal Reece?

'We'll give you morphine tablets, for when he comes home,' Valeria says to me quietly.

'Comes home?'

'Yes. Now he's stabilised, he should be coming home soon.'

I must get on with sorting the power of attorney and getting the house ready. I pull out Marcus's business card and WhatsApp him.

Hannah here. If you're free in the next day or two, could you help me with the house? Sorry for the short notice – but Dad's taken a positive turn.

I put an *x*, then take it off, then put it back. Then take it off.
Send.

He replies instantly.

Sure, are you in tonight? X

A big kiss – interesting.

Yep, in all eve, come any time. x

So, this is what girlishly excited feels like.

As Dad sleeps, I check my messages and I'm surprised to
see a LinkedIn one from Mary Stanton, the third of Mum's
friends that I contacted. Another rebuffing no doubt.

Dear Hannah,

Thank you for your message. I was so distraught about
what happened to your mother. The world lost one of
its brightest stars. She and I were very close for a long
time, but I hadn't seen her so much before her death.
However, I would be happy to meet for a coffee.

Yours sincerely, Mary

So, she didn't hate Mum, like the other two? Since Dad
could be home in the next day or so, I cajole Mary by
text into agreeing to meet tomorrow in her lunch hour at
her doctor's surgery. Mum already isn't Mum to me after
Jeremy, and this is probably a pointless meeting that will
just underline what I already know, but I might as well face
the full glare of Mum's 'party me'.

Back home I launch into a flurry of tidying: scooping up
all my wine bottles off the floor, straightening the pillows,

hiding all the cat-haired blankets. By the time I've washed out some clean glasses and opened a bottle of wine, the doorbell rings.

As I walk towards the door, I hear singing.

'Who can take a sunrise, sprinkle it with dew. Cover it with chocolate and a miracle or two' – and as I open the door, Marcus finishes, 'the handyman can.'

We grin at each other.

'Drink?' I say, motioning with my glass.

'Oh, yes, the handyman certainly can,' he laughs.

After the disconcerting intensity of Jeremy, being with Marcus is such a relief. I gulp my wine, then catch Marcus clocking me and put my glass down.

'Before we start,' I say, 'I need to check something.'

He frowns.

'I don't want to put you in a tricky position with doing this work. Both your parents seemed a bit odd about you helping me?'

'Ah, ignore them,' he says, waving away my concern. 'They just—'

'—think Dad did it?'

'I can't say for sure,' he says, twisting at the button of his jeans, 'but it was such a difficult time back then – obviously mostly for you, but for all of us. And they're both very into dealing with difficult stuff by moving forward. Not dwelling. I think they're scared of me being pulled back into your sadness. Sorry. I'm not scared.'

I nod.

'I want to help as much as I can.'

'I know you do, thanks,' I say, touching his arm.

'But it's probably better if I get this all done before your dad gets back – for my parents' sake.'

'He could be back in a couple of days.'

'Then I'll start tomorrow?'

'Are you sure?' I could cry, he's being so nice.

'So,' he says, pulling out a pad from his back pocket and theatrically licking his pencil. 'Mobile?'

'Dad's not really up to using a phone.'

'No, I mean walking. Or does he use a wheelchair?'

'Oh right. I suppose he may well be in a wheelchair,' I say, realising what I'm taking on.

'Then you'll need a ramp. Those stairs at the front are really steep.'

'I guess.'

'And a smaller ramp for the lip of the porch. You're lucky these houses have big wide doors, so it'll be easy getting in and out – and you've got a downstairs loo. What about a bed downstairs?'

'Oh God – how do I get that?'

'No problem, you can hire a hospital-style bed – I can sort it,' he says, pulling out his phone. I'm both appalled at all that needs to be done and relieved and impressed that Marcus is so capable.

We set off round the downstairs of the house, me indicating curtain rails that are hanging down, wonky floorboards and the broken toilet seat.

'Yeah, all this is easy – I'll put a new seat on first thing tomorrow – with a slow close. God, all these photos in here!' he says, peering at the toilet walls. 'They used to make me snigger.' The toilet and all the bathrooms in this house are full of Mum's series called 'God Says' – church signs she snapped all over the country: garish printed posters, messages picked out in individual Scrabble-style letters, and hand-drawn cursive script on A3 sheets under glass on formal church noticeboards. The unifying theme is the inadvertent smuttiness of the messages.

'Are these all really real church signs?' he asks. 'I always wondered if she made some of them up.'

'Oh no, all real,' I say, but now wondering if that's true.

Marcus squints at one. '"PRAY FOR A GOOD HARVEST, BUT KEEP ON HOEING",' he reads with a slight snort.

'"YOU CAN'T ENTER HEAVEN UNLESS JESUS ENTERS YOU",' I read. 'How did the priests or congregations never see the blatant innuendo? Look at this one: "FORGIVENESS IS SWALLOWING WHEN YOU WANT TO SPIT".' I giggle, then clock Marcus's awkwardness as he steps back. Maybe these aren't so funny, now we're older, with this attraction between us.

'Shall we get on?' he asks, looking up the stairs.

'I just need to get the ground floor habitable,' I say, brushing a large cobweb from between the banisters. 'Dad'll be living downstairs from now on.'

'This place is like a house in a scary movie,' he says, pulling away more cobwebs.

'And we're the innocent kids wandering round,' I say. 'The call's coming from inside the house, aaagh,' I laugh, making a *Psycho* slashing motion.

Marcus looks at me, horrified.

'Sorry. What's wrong with me.'

'It's OK,' he says, touching my sleeve. I lean into his shoulder and he tightens his arms around me.

'Are you OK?' he asks gently.

I nod into his chest. 'Sorry, it's been a difficult day,' I

mumble. 'You said before that you hadn't heard from Reece recently?' I ask, straightening and scrabbling for conversation.

'No, not since – you know.' He shrugs. 'Lives diverge. He's not here, is he?' he asks, looking round sharply.

'No, he won't ever be here – he and Dad don't get on.' I thought Marcus would be interested to hear about Reece. It makes me feel even closer to him that we've both been dumped by my brother.

'Well, I've got your list,' he says.

'And you know I'm going to pay you properly for all this work.'

'No, you're family. It's the least I can do.' As I open my mouth to disagree, he waves me away, picks up his glass and drains it.

'We're not actually related though,' I say, instantly kicking myself at how suggestive I sound.

'I better get going.' Ah, no, he's embarrassed.

But then he smiles warmly, his eyes crinkling at the sides. 'I'll see you tomorrow, bright and early.'

As he drives away in his purple van, I touch my arm, where his hand squeezed, and remember the feel of his broad chest under my cheek. Perhaps I'm not so alone without Reece.

I spend the evening watching Evel Knievel videos, taking a gulp of wine with each jump. According to the documentary Knievel was always a risk-taker, up for any dodgy escapade, who then reinvented himself as a showman who tapped into people's love of daredevils. With all I'm discovering about her, I can so see why Mum loved him. The grainy footage of the jumps is still breathtaking and I do what Jeremy said Mum did and freeze the film at the height of a jump – the white-leather-clad guy on his heavy bike is miraculously suspended in the air, stars-and-stripes cape splayed out, totally defying gravity, but I'm drawn to all the spectators, the mechanics, the cameras – everyone looking, leaning, yearning towards him. Just like in all those photos in Mum's scrapbook.

Mum was right about Knievel's infectious joy mid-air, but as the night lengthens, I find myself haunted by all his terrifying crashes.

CHAPTER SIXTEEN

It's hard not to grin stupidly as Marcus arrives to start the renovations the next morning. He strides back and forth to his van, all loose-limbed, ruffle-haired and muscle-bound. This morning he seems even more ridiculously attractive than yesterday.

'Hi,' he says, smirking at me from beneath his blonde fringe.

'Hi yourself,' I say, cocking my head girlishly. Jesus.

'I've got your list, so you just get on with whatever and ignore me.' As if.

'Actually, I'm off to the hospital to see Dad, so here are the spare keys.'

'Thanks,' he says, catching them in his broad left hand while simultaneously lowering two planks of wood against the front porch with his right and swiping sweat off his brow.

Christ on a bike.

* * *

As I walk down the hospital corridor later, Loreta approaches with a plate piled high with what look like slices of fried dough. The sweet, greasy smell makes me nauseous with my hangover.

'*Skruzdėlynas*?' she says, offering the plate. 'Lithuanian honey cake.'

'Maybe later. How's your dad?'

She shrugs. 'The music stopped working so today I try taste and smell.' She's amazing; she never gives up trying to reach her silent dad. 'Your dad's up,' she says with a wan smile. 'He was telling me about your brother visiting. That's nice.'

'Oh no, that's just his confusion – I better go see him.'

Dad's sitting up in the high-backed chair again, eating one of the doughy slices.

'Hannah,' he says brightly.

'You look great – how are you feeling?'

'I saw Reece this morning,' he says excitedly. This is my fault. I shouldn't have mentioned him yesterday, definitely shouldn't have said he'd visit. I've set him off on a Reece jag. But he looks so happy I force myself to enter his fantasy.

'Umm yeah, that's lovely, Dad.'

'Will he come tomorrow?'

'I expect he will.'

I help him sip his tiny carton of orange juice, then I munch on a quince.

'Badminton racquets,' Dad says suddenly, 'we need badminton racquets.'

'Okaaay. We'll go later. New badminton racquets for all of us.'

Dad's happily off down another conversational track,

170

but leaving me floundering as usual. I chew my quince furiously, right down to the fibrous core, reminding myself that if I picked it up, then ate the flesh, then the core, then there is some bloody linear reality going on, if only at the level of my quince consumption.

I'm off at eleven, on the forest-green District Line to meet Mary. As I walk over Putney Bridge towards the doctor's surgery where she works, I pause to stare down at the rowers on the glinting river below me, feeling guilty. Today I've intensified my Mum impersonation, wearing her blue shirt with a pair of her tight ankle-tapering white trousers, sporting her black eyeliner, her bright red lipstick, and backcombing my hair. I know I'm a poor imitation of Mum, but I need more from eating the fruit of my very own tree of knowledge. Quince consumption has furthered my drastic weight-loss resemblance to Mum, which unnerved Reece and prompted revelations from Jeremy. I will now use my new superpower on Mary.

I set off again and arrive at a little row of shops on the far side of the bridge, where the doctor's is situated. I step through the double-layer doors and see a plump lady with glasses at the reception desk.

'Oh my God,' she says, flattening down her hair, 'Hannah?'

I nod, enjoying my Mum power.

'I've only got half an hour sorry, is that OK?' she asks in an oddly subservient manner.

So, it wasn't just men that Mum could entrance?

We settle in a cafe next door, me with a tuna roll, her with a massive egg mayonnaise sub. She's wearing an unflattering red ruched top and a pleated skirt and is frumpy now, barely recognisable from her uni pictures.

'I really don't know how I can help you – it was all a long time ago,' she says nervously.

'Thanks for meeting me – and at such short notice. I wanted to talk to someone who knew Mum, outside of the family life I knew her in.'

She swallows and blushes. 'I'm sorry, it's just that you look so like her.'

I incline my head and loosen my shoulders, like Mum. 'And that makes you uncomfortable?' I say in her breathy voice.

Mary visibly tingles. 'It's been a long time, but Jen was a big part of my life.'

'So, how did you meet her?' I ask, giving her a big smile and touching her hand like Mum used to. She flinches with pleasure and tries to cover her reaction with a little laugh.

'Oh, it was on the very first day of term. I was in the main hall for freshers' week, not sure what to do with myself, when I saw this bowed head – the long blonde hair of someone sitting cross-legged on the floor. Just another typical pretty clone, I thought. But then she looked up and . . .' Mary swallows and catches a stray strand of hair behind her ear girlishly. 'Well, you know.'

I nod, seeing my image reflected in her eyes and feeling almost like she's talking about me.

'And you stayed friends right through uni and beyond?'

'Yes. But at uni we were a foursome – me and your mum, Anne and Franny.' She frowns. 'I went to a uni reunion a couple of years ago – and someone said that they were afraid of us four, cos we were so bitchy. I just remember us being funny. Looking back, I think maybe we were a bit vile. Jen's alpha energy was infectious – like we were in this private little world of hers, looking down on everyone else.'

'Students can be a bit self-involved.'

'I think I became a worse version of myself with her,' she says, but smiling, like she's proud of it.

'And boyfriends?' I say, trying to keep my face unreactive.

'Oh, Jen broke lots of hearts, had whoever she wanted, but it was never serious. Till your dad, of course.'

'Why was he different? Cos he was older.'

'Oh no, she'd had older before – professors, club owner, mature students. But with Philip it was instant. He walked into the student bar, all serious and gangly, followed by his adoring students, and she said, "That's the man I'm going to marry." She didn't know anything about him, only later found out that he was a bit of a star with his little physics books. She didn't even care he was married.'

'He was married before?'

'Yes. Jen showed me their photo at some uni dinner: "Ooh, look at Mr Davidson and the future ex-Mrs Davidson",' says Mary, throwing her head back and laughing like Mum. 'She was having an affair with him within a week. He tried to keep it quiet but she was pretty brazen.'

'But he'd had affairs with students before?'

'When?'

'The "Sleazy Killer" headline? That was based on the student nickname for him.'

'"Sleaze"! That was ironic – cos he was so strait-laced – one of the few married-married profs, not up for anything extracurricular.'

'Then – why with Mum?'

She shrugs. 'Jen always got what she wanted.'

'And then she got pregnant,' I say wearily.

'Ah yes, the "pregnancy".'

'I know about the miscarriage.'

'Well—' she says, drawing out the word. 'She told him she was pregnant, cos he was having second thoughts about leaving wifey.'

'You're saying she faked it?'

'She couldn't get pregnant – tried getting him too drunk to be careful – was even putting holes in condoms and laughing at him being so careful rolling them on.' She stops laughing when she sees my appalled face. 'Eventually she just told him she was pregnant.'

'And that's why Dad left his first wife and married her?'

'Sort of. But his wife left him. She got a letter, supposedly from Sid, a dalliance of Jen's, saying Jen was pregnant by Philip and they'd both been betrayed. But if that meathead could string together those sentences, find the address and actually post it, I'm the Queen of Sheba.'

'It was from her?'

'She kept saying "*If* I'd done that – I'd be a bitch" and then laughing uproariously. And then of course she had to "lose the baby".'

I pinch my thigh to keep calm.

'But she did get pregnant eventually,' I insist. 'With my brother. And then me.' She tongues her cheek again and I want to slap her.

'Are you sure you want to hear this?' she says, with fake reserve.

I nod mutely. I'm way past what I can bear already.

'After the "miscarriage", she told Philip she was coming away with me for a spa weekend. But we just hung out at the student bar all three nights.'

'So?'

'So, she never slept at mine. And a month later, hey presto, pregnant.'

'You're saying Dad – wasn't my brother's father?'

'I sincerely doubt it,' she says with relish.

'Nor mine?'

'No idea, but he never had kids with his first wife.'

This woman's her own bitch, however much she blames Mum. I need to get away from her, but I need to cover all my bases before I go, as I don't ever want to see this bitter harridan again.

'I tried to contact Anne and Franny,' I say abruptly, 'but neither of them would talk to me.'

'No, they wouldn't. They didn't understand Jen like I did,' she says, swelling like a greasy toad. 'Franny got so crazy, said Jen was stealing from her, that money kept going missing from her purse, then an expensive handbag went walkabout. The last straw was when she let Jen use her bank account to pay for one month of digs, and Jen paid her the money back in cash – but a year later Franny found that Jen had set up a standing order using Franny's account to pay her rent ever since.'

'Didn't you think that was wrong?' I say incredulously.

'Ah, Franny was rich, the money meant nothing to her,' she says with a giggle.

I feel especially sick at this particular revelation. Is the moral vacuum Mum had about money inherited: like mother like daughter?

'And Anne?' I ask with a cough.

'Jen shagged her husband Sean,' she says matter-of-factly. 'She told Anne it was just a physical thing, nothing to stress about – but Anne had got all suburban and righteous.'

'You thought that was OK?'

She shrugs and I want to stab my fork through her hand.

'We all shagged each other's conquests back then; it was a bit prissy of her thinking things were different cos she was married. Anyway, those two fell by the wayside.'

'But you stayed friends. Only I never met you?'

'Well, you wouldn't have, I never had anything to do with her "domestic" life.' She says the word with a sneer. 'Once she moved into that dreadful house in Highgate, and made friends with other mums, I still saw her at parties but it wasn't quite the same – it was a bit of a shock to be honest.' She takes a big bite of her sandwich.

'What was?'

'To be out of her orbit, to realise that I was somehow – optional to her.' She's talking like a jilted lover. 'Jen could make you feel so special, so important, but people were disposable to her. I'd seen her do it to lots of other people, I just never thought she'd do it to me.' She looks at me with hangdog eyes, like she thinks I'm going to be sympathetic.

I nod to keep her going.

'With Jen, you thought you knew where the ground was, but that's because you were up in her orbit with her, and when she let you go – poof – the ground wasn't there any more.' Bitterness rolls off her, like the mayonnaise running down her chin when she bites into her stuffed egg sub again, her eyes drinking me in.

I shake out my hair and feel so young, thin and beautiful,

in this woman's eyes, thrilling with an ugly visceral pleasure.

'If she left people so easily, why didn't she leave Dad?'

'Oh, he was her rock. Yeah, she was wild, but not strong. However far she pulled away from him, he was always there to pick up the pieces. But I guess even a doormat has a limit. I was shocked when I heard about what happened to her. But not surprised.'

That bizarre statement again.

'You're the second person to say that to me.'

She shrugs then glances at her watch.

'I'm sorry, but I have to get back to work,' she says.

As she stands, I catch her arm.

'Did the police talk to you at the time?'

'Oh no, I wasn't a close friend by then, I wouldn't have come up.'

'But why didn't you contact them? You could have explained my dad's motive.'

She gives me an odd smile.

'Because I kind of understood why Philip did it.'

I arrive home, relieved that Marcus is there, to save me from my thoughts. He's clearly been hard at work. There's a smooth wooden ramp over the steep steps up to the front garden and another shallower one over the lip of the porch.

'Oh, hi there, I'm pretty much done,' says Marcus, coming into the hall as I enter. The hall's bright now that he's pulled down the broken blinds. I peek into the toilet which has a brand-new seat and handrail. The curtain rail is back up in the lounge and the loose floorboards on the ground floor are all steady.

'Wow, Marcus, this is all great. You have to let me pay you.'

He shakes his head.

'How about a drink? I'm having one. Or ten.'

'Sure.' He eyes me. 'You all right?'

'It's nothing. Thanks for all this,' I say, bringing him a beer and white wine for me.

'You're the best,' he says, as he takes a swig and I sit down next to him on the sofa.

'It's really great seeing you again, Marcus.'

'You too,' he says, looking boyish and nervous. I want to lean down onto his broad chest and be enveloped by his arms again, feeling him brush the hair from my eyes as he—

'Are you sure you're OK?' he asks, looking concerned. 'I should let you rest.'

Of course he's not interested in me: I don't have Mum's power with proper men, just has-beens like Jeremy and obsessive women like Mary.

'Yeah, sure,' I say, standing to see him out.

'But why don't we go out for a proper drink?'

'A proper drink?'

'You know, in the real world. Well, down the pub.'

A proper drink for me is drinking alone till I pass out, but I smile.

'Sure.'

'What about Tuesday night? I'm off on Wednesday.'

I nod. He smiles down at me then kisses my cheek. I can't believe it. My childhood crush has asked me out on a date – a date when he doesn't have to get up the next morning. Perhaps some of Mum's power is rubbing off on me?

But as the front door closes, I am left alone with my revelations from Mary, on top of those from Jeremy. Chris is right, this accepting lark is no fun. I've clearly been too close to really see Mum – like one of her 'Look Closer' pictures, but now I'm zooming out and seeing her for who she really was.

But I need evidence beyond hearsay. I google DNA testing and find a two-day turnaround. I thrill to the tiny precise pain as I yank a hair from my crown. Then I find Dad's comb and pull a wispy grey hair from its teeth, perhaps the ones that she photographed close up like they were prison bars. This could be the proof of what led Dad to imprison himself here all those years.

CHAPTER SEVENTEEN

I've just released the hospital security door the next morning and turned towards the ward when there's a flurry of footsteps, and I have to step back sharply as people dash past. Please not Dad. But they're rushing to the left – to the bed opposite. The green curtains are swept round as I catch a glimpse of Loreta with her hands clamped to her mouth, her eyes wide. There's frantic motion behind the curtain, arms, elbows and bottoms puffing out the material, but after a few minutes, the flurry ceases. There's quiet mumbling and then a single long yelp of animal pain.

'No!' shouts Dad, who's stumbling towards me with a Zimmer frame, Valeria pushing his drip medication along with him.

'It's all right, Dad,' I say, putting myself squarely into his eyeline.

'Jen,' he says, looking wild-eyed at me. Not again. Is Loreta's scream of agony reminding him of stabbing Mum?

'Hi, Ms Davidson,' says Valeria, glancing across the ward. 'I know it's difficult. Can you stay with your dad, keep his focus off – all that.'

I nod, helping him into the white chair.

'It'll be a while till the orderlies get up here to remove – him.' She checks Dad's chart. 'Your dad's doing great and he's being discharged the day after tomorrow. He'll be more comfortable at home – and we'll be sending him back with morphine tablets along with all his other medications, to – ease things.'

'Could someone go through all this medication with me before then?'

'Yes absolutely, but umm—' She frowns as she looks at the clipboard. 'I thought so. You're not the power of attorney for Mr Davidson.'

I see Loreta's little white boots shuffling round the bed. Poor woman.

'Oh, no, I haven't got around to sorting that – I'll get it done today, I promise.'

'I mean power of attorney has already been awarded for Mr Davidson.'

'But I haven't done it yet.'

'Full medical and financial power of attorney was signed off yesterday.'

'But how? To who?'

'To Mr Davidson's son, Reece Davidson – or Ryan Patterson as we all know him,' she says with a smile.

'But that's not possible, Reece – Ryan – hasn't been here. Has he?'

'He visited yesterday – we were all rather excited to have a star in our midst,' she says, blushing. 'I got his autograph.'

So Dad wasn't delusional yesterday.

'You never said he was your brother,' she admonishes me.

'But what was he here for?'

'To visit with your dad, of course,' she says, frowning at me. 'He's got such a lovely smooth voice hasn't he.'

'They talked?'

'Of course. Your dad kept saying "You're a good boy, Reece." Which I thought was lovely. That he was reassuring him, despite being so weak himself.'

'And Reece signed the forms?' I say incredulously.

'Yes, and your dad,' she says, talking to me like I'm thick.

'How was Dad deemed competent to sign – he's so out of it,' I exclaim.

She narrows her eyes. 'Not all the time. And we apply a certain leeway with these things to move them along. Yesterday your father was certainly capable.'

'But look at him,' I snarl, gesturing to Dad.

'You'll have to calm down, Ms Davidson. There's zero tolerance to abuse here. We've got enough to deal with,' she says, gesturing to the closed curtains opposite.

'Sorry.'

'Your brother would have to give permission for us to release any medication to you. Or indeed to release your father himself.'

'What?' I blurt and she eyes me critically. 'OK. I'll – look into it.'

God, it was me that told Reece one sibling could take power of attorney. But why would he want it? Does he think me so incapable, that he can't let me look after someone he loathes? Am I even allowed to still live at Dad's? Now I'm not even a main performer in the tawdry little play Dad and I are in, I'm an extra – who's just been let go.

I escape to the corridor and call Chris. He picks up straight away.

'Yes?' he answers sharply.

'I'm sorry to call again,' I say, tensed by his tone, 'but everyone else thinks Reece is such a saint. And the man in the bed opposite just died.' I burst into tears.

'I'm sorry about the guy on the ward. What's Reece done now?'

'The man was really old, but so's Dad, so he's probably next. And Reece has been visiting Dad.'

'So what?'

'So he's been doing it without telling me, and he's taken power of attorney, which is—'

'I know what it is. But he's allowed to visit him, isn't he? He doesn't need your permission.'

'You don't understand – Reece hasn't seen Dad since Mum died – like never. Or that's what I thought anyway. I didn't want to get into it with you when I saw you before, but Reece has always blamed Dad for Mum's death, indirectly – or even directly.'

'So that suicide theory of his?'

'He never thought that – it was just to deflect the press.'

'Good to be kept in the loop finally,' he says sarcastically. 'Maybe you're being a wee bit paranoid. He's allowed to visit your dad without telling you – but is it that you think he's taken power of attorney to steal the inheritance?'

'No, of course not, he's filthy rich,' I snap.

'Well the rich can be greedy. But if not, then maybe –

he's trying to help you. Taking over some of the burden.'

'That's ridiculous.'

'Why?'

'You don't really know anything about him,' I bark at him.

'Well why don't you just ask him. You have equal rights in these matters.'

'It doesn't feel like that,' I whine. 'He's the adult and I'm the child. Clearly he's been doing all sorts behind my back and yet again I'm shut out.'

'If you don't like what's going on, then take action,' he says, sounding really irritated.

'I have been taking action,' I say petulantly, 'you know that.'

'So keep going and ask your brother what he's doing.'

'But he's so hard to deal with.'

'Life's hard,' he says aggressively.

'Obviously, but not everyone's a terminator like you.'

'Fuck off. You just thrive on thinking you've been dealt the worst hand.'

'So now you agree with Reece: I'm just a messed-up child.'

'Oh for heaven's sake. Stuff happens. How we react is a choice. You're choosing to be stuck.'

'Says the man still living in his parents' ugly house.'

'I take it back, you are childish,' he says witheringly.

'Me? You're the one hiding from the world at Mummy and Daddy's.'

The line goes dead.

I phone Reece but of course he doesn't pick up. I keep phoning all afternoon, propelled by my anger with Reece and Chris, sitting by Dad as he dozes, the curtains opposite staying closed. All the ward business is plodding along as usual – but everyone has their antennae tuned in to what's behind the curtain.

Chris rings back but I let it go straight to voicemail, then listen to his message.

'Er, look, sorry we got so heated earlier. I was in a dark mood before you rang and you pushed the wrong button. Are you OK? You're sounding pretty out there. I'm worried about you. Please call me back.'

Oh so now he's worried about me. Because of course, everything is just my deluded imagination. Nothing's a real problem or danger. I just need medicating. I erase the message.

Eventually, a whole two hours later, a trolley is pushed down the ward and swallowed by the curtains. I hear someone counting 'three, two, one', then a hefting and lowering, followed by the sound of a long zip being pulled. The curtains are pulled back and the trolley, draped in a sheet, is pushed away. Loreta follows, carrying the folded Lithuanian flag, like an American military funeral. Our eyes meet. I mouth 'sorry' at her. She walks over.

'Thank you.' She glances over at my dad. 'Do whatever you can to make this last bit good for him. Life's so short.'

At home I drink heavily, trying Reece's phone over and over. I remember the drill from the old days and set up a Google alert for 'Ryan Patterson', and immediately receive one.

Ryan Patterson Official Facebook: Ryan is in London

tomorrow, filming London scenes for the highly anticipated new series of Muerte – watch this space for photos, #RyanPatterson.

Annoyingly vague – but I know the fans won't let me down.

CHAPTER EIGHTEEN

Deep in my fug of sleep, I register a distant bleep. I'm on the lounge floor, the lights are on and it's dark outside – the clock reads 6.33 a.m. My phone bleeps again. And again. It's a deluge of 'Ryan Patterson Notification Alerts'.

The first, from 'Lucycat233', shows a picture of a thumbs-upping young woman with a bleary Reece behind her:

Me with super-sexy Ryan Patterson – filming by Oxford Street Topshop – NOW!!!!!! #RyanPatterson

One from 'VeganVi666' has a picture of what could be a tramp with Reece's hair.

Star without airbrushing, bless. #RyanPatterson

And another from 'BeaneryBen77' shows a bearded bloke, cap backwards, near an exhausted-looking Reece holding a coffee cup.

That plonker Ryan whatshisface from Muerte, drinking tasteless chain coffee in Oxford Circus. For a real coffee, visit The Beanery. @thebeanery

I try Reece again.

'Hi, I'm not available right now, please leave a message.'

I stab the red disconnect key. He sounds so proper. So measured. So butter-wouldn't-melt.

So. Game on.

Forty-five minutes later, the tube regurgitates me and a spew of early commuters at Oxford Circus. Reece is so easy to find, with the white production trucks and all their snaking wires, the huge silver tripoded umbrellas and the craning crowds. I balance on a stone bollard and see they're mid filming. Reece rushes out of a green shoe shop on the corner. He's unrecognisable from the earlier tired tweet photos, now suave and impressive in a short Italian-style mac, his dark curls glossy, eyes alert. A striking redhead follows him out, screaming at him as she throws a red stiletto. He gives his trademark smirk as she rushes at him. They are just about to embrace, or fight, when they freeze mid lunge, then look over to the director. The technicians reset and the scene repeats. The redhead has just chucked the shoe again when I shout.

'Ryan.'

Reece doesn't react.

'Ryan,' I shout louder and he glances at the director, with a tired smile.

'Reeeeece, up here.' He snaps towards me, clocks me, then strides away. A bulky bald-headed man wearing a massive black puffer jacket and headset comes barrelling towards me.

'Please keep quiet during filming, madam.' He holds out his hand to me, like he's fricking Prince Charming.

'Reeeeeeece,' I shout and am swept off the bollard.

'It's OK, Ed,' says Reece, approaching at speed. 'Just an old friend.'

'Are you sure, Mr Patterson?' says Ed.

'Yes, are you sure, Mr Patterson?' I parrot.

Reece pulls me to an empty doorway. Ed hovers.

'What the fuck, Hannah?' hisses Reece. 'Are you drunk? Some people are busy working, you know.'

'Are *some* people? Yet *some* person, had time to steal power of attorney for Dad?'

He sighs. 'Wait till I finish this scene and I'll explain.'

'No, I . . .' But I'm suddenly aware of all the fans looking on, cameras trained on us. 'Fine, but you better come.'

'Could you show my friend to my trailer please, Ed?'

'This way, madam.'

Reece strides off and I follow Ed through the sea of curious fans. He opens the door of a large prefab dressing room on wheels and follows me in.

'Is it company policy for you to be here alone with a single female, Ed?' I ask. 'It rather leaves you open to accusations of harassment if I feel threatened – and oooh,' I feel my forehead theatrically, 'I do believe I'm feeling harassed.'

He frowns and backs out.

189

'I'll be right outside,' he says as he closes the door.

'Be still my beating heart,' I call.

It's easy to work out which section is Reece's, with the stylish clothes thrown over the chair, and a leather satchel I recognise from the earlier tweet images. I clock a comb with Reece's dark hairs caught in the teeth. His DNA. After Mary's claims, I have to know for sure. I pull a clump of tissues from a box, and sweep the hairs into it and then into my pocket. Glancing at the closed trailer door, I lift the satchel flap. His phone is on top, huge and glossy with bevelled edges. I flick it to life to reveal the bright red Rothko print as his screen saver. He's obsessed with that image. I flick the screen but it's locked. I try my face for the recognition, but nothing – guess we aren't that similar – different fathers maybe? I glance at the metal door handle of the trailer. He'll be back any second. I try the number lock. He's lazy with this kind of stuff so I try: 123456. No. 654321? No. I wonder? 041096. The date of Mum's murder. And I'm in.

Reece has so much power by ignoring me; I need to find some back way into his life, to track him. Twitter? Facebook? Find My Phone? I'm struggling with the settings, when I remember Dad's 'Here then There' tracking app. I download it to Reece's phone, and accept my phone following him, but not him following me. Now I'll be able to see where he is whenever he's got a signal, but he won't get any notifications, so will be unaware – as long as he doesn't notice the icon.

The icon is on the last of the six pages of Reece's apps, but it's bright pink and very obvious against the Rothko red background – he'll see it straight away. I hear applause outside as I glance at the door handle. If I move the app into a folder, he'll never know it's there. I press on the icon to make it moveable, but my hands are sweating and I can't seem to get the pressure right. Come on. I hear commotion behind the door, muttered voices. I push again. Nothing. I hear a footstep on the metal step outside. Finally, the app gets a + symbol and I slide it into the nearest group folder, chuck the phone in the satchel and step away – just as the creaking trailer handle is depressed.

'Thanks for waiting,' says Reece as he enters. 'I've asked Suzanne to give us five minutes.' I presume that's his red-headed co-star. He pulls the door to firmly, walks to his chair and motions me to sit opposite him, like we're about to do an interview. I stay standing.

'Why the fuck did you take sole power of attorney?' I spit. 'What are you so afraid I'll find out?'

'What?' he says, acting all confused.

'You warned me not to investigate – and when I do, you steal power of attorney and take control of Dad.'

He reaches out to a little fridge beside him, pulls out a bottle of water, and hands it to me.

'Sit down, and have a sip,' he orders me. 'You look awful.'

'I'm fine,' I shout, slapping the open bottle out of his hand so the water balloons on his shirt and flecks his face.

'Calm down, you're hysterical. And delusional. You're clearly drinking too much, off your pills again and spiralling.'

'You've been visiting Dad in the hospital, haven't you? When you told me over and over that you never wanted to see him. Why?'

'I don't need your permission,' he says, haughtily, sounding like the pig-headed teenager I remember.

'And you've been to the house too, haven't you?' I accuse him.

'No. Why would I go to the house?' he says, looking almost genuine, and his pretence infuriates me.

'I know you've been there, looking through stuff when I'm out, letting the cat escape.'

'What? I have absolutely no idea what you are going on about. But yes, I did take power of attorney.'

'Why?' I shout.

'To protect Dad.'

'From what?'

He pauses, staring at me, then shrugs.

'From you.'

I stare back at him, unable to compute this.

'You said I wasn't helping enough,' he continues in a steely voice. 'I felt bad and yesterday morning asked my accountant to look at Dad's assets, to get an overview – and he discovered some very worrying irregularities.' He tilts his head.

My chest contracts.

'Very sizeable irregularities that were present even yesterday.'

The trailer door opens and the red-headed actress from the scene enters.

'All right to come in?' she asks, eyeing me with interest.

'I'm so sorry, Suzanne, but could you just let us have a few more minutes?'

She purses her lips, clearly wondering why Reece is spending time with some difficult fan.

'Sure, no problem,' she says, backing out while smirking, then closing the door.

Reece turns back to me. 'Where were we? Oh yes. My accountant uncovered that thousands of pounds have been disappearing from Dad's account over the last six months – and going straight into the account of a certain Mr Wilkes. It added up to over seventy thousand pounds.'

The inside of my head is folding in on itself and I raise my palm to him, but on he goes.

'I took financial power of attorney yesterday to protect Dad from this criminal. I was going to tell you as soon as I'd got to the bottom of what's been going on. I got hold of this Mr Wilkes last night, assuming he was some fraudster, illegally siphoning off money after hacking Dad's account – only to discover that the fraudster – was you.' I break eye contact but Reece carries on. 'Mr Wilkes explained to me that he was your old boss and that he sacked you from your stationery shop job six months ago, after uncovering your, and let me get the exact words he used, "widespread financial fraud and serious criminal damage".'

Reece pauses, to let the words hang in the air between us.

I think of Mr Wilkes's fury as he slapped me hard across the face.

'He explained that because of your many years of impeccable service, he agreed not to involve the police, despite your theft from his business, your arson attack on his shop and the subsequent risk to life.'

I think of lovely Mrs King from the flat next door, standing in her nightdress in the street barefoot, as she cradled her baby, weeping silently, staring up at the flames and the black smoke billowing out of her flat.

'He said he agreed to a cover-up and private repayment scheme with you for the money you stole – but even then, he had to forcibly evict you from the flat upstairs.'

I think of the rough hands peeling my fingers from the door of my flat, the thick arms hoicking me up, and the gruff laughter as I was manhandled down the stairs and dumped onto the pavement.

'I thanked him for not pressing charges and said it sounded like he'd bent over backwards to help you – in the circumstances.' He pauses. 'Any thoughts?'

'It was just a loan from Dad,' I say hoarsely, 'to pay off a debt that was due to my – mismanagement. Other than that, I've only used Dad's money for food and basics. I'm not a thief.'

He snorts.

'And the two thousand pounds yesterday was for Marcus.'

Reece's eyes flare. 'I told you not to have anything to do with that piece of shit.'

'Dad's coming home – I need to make changes, bed downstairs, ramps—'

'That arsehole should be nowhere near our house.'

'Why not? He's been great. What have you got against him?'

Reece narrows his eyes at me. I feel my cheeks redden.

'You're not – oh my God you are! You're imagining that he's interested in you? You're totally spiralling like you were at uni. Marcus is a loser. You're not to have anything to do with him.'

'You can't tell me what to do,' I snap at him.

'Apparently I need to,' he growls.

We glare at one another.

'Am I still allowed to stay at Dad's – to take him home? Because you've taken medical power of attorney too, you know.'

'It seemed safer to do so, in the circumstances.'

'What!' I explode at him. 'Because you think I'm a danger to him?'

Reece shrugs.

'Seriously, that's what you're suggesting?'

'You committed arson and attempted murder.'

'It wasn't attempted murder. I was just burning some papers. The fire spread. Obviously, a beyond-dumb thing to do, but I never in a million years intended to hurt anyone.'

'Given these financial shenanigans of yours, it's not a huge leap to think that it would be awfully convenient for you if Dad died sooner rather than later.'

Now I laugh out loud. 'Reece, this is me. Are you kidding?'

We stare at each other – our eyes clicking for real at last. He swallows, and breaks eye contact first.

'Do you really believe that I'm a danger to him?' I say quietly. He looks back and shakes his head. 'And about the money, I can explain, I—'

'I don't care about the bloody money,' he says, sounding suddenly tired. 'I've paid off Mr Wilkes in full, the fifty thousand pounds you still owe apparently, plus another fifty thousand for his silence.'

'You didn't need—'

'Yes, I did. Grow up. I have to be ultra-careful in my

position. Half Dad's money will be yours, quite soon I imagine – and he's got loads in his account, what with his totally undeserved university pension and never going out. There was never any need to steal it.'

'It was a loan,' I say dully. 'I can explain what happened at the shop – you see—'

'I don't need the details. In fact, I don't blame you for whatever you got yourself into.' He fiddles with the corner of a script. 'I know I haven't been there for you,' he says eventually, his voice breaking slightly.

I am gobsmacked by this moment of kindness.

'I'll help you now, however I can, but you've got to meet me halfway and admit you need help. All this I've discovered about your past, and all the obsessive sleuthing you're doing—'

'I'm fine, honestly I am. You're twisting everything. I've been finding out so much about Mum. I—'

'Stop it,' he roars.

I flinch.

'Have you really found anything genuinely concrete about her?' he says with contempt.

'Yes – that Dad had every motive to kill Mum.'

'Oh well done for proving the blindingly obvious.'

'But don't you want proof?' I say quietly.

'No, he'll be dead soon. Surely you see that you need to move on?'

I stare at him, then nod.

'Thank God. This is all so bad for you. Look, I've spoken to a therapist who's willing to see you – he's one of the best in this field.'

'What field is that?' I ask, my voice hardening again.

'Your emotional problems. Come on, you know you need help.' Reece knowing about my awful secret has rocketed me back to the role of his annoying, vulnerable little sister: who cried when he closed our late-night Curly Wurly-eating club; who got moody when he ignored her as he passed her on the street with his mates; who could never get her life going and bombarded him with cries for help till he got sick of her and dumped her for good.

'I'm sorry I didn't tell you about my money problems,' I say, 'about what happened. But we weren't in contact. Hadn't been for years.'

'I know, that was my fault and I'm sorry.'

'But I have to stay at the house, to be there for Dad – till the end, unless you want to?'

'I could pay someone to do it,' he says, his voice combative. 'If you're not—'

'Dad's only got a few weeks at best – you're going to let him die alone? Without either of us. Or is that your final punishment? What you think he deserves?'

He shrugs; I widen my eyes, then he slumps back.

'OK, but you have to cut down your drinking.'

I open my mouth but he silences me with his hand.

'Come on. And you have to agree to see my doctor.'

'Fine.'

'Is that a yes – to both?'

'Yes. OK,' I agree sullenly.

The door handle squeaks open and Suzanne steps in.

'OK,' Reece whispers to me. 'Anastasia will sort the shared power of attorney so the hospital will engage with you, and she'll forward you the doctor's details.'

I nod.

'Bye, then,' I say quietly.

He nods.

Suzanne smirks as I pass her.

I've always thought I was a basically decent person. Wary, self-protective, unadventurous, yes. But deep down, basically decent. But this last year has proved me wrong.

In my first year at uni, we all had to fill in a mental health assessment form. For the question 'What do you want to be in the future?' I thought of the most unattainable, fantasy goal I could imagine and wrote 'Not unhappy'. My university adviser summoned me to her office. She was a young woman, with long Pre-Raphaelite hair and wide, hopeful eyes, brimming with enthusiasm.

'You're a bright girl, you could aim high,' she said, frowning at my answer as if it hurt her. 'What do you *really* want to be?'

'Not unhappy,' I replied doggedly.

'But surely, there must be something?'

I shook my head.

'Shall I just put "the world is my oyster"?'

I shrugged.

I dropped out of university one week later, relieved to be leaving behind the work, the frenzied socialising, the competitiveness, the dating. My disappointed adviser had crystallised a goal for me and to reach it I had to make my life smaller. Much smaller.

The ad for the job in the stationery shop had the tantalising phrase 'long hours working alone' along with 'live-in position for security'. I snapped it up and gradually discovered that less is so much more. Five-thirty every morning: sea swim, marvelling at the shocking blues, smudged greys and cooked egg whites of the sky, adjusting to the ever-shifting water, serene, choppy, or wind-whipped into a fine spray, my body feeling powerful or powerless, but powering on anyway. Then home to All-Bran and semi-skimmed milk in the same blue bowl with the white ring and putting my packed lunch of sliced-cheese sandwiches and an apple into the same rectangular Tupperware with the pink clicking handles. All day at the shop, six days a week, unloading, stacking, checking, arranging, and chatting with regulars. By the time I closed up at six, the shop and I were one symbiotic organism of order and efficiency. Evenings were alcohol, convenience food and Netflix, through to the oblivion of sleep. A couple of years in, I was amazed to discover that I had attained my goal – I was 'not unhappy'.

I stuck with my winning formula, despite the agony of repetition, and for years the shop made a decent profit. But gradually everyone was buying stationery online and at the supermarket, despite my endless schemes to bring in customers. Mr Wilkes would nod and pat my shoulder.

'We'll see how things pan out,' he said. But I knew I was losing my precious sanctuary. At first, I used my own savings to buy our merchandise. Then I started faking the order receipts and transferring the money for the fake orders into my account and used it to buy more shop merchandise, which I stacked upstairs in my flat. Soon our stock was drastically low. I stopped sleeping, stopped eating, upped my day-drinking, cooked the books and re-arranged the merchandise. I couldn't put the stock upstairs through the tills again, because of the codes, so I sold it on eBay at inflated prices, and used the money to buy more stock at cost.

One little step leads to another and before you know it, you're dressed head to toe in black, disabling the shop alarm, using your gloved hands to swipe the carefully organised pens off the racks, tears pouring down your cheeks at the wrecking of the beautifully arranged colour-graded displays, forcing the cash register open, pocketing the measly takings, and taking apart the supply room to pretend the merchandise has been nicked. Then, like you've seen in countless crime dramas, you're chucking a struck match into the storeroom to start a harmless fire diversion, reactivating the alarm and then using a screwdriver to break the lock on the back door. The security alarm and smoke alarms start blaring immediately. You're the emergency contact, so the alarm company call you, just as you're pulling off your black hoodie and walking back down to the scene of your crime, where you weep at the destruction you've wrought.

I'd thought the fire would be easily extinguished before any real damage, but it accelerated terrifyingly fast, and the people in the adjacent flats barely escaped in time. I nearly killed four adults, three children and a newborn. The police had no leads, but Mr Wilkes deduced my financial scam in no time, assuming I'd done it for profit, had me forcibly evicted and sold everything I owned. He agreed to a private deal to pay back the money plus one hundred per cent interest in exchange for covering up my arson, because his own business practices were less than squeaky clean and he wanted to collect on the insurance.

That evening, I sat on Brighton beach, bruised, penniless and ashamed. I stared out at the surging sea that had always grounded me. I had been content here in Brighton, a lowly pebble on an endless beach. I picked up a misshapen stone of mottled grey and white with a hole through the centre, and added it to the chain holding my Dolores cross from Mum, as a tiny reminder of my Brighton peace. Then I used the final cash I had in my pocket to get a train to London and moved back in with Dad, with no job, no home, no possessions, and nowhere else to go. And ever since, I've lived off Dad's money and used his account to pay back my enormous debt to Mr Wilkes.

What a bloody saint I am.

CHAPTER NINETEEN

I experience the oblivion of a ten-hour dreamless sleep. I know the truth about Dad's guilt and Reece knows the truth about mine, but I feel deadened. Chris is right, 'closure' is vastly overrated.

Checking my mobile, I see that Anastasia has sorted the power of attorney and already forwarded me the details of a therapist and the address of my closest AA meeting. I erase both. I see another missed call from Chris and that he's left another message.

'Hi Hannah, I just wanted to say that I get that you ignored my last message. Hanging up on a phone call is a serious violation of finishing-school etiquette. *Hence* – you were right to ignore my first apology. But please accept my second one.'

I smile but erase the message.

I go round the house collecting up every bottle, empty and full, and deposit them all in the bins outside. Reece is right about one thing: me stopping drinking. I'll need all my reserves to help Dad through these last days.

I hear some post dribbling onto the floor downstairs. The usual guff of flyers. And a sharp-cornered official envelope. DNA results. I edge my thumb under the sticky flap and pull out the folded white paper. Skimming over the words, I zero in on the bolded section: *0% Chance of Paternity.* 'Dad' definitely isn't my dad. Nothing's changed and yet everything's changed. He still brought me up, he still feels like my dad. But a solid truth that I never doubted has been exploded. It's like someone saying that Hawaii doesn't exist. Nothing's changed per se, cos I've never been there and never plan to go – but how did I believe in its existence for all these years. As I dress, I chuck the tissue with Reece's DNA in the bin. He's right: looking back only destroys me and alienates everyone. I need to move forward.

Marcus arrives at midday to oversee the delivery of the hospital bed. He's in his element lugging stuff about, so confident, so capable. He directs two bald-headed, paunchy men to bring the bed into the lounge, where he's pushed back the settee to make room. It's a big professional-looking hospital bed and looks imposing even back against the wall.

'Sign here, Mr Roberts,' says the taller guy, and Marcus signs the proffered forms.

'Are you happy with it all, Mrs Roberts?' says the smaller guy to me. I lock eyes with Marcus and we both smirk at the man's mistake. Marcus puts his arm round me in a husbandly fashion and I look up at him like a loving fifties wife in an ad, then we giggle conspiratorially.

'Yes thanks, it's great,' I say. Marcus is the one sliver of silver lining left after all the hurricanes have passed. Reece and 'Dad' can't take him from me.

'So, are you all set, Mrs Roberts?' asks Marcus as the front door closes behind the departing men.

'Pretty much, Mr Roberts.'

We grin at each other.

'Oh, but before you go, could you un-jam a couple of doors for me?'

I don't want any more locked doors or secrets in this house.

'Sure, what are husbands for?'

'The gate in the back garden. I don't have the key for the padlock.'

'No problem.'

He uses an enormous pair of pliers to break the rusty chain, but the door is still wedged shut.

'The entwined bindweed and accumulated mud are holding it tight,' he explains.

'It's like the Sleeping Beauty story,' I say with amazement. 'The forest growing up around the princess as she slept for a hundred years.'

'Well then, I shall release you, milady,' Marcus says, bowing low.

'Thank you, kind sir,' I reply with a curtsy.

As he slices away the bindweed, I think of the Sleeping Beauty illustration in a book that 'Dad' used to read to me – a strapping prince with a feather in his hat scythed away the twinned trees that had grown up around the castle where the princess slept. I've been under a spell for so many years, not knowing who my parents were in so many ways, struggling with my own secrets, but now perhaps finally my prince has arrived to release me.

He finally clears everything and wrenches open the rusty gate.

'After you,' he says with a flourish of his hand, and I step through into the wood.

'Are you OK?' asks Marcus as I look back through the gate at the house – which looks smaller somehow.

'Yep, onwards,' I say confidently. 'Now the cellar.'

He frowns. 'What?'

'I want all the doors in this house opened. Dad locked it after—'

'Umm, I've got a job to get to right now. Another time?'

'Please Marcus? I need everything open now.'

'OK, sure.'

We go back in, and he bends down and peers at the cellar lock.

'You don't have the key?'

'No. Can't you force it?'

'It'll ruin the door,' he says.

'Fine.'

He shrugs, then picks up his crowbar and forces it between the door and frame. Glancing at me, he takes a deep breath and pushes his whole weight onto the lever. There's a cracking as the wood gives a little. I think of another fairy-tale locked door – the one hiding Bluebeard's dark secrets, and the curious wife whose prying led to the horrific discovery of all her husband's murdered ex-wives.

'Should I?' asks Marcus. I nod. He lifts his boot and kicks violently, and with a terrible splitting, it cracks open.

I flick the light switch, but nothing happens. Marcus hands me a large black torch and we walk down the rickety stairs into the dark. At the bottom, I play the beam over the room. Every surface is covered in a thick layer of grime, but it's all as I remember it – the wooden work surfaces along one wall, with a sink and basins for developing pictures, and along another wall, a work area with two large magnifying machines. There are still a couple of dusty curling photos pegged up along two wires strung up across the ceiling – old 'Falling' photos from Mum's last collection – a wine glass spilling as it falls in a series of time-lapse shots.

'Dad must've spent a fortune on all this,' I say as I swing the torch around. On the bottom shelf of the large metal unit on the third wall, the yellowish beam illuminates the carefully labelled files of each of Mum's photography collections, in date order – 'Family', 'God Says', 'Look Closer' and 'Falling'.

Marcus coughs. 'It's really dusty down here,' he says as I notice a final thin file, dated the year of her death.

'Michelangelo?' I read as I pull it out. 'I don't remember a photo series with that name.' I lift a sheet of negatives in front of the torch, screwing my eyes to focus – they're photos of torsos, in Michelangelo statue poses. Just like the ones of Reece in Mum's last roll of film, that he has on his mantelpiece. So that wasn't for the 'Falling' series? Even in negative form I can see these are clever living pastiches of decapitated sculptures, astutely recreated by Reece and framed by Mum; the sheer marble effect of Reece's smooth torso, his small precise nipples on his slabs of chest, his undulating rib muscles and his ridged abdomen either side of the raised knot of his belly button. I am embarrassed by these near-naked images of Reece, but also jealous of Mum's intense focus on him, recalling the ridiculous, sensual pleasure I got from Jeremy photographing me.

'I thought this was going to be some awful Bluebeard's trove,' I say. 'But it's just photos of the favourite son.'

'She loved you both,' Marcus says gently. 'Come on, we should get some fresh air.'

'You were lucky being an only child,' I say to Marcus as we shake off the dust upstairs. 'No comparisons.'

'Ha,' he snorts. 'I was jealous of you two, you were so tight. I guess we're always dissatisfied with our lot?'

'At least there was nothing Bluebeardy down there,' I joke.

'Just as well given that Bluebeard stabbed his snooping wife.' He seizes. 'Sorry – I didn't mean anything about your mum. Or that you shouldn't snoop in your own house.'

'No it's fine, but Bluebeard's wife was saved at the end – by her brothers.'

'Not in the version I remember,' he says, frowning. 'Well, lucky you've got a brother then.'

After Marcus leaves, confirming our date on Tuesday night, I feel fidgety and unsettled. I do have a brother, or perhaps just a half-brother, depending on who our fathers were, but still not one who would rush to save me. There were no secrets in the cellar, yet something's still nagging at me about it. But I can't put my finger on what.

My mobile starts ringing and I rush to answer, thinking it's about Dad. But it's Chris again. I let it ring, then just before it clicks off, I stab the button.

'Hey,' I say.

'Hey,' he says, 'thought you were going to ignore me again.'

'I thought about it.'

He laughs. 'I'm sorry about before.'

'No, I was really rude. I'm sorry.'

'You were upset but you were also right. And I've put my parents' house on the market.'

'What? You're kidding.'

'Nope, and I feel great – I needed a rocket up me – thanks.'

'Ah don't go on what I say, I'm hopeless.'

'You're not. But don't stress, I made the decision. How's all the sleuthing going?'

'Oh, I'm done with all that,' I say flatly, feeling like I'm letting him down somehow.

'Okaay?'

'I've only confirmed what you thought – Dad killed Mum – she was a cheat at everything, work, family, parenting – oh and best of all, Dad wasn't even my real dad. I did a DNA test.'

'Well that's new. Your brother?'

'Doubt he's Dad's either.'

'Some studies say that up to one in three men are most likely not the fathers of the children they think they are.'

'That seems crazily high.'

'People are very . . . pragmatic . . . liars. They go with the easiest answer that will keep life bubbling along. It's not necessarily wrong. Just practical.'

I give a sarcastic snort. 'Are policemen allowed to be such morally ambiguous pragmatists?'

'Lucky I'm not one any more then, isn't it? Do you think your dad knew?'

'He never had kids with his first wife, so maybe – perhaps finding out about me was the straw that broke the camel's back?'

'I don't think "maybe" and "perhaps" would stand up in court.'

'Everything I've discovered is circumstantially overwhelming. I'm now convinced that the bloke I called "Dad" killed Mum. Sorry to go on.'

'I told you, I want a resolution too. And don't ever forget how truly, madly, deeply bored I am!'

'Thanks,' I say, centred by this almost-stranger who I feel more comfortable talking to than most people.

'I'm sorry,' he says gruffly.

'Why are you sorry?'

'It's hard to see parents as less than ideals.'

I laugh. 'That's putting it mildly. I didn't know Mum at all. And I certainly had no idea of what Dad was capable of. And that he wasn't even my dad.'

'They were still your parents practically. It wasn't all a lie. Just cos people play one role, doesn't mean that the other role isn't true when they're playing it.'

'That's very woo-woo of you.'

'I try. But if you're now certain it was him, how do you feel about him evading justice?'

'Well obviously murder is never forgivable, but—'

'I don't think the law allows for "but"s either.'

'But—'

'Fair enough,' he laughs. 'Motive is usually a whole heap of "but"s. So what now?'

'I guess I try to be with him here till the end.'

'Do you think you can do that, with what you know?'

'We'll see.'

'If you need anything – well you know.'

'Thanks, you too.'

After we say goodbye, I stand plumb centre in our family lounge and rotate slowly, memories adhering to me like candyfloss onto a stick. As I speed up, sticky tendrils swirl from every laughing photo, every clumsily made clay ashtray, and every indent in a chair. Dizzy, I steady myself with the mantelpiece, my fingers smudging its thick layer of dust, and I inscribe MUM WAS HERE. 'Dust,' as 'Dad' used to say, 'is dirt, pet hair, insect waste and dead skin cells.'

Tomorrow, that 'dad', who is not my dad, is coming back to live in this filthy house, speckled with Mum's dead cells.

I erase my mantelpiece inscription, wipe my blackened palms down my jeans and set off for the shops where I select my weaponry of brushes, mops and scourers, my ammunition of heavy swan-necked vessels and industrial-sized spray cans, and my big black rolls of extra-strong body bags for the vanquished filth.

That 'dad', who brought me up as his, despite not being my dad, and probably knowing it, is coming home to die.

Back home, I sweep away all the crap littering every surface into the welcoming plastic sacks: the towering piles of magazines and newspapers, the trinkets and art projects, the sports medals, the photos. This house is moving on – without Mum. It feels so wrong, so sacrilegious – so exciting. I forgot to buy rubber gloves but am galvanised by the stinging of my red, blotchy hands.

That 'dad', coming here to die, murdered my mum.

I pour two full bottles of thick gelatinous bleach into the downstairs shit-encrusted toilet bowl, looking at Mum's church sign photos, the one above the cistern reading: 'JESUS HAD TWO DADS AND HE TURNED OUT FINE'. Mum must have laughed at her private sick joke every time she came in here; Dad must have died a little more inside.

But that 'Dad' murdered Mum after years of her cheating, lying and manipulation, leaving him a cuckold raising someone else's kids and paying for her vanity projects and infidelity. She missed our childhoods, not busy with some stellar career, just shagging in cesspits like that crummy photography studio. And she lied to Reece and me about who our dad really was.

I spray multiple times the advised volume of foam onto the thick, gritty layer of grease on the old standing gas cooker, inhaling the heady fumes. I watch the dirty lather bubble away, and when the potion has wrought its spell, I swipe away the grease of years' worth of lonely meals that poor Dad cooked here in his self-imposed prison.

Sometimes moving furniture is just re-arranging, but sometimes it can smash calcified patterns, shifting thought, allowing hope. It's 1 a.m. when I finally haul the endless bags of rubbish out to the bins, and the entire ground floor of the house is unrecognisable. It and I have shed our skins – and her skin.

I, of all people, understand how you can find yourself down a disorientated cul-de-sac of confusion and in the heat of the moment do something you regret, the second you've done it. I could have killed all those people in my moment of madness. 'Dad' killed Mum, *but—*

Thinking of Mum's skin cells still present in this house, still trapped amongst her clothes, makes me shiver. I can't face cleaning upstairs, but I need to keep her as far away from me as possible, so I use masking tape to seal shut every drawer in Mum's bedroom and tape across the slatted

211

cupboards, till they are big ugly silver rectangles of tape. Mum is completely erased from downstairs and walled-in upstairs.

I finally accept what Reece said all along – in the one true film version, Dad killed Mum – *but* it was a moment of madness after extreme extended provocation. If I can live with my terrible moment, I can accept 'Dad's' *but*, can live with the secret and can give – my dad – a good end.

CHAPTER TWENTY

'Welcome,' I say dramatically, slamming open the front door for Dad's wheelchair the next morning. The hallway is bathed in sunlight with the broken shades over the side window gone and it all smells so gloriously lemony. Dad doesn't respond, so I plant my feet into the gravel and heft his wheelchair up Marcus's new wooden ramp. To quash any similarity I have to Mum, my hair's pulled back starkly with clips, I'm wearing Dad's garden dungarees and I'm make-up free – she wouldn't be seen dead in this get-up. I'm determined that Dad and I will make a fresh start with zero reminders of her. Dad's disappointingly unimpressed with my home improvements in the hall, so I push him through to the newly configured lounge, thrillingly clean and streamlined and with Dad's new hospital bed in pride of place.

Dad's eyes are glazed and unfocused. I'm deflated, but what did I expect? I settle him into the bed, put his adult nappies under it and line up his pills. He's got an impressive array: morphine tablets, blood thinners, cholesterol and blood pressure medication, and anti-constipation gel pills. I momentarily relax as I order them into his plastic pill caddy marked with the days of the week in big letters. He's got two slow-release morphine tablets per day and a small store of fast-release ones for emergencies. As morphine is a controlled drug, I've only been given one month's supply. '*If* you need any more,' Valeria told me, 'you can get them through the GP.' She clearly thought the idea he would last beyond a month was hypothetical.

I'll be doling out all the pills, so Dad doesn't actually need this days-of-the-week caddy. But no point risking giving Dad an overdose by mistake. The vet thinks Schro deserves to be set free – yet Dad has to limp on to the end. What if I did it subconsciously? In a fit of Jen-ness for him killing her? Her presence feels so strong that I have to actively remind myself not to carry myself and speak like her now. I fill the pill caddy and lock it and all spare tablets in a large metal box that I purchased at WHSmith's, where I had to stop myself reorganising the shelves and aligning the pens. I place the key behind the carriage clock on the mantelpiece – where Mum and Dad always put important things, like passports or season tickets.

I switch on the TV to fill the void. My finger hovers over the channel choice, but Dad looks so forlorn that I swallow my aversion and tune into a random *Muerte*. *Episode 4: An expat coffee shop owner is murdered. He refused to learn a word of Spanish despite ten years' residence. Have the locals finally had enough?* I watch as a straw-hatted elderly couple order coffee in English from a bald-headed guy in Union Jack shorts.

Then a young man makes a complex order in Spanish.

Union Jack stares at him in shock. 'S-sorry?' he stammers.

'Coffee?' the young man then says in English.

Union Jack laughs.

'Got me there, mate, I thought you were one of "them",' he says, nodding towards a Spanish family.

The young man's eyes flash and he starts abusing Union Jack in Spanish, calling over other locals who become equally incensed.

Cut to Union Jack on the floor of his shop, blood pooling around his head beneath his heavy coffee machine. As the jangly credits kick in, I leave Dad to enjoy the celluloid return of his prodigal son to solve the caffeinated crime.

Dad's asleep when I bring him some tea, so I click off Reece, who's now elbow deep in coffee beans. Dad and I always liked the milk poured into our tea first. Mum put it in last. I make two cups as an experiment and – they do taste different: hers is substantial and intense, mine thin and unbalanced. I so want to drink hers, but force myself to stick with mine.

'Reece,' Dad calls out as he jerks awake, reaching both arms out to the TV. I'm right here – a flesh-and-blood child, if not a blood relative. Why does he yearn for my celluloid sibling? Was Reece more inherently loveable? Or is Reece his actual son and Dad knows I'm the cuckoo in the nest? Dad continues to moan and gesture to the black TV, and eventually I have to turn it back on and suffer more of Reece's smarm.

* * *

'Aaaaaagh!'

I wake from a nap to a huge roaring from Dad who is thrashing back and forth in his bed.

'Where am I?' he says, looking round in confusion.

'You're back home from the hospital.' I smile, but he looks panicked.

'Why's the bed in here?' he says, looking round. 'It's all wrong, all wrong.'

'This bed's just temporary, till you get the strength for the stairs.'

'No, no, no,' he says, swinging his head back and forth.

'I've just tidied up a bit,' I say, putting my hand on his arm, but he shoves it away.

'No, no, no,' he moans. 'I don't like it. I want it back.'

He's going to hurt himself if he doesn't calm down.

'It's fine Dad, it's just different—'

'Change it all back,' he shouts, his body sloping off the side of the bed so I have to haul him back up.

'OK, OK, fine, I'll change it back.'

'All going back?' he says desperately.

'Fine.'

I start lugging pieces of furniture back into their original places, feeling utterly defeated. Then I remember it's bin-collection day, rush outside and drag in the bin bags of filth. I have a pretty good recall of the old landscape of junk, if not the content, as it's been the same bloody outline for so many years. Dully, I start recreating the oh-so-familiar silhouette. Dad moans in pain throughout, despite the two fast-acting morphine tablets. After I finish, I feel heavy and hopeless and slump down on the floor next to Schro curled up on his Spurs blanket under the coffee table. His

216

cancerous leg is rotting and reeking and his food has stayed an uneaten coagulating sludge since yesterday. He registers my presence with a slight lift of his head, like an old yogi gracefully acknowledging a young student's trials. Schro's clearly 'ready'. That bloody vet said I'd know when.

When – is now.

He's like an old, desiccated fur stole as I settle him on Dad's lap for a final pat. I don't tell Dad it's the last time ever – why give him the wrenching experience of bidding farewell when it'll be senseless pain that he'll forget entirely. If you don't know a horror has happened, has it happened at all? They seem to register each other. A final gentle moment between these old dying friends. Will I get this moment with Dad before he goes? I wipe away a maudlin tear and steel myself to get on with the process of killing.

'Will Reece be coming again soon?' asks Dad as I lift Schro.

'To visit? I've no idea.'

'No, coming home for tea.'

'Dad, Reece doesn't live here any more.'

His eyes fill with tears. I think of Loreta doing anything she could to keep her dad happy and telling me to do the same while I still had time.

'Yes,' I say with a sigh, 'he'll be home later.'

'Where is he now?'

'Umm, he's – he's playing football with Marcus.'

Dad pulls back his right arm and punches me violently in the face.

My head slams back as I yelp, then I lurch forward, trying to get my balance.

'You fucking bitch,' he shouts.

I freeze in shock. Dad's face twists into a grotesque sneer, he bares his teeth, and then he snarls at me and I'm propelled backwards by his hatred. I knock my hip on the wooden arm of the settee and an intense jolt of pain shoots through me as I struggle not to drop Schro. Dad's pulled the bedcovers back and is getting up.

'Dad, stop it—' I shout, as I try to shield Schro from him.

'You fucking bitch,' he shouts again as he lurches to his feet, raising his walking stick. I throw Schro to the far corner of the settee and he lands with a terrible strangled squawk as Dad brings the stick crashing down on me. The tip catches my forehead, my feet slide out from under me and my head slams onto the wooden floor. I am momentarily paralysed by the intensity of the pain ricocheting through me. Dad's standing over me, his face contorted. I roll sideways into the base of the settee then squirm backwards towards the door. My head's throbbing, my vision's blurred and I can't coordinate my limbs. I use the door frame to pull myself up as Dad steps towards me, raising the stick again, his eyes bulging.

'You'd be better off dead,' Dad shouts at me. He thwacks my shoulder and I crumple to my knees. He lifts the stick again, straining upwards to deliver the killer blow. Then, as quickly as it arose, the anger floods out of him as his shoulders sag, his gaze disconnects and the stick falls from his bony hand. He stumbles backwards and falls back to lie widthways across the bed.

Everything is still. I hear the carriage clock ticking, feel the bobbly painted wood of the door frame and see a drip falling onto the floorboards in front of me. When I touch my face, my hand is slick with blood.

Dad isn't moving. I carefully inch forward, close enough to see his bony chest rising and falling with a laboured breathing. I am numb, every nerve ending cauterised. I know what I've just experienced. Dad killing Mum. Experienced it, as if I were Mum. Now I have a soundtrack for my one true film cut – as Dad violently stabbed Mum, he was shouting, 'You fucking bitch, you'd be better off dead'.

Schro mews. He's hunched into the corner of the settee, looking up at me with rheumy, pained eyes. On autopilot, I move towards him. At least I can put him out of his misery. I retrieve the Spurs blanket and use it to gently gather up Schro's fragile body. Glancing at Dad, who hasn't moved, I put the blanket at the bottom of the white wire cat box, then lower Schro in. My blood-streaked hands shake as I feed the long locking pin through the mesh hoops.

'It's all OK, Schro,' I say, like some robotic Stepford wife, 'it's a lovely day, the sun is shining and we're going for a short walk.' I drape a towel over the back and sides of the box so that Schro won't be upset by the rush of life outside but can still see me.

Dad still hasn't moved.

As I open the front door, I see Marcus walking up the street. He smiles, then stops in his tracks.

'Are you all right?' he calls. When I don't react, he breaks into a run.

'What's happened? You're bleeding.'

I can't tell him. It's too grotesque. I do what I always do: seize up, harden and bludgeon on.

'It's Dad, he's – upset. Can you go and check he's all

right? Make sure the sides of the bed are up.'

'I'll call Mum, she's better at that stuff than me.'

'No, it's fine, I—'

'I'll get her,' he shouts, leaping across the dividing wall. 'Wait there.'

I slump onto the steps, lowering Schro's box.

Mrs Roberts follows Marcus back out moments later, wiping her hands on a dishcloth.

'Oh my God, you're bleeding everywhere.'

Marcus dabs my face with a big wad of kitchen roll he's brought out.

'I'm OK. But could you just check on my dad, Mrs Roberts?'

She exchanges a look with Marcus.

'I won't be long,' she calls as she hurries up the path and enters, leaving the front door ajar.

'What happened?' Marcus asks gently.

I shake my head and he tends to me quietly, as we wait.

'Your dad's absolutely fine,' Mrs Roberts says when she re-appears. 'He was lying across the bed in an odd way, but I've got him back in.'

'Thanks so much. It was an accident,' I gabble. 'I was trying to help him, and he flailed his arm out and I caught my head on the table. I'll be more prepared next time. Not that there will be a next time. You couldn't stay with Dad for a bit could you – I just really need to go to the vet's – for Schro's boosters.'

'No problem,' she says, frowning at me for a moment, then going back in.

'You sure you're OK?' Marcus asks.

I nod.

'We still on for that drink?' he says as Mrs Roberts closes the front door.

I nod again, giving him a weak smile.

After refusing a lift, I set off up towards Muswell Hill, holding the box in front of me so Schro can see me, and he shifts up to the mesh.

'What a lovely day, Schro.' I must keep going. I can't think about what's just happened. I will do this one thing right. Give Schro an easy death. 'Can you hear the birds, Schro? Silly little twits. You'll be bounding after them soon. They won't know what's hit them.' I'm sweating and crying quietly. My arms hurt and the cage is digging into my ribs. The sun is a deep burnt orange and the sky is splattered red and purple – like the eyeball of the sun is leaking. I keep trudging, taking Schro to be murdered.

At the surgery, the matronly vet is behind the counter in her pale purple twinset.

'Ah, it's time,' she says as she sees me.

'Yes,' I say, dully.

'I'm free now. Do you want to come into the room for the procedure?'

'Yes.'

'It can be unpleasant.'

I still nod. I have to be there to the end.

'OK, then bring him in.'

'Come on, lovely Schro,' I say quietly as I lift him out onto the examination table. He's so light, so other-worldly.

She places her right gloved hand firmly onto his neck, reaches back to the counter for a small syringe and pauses. I nod and she injects him at the neck.

He shudders. His body locks and he gives a strangled

yelp, louder than any sound he's made for months. He coughs. He gurgles. He chokes. I turn my head away – but still hear him gurgle.

And finally, everything is silent. I turn back. The room is quiet and there is a still, lifeless curl of fur on the table.

'All done,' she says. I reach out and touch the very tip of the fur of his tail. All of me is there in my finger, touching the tiny filaments.

I break contact, pay on autopilot and stumble outside. The sun has sunk and the sky is a dark, glowering purple. I double over and weep. Poor poor Schro. Death like this isn't some clichéd 'blessed relief'. It's a violent, disgusting wrenching. Death like Mum experienced it would have been unthinkably gruesome. Her own husband screamed, 'You fucking bitch, you'd be better off dead,' as he lifted a massive kitchen knife and plunged it into her, the tip piercing her skin, the blade shoving in, shattering her ribs as it drove through her tissues, her veins, her arteries and finally pierced her still-beating heart. The pain, the shock, the disbelief that Mum must have felt as she realised what was happening, seeing who was doing it, grasping onto the final seconds of consciousness as life was obliterated, was all beyond horrific and unforgivable – whatever Mum had done.

'Give me my cat!' I shout as I fling the vet's door open again, the glass rattling violently. I stride towards the back room.

'Stop,' the vet shouts, stepping in front of me. 'What d'you think you're doing.'

'I need my cat's body,' I shout.

She frowns as a wave of panic engulfs me. What if

Schro is being burnt in some pet incineration oven this very second?

'You put down our dog Feynman here and let us take him home to bury him,' I wail, 'and now I need Schro's body back to do the same. Please.'

She frowns then motions me into the rear room.

'I do understand that the death of a pet is upsetting,' she says as she closes the door, 'but you need to calm down. Wait here.' She disappears out a back door and returns with a sealed bag, like something you'd get cooked chicken packed in from the supermarket hot food counter. It's so crushingly mundane and feels so light, as if Schro's departed essence had weight.

'I would recommend that you deal with the remains within the next twelve hours,' she says officiously.

'My high priestess robes are still at the dry-cleaner's, but I'll try,' I retort sarcastically, then falter when I see her appalled expression. 'Look, I'm sorry I'm so upset,' I continue in a more placatory tone, 'but how is this any different to what you did with Feynman?'

'I didn't put him down,' she snaps.

'But—'

'Yes, he was booked in by your mother, but then—' She tuts and looks away.

'What?'

'It was all rather distressing if you must know,' she says, blinking at me. 'I knew that lovely dog so well from his many appointments here, so beautiful, such a lovely temperament.' Her brief smile of memory evaporates. 'Your mother phoned to cancel the procedure that morning.' She squirms. 'I don't want to pass on hearsay . . .'

'This isn't a court—'

'Your dad murdered him,' she says abruptly. 'I'm sorry to say it like that, but those were your mum's exact words. I've never forgotten them, especially after . . . what happened to her, just a few days later.'

'Murdered him?' I mumble.

'She was utterly distraught, said he had – and I'm using her words here – "violently smothered him as he fought for his life". Unforgivable animal cruelty in my view. I'm sorry, I shouldn't really be telling you this. With what happened to your mum just the next week, I realise it seems—'

I clutch my bag of Schro and sweep out.

I was so cataclysmically wrong. I can't forgive 'Dad' for what he's done. I must expose him to the world's judgement and make him pay. All those tools that Loreta used to reach her dad, igniting his memories with sight, sound, taste, touch and smell, I will now use to prove Dad's guilt to the world. And not forgetting the best tool of all – me.

CHAPTER TWENTY-ONE

As I open my eyes, I register the dirty brown of my soil-stained hand against the white sheet of Mum's bed and the swollen red edges of my torn fingernails. Last night, I vaguely recalled where we'd buried Feynman in the garden, though the ice-cream-stick cross had long since rotted. After slicing a couple of worms in half while breaking up the rock-hard earth with my spade, I scrabbled at the ground with my bare hands and finally unearthed a piece of pitted purple plastic. I gulped out a sob and held it to my cheek. I was in the right place. This was Feynman's chew toy that I'd chucked in during his funeral the week before Mum died. That funeral where Dad had appeared so grief-stricken and Mum had appeared to be clinging onto him for balance. Now the whole scene dissolves and reassembles in my memory: she was rigid with tension, desperately trying to control Dad's seething anger after his violent murder of poor Feynman.

Mirroring the actions of Feynman's funeral, I lowered Schro's fragile furry body into the hole, then added his favourite toy, an electric-green feather that he had never tired of leaping to catch.

'Bye Schro. Love you,' I sobbed.

Feynman and Schro are finally buried together, but I will not be following Reece's suggestion: I will not let sleeping dogs lie.

Today, I step through the looking glass and become Mum, moving from understudy to lead. To start my transformation, I slept in my parents' bed last night – well Mum's, as Dad usually slept in the spare room. Sunlight is darting over the ceiling above me, flickering on the chipped ceiling moulding and dusty red Chinese lantern in the centre. I know this big bed so well, with its Chinese-style painted headboard, and the heavy red-and-orange bedspread.

How appropriate that I am waking up with the sunlight – drawn to the light as I emerge. This must be what it's like for a real butterfly. The final transformation isn't an effort – it's an effortless momentum towards the inevitable. I lean into my forearm, which still has the powdery, perfumed smell of Mum from the sheets. I bury my face in the scent, embodying Mum's languid body draped here.

I was wary with Dad last night, but as before, it was as if nothing had happened and he was his old fragile self. From now on, I'll stay hyper-alert, ready for the slightest sign of his Jekyll and Hyde shift. But now I don't fear it. I want it. I will be Mum 24/7 to bring my Jekyll dad forth and finally get answers.

Once Dad's fed, propped safely between cushions and smiling at Reece on screen, I sprint to the chemist and select a box of hair dye displaying a young woman smiling enigmatically with cascades of 'Honey Blonde' hair. But the pictures on the back showing 'if you've got this colour' then 'you'll get this colour' clearly show I'm not going to get anywhere near her shade. So, I buy two packets of hair bleach.

Dad's still watching TV as I take my purchases up to the bathroom. I know the advice for bleaching brown hair – patch test then do it carefully or you can hurt yourself. I use two packets at once, which reek and sting like mad on my head and eyebrows, but I double the time advised, screwing my eyes against the pain. I squirt Dad's shaving foam on my legs and armpits to shave them and catch my reflection: a freaky yeti-poodle, with foam on its face, head and legs. Once I've shaved my dark body hair and can't take the agony of the bleach any longer, I leap into the shower and drench myself till I'm pain-free. I towel-dry my hair, apply the honey-blonde dye to my hair and eyebrows, and let it ferment while I file my jagged nails into the pointed arches that Mum favoured.

In the bedroom, I rip off the swathes of silver tape on the bedside drawers, to reveal a tangle of pants and bras: baby blues and pinks, vivid scarlets and intense blacks. I take out a delicate pair of pink pants and a matching bra, both with fine lace panels, and marvel that they fit me. I've only ever worn waist-high M&S pants and sturdy underwired bras that come in packs of three. These spiderweb silk garments are like fairy clothes. I pad over to the full-length mirror and admire how these fripperies adorn and accentuate my lithe figure.

After my final hair sluice, I use Mum's close-up hand

mirror to tweeze my thick, now blonde brows to Mum's thinner, more arched peaks.

I use my phone to play one of Mum's favourite tracks: Cyndi Lauper's 'Girls Just Want to Have Fun' as the soundtrack for her full exhumation, and I feel her rising in me as my shoulders jerk in time. I drag the masking tape off Mum's wardrobes, big patches of paint peeling from the doors and bits of plaster flying from the walls, then splay open the doors to – Pandora's closet. This time I lean in, breathing Mum into me, getting every last atom of her stale breath into her new host body. I pull out a huge handful of dresses and fan them across the bed. They're a rainbow of beautiful colours, grass green, setting-sun orange, early-morning sky blue. I select a sky-blue silky dress with a full skirt, white netting underlay and white lace hem. I put my head through the boat neck and it floats down over me, fitting perfectly. At the bottom of the wardrobe, there are row upon row of dusty shoes. Mum loved heels: high Italian spikes, red-soled patent leather stilettos and black Minnie Mouse platforms with red bows. All stupidly high.

'They're far more comfortable, darling. My feet hurt in flats,' I say out loud to the empty room, feeling her sensuous smile flickering on my lips.

I put on her white-and-gold strappy sandals with high wide heels and dance along to Cyndi. Then I sit at her dressing table and imitate the make-up routine that I watched so many times as a kid: a light powder, mascara and red lipstick. I can't do it properly as everything is so dried out, but I do my best. I dust a hint of powder over my skin and as I inhale the powdery aroma, I feel her kissing my cheek. I spit on the mascara to darken my lashes. The deep-red lipstick stains my lips when I push hard. I brush my damp now-blonde hair back and twist it up in a French pleat, feeling Mum's motion in my arms, and automatically pull two strands free either side of my face. It's like I'm focusing my childhood kaleidoscope: I go out of focus and she comes in. I take her almost empty bottle of Chanel No. 5 and dab it on my wrists and behind my ears, and the musty but still-floral smell ignites my transformation.

Hi Mum.

Who knew I had this identical version of you inside me. But I think you've always been there, waiting patiently, biding your time, unwilling to be limited by mere physical death. Your beautiful butterfly form has always been curled inside my swollen cocoon and now you've shed my chrysalis and are spreading your wings. And you're not a fragile butterfly, like I always thought my butterfly self was – you're strong.

I walk downstairs, gripping the banister so I don't fall in the vertiginous shoes. I am tilted forward into Mum's stance, tits up, bottom up, chin raised. 'Girls Just Want to Have Fun' is still playing on repeat as I turn the corner into the lounge. Dad stares at me in the doorway. Who is he seeing? I dance for him, like Mum did, grabbing my skirt in my fists and swishing it. Then I stop the song, find the voice recorder app and press record.

'Hi Philip,' I say, lowering the brashness of my voice to Mum's breathiness.

'Mmmm,' says Dad. I walk closer and sit on the end of the bed. I pull at a strand of my blonde hair and suck it, like Mum used to do.

'Where are the kids, honey?' Dad asks.

I hardly dare breathe.

'Umm, Reece's playing football and Hannah's upstairs,' I say, cautiously. That's exactly what we were doing on the afternoon of the day Mum died. This is it.

'You said you were sorry, Philip,' I say gently. 'What are you sorry for?'

He swallows and his Adam's apple undulates in his scraggy neck.

'I think you're the one who's sorry,' Dad says, with a strange smile.

'What do you mean?' I lean in, but am ready to leap away if he looks like he's going to strike me.

'Naughty girl,' he says, reaching out to touch my breast.

'Ooh, no,' I yelp as I leap away. How gross. But I hover by the door. I don't want to lose this channel of communication.

'Hannah's upstairs,' I say evenly.

'Ah come on, she's busy with her Sindy,' he says. I had a thin, impossibly long-legged Sindy way back when, but not at fourteen, more like eight. Of course. He's seeing me as a much younger version of Mum. Not Mum when she died.

'But she could come down any moment,' I continue, trying to buy time, thinking I can somehow shift time frames.

'You're such a tease,' says Dad, reaching out to me. I back out into the hall. This is hopeless. And vile. What was I expecting? I'm not Marty McFly in *Back to the Future*. I can't just set the year in my time machine and step out into the one I want – 1996. This reality Dad's in is more mid-eighties. No use to me. I switch off the recording app. Looking at my phone, I realise I was playing Cyndi Lauper

230

from the eighties earlier – was this the problem? Why he's gone back to that memory? Is it to do with this dress, the time of day, what I've said? How do I get him back to the day of the murder? I think back to when Dad hit me. I wasn't even dressed like Mum then. So, what sight, smell, sound or touch was the key that opened that door? I picture what he was doing. He was stroking Schro. Is that sense memory the key? But Schro's rotting in the garden with poor Feynman. I need some sort of cat substitute.

When in doubt, look on Amazon. Using the search term 'realistic cat' I find a thriving market for such things, with options varying from £5 for a basic stuffed toy, all the way up to £105 for a creepy specimen that purrs and has inbuilt sensors so it responds to being touched. I order an orange-furred version and click the expensive next-day delivery. Apparently, it's 'so much more than a stuffed animal, it's a companion'.

CHAPTER TWENTY-TWO

The world is unpleasantly three-dimensional. After not drinking again last night and sleeping deeply, the undulations of Dad's Rice Krispies as I serve him breakfast are intense, the snap, crackle and pop disconcertingly audible. I'm wearing Mum's candy-pink dress with the full pleated skirt, a wide white belt, white sunglasses on the top of my head and high pink shoes on my feet. I've corrected my music era today and I'm playing the Spice Girls' 'Wannabe', released just before Mum died. She played it all day long, dancing round the living room, driving the rest of us mad.

I'm excited about the arrival of my robot-Schro, having received an email update that it's being delivered this morning. I'm flouncing about, gesticulating and lip-syncing along to the music like Mum, but Dad is totally unmoved by my efforts.

The bell rings. I momentarily consider pulling on my

Hannah sweats for the driver, but it's only a stranger who'll see me all mummed-up.

I pull open the front door, music blaring, and see not a delivery driver but Mr Roberts. I stab off the music. His dry lips part and he goes bright red, to match his ugly Hawaiian shirt. Ha. If he fancies me when I'm in my sweats, this get-up would be way too much for him.

'Hello,' I say aggressively. 'Did you want something?' I push up Mum's white sunglasses which have fallen over my eyes.

'No, no—' he stutters.

'Then why did you knock?'

'I – isn't that her—'

'Mum's? Yes. I'm short of clothes. She's hardly going to mind, is she?'

He shakes his head as if to break up the snow-globe reality in front of him, then starts to turn away. I see. Because I'm more confident today, not some drunken easy prey, he's off?

'Why did you ring the bell?' I ask, touching his arm, to show the tables are turned, and he flinches like I've burnt him.

'Umm. I was off to the shops and Libbie said I should check if you needed anything,' he stammers.

'Don't rush off. You should say hi to Dad since you're here.'

'Umm, well I—' He looks at his watch. He's a dirty old man, but he's a voice from the past and he might jolt Dad into some useful memories.

'Come on in,' I say, stepping back.

'OK sure, just for a minute.'

Dad smiles as we enter the lounge, but I'm not sure which reality he's in.

'Philip, how are you doing?' Mr Roberts says.

'Jen, can you get a cup for Frank?' Dad replies.

Bingo.

Mr Roberts' eyes widen.

'He confuses me with Mum sometimes,' I whisper to him, excited by the effect he's having on Dad. 'Go on,' I say, pushing him towards a seat. 'I'll be right back with the tea.'

When I return, they're talking about the weather and how the temperature's dropped. Mr Roberts looks confused as it's still quite mild. But the temperature did drop noticeably in early October 1996 when Mum died. I try not to get my hopes up.

'Do you think we should stick with Southgate?' asks Dad.

'Errr. Yeah, seems like a good bloke,' Mr Roberts replies haltingly.

'He's an idiot,' barks Dad.

'Oh I don't know, he's doing OK,' Mr Roberts says.

'Are you kidding. How could he miss?' Dad explodes.

'Miss what?' mumbles Mr Roberts.

'The goal, of course,' says Dad.

The hairs on my arms prickle. Dad isn't talking about the Gareth Southgate of 2019, England manager. This is the Gareth Southgate who missed the penalty in '96. I think of us all in the lounge, cheering England on that last summer together, Mum and me on the floor, Reece sitting on the settee next to Dad, whose fingers were tightly crossed with desperate hope.

'Bloody Germany,' continues Dad.

'What have they done?' says Mr Roberts, even more confused.

'Knocked us out, of course. Again!' says Dad, gesticulating.

'I think it's the nineties for Dad,' I say to Mr Roberts. 'It's coming home,' I whisper before starting to sing the anthem of that competition, Skinner and Baddiel's 'Three Lions': Reece and I used to belt it out all round the house.

'Euro '96,' whispers Mr Roberts, his gaze sweeping over me, and I have an intense déjà vu sensation.

'Just go with it, Mr Roberts,' I say. 'It's good for Dad to unearth memories.'

'What memories?' he says, his eyes darting around.

'Whatever comes up. Say yes to everything,' I whisper. 'It's a technique for dementia,' I add, leaning in to pour the tea.

Mr Roberts swallows as a bead of sweat drips down his cheek.

'One all in the semi-final, wasn't it,' says Mr Roberts nervously, turning back to Dad.

'Yep, five good penalties then that big-nosed idiot shoots straight at the goalie,' says Dad as I pass the tea and my hand brushes Mr Roberts' own. He flinches violently, his cup crashing to the floor, tea spilling everywhere.

'God, sorry,' he says, standing abruptly. 'I-I really should get back. I promised Libbie I'd do the shopping. It was good to see you, Philip,' he says in a bizarrely upbeat voice as he rushes towards the front door.

'No, please, you're really helping Dad,' I say, chasing after him, desperate to push the experiment. But he's out the door.

'Mr Roberts,' I shout and he freezes in our front garden, staring back at my pink dress, and I feel the weird déjà vu again. Of course. That's what I'm remembering. I was at uni, chatting to a girl on my course, Bella something, and this boy joined us, who I'd been shagging for a few weeks. I registered this exact intensity I feel from Mr Roberts now; they were hyper-aware of each other despite barely interacting, like when a cat's fur suddenly springs up and though it hasn't moved, you know it's engaged all its muscles and is ready to spring. When I discovered they were shagging a couple of weeks later, I knew it had been inevitable from that moment.

I look down at Mum's dress and then just as Mr Roberts steps over the little wall dividing our gardens, I call out to him in Mum's breathy, innuendo-laden tone.

'Fraaa-nk.'

He stops, foot mid-air, like he's been shot. Then he lowers his foot and turns back to me, eyes wide, jaw slack.

Of course. His fascination with me wasn't actually with me.

'How long were you sleeping with her?' I ask.

He shakes his head.

'How long,' I shout.

His shoulders drop. 'Please. Not here. My wife—' he says, gesturing back at the house.

'My *dad*,' I say, gesturing to our house.

'God,' he mumbles.

I look at our two houses, indivisible at their party wall. What an apt name for this particular wall. Mum's 'party me' wasn't just busy outside the home apparently.

'Let's go to a coffee shop, to talk. Please,' begs Mr Roberts.

'Fine,' I say eventually. 'Give me a few minutes to change.' I race up the stairs two at a time and get into my Hannah slob look. I check on Dad, who's looking into space. The sides of the bed are firmly up. I put on another episode of *Muerte* and leave him watching Reece dancing flamenco – brilliantly of course.

'Name?' asks the coffee shop barista.

'Jen,' I say.

Mr Roberts winces.

'So, lover boy,' I say sarcastically as we finally sit down with our coffees.

'Hannah, I—'

'You had an affair with Mum!'

He stares down at his hands and speaks without looking up. 'It was years ago.'

'Well, she died years ago, so that doesn't really nail it down.'

'It was only once,' he gibbers, 'when you and Reece were – Reece had just started secondary, so eleven, and you would have been—'

'Seven.'

'It was totally stupid. Meant nothing,' he mumbles.

'Hardly worth doing it then,' I snap.

'No,' he agrees. 'And I regretted it hugely.'

'Oh, well huge congratulations for your morality – after the fact. Does your wife know?'

'God, no. Jen and I agreed to never mention it again.'

'How thoughtful of you both. And my dad?'

'No, I don't think so.'

I lift my coffee, scalding my tongue and crashing it back down, slopping it onto the table.

'How the fuck did you go on living next door?' I demand.

'I did suggest moving, but Libbie couldn't understand why. Marcus had just started at a good secondary and she wanted to keep him there,' he says sheepishly. 'And then later, after what happened to your poor mum, we wanted to be here to help. I'm really sorry.'

'Oh well that's all right then. If you're *really* sorry.' He's not sorry – he's proud he fucked my beautiful mother – it's so obvious. 'You were cheating on your wife, your son – on all of us. You were part of our family.'

'I know. But please,' he begs. 'Please don't tell Libbie. It would destroy her . . . and for what?'

I laugh.

His eyes run me up and down. 'Why've you made yourself look so like her – the hair, the clothes. It's so – creepy.'

'I'm creepy! You're a grotesque perv – lusting after the daughter of your ex-lover cos she reminds you of her.'

Mr Roberts shakes his head and reaches out to touch me.

'Are you fucking kidding.' I bat his hand away and swipe my cup onto the floor, an arc of coffee splattering across it. I run from the shop, tears pouring down my face, drenched in self-disgust. I was revolted by Mr Roberts' leching over me. But there's always another layer of horror. Now I see how pathetically full of myself I was to believe I was worth being leched over – he was only ever leching over Mum. I am ultra-pathetic to be upset by this ugly slight.

* * *

As I approach the house, Mrs Roberts is in her front garden picking at weeds, kneeling on a little green plastic mat and using green coordinated tools. I look back down the street and see Mr Roberts racing behind me.

'Oh, Hannah dear,' she says, with a broad smile. Then she registers my tear-stained face. 'Are you OK? Is it your dad?'

I am shaking my head as Mr Roberts arrives, his eyes darting between us.

'Frank, there you are. Oh, you haven't done the shopping?' she says, looking at his empty hands.

'Yeah sorry, I forgot my wallet. I was just coming back for it.' He's not looking at me but his whole being is tuned into me, terrified that I'm going to tell her.

'Ah, what's he like,' she says fondly, shrugging at me.

'What an idiot,' I say pointedly.

She laughs. 'Well go on then,' she says to him, gesturing into the house. 'Go and get it.'

'What?' he asks.

'Your wallet?'

'Oh, yes of course.' He walks past me slowly, trying to listen to what we're saying as he gets further away.

'I just feel so sorry for Dad,' I say, loud enough for Mr Roberts to hear. 'He's had to deal with so much and now he's so very unwell.'

Mr Roberts can't walk any slower and finally disappears from view.

'You poor thing,' Mrs Roberts says to me. 'Can I do anything, dear?'

'No, I'm fine, I just need to – let my thoughts settle,' I say as I walk back to our house.

'Oh, Hannah,' Mrs Roberts calls after me, 'I almost forgot, there's a package for you – it was delivered while you were out and I signed for it. Frank,' she shouts back into the house. He rushes out.

'Yes?' he says, his face ashen.

'Can you bring that parcel in the hall out.'

'Parcel?' he stammers.

'Yes. Just inside the door.'

He turns back and returns with a large Amazon box.

'Thanks,' I say, taking the parcel. Our eyes meet momentarily. My back is turned to Mrs Roberts and I silently mouth '*Fuck you*' at him and step back over the wall.

'Thanks so much, Mrs Roberts, we must have coffee soon,' I call out, staring at Mr Roberts' pained face. 'It would be great to talk to you more about Mum.'

He drops his gaze.

'Any time, dear,' she says, walking back in.

I close our door and tear violently into the parcel. Inside a ludicrous amount of plastic air-pocketed sheeting is a rectangular box with a glossy picture of a sleeping orange cat. I open it and there's my fake Schro – a frighteningly lifelike cat, with a control panel in its tummy covered by a Velcroed flap of fake fur. I pull out the plastic fob protecting the batteries, flick the switch and place it on my lap, feeling like a fairground version of a Bond villain. Fake Schro breathes and shifts as I stroke him. It actually is calming! Eventually, I take it through to Dad and put it on his lap. He starts to stroke – and I see his body is relaxing with the muscle memory.

'Have you fed him?' Dad asks.

'Yeah, he's fed,' I reassure him, marvelling at how easily he is manipulated by his senses.

I will redouble my efforts.

CHAPTER TWENTY-THREE

It's date night. With Marcus. The thought makes my head flicker like it's being brushed by tiny wings. Of course, I should cancel. But Marcus and I grew up alongside each other, and it's very possible that he has memories of my parents that can help me. Yeah, yeah! The fabric of my stultifyingly dull, endlessly disappointing reality has ripped open and I've been gifted the rare chance to slip through the tear into my very own fairy tale – me, frumpy old Hannah could finally be the princess, desired by the prince. How can I not go?

I have a long, ludicrously over-bubbled bath. I feel weird dating Marcus, given his dad's perviness, but why should he get in the way of my chance of happiness? I rub thick, creamy body lotion over my every limb, undulation and crevice. I've bought new make-up, just Boots stuff, but it was still childishly exciting to pick out and now I cascade the little pots and wands all over my bed, like the teenager

I should have been twenty-odd years ago. I tried to diverge from Mum's colours, but I know they suit me now, with my blonde hair, and I try to ignore Mum's presence in the pale cream of the foundation, the burnished pink of the blusher and the deep red of the lipstick.

I want to have a night off from being Mum tonight, and thankfully I found an unopened packet of Mum's underwear and slide the red silky garments on – in case things take a fortuitous turn. As the material skims my goosebumps, I thrill at the thought of his hands on me. I haven't had sex for years – the last time was with some ponytailed hippy that I picked up in a Brighton club when I was out on a bender. It only underlined what I already knew – that loneliness is underrated. But this is different. I am finally the prize fruit, not the scrapings at the bottom of the barrel.

There are no unworn dresses in Mum's wardrobe and the long multicoloured hippy dress, the formal fitted Grace Kelly, the many full-skirted sundresses, are each dripping with memories. But eventually I find a long pink silky sheath at the back, which I don't remember. As it cascades down over my body, I grasp what a well-cut dress does on a slim form – it hangs off my limbs, slithering as I move, making me intensely aware of my body beneath. Finally, I dab on a free flowery perfume sample of a younger scent from a magazine and brush out my hair.

I look in on Mrs Roberts, who has come round to sit with Dad tonight. She seems the same as usual, so presumably Mr Roberts didn't feel he had to come clean.

'You have a lovely time with your mate,' she says, waving me off. I've told her I'm out with a girlfriend, since she and Mr Roberts are so awkward about me seeing their beloved son.

'Thank you, I shouldn't be too late.'

'Oh, I'm fine, no worries, you have fun.'

Would she be so kind if she knew the sort of fun I hope to get up to with her son?

I'm convinced this date is a cruel trick and Marcus won't come. But as the Woodman Pub door creaks back, I clock him lounging on the bar. He straightens as he sees me, his eyes widening as he takes me in.

'H-hi,' he says as I approach.

'Hi, yourself,' I say, intoxicated by the effect I'm having on him. This is like Jeremy, but a billion times more appropriate. He's seeing me, Hannah. He only knew Mum as a child. He tentatively holds out his closed fist for a bump, like we used to do as kids. I bump back, enjoying the newly charged experience of this old familiar greeting.

'You look so – different,' he says, 'your hair.'

'Blonde bombshell?'

'Yeah. And – that dress.' He swallows.

'The new me.'

'What'll you have?' he asks, looking impressively disorientated by me.

'Just fizzy water thanks.' I watch him ordering – his rangy denim-clad legs, his tight white T-shirt across his broad shoulders, the stubble already pushing through his recently shaved face. As we settle on our stools by the window, he doesn't take his eyes off me.

'So, little Hannah Davidson – all grown up!' he says.

'Hard to avoid doing it,' I say, aware of the hypocrisy

of this statement, given how my inner life has stalled even as my limbs have lengthened. But tonight, I am a proper grown-up, in a pub, on a date.

'It's so amazing seeing you again after all this time. I'm only at Mum and Dad's occasionally,' he says.

'Same, I'm just home now while things are so—'

'I know,' he says, putting his hand on mine. I want it to rest there for ever, but he pulls it away and sits back.

'It is really strange being back home,' I say, 'all the memories.'

He nods with kind understanding.

I've watched endless storylines on Netflix like this – childhood friends reunited in the town they both grew up in before one of them moved to the big city, the mismatched pair seeing each other anew, the awkwardness between them eventually leading to the moment when they admit their attraction and finally kiss. And now I'm living it.

'I think I'm grown up and then I come back home and feel like a kid again,' he says. 'And I sort of like it: Mum cooking shepherd's pie, doing a few pull-ups on my old bar . . . Oh God, I know it's different for you. Sorry—'

'No, I do have some of that contented recognition thing you're talking about. But,' I shrug, 'I have a load of crap too.'

'Who doesn't?' he says darkly. I let it pass – his version isn't even in the foothills of my Everest.

'Did you see that Reece published an autobiography?' I ask to change the subject.

'Yeah, caught him on *Good Morning Britain*,' he says, 'tragic hero confounding the odds! When all he does is dress up and prance about.'

I grin.

'I haven't seen him since the day before it happened,' he says nervously.

'When you were playing football with him—'

'No, the day before that. I'd pulled my hamstring, so I didn't play with him that night.'

'Oh. OK. Reece described that night in his book, and I just assumed that you were one of the friends he mentioned.'

He shakes his head. 'Not that night, no. And I haven't read it.'

'Oh it's all about having some last golden moment of innocence at a football match and then coming home. I was there for that bit and—' I frown.

'What?'

'Well what he described – was kind of what happened, but it wasn't like he made out – it wasn't just a regular easy evening. Dad and Reece were in such foul moods. I don't know why. I've gone over and over it all in my mind so many times—'

Marcus is looking away.

'I'm sorry, I'm going on, it's being at home at this time of year,' I laugh, desperate not to mess up this date.

'I don't mind.'

'No. Forget it. Now come on, tell me about this handyman business of yours?'

He relaxes as he launches into anecdotes about all the eccentric clients he's worked for and the useless poshies who can't even change a light bulb.

'Do you want a smoke?' he asks as our drinks are running low.

'I don't smoke, but I'll come outside if you want to.'

'I meant smoke smoke,' he says, conspiratorially.

'Sure, why not,' I say, trying to sound nonchalant, though drugs are not really one of my vices.

We move outside the pub to the street, going across the road to lean on the wall. He expertly rolls a joint, adding a big helping from an impressively large lump of black resin. He lights it, takes a long drag and passes it to me. It's really strong, but I'm so hyper already, it barely touches the sides. I lean back against the rough brickwork.

'You OK?' he asks, putting his hand on my shoulder and looking down at me.

'Yeah, lovely.' It's such a warm night and the lights strung in the trees of the pub make everything look magical. We puff away in companionable silence. Staring at him, I notice a puckering in the skin above his right eyebrow.

'What's that?' I say gently, reaching up to touch it. He catches my hand and smiles nervously.

'It's nothing – I got hit by some scaffolding at a job years ago.'

In Netflix romances there's always that moment when the star-crossed lovers' bodies are suddenly thrown together: they're pushed into one another by a jolting lift; he pulls her from the path of a speeding taxi; they fall onto each other tripping in the snow – and in that slow-motion moment, they look into each other's eyes – and then they kiss.

And now Marcus is brushing the hair from my eyes and I realise that we're in that moment right now. I'm the girl. And all those films were so spot on. When it finally happens, it's so easy and so right. I turn my head, stare at him, then close my eyes, and as my lips reach his, he – recoils and shoves me so violently that I'm slammed back onto the rough wall, grazing my shoulder and falling to the ground.

'Fuck,' he says as he rears away from me, wiping his mouth, looking at me with disgust.

I blink back at him. 'Sorry, I thought—'

'Fuck,' he shouts out into the darkness. I slam my head back against the wall then rock forwards onto my knees. I'm disorientated, shock intensified by the high that the clearly very strong drugs are inducing.

'God, Hannah. I was just being brotherly,' he says as he strides back to me and offers me his hand. I hit it away and stagger up on my own. I'm so familiar with self-disgust, but this is a new, elite level of self-loathing.

'I wasn't being serious,' I say, every bit of me closing down. I'm like a speeded-up film of water freezing, as my familiar impenetrable icy layer re-seizes and groans around me. 'It was a joke, lighten up.'

'Yeah, of course,' he says, letting me have my lie. 'You're like my little sister.'

'Of course,' I say, smiling madly. 'It was just a joke, Marcus.'

'A dumb joke,' he says forcefully.

We stare at each other.

'I've got to go,' he says abruptly.

'Yeah, me too.'

He strides off in the opposite direction to my house. I float home, disembodied by the cocktail of drugs and horror. When I reach our gate, I see that a couple of the quince have fallen and are starting to rot in the grass below. I slump down and bite a soft rotting specimen. It's disgusting, but I keep on chewing, revelling in the vile fermenting pulp.

CHAPTER TWENTY-FOUR

Through the long sleepless night, all I see is Marcus's face scrunching with disgust; all I feel is his violent shove; and all I taste is his beery, smoky breath being sucked out of my mouth with his inhale of revulsion. How gobsmackingly pitiful. To imagine that I'm one of the real people. I am a shadow person.

My phone bleeps. It's Anastasia WhatsApping me again with the contact details for Reece's doctor, which I instantly delete. I must fully re-embrace my Mum-self: she is all-powerful, admired and desired.

I stumble through the routine of the morning, my head thick with spliff, thinking of Loreta trying to reach her father via his senses. I'm playing more of Dad's music from the nineties – Nirvana, Green Day, Blur. Perhaps this music can reach down deeper into Dad's non-verbal depths. I put on Radiohead's 'Creep' and turn the volume right up, good for Dad's era but mainly as a soundtrack for my grotesquery. I feel so tantalisingly close, so sure that when I finally recreate the right version of Jen, when everything lines up, then, like images in two facing mirrors, we will ping back and forth, over and over and indivisible, and I will be entirely her for Dad. And unlock the truth.

The music swirls. Dad's swaying along with it, stroking Fake Schro. I've used sight, sound and touch – but I'm still not there. I think of Loreta's little Lithuanian cakes – the doughy aroma, the saliva-flooding sweetness. Taste and smell. The more overlooked senses. Worth a shot. I leave Fake Schro purring on his lap as I prepare a lunch of burgers and chips, one of Dad's favourite meals that Mum used to make for us. The house reeks of grease as the burgers sizzle on the grill. I dress as Mum yet again in a yellow full skirt and white shirt.

'All right, Philip?' I say as I enter the lounge with his tray – all hostess-with-the-mostess. He nods, taking a deep inhale of the fatty feast. I cut the burger into pieces and he tries a tiny mouthful but gives up and nibbles a chip. Hamburger was a ridiculous idea as he has no upper teeth and can't chew easily. I take a big bite of mine, but I have to force myself to swallow the greasy flesh. Why can't I make any of my memory recreations feel as good as the original experiences? Has memory sharpened the experience beyond the reality? Or can I never really go back? Because I can't recreate anything exactly and because I am fundamentally changed by living so can never re-experience anything as the person I was back then. The nineties music mix has moved on to Green Day's 'Basket Case'.

I dunk a long chip into the tomato sauce and am about to bite into its oily crispiness when a large dollop of ketchup plops onto my white shirt.

'I'm not ready,' says Dad in a whisper.

'No rush, take your time.'

God, I've ruined this shirt with this doomed experiment.

'Why are you back?' he whispers.

'To look after you,' I say, swiping at the mark.

He moans.

I look up to see him staring at me, sweat glistening on his forehead, breathing fast. My eyes flick to where he's focused.

The red sauce is splodged on my white shirt, over my heart. Like blood. Like blood spurting from a stab wound. With my free hand I feel for my phone, swipe the music off and click the voice recorder on. Keeping my eyes trained on Dad, I carefully lower my right hand down to grasp the bottle of sauce, belch a handful into my left palm and splodge it onto my chest, and the pungent red goop oozes through my fingers.

Dad shakes his head, sweat beading on his upper lip.

'Jen,' he whispers with awe, his eyes hungrily scanning my face, my hair, my body. I tentatively extend my dripping red hand. Expecting it to be grasped violently, I plant my feet ready to pull back. But he shudders and shrinks away – from what perhaps he thinks is a ghostly hand trying to pull him from this world? I extend my red forefinger at him, and a bead of red drips onto the white sheet.

Dad's eyes widen.

'Time for the truth,' I say darkly. All very cheap–TV–Christmas–Carol – but Dad nods solemnly as his shoulders slump.

'Take me, then,' he says with resignation.

'Free yourself by admitting your guilt,' I intone theatrically, wishing I had Reece's improv skills.

'But just take me – and leave him,' he pleads.

I'm wrong-footed in my panto script.

'Who?'

'It wasn't his fault. Just take me,' he pleads.

I'm losing my thread. 'What wasn't whose fault?' I say, stepping in and lowering my arm.

'He didn't mean to do it.'

I'm not quite sure how to proceed.

'Reece!' he wails, then his head flips back and he stares up at the ceiling, his body rigid. He's not breathing.

'Dad? Are you OK?'

Nothing. I've killed him. I reach for my phone and dial 999.

'Which service do you require?' asks the operator's voice.

'I—'

Then he sucks in a huge breath and snaps his head back and . . . smiles.

'Hannah,' he says as colour floods back into his face.

'Oh, sorry, false alarm,' I say, hanging up.

'We have to get a badminton racquet for him,' Dad says, calm and upbeat.

'Who?' I beg, willing him to vault back into the track he was on before.

'Reece. He needs a new badminton racquet,' he says, smiling at my confusion. Dad's firmly down his new track and I'm left flailing in the other.

I replay the sound file: 'It wasn't his fault.' And then the wail of 'Reece'. Then on to badminton racquets. Was the desperate 'Reece' linked to the first track of thought about something not being someone's fault – or to the second track, the innocent need for a new badminton racquet?

I ring Reece, who picks straight up.

'Hannah? Are you OK?'

'Yes, I'm fine. But listen. Dad's really opening up. He just said about something not being your fault, or it could have been about badminton racquets?'

He's silent.

'Reece? Did you hear what I said?'

'Have you made that appointment with the doctor yet?' Reece says stiffly.

'No, I'm fine, I told you. What do you think Dad meant?'

The line goes dead. I ring him straight back but my call is disconnected after one ring. Each time I try, it's actively disconnected.

I try the 'Here then There' app, and see his flashing dot in Soho. Google Earth shows me that the address is an office block on Soho Square. I remember the grey curling font on his agent's website and look it up. Yes, the office of the Anastasia Rudd Agency is in Soho Square.

It's a tall, narrow white building, near the top corner of the square. Reece's dot is still flashing here when a taxi drops me off twenty minutes later, in the pouring rain. As I go to press the top buzzer, a young sharp-suited man is leaving, so I slip in behind him. I climb up the narrow stairs, passing a voice agency, a confectionery business, and various company names and logos. There's only one way in and out of these old walk-ups – so he'd have to pass me to escape. At the top floor, breathing heavily, I see a white painted door with the same stupid grey curling font from the website: *Anastasia Rudd Agency*. It creaks open to a small hallway with a receptionist, very tastefully decorated in pastel blues and greys, and surrounded by several small glass-partitioned offices. A young man is typing in one, and down a little corridor is a closed office door. Who could possibly be in there?

'Hello, can I help you?' says a pretty girl with ironed-blonde hair like her boss, sitting at a desk facing me.

'Could you tell Anastasia that Ryan's sister would like to have a word – with Ryan,' I say tensely.

She speaks into her headset. 'There's a lady here saying she's Ryan's sister?' She swallows and looks chastened.

'I'm afraid neither Anastasia nor Ryan are here at the moment, would you like to leave a message?' she says, attempting to sound authoritative.

'No worries, I'll just wait. And I didn't ask if Ryan was here,' I say pointedly, plopping down on one of the three padded chairs near the door. The girl's eyes flick to the closed door. We both know they're both in there.

'I've got all the time in the world,' I say loudly. The closed door opens and Anastasia strides out. At the reading she was in a muted grey dress, but now her tall, slim physique is draped in a beautifully cut bright fuchsia dress.

'For heaven's sake, Suzie, I'll deal with this. Ms Davidson, my agency is not an answering service for your brother.'

'But he won't answer my calls.'

'Which would suggest that he doesn't want to speak to you.'

'Is he here?'

'No.'

I don't want to give away my app tracking, so can't call

her on this.

'Are you sure? I should warn you that this conversation is being recorded,' I say, raising my phone to show the red 'on' of the voice recorder app. She raises her eyebrow, lifting up her own phone and starting to record herself.

'That's a bit *Reservoir Dogs*,' I say.

She gives me a withering look. 'I will be advising Mr Patterson, when I next see him, to instruct his lawyers that you are harassing him.'

'Please do – the press will be breaking down my door.'

'I think you'll find that my relationship with the press far exceeds your influence, Ms Davidson.'

'Twitter's harder to put pressure on,' I say, stepping towards her.

'Please keep back,' says Anastasia, sounding weirdly nervous, as if I am threatening her while speaking directly into her recorder. There is a loud smash as Anastasia's office door is thrown open and Reece strides out.

'I told you I—' he shouts as he steps out, but then stops dead when he sees me. 'What the fuck have you done to your hair? And are you wearing Mum's clothes?' In my rush to catch Reece, I have forgotten to get changed out of my Mum look.

'Suzie, Max, get out,' snaps Anastasia.

'But—' says the receptionist.

'Now,' she barks. 'And remember your disclosure agreements.' The receptionist and the young man behind the glass partition scurry away.

Hot after the stair climb, I unbutton my jacket.

'Oh my God, are you OK?' Reece says, stepping towards me and reaching for me. I look down, realising my top is still drenched in tomato sauce. Reece stops abruptly and smells his fingers. 'Ketchup? What the fuck! I can't deal with your craziness any more, Hannah.'

Anastasia takes a deep breath and flexes her beautifully manicured hand to show me the door. I slap away her hand and Reece pushes me violently. I start to fall back, but no way am I being knocked to the ground again this week. I lurch forward, reaching out to steady myself, and there is a ripping sound as Anastasia's fuchsia dress tears with my grasp, the shoulder seams splaying open to expose her bony shoulder and white bra strap, looking like red meat peeled back from the bone.

'Are you OK, Stasia?' asks Reece.

What about me?

'I'm fine,' she says, sounding almost bored. She lifts the recorder, then tugs at the frayed stitching of her dress, so it audibly rips further: 'Oh my God, you've ripped my dress, Ms Davidson.'

'What is the matter with you?' Reece growls at me, poking me violently in the chest. I kick out at his shin as hard as I can and he hops backwards with a yelp. Anastasia clicks her recorder off.

'Stop it you two,' she says firmly as she steps between us like a mother separating children, gently backing Reece up, her face close to his.

'Breathe,' she whispers to him. 'Go back into my office.'

'But—' he murmurs.

'It's OK, I'll deal with her,' she says as she pushes him gently and he turns away.

'Reece,' I call, 'Dad said that something wasn't your fault. What did he mean?' He turns slowly, his eyes almost black.

'Dad's senile – he's just rambling. Have you phoned my therapist yet?'

I make a face.

He glowers back.

'I'm not drinking, but I don't need a therapist, OK?'

'I've been really understanding, I've offered you help – but this whole Mum dress-up thing is too much. It is clearly unsafe to have you looking after Dad. Since you won't accept help, I take it back about you staying at his. I'll arrange carers.'

'But Reece, I—'

'I'm not Reece any more,' he spits, then strides to the back office and slams the door.

Anastasia lifts the ripped flap of fuchsia material and tucks it into her bra strap.

'I will be advising my client to take out a restraining order. Please leave.'

I turn and stumble down the narrow steps, my hand rubbing the sore point on my chest where Reece poked at me. In all our years of play-fighting, we both had that carefully calibrated ability to wound without lasting effect. He hit out at me just now to cause maximum pain. He's right, that wasn't my brother Reece.

The rain's stopped and everything's glistening in the bright sunlight. I cross the street to the gardens at the centre of the square, collapse on a wet bench on the other side of the railings from the office and call Chris.

'It's me,' I say.

'You OK?'

'The more I find out, the less I . . . I hardly know who

I am – or who anyone else is any more.'

'Reece?'

'How has he changed so much?'

'What happened?'

'Dad's attention was jumping about like usual, but he seemed to make an odd connection between Reece and Mum, so I wanted to find out if Reece knew what he meant, but he looked at me like I was a stranger – and pushed me really hard.'

'Fucker,' he says aggressively.

'I feel like I'm nearly on to something, but I can't quite grasp it.'

'You need to breathe and do something to calm down. Don't try to make sense of what you're thinking. Your brain will sort it without you trying. When I used to be stuck in an investigation, I used to go swimming.'

'Me too! Back in Brighton.'

'Well that's tricky now, but do something oblique, non-thinking. Your thoughts will fall into place. OK? Hannah?'

'Yes, I'm nodding. You're right. Thanks.'

'Talk soon?'

'Yes.'

I think of Reece waltzing back to his gorgeous white palace, sitting in his comfy white chair and staring up at his joyous red Rothko print. Perhaps I can find peace in that image that he loves so much too. I google Rothko's paintings, clicking the image tab and scrolling through the endless repetitive blocks of colour in search of his. I can't find Reece's particular red rectangles and almost give up, but suddenly there it is – on a website called 'Last Ever

Paintings'. My chest clenches.

I click on the link. Yes, it's the painting – the exact same vibrant red rectangles – so bright and life affirming. How can this be Rothko's last painting when he painted so many other far more depressing canvases? I read the blurb: *Untitled 1970: the bright red colours noticeably contrast with the bleaker browns, blacks and rusts of Rothko's preceding works. But while vibrant and joyous looking, this final painting by Rothko is anything but. On 25 February 1970, Rothko's assistant found the artist lying dead on the kitchen floor, covered in blood, this painting a few feet away. He had overdosed on barbiturates and cut an artery in his right arm with a razor blade. There was no suicide note, but perhaps this intense canvas, painted in the pigments of smeared blood, expressed his final emotions.*

Why on earth has Reece chosen this painting, with its suicidal connotations, to stare at every day? Something about Mum or about himself? He has a perfect dream life, why would he be suicidal?

I glance up and flinch away as I see Reece exiting the door to Anastasia's office. I'm across the road but hidden by the railings and some bushes, so he doesn't see me. He pulls up the collar of his jacket and tilts his cap down over his face, glances furtively about and then makes his way towards Tottenham Court Road, with his familiar lollop.

What is he hiding?

CHAPTER TWENTY-FIVE

Back home, I upend the bin in Mum's bedroom and scrabble through the detritus to find the scrunched-up tissue with Reece's hair from the trailer. I have to know whether Reece and I are full brother and sister. I send off another piece of Dad's fine grey hair, along with an undyed strand of mine from a brush and Reece's dark, bouncy strand. I'm sure I've seen mannerisms and nuances of Dad in Reece and me over the years – but perhaps that was only ever my mind finding patterns to fulfil the presumed result.

My stomach's tight, my skin's crawling, but Chris was right: my mind's whirring away. Reece took power of attorney because I was getting too close. Clearly he knows a lot more about Mum's death than he's told me. That's why he never comes back here to the scene of the crime, why he pushed for the simple idea of Dad's guilt without explanation – and why he's going to turf me out of here and cut me off from Dad. I have to talk to someone who really knows Reece for another angle on him.

I call Mrs Roberts and she picks up straight away.

'Hannah?'

'I-I—'

'I'm coming round right now, stay put.'

I open the front door and she hugs me to her. 'There, there, come on now, let's sit down.'

We move to the lounge and face each other on the settee.

'Tell me,' she says gently.

'OK. So, I know this is out there, but do you think – that Reece might know more about Mum's death than he's let on?'

She cocks her head and looks puzzled.

'Why would you think that?'

'I . . .' Saying the words out loud and seeing her bewilderment, I'm embarrassed and relieved at the same time. 'It's just that Reece has shown no interest whatsoever in Dad for years, literally nothing since he left for Cambridge, but when I start looking into what happened to Mum, suddenly Reece's taken over power of attorney, and cut me out of everything and he's so distant – aggressive even. And Dad said something odd about Reece.'

'What?'

'He said that some "he" wasn't to blame – and I'm sure he meant Reece. So, something wasn't Reece's fault – but what?'

'Your dad gets very confused and jumps about. He doesn't mean anything – but you're trying to find order. Like those ink blot picture tests – where everyone sees something different – I always see bats!'

'Have you never thought that Reece, might – that there's

something dark about him?'

She breaks eye contact.

'What?' I ask sharply.

'Nothing,' she says, picking at the weave of her cardigan.

'What's nothing?'

'I . . .' She stands abruptly and walks over to the French doors. When she doesn't turn back, I follow and stand beside her. She's staring out at the dark trees silhouetted against the sky.

'I haven't known whether to talk to you about all this,' she says slowly. 'But now, I guess I have to.'

I stay silent.

'When you were born, Philip and I were really careful from the get-go. I looked after you from day one. You got all the contact and love a child needs at that age. At any age. But before, with Reece, we didn't realise—'

'What?'

She glances at me then continues.

'I'd seen Jen with him in the garden in the month after he was born and assumed she was coping. But Reece looked so sickly and he cried all the time. I kept popping round, but she said she was fine. Your dad was really worried. He was doing all the baby care when he was there, mornings and evenings, but he'd had to go back to work, so she was alone at home with Reece in the day. A couple of months in, Philip got a call at work from Jen, heard her cry out, then the line went dead and when he rang back, he couldn't get an answer. He was terrified, tried to reach me, but I was out for the day so he rushed back.'

She swallows but I nod at her to continue.

'He found Jen sitting in the lounge – drenched in blood.

She was rocking back and forth, with a kitchen knife on the floor in front of her, next to Reece who was also covered in blood, screaming away.'

I clutch at my throat but wave Mrs Roberts to continue.

'Philip called an ambulance, bound Jen's wrist and searched wildly for Reece's wounds but found nothing. She was lucky, her wrist wound wasn't too deep. The hospital diagnosed severe postnatal depression, she was heavily medicated and given a therapist and I agreed to take over looking after Reece. Reece had no actual injuries at all, but he was malnourished and listless. Jen admitted to the therapist that she'd been shutting Reece away upstairs every day because she was afraid of what she might do to him, leaving him unfed and soiled. And then that day, she said she'd reached the point where she thought the world would be better off without her.' Mrs Roberts breathes and gathers herself. 'But with help, she got better gradually. Reece put on weight and I did my best to show him love, but – well, those first months of severe neglect at a really vital time, when kids have to bond, and he'd seen his mum all covered in blood.' She shudders. 'I told myself that he was so young it wouldn't have any lasting effect. And in so many ways, he grew up into a lovely child, and a fine young man. But—'

'But what?'

'I don't want to make something out of nothing – and well, I suppose it's why he's become such a good actor – but Reece is complicated, manipulative, impulsive.'

I make a face.

'No, he is, he clashed a lot with your dad as a teenager, more than the usual stuff, got into lots of scrapes before he learnt to control – whatever it was – to be what people wanted. Your mother always defended him, said he was artistic. They were so close. And then when he lost her – his protector, his soulmate – it destroyed him.' She turns to face me. 'So I guess I'm saying, you have to forgive him for all the walls he puts up. Of course he doesn't want you looking into her murder, it's too painful for him. But that's all this is, nothing more sinister.'

I feel something beyond words, bubbling up inside me.

'But wouldn't Reece being so adamant that Dad did it, be a great cover if – he was involved?' I say slowly. The thought's so slippery, I can't quite catch it. Dad once said to me: 'We cannot think outside the dimensions that our minds allow, but the world may have more dimensions than we can conceive of'.

'No, God, that's not what I'm implying,' says Mrs Roberts. 'Of course he had nothing to do with your mum's death. I'm saying it traumatised him worse than anyone else because of his difficult start.'

'But after Mum's death, Reece was so strange, wound so tight. Have you never . . . ?'

'You're scaring me,' she says, her voice trembling.

'But it's possible?'

'I don't . . .' She swallows. 'On the evening of your mum's funeral, we were in the garden out there,' she says, motioning, 'and Reece had had way too much to drink. He was bristling with anger. I went to put my arm round his shoulders, and he shrugged me off violently and said, "Do you ever think that maybe – she deserved it." Said it so coldly. It really shocked me. Then he left for Cambridge the next day. But that doesn't mean that he was involved.'

She's willing me to disagree.

'It makes sense of everything,' I say slowly, 'if he did it.'

She shakes her head.

'And if it's true, he's escaped scot-free,' I say.

'But—' she says, shoving her hands through her hair, the right one catching on a tangle, which she tugs at. 'If, and it's so unlikely, but if he was involved, it would have been because of the stress of those terrible first few months, intensified by teenage hormones, leading to momentary madness.' She gives a sharp intake of breath. 'He's like my own son,' she continues desperately. 'He's gone on to build a good life. Why would you want to destroy that?'

'Me?' I say incredulously.

'If you persevere with digging up the past, if you confront him, if there's even the slightest possibility that it's true – you'll destroy his life.' She clasps my hands. 'You were the lucky one growing up in your family, you have to let this go.'

I stare at her in disbelief. Me, the lucky one?

'It's not true. But do you really want to take that risk?' she says as she walks back to the couch and falls back into it. I follow her, worried by how white she's turned.

'I'm sorry,' I say gently, kneeling down in front of her. 'Are you OK?'

She coughs, trying to clear her throat. 'This is ridiculous. We're letting our thoughts run away with us,' she says, breathing heavily.

'You're right,' I say, to quell her panic. 'I'm sorry, I've been on my own too much. You should go and have a lie down, Mrs Roberts – Libbie.'

She smiles and pats my hand.

'Maybe I will. Will you be all right?' I nod and she struggles to her feet, kisses me on my forehead then shuffles out, looking ten years older than when she arrived.

Me the lucky one? Is everything back to front?

I was often frustrated with homework as a child, so incensed that I hadn't been given enough information to deduce the density of some stupid gas that I would stab at my exercise book with my sharpened 2HB pencil, drilling craters till I snapped off the point. Dad would shake his head as he handed me a crisp white sheet of paper.

'Come on, Hannah, forget what you think you know, start in a different place. What did Einstein say?'

And I would roll my eyes as I parroted his advice:

'The definition of insanity is doing the same thing over and over again, but expecting different results.'

Maybe I need to start in a different place. I am so very tired of driving the dodgem car of my mind round and round, of endlessly hitting the rubberised edge of the fairground rink, of swinging the wheel back to reverse, and depressing the pedal to the grimy floor yet again. I knew my dodgem car wouldn't work off the rink, disconnected from the sparking electricity of the metal grill above, but it never occurred to me to leave the car.

Now I lift the frayed loop of the safety belt up over my head, uncurl my hunched frame from the low black seat, and step out of the car.

Reece is not on my side.

I walk across the scuffed rink floor, step over the lip of the track, and walk across the matted, sun-dried grass between the rides.

Reece knows more about Mum's death than he's telling me.

I look back at the flashing dodgem lights one last time, then push through the turnstile and leave the fairground.

Reece killed Mum.

I've been so misdirected by Reece's anger about Dad's guilt. So limited by my certainty that Reece loved Mum. So blinded by my belief that my brother is a better person than me.

After Reece's book reading I chastised myself for my knee-jerk victim mentality of imagining that Reece was talking directly to me, taunting me by saying he wasn't making the mistake of living his life looking back.

But what if he had written all that especially for me?

Reece called his autobiography *Solving Me*. I groaned at his self-importance, but what if that title wasn't just theatrical self-aggrandising. What if it's a direct challenge. To me.

What if Reece has been hiding in plain sight all along. And he thinks he's so clever, and I'm so thick, that I'll never see the truth.

That he killed Mum.

CHAPTER TWENTY-SIX

When we were children, I rarely beat Reece in our games in the woods. He excelled in the sheer physical feats: the racing; the exhausting hopping on one foot till numbed collapse; and the always popular rib-poking tag game of hide-and-seek, with Reece screaming, 'I'm gonna stab right through to the other side!'

I excelled at the mental endurance games: the wide-eyed no-blink competitions; the agonising forensic hair-pulling; and I could almost always beat him in the 'Tickling Trials'.

Success in a Tickling Trial is all about preparation.

If you get tickled unawares, forget it, you're doomed.

Knowing it's coming makes it way worse. You're anticipating the upcoming agony, tensing your muscles and heightening your sensitivity, confirming the inevitability of failure. And at the first flick of a finger, BANG, the excruciating, all-enveloping intensity floods you, zero to unbearable, and you jackknife away screaming.

But you can win. *If* you know it's coming, and *if* you prepare. I'd be lying flat out and barefoot on the rough ground of a secluded area of the woods and Reece would be taking his time circling me.

'God, how do you walk around on those mutant trotters, *oink, oink,*' he would say, inspecting my feet.

'Better than your tree-swingers, *ooh, ooh, ooh,*' I would retort.

He would wriggle his equally long fingers over my face to heighten my anticipation. But I would breathe out, flop my feet and disconnect all my muscles. Not some simple loosey-gooseyness. I would gather myself and lift up out of my body entirely, sitting up above my head in the trees.

'Ready?' Reece would say with a smirk.

'Bring it on,' I would smirk back. And whoosh, Reece would swoop in and scrabble his fingers onto my bare soles, like a dog digging furiously for a bone. My old body would register his fingers' lacerations, but I would remind myself that those unbearable sensations were only in my husk: 'I'm up here,' I'd tell myself, 'you hooo. She's not me.'

'How?' he'd pout, tickling more furiously. I would give a bored shrug. Finally, he would give up in a huff and I could slide back into my husk once more, triumphant.

To beat Reece now, I have to think ahead and take myself out of my body entirely, so I can manipulate him and be untouched. I've been dressing up to try to take Dad back to that day – when all this time, I should have been trying to take Reece back there. And I have to do it now, before he throws me out of here. I saw the power of my Mum-ensemble on him at his agent's. Now I need to go all the way.

I need to be Mum for Reece.

Another thick envelope is lying on the mat the next morning. The second DNA results: *Matching Maternal Sibling DNA, Different Paternal Sibling DNA with 0% Match to Father's DNA*. Reece and I had different fathers, and neither of them were 'Dad'. Have I always known that we were not fully brother and sister? Neither by nature nor by nurture. We have different DNA swirling through our every cell and though we lived in the same house, we experienced different childhoods. Who is he, and what was he capable of?

'Reece might be coming over today,' I tell Dad as I serve his Rice Krispies.

He nods. I don't know if he understands.

'The prodigal son finally coming home.'

I check my tracking app to see where Reece is presently and he's at his Chelsea palace. I check Google alerts for news of him – but he's not booked for any public events. It's now or never. There is no ground beneath my feet any more. I'm mid-fall.

I spend the morning shopping and then luxuriate in Mum's bath oils. At lunchtime I WhatsApp Reece to entice him round. I could tell him that Dad's dead, but he would just be relieved it's all over. Any request for help would be rebuffed. I finally settle on my message.

Dad has admitted your involvement in Mum's death. If you want to discuss, I'll be home by 5.30. I'm going to the police tomorrow whatever. Hannah.

I don't want him to come any earlier. Five-thirty was the time of day I came home and found Mum, Dad and Reece all standing looking daggers at each other and then Mum went out, swiftly followed by Reece. That was when everything started to feel so off and when Reece started lying in his autobiography. I watch the little ticks appear at the bottom of the message:

Tick, the message is sent.

Second tick, the message is delivered.

The ticks go blue, the message is read.

But no reply.

I have a few more hours to prepare. Assuming he comes.

I need to employ all five senses for full effect.

Sight – check. The house is eerily identical to that afternoon. I've cleared away anything that wasn't around then. All my adult stuff: clothes, books, bags, and Dad's new paraphernalia: his stick, the pill pots, the pill divider, the bedpan, the nappies, everything except for the bed, which I push as far into the corner as I can. I cover most of the bed with a familiar rug. Dad looks on, nonplussed. For the first time ever I'm glad Dad's maintained this place like a mausoleum, ready for today.

Sound – check. The house has the exact heavy silence and occasional traffic sounds from childhood. I put Mum's 'Wagner Hits' and Madonna CDs by the music centre for when Reece gets here, but for now play Dad's music from that era – Nirvana, Green Day, Blur.

Touch – check. Every surface is a braille map of our youth – the overstuffed settee with its shiny worn patches, the wooden floorboards, the heavy velvet of the curtains. I can't put a hand down without a memory shimmying up my sleeve. Dad is stroking Fake Schro on his soft Spurs blanket. And because the chillier weather today is identical to that Friday in October, even the hairs on my arm feel like they're flexing to the same air.

Smell – check. I'll put on her perfume later. I've piled quince in a bowl in the lounge for their exotic fragrance. I've grilled some mackerel, cleaned the grill to erase the stink and encased the fish in Tupperware ready for later. I couldn't find Mum's favourite Embassy cigarettes, but I take an ashtray outside and smoke several Benson & Hedges, carefully collecting the ash, and then put the full ashtray in a Tupperware box. I want to wash my hands and brush my teeth, but I let the familiar woody aroma linger on me.

Taste – check. I've set out plates of familiar biscuits: Bournville, Custard Creams, Jaffa Cakes. Not that I think any of us will be eating. But taste is evoked by thought and memory. Saliva gathers in my mouth as I pull the foil wrappers off some Tunnock's Teacakes. And I have honey and pancakes ready for when Reece arrives.

I keep having to go to the loo, I'm so nervous. One of Mum's church signs on the ceiling reads: 'DON'T GIVE UP. MOSES WAS A BASKET CASE ONCE.' Oh, I'm not giving up. I'm all in. Bring it on.

Once the scene is set, I carefully bring Mum to life: I paint my toenails bright red and put on her silver toe ring; I do her full make-up, the smooth pale base, the thick black eyeliner, layers of mascara, swipes of rouge and her trademark red lipstick; I backcomb my hair massively, as Mum's was so wild and messy that day. The Cranberries' 'Zombie' plays loudly on my phone and I sing along, feeling

Mum belting it out with me as she coalesces in the mirror.

The actual clothes Mum was wearing when she died were kept for forensic tests, still bagged and tagged in some police storage unit no doubt, but I find the best approximation of what she had on that final morning – a cream blouse with a delicate filigree neckline and a pale green skirt. This outfit is almost identical to the one she had on at breakfast and when her body was found. I also prepare the clothes she wore mid-afternoon and hide them in the hall cupboard.

I've even bought a new small bottle of Chanel, incredibly expensive even in the tiniest volume, but it's worth it as the powdery floral scent is so much stronger and more complex than her old supply – and as I put it on, it's as if I've released her genie from the bottle.

At three-thirty I still have two hours left. I check Reece's location on the app. But he's already left his flat. I watch his dot intently. Going for a coffee? But he's moving in the direction of the station. If he's coming to us, he could be here in under an hour. I speed up my preparations, dropping one of Mum's many tasselled bags on the floor of the lounge and lining up some bottles along the side of the settee, constantly checking on Reece's position. He's out of range for half an hour – underground perhaps? Then he's suddenly flashing again – at Highgate station. It's only four-thirty – Reece is coming when he thinks I'm out. He's only a few roads away, moving towards us. I've got ten minutes tops, if he's walking.

'OK, Dad, it's showtime. Shall we get you sitting to receive our guest?'

'Hmmm?'

Dad is disconnected but he doesn't resist, and soon he's in his place on the settee. I pull back the heavy curtains, so that bright sunlight bathes the room.

Having a final nervous pee in the downstairs loo, I look to the top of the toilet door as I leave, and read: 'WHAT IS MISSING FROM CH–CH: U R.' Well, not tonight Mum. You're right here, ready to party.

I put two shop-bought pancakes in the toaster and as soon as they pop up, I carry them through to the lounge with a squeezy bottle of acacia honey. I remove Dad's Nirvana CD and put in Mum's Wagner as I see Reece's dot flashing at the front of the house.

He's here.

I fast-forward the music to twenty minutes in so that the track will reach Mum's favourite bit, just as Reece enters: that bit of the track that Mum played over and over again that summer she died, the end of 'Love Duet' from *Tristan & Isolde Act II*, 'O sink hernieder, Nacht der Liebe'.

I stand next to the CD player, by the lounge door. The music swirls and rolls, the voices overlapping as they circle and blend, and wave upon wave of music surges orgasmically towards climax.

I hear Reece's key in the lock. He's not using the bell? I press record on my phone and place it in my pocket. The front door creaks open. Steps shuffle forward. I stare at the scratched bulbous doorknob, and watch the blackened metal turn slowly. Reece is hidden by the door as it opens but I watch him through the crack, and then peek round as he steps into the room. He's wearing tight black jogging gear and a black cap, and carries a black holdall. He's looking straight at Dad and doesn't register me behind him.

'Hi Dad,' he says, raising his voice above the music.

'Reece?' says Dad, raising his hand to his eyes as if to shade them.

'So, I hear you've been chatting with Hannah.'

Dad frowns. Reece leans in.

'Did you hear me?' he asks coldly. He straightens up. 'Why are you playing this stupid music? I can't hear myself think,' he says as he turns towards the CD player behind him.

'Hi, Reece,' I say in Mum's breathy tone.

'What the fuck,' he says.

'You're early, darhling?' I say, imitating Mum.

He backs up as I stretch out my arms above my head, like Mum always did at this particular moment in this ludicrously sexual music. I flick my hair, bending and undulating my body like Mum, a massive grin on my face. Reece tries to get to the stereo but I dance in front of him and turn the volume up. The music surges to its final crashing chords.

I turn back to Reece in the silence.

'Cat got your tongue?' I ask. 'Not Schro sadly, he was put down this week – the only decent member of this family gone now. Though you probably know that from your secret visits here.'

'What are you talking about? I haven't been back here since Cambridge, I told you. Hannah—'

'I'm not Hannah, don't you see it?'

He frowns. 'Look, you're totally spiralling, let me get you some water,' he says, making for the kitchen.

'No, son!' I shout and he stops dead.

'You're sick.'

275

'Sit down, Reecey,' I say, using Mum's pet name for him. He falls back on the settee, the other end to Dad.

'The temperature had dropped a little that last morning that Mum was alive,' I say, like I'm reading on *Jackanory*. 'The day before you were meant to leave for Cambridge. I had school and you three were meant to be off on a special shopping trip for last-minute uni supplies. But at breakfast time, Mum said she hadn't slept well, so she wasn't going to come shopping as planned. Dad wanted to cheer her up so before we all left that morning, he made her favourite breakfast of pancakes and honey.' I flip the lid on the squeezy honey and pour it onto the warmed pancakes on the coffee table. 'Mmm, that lovely, sweet smell. And Mum was playing Wagner, yet again – standing at the window and dancing. Everything was normal, the room bright, the air sweet with honey – the very last moment of normal for our—'

'Why am I here?' interrupts Reece suddenly, but I ignore him.

'So, after our honeyed breakfast, you two went off to town to buy things and have lunch together, while little Pollyanna Hannah trotted off to big school.'

Reece is staring at the floor.

'Now on to the afternoon,' I say brightly. I pull the lid off the Tupperware box of grilled mackerel and the stink floods the room.

'Ugh, what's that?' says Reece and Dad wrinkles his nose.

'Yes, that's the face I made as I came in that afternoon – back early cos choir was cancelled. Mum had cooked mackerel for lunch and left her greasy plate on the kitchen counter. We didn't tidy it up till the day after her body was found and now I loathe this smell – like it's the stink of Mum decomposing.'

'Jesus,' mumbles Reece.

'Oh, mustn't forget the curtains,' I say, pulling the curtains almost closed, and the room becomes gloomy – just like it was that afternoon. I turn on the low art deco lamp next to Dad and it sheds the fan of yellowy-green diffuse light that I remember.

'So, Pollyanna Hannah got back from her fifth day in Year 10, all jolly cos she was in the top set for maths, and she walked in on you three here in the semi-darkness, with the little lamp on and nobody wanted to hear her maths news, did they? Oh, I forgot the soundtrack.' I swap the CDs and start playing Madonna's breathy 'Justify My Love'. The long chords and tinny drums roll out. 'Remember? You were both standing just in front of where you're sitting now, looking thunderous, that oily rich smell of grilled mackerel swirling round the dark room – oh and bottles strewn everywhere,' I say, knocking over the row of bottles I've set up along the settee. 'And a kicked-over ashtray,' I add, opening the second Tupperware of cigarette ash and throwing it down. 'And Mum? She – I – was standing here, having changed into my white Chinese robe for some reason.'

'Red,' blurts Reece.

'Ding, ding, ding, top marks, son.'

'I'm not your fucking son.'

I dart into the hall, drag open the cupboard door and pull on Mum's long red Chinese gown, the wide-sleeved silky material making me shiver. I stride back in and they both stare at me in horror.

Dad's hands have balled into fists.

'Stop it,' says Reece, 'you're being cruel.'

'Me cruel?' I blurt. 'You're here an hour early, dressed like a serial killer.'

'I – God no, I just didn't want to be recognised and I wanted to talk to Dad without you.'

'Really,' I say sarcastically.

'Yes, really. What are you—'

'Okey-dokey, on we go. Reece, you turned off the CD when you saw Hannah enter. Remember.' I flick the volume of Madonna's panting up for a second and then snap it off. 'And you three all stood there, no one speaking. Then Mum left the room.

'"All right darhling," she said to Pollyanna Hannah as she walked past her and stroked her hair. That was the last time Mum ever touched me. And then she looked back at you two and said "It was nothing," picked up her bag and walked out the room and out of the house. So here I go.'

'It was nothing,' I say as I pick up the tasselled bag from the floor. 'What was nothing?' I ask, searching their faces. They stare back. I walk out, willing one of them to react. But there's only silence.

It was all pointless – I'll never know.

CHAPTER TWENTY-SEVEN

'You fucking bitch. You'd be better off dead,' Dad shouts on the other side of the door.

'Shh, Dad,' Reece says desperately.

I walk back in and Reece looks at me with wild eyes.

'You fucking bitch,' mumbles Dad and Reece instantly looks up and to the left. One of Dad's many fascinations was 'neuro-linguistic programming', or NLP – 'When people look up and left, they are remembering an actual image or experience,' he told me.

'You fucking bitch,' Dad repeats and Reece drops to his knees in front of Dad. I clasp my body to hold myself together.

'I'll never tell,' whispers Dad, looking down at Reece, patting his head. 'Never.'

'What happened?' I ask.

Dad stares back blankly.

'What happened? Reece. Did you – kill her?'

His shoulders start to judder and I think he's crying. But then he stands and a horrible sarcastic laugh rumbles up out of him.

'Get out,' he says, pushing me out the door.

'No,' I protest, shoving back at him.

'I mean get out of the lounge,' he says, looking back at Dad. 'Let him be. I'll tell you, just get out,' he growls, pushing me into the hall. I stumble out with him, banging my arm on the sharp edge of the door, but impervious to the pain. What has Reece done? What is he going to do?

'You'll never stop till I tell you, will you,' he says dully.

I shake my head.

He slumps back on the wall and I crumple onto the stairs.

'What a fucking sliding-doors mistake that was,' he mumbles.

'What?'

He raises his hand sharply to silence me.

'Coming back early. Mum thought she'd be alone that afternoon,' he says with an ugly smirk. 'Dad and I were going to shop some more and then I was going straight on to football, Dad was going to a concert at the Wigmore Hall, and you had choir practice after school. She thought she had the whole house all to herself.' He takes a breath, girding himself. 'But after lunch Dad was tired, so we cut our shopping short. It was too early for football so we came home together, walked back through the woods to come in by the garden gate. We were talking about Spurs' chances for next season.' He gives a little snort and smiles. 'Dad had pushed the boat out trying to make the day special before I left for university – he'd got me this posh new badminton racquet to take with me – dark blue, carbon alloy, so light. It was the most beautiful thing I'd ever seen.' He smiles, then his face darkens. 'It was about five by the time we entered the gate, still light, but the lounge curtains were closed. I was bouncing my new racquet on the heel of my hand, enjoying the ping of the taut strings – and then I realised I was pinging them in time with – something else – something rhythmic.' He glances at me. 'I couldn't work out what it was. Some echo off the wall? But it kept going even when I stopped bouncing. Squeak, squeak. Some kind of – spring? As I got closer, I heard them. Panting.' He shuts his eyes. 'I opened the lounge door, pulled back the curtain – and there they were. Him sitting back on the settee, her straddling him.'

'Who?' I whisper.

'Mum.'

'With?'

He opens his eyes, and looks straight at me. 'Marcus.'

I shake my head.

'Oh yes,' he says, jutting his chin at me. 'Old dreamboat Marcus. Dad came up behind me and I tried to get in his way, to stop him seeing, but' – he gives a little snort – 'people always spout that cliché about things going into slow motion, but it's true – I saw them, then I turned my head a fraction and caught the look on Dad's face just as he clocked them, then saw him grasp what he was seeing.' Reece is lost in the moment, re-enacting the turn, seeing Dad. 'They hadn't even registered us. She kept on pounding away, her hair flying out, and they were making these disgusting moans. Like animals rutting, on and on – till I shouted at them. That got their attention. He froze,

horrified, but she seemed dazed, she even, kind of, smiled.'
His voice breaks.

I reach out to him, but he waves me away and speeds up as if desperate to get it all out, now he's started.

'She leapt up and Marcus clutched a pillow to himself like he was in a fucking West End farce. I ran at him, sending bottles and ashtrays flying, and hit him across the face with my racquet.' Reece is swiping at the air with his clenched fist. 'He was trying to fend me off but I kept thwacking at him, blood everywhere. Then he darted away and I hit the bureau, snapping the racquet. He dragged on his jeans and legged it.' He gives me a dark smile. 'And he left his Y-fronts on the floor – there, right in the middle of the carpet.'

'What about Mum?' I ask quietly.

'She was just standing there with that glazed look she got when she was really drunk. As the front door slammed, Dad stepped up to her – and I thought he was gonna scream at her, but he just sounded defeated.

"Aren't there enough men in the world – you had to have him too?" he whimpered. I mean, it was his wife, with the kid from next door. How pathetic.

"It meant nothing, just a stupid mistake,"' Reece parrots in Mum's breathy tones. '"They're just bodies," she said and she put her hand on my chest as she said it, "just beautiful bodies." I shoved her so violently and screamed at her: "You fucking bitch, you'd be better off dead."'

'You?'

He's nodding, hunching his shoulders and squirming away from me. All this time, Dad's been describing and enacting what he saw and heard, not what he did or said.

'Then we heard your key in the lock and in you breezed, chattering away, and we all just stared at you.' I see that tense grouping of Mum, Dad and Reece that's been lodged in my memory all these years, and finally the seized faces, the monotonal replies, the dark energy make sense.

'Why didn't you tell me all this before?' I demand.

'Because you were a child.'

I snort with frustration. 'But why not later?'

He shrugs and looks down.

'Oh God. What did you do, Reece?'

He frowns at me and then jerks with realisation.

'No! I didn't kill her. How could you think that? I've told you all along who did it.'

'You don't know that,' I say, but see his look. 'Or do you? What happened next?'

'Dad and I were trying to fake normal for you – Mum had gone. And once I was sure Dad wasn't going to do anything awful, I had to get out of there too. I played the most aggressive game of football of my life that evening, really hurt people, and then I got totally smashed. You and Dad were in the lounge when I rolled in, no sign of Mum – and you were rambling about cheese on toast.'

'Lasagne,' I say flatly.

'Was it? Well, anyway, I went upstairs and passed out.'

'Go on.'

'I woke up about half twelve desperate for water and as I came downstairs, I looked out the landing window, and saw someone coming through the back gate from the woods.'

'Dad?' I whisper.

'Yeah. He tripped through the doorway, really drunk

and pathetic. I somehow got him to a chair. He slurred "She's gone," over and over. He was drooling. I'd never seen him look so pitiful. And stupid me, I felt sorry for him,' Reece laughs, 'the cuckolded husband, replaced in his younger wife's bed by their son's best mate. It was a fucking Shakespearian tragedy.' He narrows his eyes. 'But the next morning, I realised what he'd done.'

'That look.'

'What look?'

'Between you, when Chris, Detective Manning, told us it was Mum's body.'

He gives an ugly smile. 'I saw the naked panic in his eyes straight away – he knew I knew he'd done it.'

'But did you never ask him outright?'

'Didn't need to.'

'And Marcus?'

'Haven't spoken to that toilet since. I'd smash his face in.'

'But why didn't you ever tell me any of this?'

'I was protecting you. Do you feel better now you do know? That Dad is a murderer. That he stabbed Mum because she fucked the boy next door, who we grew up with. That nothing was off her menu. Does that knowledge give you some sort of closure, Hannah? You think you'll be able to process and move on?' he says sarcastically. 'Yeah, well, good luck with that. I've had a bucketload of therapy and I'll still drink and take any drug I can to block out my thoughts when they get too bad.' He glances in on Dad then turns back to me. 'Now, do you get that my autobiography was positively vanilla compared to what really happened? You'd get a hefty fee for this kind of tabloid juiciness.'

'I wouldn't do that.'

He shrugs. 'Your choice.'

'No! You never gave me any choice at all,' I shout. 'And it still doesn't make sense. If you understood why he killed her, why do you hate Dad so much?'

Reece throws back his head and gives a loud, guttural cry.

'Because he did it for me. Don't you see? I was so out of my head with shock when I saw them together. So disgusted when she touched me like that. When she didn't mean anything by it. She didn't,' he beseeches me. 'You said yourself, over and over, that Dad would never be roused to murder. And you were right.' Tears are streaming down his face now. 'On his own he'd have pushed it all down, like he did all her madness – but that day I blew his safety valve with my disgust, my anger. I screamed that she'd be better off dead, and he killed her – for me.' He hangs his head and shudders as he cries silently.

I put my arm round his shoulder and this time he lets me as he gulps out sobs.

'I don't think that's true. He killed her cos he'd finally had enough – cos she cheated on him with someone she knew as a child.'

'No, I drove him to it.'

'But why didn't you tell me? I could have helped you.'

Reece gives a strangled half-laugh. 'Because you would have gone to the police and turned Dad in.'

'So? He should have been made to pay, of course he should.'

'Just one more day,' he mumbles.

'What?'

'Just one more day and I would have been free from this family for ever, off to Cambridge with my shiny new badminton racquet,' he says, spittle flying out of his mouth.

'You did go, eventually.'

'But if Dad had gone to jail, I couldn't have gone at all. I would have had to stay home to look after . . .'

I stare at him as the truth dawns.

'Me,' I whisper.

Oh my God. After all these crimes – it was *my fault* all along? My fault that Dad didn't face justice. Because Reece didn't want to be saddled with – me. The horrifying truth that I have always feared is real. Everything is my fault – I haven't held my breath long enough and the universe has taken revenge.

'I made Dad kill her,' Reece mumbles, turning away from me. 'I abandoned you,' he says, walking towards the door. I think he's leaving so I follow to try to stop him. 'And the last thing I said to Mum was "You fucking bitch, you'd be better off dead."'

He turns and draws back his fist to punch me. I don't duck. I want it. But he swings and his fist pumps out at the stained glass of the door. It shatters and Reece's arm is ripped apart.

'No!' I shout.

Reece stumbles back and crumples at the bottom of the stairs, his left arm lying floppy in a widening pool of blood.

I drag a scarf from the coat rack and tie it around his arm above the wound, like I've seen in so many police dramas. I tighten my scarf tourniquet, raise his arm so that it's above his body on the stair, and then apply pressure to where most of the blood seems to be coming from. He's wearing a tight long-sleeved black top, so it's hard to see the extent of the wounds as the blood is soaking into the black. I lift his good hand and press it on the wound.

'Push hard here. I'll call an ambulance,' I say but Reece grabs my arm with his uninjured one, moaning with the effort.

'No,' he says, 'no ambulance.'

'I have to.'

'Are you deranged? Think of the press.'

'Forget the press, you could die.'

'Don't be so bloody melodramatic,' he says with a weak smile. He struggles as he tries to get something out of his right pocket with his left arm. 'Don't just stand there like a numpty, get my phone out of my pocket.'

I pull his mobile out and wipe the smeared blood off on my front.

'Unlock it,' he orders me. I know the code but wait for him to tell me. '041096' he says dully. Our eyes meet as we both register the date of Mum's murder. 'Go to contacts. Go to Doc and ring.'

I follow his instructions.

'Put it on speaker and hold it up to me,' he says, his face very white and drawn.

The phone is answered as I'm fiddling with the slimy volume controls, and a tinny little voice is saying, 'Hello, Hello, Ryan, can you hear me.'

I eventually find the speaker icon.

'Ryan? Ryan are you there?' says a worried Irish voice.

'Patrick, it's me,' says Reece. 'I need you to come right away.'

'OK,' the voice says, seeming unfazed. 'Where are you?'

'By Highgate Woods – I'll WhatsApp you the address,' he says raising his eyebrows to me. I nod.

'What have you taken?'

'It's not that this time. I've put my arm through a window.'

'Jeez, Ryan – you need an ambulance.'

'No, it's just scratches, but I need it dealt with.'

'I'll be there in ten minutes – are you sure it's not serious?'

'I'm fine, my sister's here.'

'Put her on, I'm coming,' says the voice, who is clearly slamming doors and getting in a car as he speaks.

'Hi,' I say cautiously.

'You need to bind his arm above the wound,' he says with no preamble.

'Yeah, I've done that.'

'Is he losing consciousness?'

'No, but he's bled quite a lot.'

'Just keep the tourniquet as tight as you can. I'll be there in a few minutes. If he loses consciousness, call an ambulance.'

I send the address then put the phone on the stair beside Reece and tighten the scarf. He groans. There's so much blood. Please, please, please be all right. I exert as much pressure as I can. I haven't been this physically close to my brother for years. Not since we lay next to each other at night biting the chocolate off our secret stash of Curly Wurlys, bitching about the day. Reece has his eyes closed.

'So Schro's dead?' he asks quietly.

'Yeah, cancer, it was really bad, I didn't have a choice.'

'He was a good cat,' he says with a catch in his voice.

'A fatty fat cat,' he says, invoking our old name. He winces and jerks his arm.

'What is it?' I say in panic.

'I guess the adrenalin's wearing off.'

'He'll be here soon – whoever he is. You've needed this guy before?'

'Medical student friend from Cambridge, lives in Crouch End – who unlike me, actually followed through and became a doctor. He's helped me with the odd – drug problem.'

'God.'

A few minutes later, there's a loud knocking. I leap over to the door, my shoes crunching on the shattered glass, and open it to reveal a tall guy with floppy hair and round glasses.

'Patrick?' I ask.

'The sister?'

'Yeah, Hannah.'

'Who knew old Ryan had a sister,' he says as he walks towards Reece.

'All right, mate,' says Reece with a slight smile.

'Better than you,' says Patrick, unpacking a large rucksack on the floor.

'Close the door, Hannah,' says Reece.

I push it to and some more glass falls from the hole.

Patrick eases Reece's jacket off and cuts away his black top. His left arm is covered in slicing cuts and there's an especially large ugly cut down his forearm.

'You're bloody lucky, you haven't cut any major arteries,' says Patrick. 'Most of this is superficial but I'm gonna have to stitch this big cut on your forearm right away. This is a topical anaesthetic, but it's still gonna hurt. I can't guarantee it won't scar.'

'Just do it,' says Reece, turning his head away. 'Don't watch, Hannah.'

But I can't drag my gaze from his shockingly skinny body, my eyes sliding over the sharply defined ridges of his ribs on his hairless chest, across his taut stomach and finally resting on the intimate inward twist of his belly button.

'You're so thin,' I say.

'Gastric band,' he says with a smirk.

'What?'

'Yeah, got it cos I was losing teeth from my bulimia.'

'Jesus.' For the first time, I see not the fit film star from the billboards, but a fragile middle-aged man, trying to hold onto his youthful beauty.

'You were telling the truth,' I say to Reece, 'when you said you haven't been back to the house since Cambridge?'

'Of course. Why?'

'Nothing.'

I sweep up the broken glass and fix a piece of cardboard over the hole, while Reece makes strangled noises as Patrick stitches.

'These are dissolvable stitches, and I'm doing the tidiest job I can do, but you may still have some scars,' says Patrick.

'Get on with your needlepoint, I can see a plastic surgeon later,' says Reece.

'Evel Knievel thought his scars made him more attractive to women,' I say.

'Well, let's hope so,' he moans, as he arches his back.

'Keep your arm still,' says Patrick. 'Could you get him

some water, Hannah, he needs fluid.'

I hold a brimming cup up to Reece's mouth to sip.

'Thanks. You're doing great,' Patrick whispers to me. He puts a large gauze dressing over Reece's arm and binds it.

'There, not as good as new, but you'll do,' says Patrick.

'Thanks, mate,' says Reece.

'Are you on anything, Ryan?' says Patrick, glancing at me.

'Nope,' says Reece, 'I did this clean and stone-cold sober.'

'Impressive,' says Patrick. 'OK, so you need to keep vigilant tonight,' he says to me.

'Oh, I'm not staying here,' says Reece immediately. 'I'm going with you, Pat,' he says, brooking no discussion. Patrick steps back and shrugs.

I open the front door in a daze.

'You OK?' says Reece, frowning at me.

'Yeah,' I say.

'Hannah, I—'

'It's OK – I know.'

I touch his shoulder gently and smile. He nods back.

'Here, have a jacket,' I say, draping one of Dad's jackets over Reece's skinny naked torso. A torso which has a belly button which is a curling innie, not a raised outie.

'Goodbye,' says Patrick. 'Good to meet you, if under less than desirable circumstances.'

He supports Reece down the path and into his car, which is parked directly in front. As I walk back in, I notice the curtains next door fall back, obscuring whoever was watching.

Dad is sitting in the darkened room making odd moaning sounds.

'Are you OK, Dad?'

'It hurts,' he says, clutching his stomach. He's had his slow-release morphine for the night, but the doctor said that the pain was going to increase. I give him two fast-release pills, help him into bed and sit next to him stroking his hand till the drugs kick in and he falls asleep.

Once I'm sure he's out, I walk down the rickety stairs to Mum's darkroom. I pull out the sheet of negatives and shine a torch through the sepia images. Beautiful shots – of a lean athletic body, bending, arching, straining. Reece and Marcus were so physically similar – same height, same broad chests. But it was Marcus who had a peaked outie belly button.

All these Michelangelo photos are of Marcus.

And that final developed roll of film on Reece's mantelpiece was of Marcus, not Reece. And Reece knew it. Reminded himself of what happened with Marcus and Mum every time he sat in his white chair staring at his Rothko. It was a roll of film from this final Michelangelo series.

So many photos of Marcus in so many different scenarios. Whatever went on with Marcus and Mum wasn't some drunken one-off.

CHAPTER TWENTY-EIGHT

The next morning, I stare up at the oriental artwork that Mum cajoled Dad into having painted on the ceiling above their bed, presumably at great cost – delicate blossoming trees, rolling hills and ornate bridges over winding streams, with beautiful women scurrying across the bridges, their long robes clinging to their perfect figures, their demure eyes outlined in black, their dark hair piled high, with tendrils escaping in the wind. As a child I thought it was a magical world, peaceful and scented, with beautiful women gliding by – but now, all I see is Mum's racist, stereotypical fantasy of glamorous concubines scurrying to assignations – wearing tacky red robes like Mum did on that final afternoon.

Mum was some kind of sex addict, I guess. Not exotic and complex. Just utterly selfish in fulfilling her needs. Am I being unfeminist in not accepting Mum's unfettered sexuality? No, hurting others does matter. But maybe she couldn't help herself. I know a heightened sex drive can be a symptom of being bipolar and I wonder if Mum was undiagnosed. When I saw a therapist at university very briefly, she suggested this as a possible diagnosis for me because I was so manic and, as she put it, 'had an increased need for sexual gratification'. I was too embarrassed to explain that I just didn't want to be alone at night.

But who is not in this picture above me? All those men these clichéd concubines are scurrying towards. What about the choices they made? However attractive Mum was, however manipulative, what about them? I fumble for my phone and WhatsApp Marcus: *Could we meet up tonight? Same time, same place?*

The message is double blue-ticked immediately, so he's read it, but there's no reply. He's wondering how to politely let down the smitten daughter of a murdered ex-lover – but I guess there are too few examples in the interconnected area of that particular Venn diagram, for any precedent. Eventually he responds.

Ping. *Don't think that's a great idea after last time. Sorry.* *Be there.* Send.

Ping. *Sorry, no.*

You better be, I type, biting my lip, adding: *Mother-Fucker!* Send.

There's an even longer pause. I feel the air shimmering all the way to whichever cell tower is beaming our messages between us.

Finally: Ping. *I'll be there.*

I drag on some sweats and march round next door. Mr and Mrs Roberts answer the door together.

'Hello, dear,' she says, smiling. 'Everything OK?'

Mr Roberts looks at me with undisguised horror.

'No,' I say blankly. 'It's not OK. Mrs Roberts, I need to tell you—'

Mr Roberts' eyes widen and he parts his lips.

'What is it?' Mrs Roberts asks. How can she not read the guilt about Mum splashed across her husband's face? And how can neither of them have read the truth on Marcus's lying face, or on my face now – it's sweating out of my pores like garlic.

'I—'

'Yes . . . ?' coaxes Mrs Roberts.

But I won't shatter their lives exponentially right now. I need to deal with Marcus first.

'I'm struggling a bit and need a night out – so I wondered if one of you could sit with Dad tonight?'

'Of course,' says Mr Roberts, relief flooding across his face.

'No problem, dear, what time?'

'Seven-ish, if you're sure it's no trouble?'

'Of course,' says Mrs Roberts. 'Is it a date?'

'Umm . . . he's a real catch.'

Marcus is already at the pub at ten to seven when I arrive, running his thumbnail up and down a groove in the table, nursing a near-empty pint. He stands abruptly as I approach, flattening down his shirt, like a little boy.

'You know,' he says quietly.

'I know.'

'How?'

'Reece told me.'

'Oh, God.' He sits back down and finishes his last mouthful of beer. His usually open, easy face is blotchy.

'I'll get more drinks,' I say, turning away, desperately needing a drink but getting water for me and another pint for him. Actual confrontation is never the same as imagined confrontation.

'I'm so sorry,' he blurts as I return.

'You were helping me out of guilt, were you?' I spit back. 'No wonder you wanted to get all the work on the house done before Dad got back.'

'I did want to help.'

'I want to know everything that happened with you and her.'

He screws up his face and rears back, but I catch his arm.

'No more secrets,' I growl. 'I've been pathetically ignorant for too long.'

He takes a huge swig of beer, then stares at the table as he speaks.

'She had me posing for all those bloody jumping photos of hers, all that last summer. With Reece, and I just thought that we were having a laugh.' He glances at me but I just nod for him to continue. 'But then one day Reece had a match and I was off with my knee injury and she invited me round to do a session alone. Your dad was upstairs, so it didn't seem that weird. But then she wanted to do another solo one – at night, in the woods.' He glances at me again but I keep my face neutral. 'I knew it was weird, that Reece wouldn't like it – but I was kind of, well hugely, jealous – that Reece had this glittering life opening up for him – straight As and off to Cambridge and all with so little effort, while I toiled away to scrape Es and was having to get a job. She'd brought a bottle of whisky. But I know it doesn't excuse it that I was so drunk.' He's jamming his thumbnail into the table groove so hard that it's bleeding. 'We kept drinking and I was taking clothes off for the pictures – and somehow we . . .' He swallows the rest of his pint. 'And then we kept on doing it at night in the woods. And I just stuck it in a separate box in my head.'

'How long did this fucking go on?'

'About a month.'

I think of that barbecue we had with the Robertses that month, of Mum and Mrs Roberts cooking and egging each other on to drink ridiculously named cocktails like Sex on the Beach and Slippery Nipple; of bare-torsoed Marcus wrestling with Reece as Mum photographed them; of Marcus laughing with Dad over football results and play-punching his arm; and of fourteen-year-old me salivating over Marcus's physique.

'And that day?'

'I'd had a huge fight with Mum and Dad that morning about paying rent to stay at theirs. And I went round to see Jen at yours, where we never met up usually, and she said you were all out for ages. I wasn't thinking straight and somehow we got really drunk and started – you know.'

'Keep going,' I say quietly.

He closes his eyes. 'God, I can see it all so clearly,' he says, his voice cracking as he hunches in. 'She was on top of me and suddenly, Reece and your dad were right there in the room – the look on Reece's face . . .' He falters to a stop again.

'And then?'

297

'Reece started hitting me, whacked me right between the eyes' – he fingers the scar that I noticed on our 'date' – 'but I somehow got out of there, got even drunker and stayed at a mate's that night – and when I came back the next day – your mum was dead.'

'No wonder you were so disgusted with me trying to kiss you,' I say, with a bitter laugh.

'I've never thought of you like that. You're like a little sister to me.'

'And I thought it was a date – how fucking sad is that.'

'Why did you have to wear that pink dress.'

I flinch. 'She wore that for you?'

He nods. 'Then it was so freaky when you kissed me.'

'Aaagh!' I shout, throwing my head back.

He looks round at the people staring.

I take a breath and settle back into my hardness. 'I can't quite decide. Is it a relief to know that it wasn't just plain old revulsion that made you rear back? So much better that it was cos I reminded you of my mum.'

He gives a low moan.

'Your parents have no idea?' I ask.

'God, no.'

I want to smash him apart by telling him about his dad and Mum, but as I open my mouth to destroy him, I catch myself. Everyone else has had power over me with their dirty little secrets. Now I have secrets and will hug them to me till I decide how best to use them for full devastating effect.

'I bet you were shitting bricks when we went down into Mum's darkroom,' I say with a little sarcastic laugh.

He winces.

'All those photos of you, naked, arching, preening for her camera. You must have had a right bloody laugh when I thought they were of Reece.'

'No, I felt – sorry for you.'

'Don't you dare pity me!' I say, slamming my hand onto the table, making the drinks bounce and other drinkers look round.

'Weren't you worried about them being found before?'

'I—'

He looks at me and it hits me.

'It was you, wasn't it? You're the one who's been breaking in – searching for them. Haven't you?'

He gives a tiny nod. 'I came when you were out. Used Mum's keys. But I couldn't find them anywhere.'

'Oh my God – it was you in the house that night after Dad first went into hospital – you who went through all the photos in the lounge.'

'I thought you were still at the hospital with your dad – you gave me such a shock, out cold on the hall floor. I had to search quickly, couldn't tidy up, cos you moaned as if you were waking.'

He saw me like that – plastered and drooling, and, oh God, now I remember – I'd wet myself. My humiliation drops like a firework into the lake of my newly exposed ignorance and barely fizzles as it's extinguished by the dark waters.

'I should have you arrested for breaking and entering, you pervert,' I spit at him.

'I was desperate. I'd thought the secret would die with your dad – but then Mum mentioned that you were back living there – it woke me up to the possible danger – so I started searching for those negatives, when you were out. Your dad saw me a couple of times, but I knew he was too out of it to say anything – he kept calling me Reece.'

So that's why Dad thought Reece was visiting him.

'And then when your dad went into hospital, I thought that was my chance to get them. If those pictures ever got to the police, they would have finally known the motive.'

'Whose motive?'

Am I sitting across from Mum's murderer?

'Reece or your dad of course. One of them killed your mum.'

'You had a pretty big motive yourself.'

He looks genuinely dumbfounded.

'How can you – I was with my mate Phil Williams, on the other side of London, if you really need to check. But you have to know I couldn't have done it,' he pleads. He seems utterly genuine, but how do I tell who's lying any more?

'But you didn't go to the police with the evidence against Dad and Reece, did you? So, either you are guilty or you let them get away with it to protect your pathetic reputation.'

He looks genuinely confused.

'No, that's not it – I didn't tell the police because I had to protect them. One of them did it. But I caused it. I couldn't let them suffer for my weakness.'

Just like Reece and Mr Roberts, Marcus stopped Dad facing justice out of guilt and self-protection.

I kick my stool back and stride away without a backwards glance.

* * *

When I get back, the house is full of the comforting smell of baking and Mrs Roberts' famous chocolate-chip cookies sit on the bedside table next to Dad. She wouldn't be helping our family if she knew what my mum did to her family.

'Oh, hello dear, you're back earlier than I was expecting. Bad date?'

'Ah you know, men,' I deflect.

'Yes,' she says with a knowing eyebrow raise.

'Thanks,' I say, amazed that I can continue this parody of sociability. 'Did he eat anything tonight?' I say, gesturing at Dad, who's sleeping soundly.

'Not much, I've tried lots of things to tempt him. Perhaps try him with another of these biscuits when he wakes. I'll fix you both some hot milk to go with your cookies and I'll be off.'

As she leaves, I see that she's left the TV playing another episode of *Muerte*. I munch a cookie as I watch Reece running full pelt at me. He swerves across a rooftop in pursuit of a chunky dark-haired quarry, who leaps between two buildings, and turns to sneer at Reece.

'Nothing ventured,' Reece mutters as he launches himself and just makes the leap, a cascade of shingle falling down beneath him. He wrestles the man to the ground, despite being half his size and strength – but this is the world of light crime drama, where leading characters always win.

'Why were you running, Mario?' Reece asks as he hauls the now-handcuffed Mario to his feet.

'I see police, I run,' says Mario in a gelatinously thick Spanish accent, 'is instinct'.

Reece taps his forehead. 'Me too. I took one look at your squirrelly face – and I knew!'

What a crock. I switch it off, discarding the remaining half of the sweet cookie. Instinct is always touted as this profound, unwavering truth that we can all access, if only we dig deep enough. Bollocks. My every instinct told me that Dad had nothing to do with Mum's death. But I have proved Dad did it. Means: a common kitchen knife. Motive: Mum cheated on him with all and sundry including his neighbour and neighbour's child, and made him raise two other men's children. Opportunity: he was in the woods at the exact time and returned drunk saying 'She's gone.' My instincts are wishful lies. Reece, Marcus and Mr Roberts all had some motive, but, however I try to reframe it all, the filthy waters of Mum's infidelities and lies always eventually swirl towards the same reeking plughole of Dad.

He stirs with a moan of pain, then mumbles, 'I'm sorry, Jen.'

I open his plastic pill dispenser and give Dad his evening slow-release pill of morphine, my hand hovering over the rest of it. How simple it would be, to give him more – to release him, to execute him. But that would be too easy an escape for him, and for everyone else and their fermenting secrets.

I'm too exhausted now but I will speak to Chris in the morning, tell everyone's secrets and get Dad charged with Mum's murder. I fumble for my phone and message him.

Can we speak first thing. Dad's time has run out.

CHAPTER TWENTY-NINE

I'm wide awake. My throat's dry and my head feels fuzzy. Why does not drinking feel so awful? Mum's bedroom is bathed in ivory moonlight and the shadows of the trees are clawing at me across her bed. I'm warm under the covers, but the hairs on my arms are standing up. Something's off-kilter in the house. No, surely it's just my mind playing tricks. Those break-ins were Marcus, he admitted it, he wouldn't come back.

Thud.

That wasn't in my head – that was downstairs.

Schro? But Schro's dead. Dad? He wouldn't be out of bed, not on all that medication. I try to take a deep breath, but choke on the thick scent of Chanel No. 5 on the bedding. As I swing my legs onto the ground, I fight the impulse to leap over any grasping hands or tendrils reaching out for me from under the bed. Grow up. I pad across the room on the balls of my feet, feeling weirdly light and dissociated as

I peer out the door. The moon illuminates the empty upper hallway from the landing window. Of course, it was just this old house shifting.

Then there's a rustling downstairs.

I step out and a floorboard creaks.

The rustling stops.

I freeze, but all I hear is my own breathing.

I slowly start to descend the wooden stairs. My skin is tingling, my stomach twisting, my heart racing. Everything feels off, other-worldly. My eyes are open but my vision is strangely blurred, my tongue huge and lolling in my mouth and I have to actively will my limbs to engage.

I turn the corner of the stairs and the dark pit of the hallway opens below me. I pause and clap my hands hard, and the sound cracks in the blackness. The air feels unnaturally cold. I peer down into the dark chasm. Is there someone – or something – there? Of course not. When you're dead, you're dead. There's no such thing as ghosts.

As the reverberations of my clap fade away, I start down the final eight stairs. But a sudden gush of cold air gives me a dizzying jolt, and my foot doesn't engage with the next step. I jerk forward, catapulted into mid-air, and I'm momentarily suspended in the dark void, arms flung out like a thief winched from the ceiling above. I am one of Mum's falling photos, nothing above, nothing below.

Then gravity kicks in and I plummet to the floor, my arms flapping back in front of me just as I slam down. I'm winded by the smack of the hard wooden floor, my body stunned rigid.

In the gloom, the shadows beside me move.

'Who's there?' I whisper to the undulating blackness. I

304

crane into the dark silence, trying to engage.

Suddenly a dark presence looms towards me.

'Mum?' I gasp.

I feel her breath on my cheek and I reach out. But she has no corporeal form and I am flailing into the air.

'Mum, please, don't leave again. Mum!'

But the presence suddenly sucks away from me, as if pulled back into another realm, and then recedes into my narrowing cone of focus. I'm grabbing at the empty air as a wave of blackness overtakes me.

I hear a click and open my eyes. How long have I been out? Oh God, was that Dad? Every muscle screams out, but I manage to roll onto my hands and knees and painfully crawl into the lounge. As I reach the bed, I see Dad's chest rising and falling. He's safely tucked in, just as I left him. He hasn't been out of bed. So what was that strange presence? Am I going through some paranoid detoxing from all the years of alcohol finally leaving my body?

'Sorry, Jen,' Dad mumbles. I reach up and switch on Fake Schro to calm him. He needs to survive till I can get him charged for Mum's murder. He can't escape justice now. As he strokes, he calms and mumbles one last thing before he falls asleep: 'I'm sorry I married you.'

My head is woozy and I wonder if I've got concussion from my fall, but I'm too tired to call for help, too sore to move and too scared to be alone – so I pull a cushion from the settee, curl up on the floor and give in to my sucking exhaustion.

* * *

My eyes open and focus on the underside of the metal frame of Dad's bed, as I realise where I am. I'm cold and painfully stiff, but daylight has dissolved the shadows, making last night seem like a dream. I fell downstairs and spooked myself with my usual overthinking. Reece is right. I need to get out of my head, to seek professional help. And I must get Chris to send the police to arrest Dad. I lever myself up, wincing and moaning.

I know immediately that he's dead.

He's completely still. Grey. Sunken.

This isn't Dad – it's a shell, something that's been shed. I loathe religion, mysticism, any mumbo jumbo about the soul, but some essence has departed.

And Dad has escaped justice.

This is real. Dad's dead. But I can't take it in. What do normal people do in these circumstances?

Despite the strange blue tinge of his lips, I mechanically go through the motions of checking for life: his bony chest stays flat; there's no flutter of breath on my cheek; his brittle hand is cold and rigid.

He's been dead for a while.

And he died right next to me.

As I did nothing.

I need to move, so I walk round the bed to look from the other side, and suck in a breath as something sharp scrapes my bare sole and crinkles audibly. I peel a blister packet off the underside of my foot, emblazoned with the instantly recognisable silver and blue stripes of the fast-release morphine tablets. Each little plastic depression that should contain a pill – is empty.

And there are empty blister packets of morphine strewn

all over the floor on this side of the bed. I reach over to the clock on the mantelpiece and feel behind it for the key to the pill safe. It's not there. Swivelling round, I see the days-of-the-week pill caddy lying open on the floor; all the morphine pills are gone and the metal pill safe is flung on the settee, my key in the lock.

I peer at Dad's open mouth. His lips aren't naturally blue – they're stained blue and I can glimpse something inside his mouth. I clench my teeth and push my forefinger between his thin lips. The pad of my fingertip pushes into a spongy ball of wet chalk. I snatch my hand back and stare at my finger's blue-and-white coating of semi-masticated morphine tablets. I cough as bile fills my mouth and turn away to vomit onto the floor.

Dad died from a huge overdose of morphine. But how?

Dad did it? Impossible for him to get the key, unlock the safe box, open the blister packets and feed them to himself. Even in one of his moments of superhuman capability, his arthritic claws don't – didn't – have the dexterity.

That presence did it? It wasn't some fantastical essence of Jen – it was a flesh-and-blood person – afraid of what Dad knew about their involvement in Mum's death or the involvement of someone they loved? But how did they know where to find the key, and how did they empty out the safe and feed the pills to Dad, all without me waking while I was lying right next to him?

I did it? Have I somehow done this in my sleep, goaded by my fleeting thoughts about euthanasia, about murder? Or am I no longer playing the role of Jen – the role is playing me, and Jen has taken her final revenge on her husband for killing her? I have committed fraud and arson, stolen from

Dad, impersonated my dead mother and pushed Dad and Reece to make revelations with cruel tricks. Now murder?

Dad's glassy eyes accuse me.

'I didn't,' I shout aloud.

But it looks so like I did.

The evidence is overwhelming. If the emergency services arrive to see the empty pill packets and Dad's foaming mouth of morphine, they'll think I murdered him, even before the hospital tells them about Dad's previous suspicious fall, for which I was a suspect. At the very least they will think me a self-important angel of mercy, at worst a cold-blooded killer, doing away with Dad to get my hands on his money, especially when Reece tells them I've been siphoning Dad's money to pay off my massive debts, caused by theft and arson.

But if I didn't do this, then someone else did, and set me up to take the blame.

I am in motion, numb but moving, focused on action, before I articulate a decision. I gather up all the packets, the pill caddy and the locked box and stash them in the laundry bin upstairs, under the huge mound of dirty clothes. I drag out the squat red Henry Hoover and suck up all the remaining pills from the floor. I fill a plastic mixing bowl with warm water and return to Dad with a large roll of kitchen tissue. Dad's pupils are small pinpoints, the surface of his eyes eerily opaque. Tears streaming down my face, I touch my fingertips to Dad's fragile skin to close his eyes. But it's not like in films: they don't gently fold down and it takes several attempts to close the right one, while the left stays half open, watching me.

I arrange the kitchen roll gently around his face, then

roll up two white squares, soak them in the warm water and poke the end into Dad's mouth. Tears blurring my vision and bile burping up into my mouth, I gently wipe and remove the now encrusted wet tissue. I repeat and repeat, mumbling 'sorry' over and over, till Dad's mouth is as free of the bluey-white residue as I can get it. Then I remove the surrounding kitchen roll and chuck the mountain of morphine-smeared tissues into the kitchen bin, digging a hole in the smelly pile of rotting food and piling the reeking mess over the top. I wash my hands three times with soap, but still smell and taste the chemical tang.

I use a clump of wet wipes to collect up my pile of vomit from the far side of the bed, move my pillow from the floor, and finally stop my manic cover-up and stand still next to Dad. I rest my hand on his cold hand, lean in and kiss his forehead. I was so gung-ho last night, so ready to turn him in to the police. Then when I saw him dead, I was appalled that he had escaped justice. But now I am covering up his murder, stunned with guilt that Dad died with me doubting him – when he could have been innocent all along. I'm either a murderer or the victim of a cruel set-up. Either way, I've destroyed the evidence of murder, so I'm complicit. I've been so angry with everyone for all their cover-ups for their own selfish protection, and now I am doing the same – so easily felled by the visceral pull to survive.

I sway, staring down at his body.

I have to keep moving, start doing what an innocent person would do. After a final panicky 'Where's Wally' for any final evidence that will convict me, I call 999.

'Hello, which services?'

'Ambulance.'

'What is the nature of your emergency?'

'It's my dad,' I say, heightening my voice to sound upset, when all I feel is numbed and terrified. 'I think he's dead, I've just woken up and he's not breathing, please come quickly.'

I stumble out the information, looking at myself in the hall mirror. I am wide-eyed and dishevelled – but worse, I have huge purple blotchy bruises all down my right arm and across my right shoulder and neck from my fall last night. After hanging up, I race to Mum's room and drag on her white roll-neck sweater. I look weird for a mild morning, but weird is better than bruised-in-combat.

An ambulance arrives ten minutes later.

'Please hurry,' I cry to the paramedics racing up the path.

They lean over Dad, while I hover, terrified that they will turn to me with accusatory looks.

'I'm afraid to say,' the female paramedic starts, glancing across at her partner – *no, no, no, please don't* – 'that your father has passed away. I'm very sorry.'

I'm safe. For now.

'What happens next?' I say haltingly. She glances at Dad and takes in the hospital bed, the bedpan, the stink of old.

'A death certificate will be issued and then you'll be able to make funeral arrangements. It will be a formality,' she says, squeezing my arm, with a knowing glance at her partner.

Dad's body is zipped into a large bag and stretchered out.

After a few more formalities, the front door closes, and I am alone.

I try to take a breath but my throat is locked. I suck desperately for air, jerking like a fish on a riverbank, slamming my body back and forth as I gulp ineffectually. I hit my chest with my fist, trying to open my lungs, but I am seized rigid, near collapse. I am going to die here, panicking and alone.

'I'm not a panicker,' I said to Chris.

'Ha,' he said.

And with that memory, I flop to the floor, my head between my knees like he told me to do, cupping my hands over my face to inhale my breath, just like I did from that wrinkly paper bag that Chris held. I see his broad hand held resolutely in front of me, hear his soothing voice, and taste one of the chocolate fingers on his cat-photo plate. My breathing slows.

Then I mentally smash the plate as I sit up. I have to tell Reece. But do I trust him? Someone killed Dad, someone with keys to this house.

I go back into the lounge to retrieve my phone and sit on the settee to call him. He picks up straight away. Unlike him?

'Hi Hannah, I'm fine, you don't need to check on me,' he says, sounding annoyed.

'That's not why I'm calling.'

'Oh. So he's dead,' he says flatly. Is this news to him?

'He died last night. The ambulance people took him just now.'

'Are you OK?' he says, sounding caring. 'Do you want me to come over?'

'I'm fine, you should be resting. I'd rather be alone.'

'OK,' he says uncertainly. 'Well my people will sort out – all the arrangements.'

'Whatever.'

'And we'll deal with the house and everything in due course, OK?'

'Yeah sure,' I say, marvelling at how quickly he is making arrangements. 'How's your arm?'

'It's fine. But look – maybe don't mention to anyone that I was there yesterday. Or about my arm. There's no point in making this into some story it isn't. OK?'

I flip the switch on Fake Schro's belly and stroke my purring orange 'companion'.

'Indeed. Why confuse anyone with what really happened,' I say.

'Meaning? Are you OK?'

Stroking Fake Schro, I'm swung back to using it to calm Dad last night, and recall his final ever words.

I'm sorry I married you.

Oh my God. That's what he's meant all along with his 'sorry's. Not sorry for killing her. He was sorry – for marrying Mum. As if he had clipped her wings and caused all the chaos that she instigated. He didn't kill her – he just felt some ultimate responsibility.

'Hannah? Are you still there?' calls Reece.

'I have to go, I'm not feeling great. I'll call you.'

I hang up on him.

Dad didn't kill himself. So who did? Everyone involved in Mum's convoluted life is a suspect, but only a few had keys for access – Reece, Marcus, Mr and Mrs Roberts – and me.

CHAPTER THIRTY

'I'm so sorry,' Chris says gruffly, when I ring him to tell him about Dad. 'Are you . . . sorry, stupid to ask.'

'I am OK actually, just a bit – lost. But he's free now.'

'Was that what your message last night meant?'

'What? Oh, yes. I thought it was nearing his time. And I was right.' Christ, that message could make me look very guilty if doubt is cast on me – I have to be very careful.

'I know you don't know me very well,' I blurt. 'But—'

'I agree with the but,' he cuts in.

'OK. So. What do you think of me?'

'Phwoar. God. Sorry, I shouldn't joke at a time like this.'

'No seriously – do you think me, you know, sane?'

'Of course,' he says. 'Eminently so.'

'And you've got a good bullshit detector.'

He laughs. 'I can usually catch the whiff of manure. Why are you asking?'

'I've been pretty out there over the last year, had some

really wild phases, disconnected – rat-in-a-trap wacky.'

'Is that the prevailing acceptable term?'

'Come on, you know what I mean – not knowing my own mind. Do you think I could have done something and blocked it out?'

'Oh, now you tell me. You're the Incredible Hulk, and when you get angry, the other you bursts out and wreaks havoc.'

'Please, Chris.'

'Of course you know what you're doing. But you've had a really tough time since your mum died, and perhaps you've let your imagination run away with itself on occasion. But who hasn't had outlandish thoughts when stressed?'

'You.'

'Ha.'

'But I've thought some really – off-kilter things.'

'Yeah, yeah, you're not that weird,' he says kindly.

'But I—'

'You know, for a long time after my shooting, when I really grasped that I'd lost the use of my legs, I used to fantasise about rolling down the high street in my chair, shooting criminals with machine guns. I found it a very soothing fantasy.'

'What?'

'Yeah. It was really detailed: how I would come upon a violent robbery and would single-handedly foil the attack, killing all the attackers. I would revel in it, the weight of my gun, the kick-back as I shot, the splatter of their blood as their bullet-ridden bodies jerked into the air, the way their eyes bulged in horror. I'd kill anyone in my way, guilty or innocent – violently. I found it a very calming scenario – I used to run through it every evening to get to sleep.'

'Nice.'

'Thoughts are not deeds. But sometimes we need to play things out – to feel the visceral kick-back.'

'So you don't think I'm dangerous then?'

'Of course not. Life's hard. Our minds swing out of orbit to cope, to consider, to experiment. But they're just thoughts, not actions. I'm a good judge of character and I – like you.'

I breathe into his confidence in me. Chris's belief in me grounds me back to earth. I know I didn't kill Dad. A real live person did it – and set me up.

'You're a decent man,' I say awkwardly.

'Ouch. Where's my "dark and mysterious"?'

I snort. 'Thanks.'

'Any time,' he says gently.

'But,' my voice cracks. 'Dad died with me believing him to be a murderer – and now I don't think that was true.'

'You were there for him – you stuck with him even when you doubted him – that's what matters.'

I cry quietly, while he listens down the line. I want to tell him that someone murdered Dad, but I can't admit covering up the crime, or being suspected. I look too obviously guilty. My message last night to him would be the final proof. I have to get the murderer of Dad, and Mum, to show themselves.

'You still there?' he asks.

'I haven't given up looking into what happened to Mum, you know.'

'What are you up to, Hannah?' he asks, nervously. 'If you have real evidence, you must tell the police. Do you want to talk through what you're thinking with me?'

'Not yet. But soon.'

'Okaaay . . . But you're not planning on doing anything stupid, are you?'

'No.'

He coughs artificially. 'You're not filling me with confidence. I would – mind if something happened to you. Be careful.'

'I will. Promise.'

As I hang up the call, I become aware of a fumbling at the front door – someone's trying to get in with a key. I stare through the new pane of frosted glass that has replaced the one that Reece shattered.

'Who's there?' I call.

'It's just me, dear.'

I drag the door open to see Mrs Roberts with a plate of flapjacks.

'Oh Hannah, thanks for your call. I know you said you were OK, but I didn't want to leave you alone too long. I'm so sorry about your dad.'

'Thanks, but I—'

'Do you want to have a little chat?' she says kindly, stepping forward, but I stand my ground.

'I'm sorry, but I haven't slept,' I say. 'I'm going to have a lie down.'

'Of course. Umm, my key doesn't seem to work?' she says with a frown, shaking it in front of her.

'Oh yes, I – lost my handbag on the bus yesterday, with my keys and my address, so I thought for safety's sake I should get the locks changed.'

She nods.

'I'll get some spares cut when I'm feeling up to it.'

'Of course, good idea, but please call me or Frank if we can help with anything. OK?'

She presses the flapjacks on me and leaves.

I've just spent a fortune having an emergency locksmith put locks on all the doors and windows on the ground floor and replacing the glass in the front door. Everyone with access to keys must be kept out while I think – and plan. This is my little fortress – where I am formulating my final campaign.

Chris said he caught suspects out by catching them off-guard with accusation out of the blue. I will let my thoughts percolate – till the funeral. I can't risk doing anything before that in case I'm arrested and can't attend. I must say goodbye to Dad and then I will unmask his killer and Mum's.

Mum's killer may have had to be a man, because as Chris said, only a man would have had the height and force to drive the knife into Mum at the angle it entered her chest. But Dad's killer could be that same man – or a man or woman protecting that man. I replay the recorded conversation between Reece and Dad. 'I won't ever tell,' says Dad. I thought he meant about him killing Mum. But what if Dad believed that Reece did it and Reece believed Dad did it, and they were both covering for each other all these years? If it was neither of them – was it a lover's tiff with Marcus or Mr Roberts? And did Mrs Roberts find out that one of them had killed Mum, and so she killed Dad to protect them?

I see an announcement online that Reece is delaying filming the new series of *Muerte*, due to the 'sad passing of his father'. Mr and Mrs Roberts keep dropping over, she bringing meals to 'pop in the oven', he saying he's available 'if anything needs doing' with embarrassed hangdog eyes. Marcus drops by to oversee the collection of the hired hospital bed, saying he's 'so sorry for my loss', avoiding my gaze.

I scrutinise each of them. Is it you?

Anastasia has contacted a firm to clear the house, lock, stock and barrel. They come round to give a quote and say that we would have to pay them five hundred pounds to clear the lot. Apparently, our family's life has a negative worth. I agree that they can come in a week.

I sort manically. Dad's clothes are especially hard to chuck. I lift all his T-shirts from the top rail in one go and collapse to the floor, tops and hangers splayed around me. I finger his classic 1994 retro Spurs top, white with a dark blue Holsten across the chest, that he wore whenever Spurs played, though after Mum's death he never went to an actual match again; his muddy-green Che Guevara top, which he claimed was shrinking (as he got fatter); his purple collared top, 'how posh can the restaurant be, Jen, a collared sports top is fine' (it wasn't); the highlighter-yellow top he claimed looked good with a tan (it didn't); and his '1936 Best Vintage' top that I gave him for his last birthday (it was the best vintage).

I leave my and Reece's stuff for the mercenary 'cleaners', who I presume will sell off anything of worth and chuck the rest in a landfill. I dump all of Mum's clothes and possessions in her darkroom – along with any photos of her. I hold the huge print of her in her green dress, that Jeremy took at the studio, admire her beauty, then slam my foot through and chuck the flapping detritus down the stairs with the rest.

Dad's desk is stuffed with manuscripts and papers, covered in his tiny, neat writing. In the end I keep only the original manuscript of the first of his popular physics books, *Unreal but Real: In a Million Places All At Once* – about the theories of multiple universes. It was an idea first mooted in 1952 by, of all people, good old Erwin Schrödinger, who posited that his equations described several different histories that were 'not alternatives, but all really happen simultaneously'. I have been struggling with the Schrödinger's cat conundrum of Mum both being killed by Dad and not being killed by Dad. But now I have multiple explanations all existing simultaneously.

The days tick by. My head is clear now that I'm not drinking. I sleep deeply at night and think furiously through the days, my mind zeroing in on one suspect, only to spiral off to another, then another. It is both credible and incredible that Reece, Marcus, Mr or Mrs Roberts are guilty. Did a single person kill both or was it some horrible family tag team? One day, when I'm so tense with my cascading clashing thoughts that I'm almost levitating off the ground, I find an axe and start hacking at my quince tree twin, which shakes its drying leaves with every thwack. The trunk is too solid to get through, so I just lop off some of the side branches till I exhaust myself.

But I can't nap, so I google quince, and find an entry entitled 'Calling All Quince Lovers', full of recipes. These lunatic 'lovers' who claim to enjoy quince jam are probably the same kind of people who also believe in star signs (bollocks), reiki (utter bollocks) and 'contacting the dearly departed' (aaaagh). Facebook's impenetrable algorithm has clocked that I've been searching for funeral dresses this week and has started offering me courses in contacting those on 'The Other Side'. *Da, Da, Daaaa.* I wish. I could just speed-dial Mum and Dad and ask them: 'Who killed you?' I post a message in the comments section for the course: 'It is impossible to contact the dead, as the dead are fucking dead, and there has never been a scintilla of proof that there is "another side", where Hitler floats around chatting with Florence Nightingale, till some living tit is deluded enough to pay £49.99 to learn how to get on the party line. How dare this course encourage the fleecing of the grief-stricken.' Which sets off an avalanche of responses deriding my sanity, my open-mindedness and my right to life. I spend an enlivening few hours arguing with these tossers.

Reece rings on Wednesday to say that the coroner has released Dad's body and issued the death certificate with cause of death recorded as 'heart failure'. No mention is made of the morphine. Perhaps as Dad was so old, they didn't do an autopsy, or perhaps such high doses of morphine in the terminally ill tip into the grey area of kind euthanasia?

'Hannah? Are you there? Do you?' Reece barks at me.
'Do I what?'
'Want to come to choose the casket with me?' he asks.
'Just go for the usual.'
'There is no "usual" – there's every kind of material and spec.'

'Spec?'

'Yep – materials, handles, decoration, padding.'

'Whatever you think.'

'A bin bag then,' he says.

'Your choice. But given the eye-watering fee you got for that pirate film last year, that might not play well in the press.'

We are both silent for a beat.

'You're being really strange, you know. I thought we were—'

'Dad just died,' I say bluntly.

'I know, I just thought that we – all right, I'll pick.'

'Good.'

'Do you want me to come over or do you want to come here?'

'Nah, you're all right,' I say, steeling myself not to be sucked in by his warmth, by my desperation to connect. 'When will the funeral be? We'll see each other then.'

'Well, not to sound too utilitarian about this, but I need to be on set next week at the latest, so is this Friday good for you?'

'But that's—'

'Yeah, I know – the fourth – the date Mum died. It's the only day the Finchley Crematorium has space at this short notice – at 3 p.m.'

'Same place as Mum was cremated, on the same date she was killed, and a Friday, the same day of the week she was killed?' I say incredulously. 'Bit frighteningly on the nose, isn't it?'

'You've always liked a pattern,' he says wryly.

'OK, sure.'

'I'll put the announcement in *The Times*. It'll just be us and the neighbours, I guess. It can be really short – I'll pick some music but if you think we need a speech, you should do it.'

'Dad would like just music,' I say, thinking of all his albums.

'Cool. And then – that'll be that.'

'Except for the wake of course, back at the house.'

'Do we really need that?' he asks, sounding put out.

'We definitely do,' I insist. 'I'll organise it. But you have to come. I want everyone there.'

'Well, OK, fine. I'll order a car to collect you.'

'No, I'll make my own way. The 102 bus takes me all the way.'

We are silent for a moment.

'Are you going to be OK at the funeral, Hannah? You sound really odd.'

'Absolutely. I'm looking forward to it.'

CHAPTER THIRTY-ONE

It's sunny with a crisp chill in the air. Perfect weather for a funeral. All the leaves in the wood are alight with intense oranges, reds and browns. Dad loved the trailing creeper on our back-garden trellis in the autumn, and today it's turned the gorgeous deep red it goes for only a few days each year, as if for him. I hoover, tidy and push back the furniture in the lounge for the wake later. The funeral attendees will be me and Reece, Mr and Mrs Roberts, and an unwilling Marcus. I insisted that he attend – told him that if he didn't, I would expose his actions to his parents.

I have a long bath using Mum's exotic oriental bath salts and for the last time ever, I become Mum. I put on her favourite 'little black dress', a short flapper frock of black satin, covered in tiny rows of black tassels, and it swings with my body's every move. I remember Dad's eyes following Mum as she danced round the living room, cocktail glass in hand, before they left for one of her photo exhibitions. I pull my hair back severely, pulling free two strands at the side, and top it with her black pillbox hat with its little black veil. The pins pull but I leave them in, braced by the pain. I look like a tense blonde Audrey Hepburn. I do my usual Mum make-up and add extra-heavy black lines round my eyes. Finally, I step up into her vertiginous black stilettos with the red soles and put my phone in her black satin clutch bag.

The Roberts have offered me a lift, but I enjoy sitting alone in the front seat on the top deck of the 102 bus as it trundles up through Finchley, past all the big houses and posh gardens. I check my dot on my phone map to know when to alight and see I'm approaching the crematorium. But Reece's dot has disappeared from the map. He must have found the app. Oops.

There is a smattering of press photographers at the gates, who I smile at from a distance while they can still snap me, but as I pass to the side of their long-range lenses, I mouth *fuck you*, at each of them. There's still a funeral going on in the chapel, so I wander round the back into the gardens. I'm perusing the wreaths, wandering awkwardly across the grass in my high heels, and remembering Mum's heels sinking into the grass at Feynman's funeral, when I catch sight of a dark-suited Mafia-Don-slash-gigolo in the distance. It's Reece, looking camera ready, impeccable in an exquisitely cut black suit, black shirt, narrow black tie and black handkerchief – with his hair stylishly trimmed and glistening. He smiles. With what looks like genuine warmth. But he's an actor. After murdering our parents, is he now playing the role of understanding brother, even down to the click of shared history in his glance? He steps forward to hug me, but I pat his arm and sidestep away.

'Good look,' he says, gesturing at my clothes. 'Dad would have liked it.'

'We'll never know.'

'No, of course.'

'No. I mean – we'll never know, because the lovely guy we're burning today, wasn't our dad.'

He blinks. 'Come on, Hannah. Isn't today hard enough.'

'I'm not being whimsically metaphorical. I'm being biologically precise.'

'I don't . . .'

'According to one of Mum's university mates, Dad was infertile.'

'What?'

'Your dad was one of her uni mates, according to her. My dad – no idea. But not that "Dad" we're saying goodbye to today.'

'That's just offensive gossip.'

'No, it's fact. I sent your, my and Dad's hair off for analysis. He's neither of ours – and we have different dads.'

'God,' he mutters, looking genuinely adrift.

I feel the glow of the afternoon sun burnishing my skin, but feel cold inside and push on.

'That "I'll never tell" that Dad said to you last week, wasn't about his deeds at all – it was about yours, wasn't it?'

'Not this again, Hannah.'

'I've listened to his intonation over and over – he meant he'd "never tell" about what you did. He clearly believed that you killed Mum.'

'That's insane. He killed her.'

'No – he didn't, Reece,' I shout at him.

A man in a long black coat by the chapel looks over at us with a frown. I lower my voice. 'Dad didn't kill her. He thought you did – that's what he meant by "I'll never tell".'

'But that can't—'

'Yes. He protected you all these years. He must have known or at least suspected that you weren't his son and yet he still protected you, let his career be destroyed, lost all his friends, even lost you – all to protect you.'

'But I didn't kill her – I promise on my life.'

I shake my head. 'How will I ever know when you're lying.'

'Because . . .'

'You lied to me for twenty-three years. You're bloody good at it. You've made a career of it.'

'Hannah, you have to believe me.'

'Why?'

'Because I'm your brother.'

'Half-brother. And a very good actor.'

'I didn't do it, I promise on Mum, on Dad, on Feynman and Schro.' His voice cracks. 'But if I didn't, and he didn't . . .'

'Indeed,' I say darkly.

The man in the long black coat is now motioning us to come inside.

'God, it's time, how can we—'

'We just do. Dad was still the man who brought us up, loved us, protected us. And it's only us and the Robertses – we can get through this.'

'No, there's way more people here than I expected – so I've prepared a few words – but I don't know if I can now.'

'Come on, it's a performance, you'll be fine.'

And for the first time in forever, I take his hand and lead him back to the front of the chapel. He seems so totally floored by what I've told him. But am I being played by a psychopath?

Mr and Mrs Roberts are loitering by the door in shabby black clothes, and next to them is a hunched, awkward Marcus, who doesn't look up.

'What's that fucker doing here?' whispers Reece.

'I insisted,' I say, putting a warning hand on his arm. 'Come on, we have to do this for Dad.'

'Christ,' he mumbles.

The Robertses walk into the chapel while we wait for the hearse. Reece, or some minion of his, has gone overboard on everything. A sleek glossy hearse pulls into the chapel forecourt, the photographers flashing away with their long lenses. Inside the polished glass compartment resides a top-of-the-range coffin in dark glossy wood with gold handles and gold entwined leaves running amok. It's nestled in a truck load of expensive-looking flowers and three huge wreath-letters spelling out D-A-D. Men in long black coats and satin top hats assemble at the back of the hearse in a well-drilled system. Reece joins them in hoisting the coffin onto their shoulders. They are all big men, but I see the way Reece takes the most weight, hefting the coffin up with his powerful arms. Arms strong enough to plunge a knife into a chest, shattering a rib?

And we're off. I follow behind, just as I did with Reece twenty-three years previously, for Mum. I'm taller, older, better turned out, but inside I'm the same child following my parent's coffin.

As we enter, I spot the curves of a wheelchair to my right and see Chris sitting there in a dark suit. He gives me an abrupt nod. I squeeze his shoulder as I pass.

The chapel is full – full of Dad's old colleagues from King's. They hadn't rejected him. He hid himself away after all the doubt and accusations but they didn't forget him. I bite down to control my emotions.

As the coffin travels down the aisle, sombre clichéd funeral music plays – like from a 'Funerals Greatest Hits' CD. Oh well done Reece, you put a lot of thought into that – what about all the music Dad loved? Once the coffin is in place, we sit down and Reece hovers at the front by a huge, purple-flowered wreath. He looks hesitant, but then smiles his winning smile at everyone as he pulls some scribbled notes out. This should be interesting.

'Thank you all for coming. My – father, Philip Davidson, was a physicist and teacher and it's wonderful to see so many of his colleagues here today. His popular books brought the wonders of science to many, opening up the subject to the layman—' Reece stops reading and puts his notes back in his pocket. 'Dad – my dad, was a devoted family man. He loved us all very much, more than I ever knew—' A single tear slides down his cheek. He's unable to go on.

I step up next to him and speak.

'We are both very grateful for you all coming to wish Dad farewell. I'd like to read something, hold on a sec.' I pull out my phone from Mum's clutch and search. 'Here it is. The Wikipedia entry – for the first law of thermodynamics.'

There is a ripple of amusement from the congregated scientists.

328

'The first law of thermodynamics is a version of the law of conservation of energy – which states that the total energy of an isolated system is constant; energy can be neither created nor destroyed. However, energy can change forms, and energy can flow from one place to another.' I lower the phone. 'Dad was a scientist through and through. He didn't hold with any idea of an afterlife, any other realm, but I' – I take hold of Reece's hand – 'we, take comfort in knowing that Dad's energy has not left us – it has merely been released into the world. Back with our mother Jennifer's energy.'

There is a sharp inhale of breath from somewhere. My eyes slide over Mr Roberts, Mrs Roberts and Marcus, and then rest on Reece.

He nods and we walk back to the pew.

'Thanks,' he whispers.

'I did it for Dad,' I say.

The awful funeral dirge music kicks in again. I race to the sound system, stopping the music mid dirge. Reece is walking towards me looking panicked.

'Dad lived in self-imposed exile for many years,' I announce to the congregation, fiddling with my phone. 'Now he's free and walking hand in hand in the park again.' I find my Dad-mix of his favourite songs, turn up the volume to maximum and press play. Guitar chords kick in, then drums and an 'Oi'. Most people look confused – but Reece smiles at me. Phil Daniels' cockney narration reverberates off the stone walls. Blur's 'Parklife', from one of Dad's favourite albums, plays as the coffin moves away from us. I remember him in those months before Mum's death, loving knowledge, loving music, loving us. Everyone's laughing and crying at the same time and the track covers the coffin's departure and the closure of the little red tasselled curtains.

We stand to file out as a clash of cymbals and strange blurts of sound emanate from my phone. It's the next track in my mix, synthesiser notes of the Who track 'Who Are You'. Guitars and drums kick in as Reece reaches to turn it off, but I pull it away and let the track play. I remember this so well from Dad playing it up in his office – but I know it even better from drunken compulsive series-watching because it's also the soundtrack for the US series *CSI: Crime Scene Investigation*. How appropriate for both Dad's farewell and as my theme tune.

I shake hands with Mr Roberts, Mrs Roberts, Marcus and finally Reece as Roger Daltrey sings.

Who are you?

CHAPTER THIRTY-TWO

I travel back to the house in Reece's sleek black limousine, trying not to inhale the rich, earthy stink of the stuffed leather seats. But the air is thick with more than the choking reek of tanned hide. Eventually, without looking at me, Reece breaks the deadlock. 'Found your little tracker app on my phone, Jane Bond.'

'I was frustrated with not being able to reach you.'

'But you've got my phone number, and we're OK now, aren't we?'

When I don't reply, he turns to me.

I shrug.

He tuts with disbelief.

'How are you in this car with me if you still think I'm a murderer? What if I snap?'

'The driver would be a witness, surely,' I reply evenly.

'Perhaps I'm beyond caring, driven to murderous rage by your accusations,' he says, turning away.

'Are you?' I say to the side of his closely shaved cheek as he stares out the window.

'I didn't kill Mum,' he mumbles.

'Why do you have that Rothko hanging in your lounge?' I ask quietly.

'What?' he blurts, swinging back to me.

'*Untitled 1970* – his final picture before he killed himself?'

He snorts.

'Are you suicidal – because you can't live with something you've done?'

He rolls his eyes. 'I find it – calming,' he says, fingering the tab on the armrest, 'to know that when I feel like exploding with the sucking, seizing awfulness of being me' – he takes a breath – 'there's a way out.'

'But you wouldn't ever take it?'

'Haven't done it yet,' he says, looking at me with his odd lopsided grin.

We stare at each other as the car pulls up outside our house.

The three Robertses are running back and forth between our two houses, stepping over the tiny dividing wall like giants, carrying huge platters of sandwiches, quiches and cakes. Marcus squints at our car with its tinted windows, not knowing that Reece is watching him.

'What's that fucker still doing here?' Reece says.

'Reece, please, I want everyone who knew Dad to be here for the wake. Do this one thing for me.'

He glowers at me and then bounds out of the car as I'm struggling to release my shiny black seat belt. I watch Reece shouting at Marcus and gesticulating. Finally, I release my belt and dash up the ramp as Reece smacks the tray of sandwiches that Marcus is holding, into the air.

'Fuck off,' shouts Reece.

'She insisted I stay,' Marcus is saying, motioning to me. 'I'm out of here.'

I catch his arm. 'No. You must stay for the whole wake. Both of you. Unless you want me to chat with your parents, Marcus, and you want me to talk to the press, Reece?'

'Fine, but keep the fucker away from me,' Reece says as he stomps into the house.

'Get on with serving,' I snarl at Marcus, who follows Reece.

Inside, the dining room table has the sides extended for the first time in twenty-three years and is covered with a bacchanalian feast of quiches, salads, sandwiches, salmon boats, crisps, dips, strawberry cake, shortbread biscuits, wine, beer and juices. There is a huge stack of plates and cutlery, which is a messy amalgamation of ours and next door's. Our families' cutlery intermingling, for one last party.

I watch Reece, now back in his groove, being the consummate host, engaging Dad's old friends in conversation. He is either amazing or demonic. I top up my glass of fizzy water.

'No heavy drinking?' asks Chris who has appeared at my side.

'I'm experimenting with not,' I say, lifting my glass.

'Heavy drinking is underrated. I'd be dead without it. Cheers,' he says, raising his own glass of wine, and we clink. 'How are you holding up?' he asks.

I shrug.

'I see you've been at it with the hair dye. Interesting move for someone who was appalled to be likened to their mother?'

'I'm – trying something.'

He frowns. 'Well, you were a hot brunette – but you're a hot blonde too.'

I laugh.

'I'm here if you need me,' he says, then rolls off to chat with Dad's friends.

'I see you've opened the back gate?' Reece says, passing me to get another drink.

'Yep, everything's wide open now,' I call after him.

The light is fading and I'm feeling light-headed as I haven't eaten all day.

Marcus is doing his best to serve drinks to Dad's doddery old colleagues. He reaches for another case of wine and lifts it onto the table like it's an empty box. Such physical strength – easy for him to plunge a knife into a chest, shattering a rib? He sees me approaching and spills red wine, which soaks into the white tablecloth.

'Which do you want?' he mumbles.

'Well, Hannah's usually red, but Mum's white – who do you see when you look at me?'

He clatters his bottle down, strides out into the garden and leaves through the gate. I turn back to the room and lock eyes with Mr Roberts. He swallows. I wave at him, blow him a kiss, the way Mum used to do, then I shoot off after Marcus, into the woods.

It's getting dark and with the full canopy cover I can barely make him out.

'Marcus, wait.'

He stops dead in his tracks but stays turned away from me. I circle round him to see tears pouring down his face.

'You look so like her,' he says. 'It's like she's back for vengeance.'

'For what you've done,' I say.

'I can never forgive myself. I knew it was wrong. I was Reece's best friend and I did that to him.'

'Never mind Reece – what about killing Mum.'

'Are you mad? I swear on my life that it wasn't me.'

'Then why did you break into ours again on the night Dad died?'

'I didn't.' He looks genuinely confused. 'I haven't been back since that night in the pub with you.'

'Hey!' There's a loud shout behind us. We both turn and it's Mr Roberts breathing heavily as he catches up to us.

'Stop this,' he shouts, looking wildly between us.

'Dad, go away,' says Marcus. 'This is something between Hannah and me.'

'No, you have to stop this,' he begs.

'What can you be talking about, Mr Roberts?' I ask, with heavy mock innocence.

'Please, Hannah, you promised,' mumbles Mr Roberts.

'Promised what?' asks Marcus.

'Don't,' begs Mr Roberts.

'Don't what?' says Marcus, looking between us. 'Does he know?'

'Know what?' demands Mr Roberts.

'You two have both told me secrets – but the price of hearing them would be to tell yours. It's a bit of a Mexican stand-off, isn't it.'

Neither speaks for a moment, then Mr Roberts steps towards Marcus.

'Marcus, you can't have anything to do with her.'

'Oh, come on,' I spit at him. 'You're actually jealous of your own son? I can't go out with Marcus, because I remind you too much of your lover – my mum.'

'What?' exclaims Marcus.

Mr Roberts punches the tree beside him, the force of his blow marking the bark. He's easily strong enough to plunge a knife into a chest, shattering a rib. He cradles his bloody fist as he raises his filmy eyes and gives a single nod.

'You fucker!' Marcus shouts at him.

'Yes, Marcus, exactly,' I say. 'Though you're hardly one to judge.'

He shakes his head at me wildly, but I wave him away. 'My mother was clearly a massive fan of Roberts men – you both slept with her.'

Mr Roberts turns towards Marcus. 'Marcus, that's not true?'

Marcus looks down.

'Oh my God.'

'There, both your big secrets are out. Though I must say – at least Marcus had the good grace to be repulsed by me because of my resemblance to his lover.'

'I—' blurts Marcus, but I raise my hand to cut him off.

'Don't bother, Marcus, I know revulsion when I see it. But you, Mr Roberts,' I say stepping right up to him. 'You can't stop looking at me, touching me, lusting after me, taking any chance to be alone with me – is that mere jealousy, or because you killed Mum and I'm her replacement?'

He blinks at me.

'You've got this all wrong.' He bends forward, letting out a slow moan. Marcus and I look at each other in panic. Then his arms drop, he straightens and he raises his head. He looks first at Marcus and then at me.

'I look at you,' he says gently, 'because you're my daughter.'

A rat runs between us then into the bushes.

I think back to all the times Mr Roberts has looked at me, smiled at me, helped me to carry things, worried about me . . .

'But you said – you said it happened when Reece had just started at secondary . . .' Of course – the best lies always have concrete details.

'It was a one-night stand. I was drunk and stupid.'

'She's my sister,' says Marcus, incredulously.

'Half-sister.'

'But she still could have been Philip's,' says Marcus desperately.

'No. My dad was probably infertile,' I say, slowly. 'And a DNA test proved he wasn't my dad.'

'Jen admitted it to me,' says Mr Roberts, 'but said she'd never tell anyone and I thought I could just bury it away.'

All that pervy interest I thought I saw from Mr Roberts dissolves and reassembles as concern – the concern of a father. I am his daughter.

Mr Roberts steps towards me, but I rear back.

'Don't,' I say darkly.

'I'm sorry, Hannah, I couldn't tell you. But when I thought you and Marcus were – I had to.'

'You're not my dad, you're just a sperm provider. I've buried my dad,' I say, tears pouring down my face. 'What a grubby little family you are. Fuck off, both of you. You're not welcome back at ours, either of you, ever again.'

I run away as fast as I can.

So much for shocking either of them into any revelation about Mum's murder. When will I ever learn that I can never hold all the cards? Just as I think I know something, I indulge in self-righteous anger and then I'm proved to be woefully ignorant, yet again. I keep thinking that despite a painful landing, I've survived.

But I'm only ever falling.

CHAPTER THIRTY-THREE

I wander in the woods till it's too dark to see where I'm going. When I finally enter by the gate, the house is streaming light into the garden but the rooms are almost empty. All Dad's old colleagues have gone. In the lounge, Reece is slumped in an armchair, glass in hand, and Chris is leafing through an old photo album. In the kitchen, Mrs Roberts is tidying up. I can see she's exhausted, struggling to lift a pile of plates. But I feel nothing. She's the last of the suspects. I burn like the white embers on one of Dad's autumn bonfires, fragile but still hot.

'Hello, dear, have you seen Frank and Marcus?' she asks me as I step into the kitchen from the garden.

'I don't think they'll be back,' I say menacingly.

'Oh?' she says, jolting at my tone. Her son and her husband both slept with Mum. Her husband fathered me. That's more than ample motive to cover up the identity of Mum's killer. And to kill Dad to keep the secret.

'They're upset,' I say.

She continues to scrape food from plates into the bin.

'Of course,' she says slowly. 'They both cared for your dad, we all did.'

'Really?' I snarl at her.

She blinks at me and wipes the back of her hand across her forehead, smudging it with cream.

'They didn't care for him that much,' I say quietly, advancing on her and wiping the cream from her face.

She smiles. 'I know this has all been a terrible strain—'

'They didn't care enough not to sleep with my mum.'

She seizes, fork freezing mid plate scrape.

'W-what?' she stammers, clunking the plate to the sideboard so hard that she chips the edge. 'What d'you mean?' The colour leaches from her face and she stumbles back and crumples onto a kitchen chair. I can see that this information is a total revelation to her.

'You didn't know?' I ask, stating what is blindingly obvious.

'I-I don't understand,' she mumbles.

I can't take my words back. I feel dirty and cruel as I look down at the woman I have just destroyed.

'What do you mean?' she asks tremulously. 'That Jen slept with Frank and – with Marcus?' She shakes her head, her mouth hanging open.

I have completed the work my mother started – I have destroyed this whole family irredeemably. I am truly my mother's daughter. No genetics test needed to prove that.

'Yes,' I say quietly. 'I'm sorry. You should go on home.'

'But I don't understand,' she says, staring at me.

'You need to talk to your family,' I say, trying to take

her arm as she struggles to her feet. She flinches away from me, looking at me blankly. I have broken her heart. Mum destroyed people in her wake – they were collateral damage. But I'm destroying people with intent.

Slowly Mrs Roberts turns, stumbles towards the front door and leaves.

This has been a grubby tale of male desire and control all along. Mr Roberts and Marcus cheating, Dad and Reece encouraging Mum's behaviour and then withholding evidence, all resulting in the suffering of the women of our two families: Mum was murdered, Mrs Roberts was cheated on, and I was ignored and stunted.

As I walk back into the lounge, Chris wheels over to me.

'Are you OK?' he asks.

'Sure. Why?'

'Sure. Why?' he parrots back at me gently, raising an eyebrow.

'Ah, you know,' I say. 'More "stuff". You've lasted well for someone who hates people.'

'Not all people,' he says, still looking at me with concern. 'Tell me. Remember I'm unshockable.'

'I . . .'

'All right?' says Reece, coming over. 'Ah, Detective Manning, still here? Well, life finally got Dad, when you couldn't.'

'Reece, don't,' I interject.

'It's fine, Hannah,' Chris says. 'I was never out to "get" your dad. Just uncover the truth.'

'Well, you failed abysmally,' says Reece, 'as has my "sister",' he adds, making air quotes with his fingers. 'But she's full of theories.'

'Truth is an elusive commodity,' says Chris cheerfully. 'Like juggling with water.'

'I think you should go,' says Reece.

'You're being rude,' I say.

'Oh, I think we're beyond polite niceties with Detective Manning. Should I call you a cab, Detective?'

'I'm fine, thanks.'

I wave Reece away and he walks back to the lounge.

'I'm sorry about my brother.'

'Look, I've got a cab waiting, but I can stay if you need me to?' he says, gesturing to the lounge.

'I'm fine,' I say, 'thanks for everything.'

'You know, I've accepted an offer on my parents' house.'

'Oh, wow. That's great. But I hope I didn't push you to do something you weren't ready to?'

'I was more than ready. And I wondered if you wanted to come flat-hunting with me some time?' he says shyly.

'Maybe, but I'm pretty busy for a bit.'

'You're not going to do anything risky are you?'

'Course not. Just packing up the house.'

'OK. Well, will you phone me tomorrow – let me know you're OK?'

I nod. I don't want to lie to him, but I know that flat-hunting with him is an impossible dream, and I won't be here to call him tomorrow. He starts to turn his chair, but I catch the armrest, bend down and kiss his cheek. As I pull away, he blinks at me in confusion, then turns slowly and leaves.

'Very chummy with the enemy,' Reece says to me as I turn back.

'Very hard to tell who is the enemy round here,' I say.

'Meaning?'

'Are you staying here tonight? Your old room's free.'

'In with my posters of Oasis? I don't think so.'

'Fine.'

'Well that's it then,' he says with finality.

'Yep, that's it.'

We stare at each other for a long moment, and then he leaves.

It'll do as a final goodbye.

I turn off the lights and step into the garden.

The sky is clear and the moon is full, just like the night Mum died, exactly twenty-three years ago today. The shadows of the trees are crystal clear, beckoning me to follow them. Mum's dead and burnt. Now Dad's dead and burnt. He died with me doubting him. I have destroyed the Robertses completely. I have finally severed the last vestiges of my tenuous relationship with Reece. Our pets are dead. The house will be sold. The truth will be hidden for ever.

I'm done. Finally, tonight, I will give myself to the woods. I bring up a photo of Reece's blood-red Rothko on my phone. He's right, there is an option when you can't bear your thoughts any more. I will walk into the woods and hang myself at the site of Mum's murder, with one of her scarves.

The white shafts of moonlight illuminate the messy remains of the wake in the house. Who cares if I tidy or leave the house contents to be chucked into landfill by the clearance firm – the house can be sold, gutted and converted into bland magnolia-painted flats. But my pattern-loving brain needs to impose my old forensic stationery-organising on the house before I go.

I walk back in and put on one light. It's eleven on the kitchen clock. I scrape the mush and detritus from the plates and stack them in the dishwasher. I handwash all the serving utensils and cutting boards. I rinse the cutlery and stack it upright to dry, forks together, knives together, spoons together. As I stack the final spoons, I feel released, lighter, I can let go. I tip the grimy water down the plughole – but realise that a single piece of cutlery was still hidden in the greasy murk.

I rinse it clean.

It's a small knife – heavy for its size, sharp, expensive, barely used – with an oriental-effect handle.

I think of the curling photo of the murder weapon that Chris showed me – much larger than this, but it's the identical handle. This knife is from the same set. And I've seen it before – it was the little photo from the frieze in the kitchen, that got removed. Somebody came into the house to remove that picture.

It's not one of our knives, so it must have come . . . from next door.

So, Mum's murderer was a tall, powerful man with access to next door: Mr Roberts, Marcus or Reece. And then one of them, or Mrs Roberts protecting one of them, killed Dad.

I sit very still.

Then I carefully create three separate identical messages – for Reece, Marcus and Mr Roberts:

I found a knife from the same set you used. Same time, same place, tonight?

The true murderer will know what I mean. It will mean

nothing to the others. My finger hovers over the green button – and then I press.

Send.

Send.

Send.

I have to look him in the eye. It doesn't matter what happens to me now. I pull on the green skirt and white blouse that I used for my recreation of Mum's last day with Reece and Dad. I strap on some high sandals like the gold ones Mum was wearing that day.

I've got about half an hour till the time of the murder.

Midnight.

Surely the murderer will still be up, tortured with guilt on the anniversary of his crime. I touch up my make-up, filling in my eye sockets with black, backcombing my hair wildly and painting on deep-red lipstick so roughly that my mouth is a bloody gash.

I check the messages.

Read.

Read.

Read.

CHAPTER THIRTY-FOUR

Tonight, the pattern completes.

At ten to twelve, I descend the creaky stairs of the empty house. I'm thirty-seven, the same age as Mum, when exactly twenty-three years ago, on this day, at this time, she walked out to these woods where she died. I am her doppelganger, thrumming with her cells, her look, her clothes, her scent. I walk through the French windows, push open the garden gate, and step through this portal to the past.

The wood is now pitch black. The tiny, eerie light from my phone torch barely stretches a few feet ahead of me. It's hard to walk in Mum's high strappy shoes and my ankle keeps turning on the uneven ground. But I persevere along the outer circle of pathway and then turn in towards the centre of the wood. The small oriental knife is gripped tightly in my right hand.

I hear a tiny, high-pitched squeaking. Bats. I know this sound so well from childhood and remember Dad telling me to enjoy it, as I would grow out of being able to – adults can't hear the frequency. But somehow, I can still hear them – perhaps because I stopped growing up at age fourteen.

My footsteps crackle on the forest floor as if I'm singeing the earth. Huge spectral trees rear up around me. Leaves rustle. A branch cracks nearby. I bristle with the sense of being watched and swing round to stare into the gloom. But if anyone's there, they're subsumed into the blackness. My mouth fills with saliva and my throat closes. Each step takes me further into the black void, as the forest sucks me in, pulling me forward and then closing off the path behind me.

I finally reach the corner of the children's playground fencing, feeling the hard cold of the metal railings with my left hand. I bounce my hand from railing to railing, making a metallic rhythmic clanging. There is a faint light from the perimeter of the woods, but only sheer blackness in the direction I must travel. Suddenly there are footsteps nearby. I freeze, holding my breath, but they've stopped. Perhaps it was just an echo of my own steps?

My phone goes dead, and with it my torch, plunging me into a silent black void. The blackness is so thick and all-enveloping that someone could be standing right next to me and I wouldn't know it – till they reached out and grabbed me.

But I can't go back now. I have to let go of the cold safety of the metal fence and step into the tarry gloom in the direction of the hornbeam tree. I inch forward, arms outstretched.

Something scrapes across my face and I fall forward

hard, rolling to try to avoid the next blow, and slam into a log. But nothing happens. I must have hit a branch. I lie still and hear an agonised cry. A fox? Or is it laughter? We used to joke that a yelping fox sounded like Mum laughing. I roll onto all fours and force myself back up. I'm disorientated but start inching forward again in the direction I fell. The canopy above me is thinning and I make out the silhouette of the double hornbeam ahead, with its skyward form and its low, grovelling twin.

I cross the last few feet and stop.

'I know you're there,' I call into the inky darkness. 'Come on. It's only me.'

The contorted scream of a fox cries out to my right and my head snaps towards it. Then a dazzlingly bright light shines straight at me from the left and I swing back towards it, shading my eyes to see who's holding it.

'And the mystery guest is . . .' I say.

The torch beam is snapped up to ghoulishly light up the face of—

'Me,' says Mrs Roberts with an apologetic grimace, her eyes huge and wild.

'But I didn't message you,' I say, shocked and confused. Surely the killer was a man?

'Frank sleeps like a log. Being a mum ruined my sleeping for good and now I'm tuned in to every cry – and every mobile bleep with a message about a knife. How did you find it?'

'Amongst the cutlery at the wake,' I say, lifting the blade as she manoeuvres her beam to light it.

'Of course – I shouldn't have let Marcus sort the cutlery,' she says with a sigh. 'I'd got rid of that stupid photo in your kitchen but I was silly to keep the remaining knife set, as a memento of her. Marcus was so desperate to do a good job for you that he must have unearthed that old knife block stacked at the back of the cupboard, with that one knife missing. I shoved it there that night – after the set became incomplete. Should've disposed of it years ago, but I'd only bought it recently, copying your mum's love of all things oriental.'

She has inched towards me, and I step back over the horizontal tree trunk so that it lies between us. I brandish my small blade at her. She swings the beam of light away from me and to her right hand, which is gripping a large kitchen knife.

'David only fells Goliath in a fairy tale,' she says.

'So you killed Mum? Why?'

'It was an accident – I promise,' she says, stepping forward and stabbing at me as I rear backwards. 'A single moment of hatred, in a lifetime of devotion.'

'Please let me go.'

'I can't,' she says desperately, 'you'll destroy us all.'

'No, I won't. Of course I won't.'

She is circling round the taller tree and I move anticlockwise away from her, glancing down at her knife and then returning to her wild eyes.

'But she was your best friend?'

'Yes, and I've missed her every day since. I hardly feel I'm me, even after all this time, without her to reflect myself off.'

She takes another few steps towards me and I circle away in unison.

'You know you really are quite like her, my dear,' she

says warmly, sweeping me up and down with the beam of her torch. 'It's like she's stayed young and beautiful, while I've got fat and old.' She takes a little run at me, but I swerve and circle around so we are now on opposite sides of the tree from where we started.

'But why would you kill your friend?'

'You don't think her stealing Frank and Marcus were enough reason?'

'So you knew – when I told you at the wake! You were – so believably destroyed.'

'I guess Reece isn't the only actor round here,' she says with an odd laugh, looking nothing like the woman I thought I had destroyed. 'But no, that wasn't why it happened. I could eventually have forgiven her for taking Marcus, even after I'd already given her Frank.'

'Given?'

'And given her you, too,' she says malevolently.

'You knew I was his? All the time I was in and out of yours? All the shared family events?'

'I suggested it,' she says, with a proud smile.

'What?'

'Oh, I didn't mean to. Jen was bleating on and on about how she couldn't get pregnant with your dad – no matter how much they tried.'

I wince.

'He was the rock that let her lead her wild life and she was terrified of losing him, thought another kid would seal the deal. One night, we were in her garden on those green loungers, both quite drunk on cocktails, Sex on the Beach, Slippery Nipples.'

She smiles, lost in the memory. I stay as still as I can,

but carefully edge off the back strap of my right shoe and imperceptibly lower myself down till I'm barefoot on the right.

'I'm not much for drinking,' she continues, 'but I went along with it all cos it made her happy. I joked "Oh God, you should try Frank, I got up the duff the very first time." It was just a flippant remark. But then he came back a few evenings later, when I'd been up at the church, reeking of that cloying perfume of hers, and a few weeks later she tells me she's pregnant and gives me that special smile. As if she'd followed my advice.'

'But how did you stay with him – go on living next door to us?' I ask, shifting my weight imperceptibly slowly, so that it's fully onto my right bare foot as I edge the left back strap off.

'Oh, I was beside myself, but I think she really believed I had given her permission. And in fact, in a funny way she saved my marriage. Frank and I were drifting, especially with the stress of my hysterectomy after Marcus. Frank decided for me while I was anaesthetised, and I woke up barren. We were heading for divorce, but after his "dalliance", he felt so guilty, it was like old times. Except that I couldn't have any more children. But she now had two she couldn't raise.'

I've managed to ease off my left shoe now, and I'm lowering my foot very slowly to the ground.

'Jen was an amazing person, but a truly terrible mother – with no intention of letting kids cramp her style – so I got to raise you two – you were my reward.'

'But wasn't I a constant reminder of how your husband had betrayed you?'

'Ah, you have such a childish view of life, my dear. Haven't you learnt that it's all compromises and priorities as an adult. I'm dowdy and plodding and always had to work really hard at life – but then Jen turned up, so glamorous and charismatic, everything came so easy. We were a great team. Yin and yang. We had an unspoken pact: I looked after the children, made the happy home; she led the exciting life and I got to bask in her energy. Until . . .' My hand tightens on my knife.

'Marcus.'

She nods. 'Reece told you finally?'

I nod.

'I put them through hell,' she says sadly. 'He and your dad both thought each other had killed her, and in protecting the other, never told what happened with Marcus – protecting me.'

'Marcus thinks you don't know.'

'He has no idea at all. Jen told me herself, came round near midnight, throwing stones at my window like she often did after a night out, so she could wind down with me. I didn't mind.' Mrs Roberts has that same glow I saw in Mary Stanton, another dowdy woman my glamorous mother entranced. 'But that night she was drunk and in a terrible state, gabbling about how this time she'd gone too far – didn't dare go home. She didn't even apologise, she was so caught up in her panic. "It was nothing, just a dalliance with Marcus," she said to me, "but then Phil and Reece came in and saw me and oh my God what am I gonna do, I know he's going to leave me this time." All her, her, her. You of all people should understand why I did it.'

I frown, and her eyes bulge as she raises her hands up

and then slams them down.

'Because I saw that I was nothing to her,' she shouts, the point of the knife now pressing into her thigh. I marvel at Mrs Roberts' shimmering fury – she is the physical manifestation of all my own pent-up despair and anger at being ignored by Mum. All this time I've focused on the effect that Mum had on the men in her life, when the most insidious, dangerous relationships were with women. I know only too well the highs of hero-worshipping Mum and the agonising lows sparked by her indifference.

'I'm not nothing,' she snarls, the knife cutting into her leg and blood blossoming on her skirt.

'Of course you're not . . .'

'So I slapped her – there in my kitchen.' She snorts. 'You should have seen her face – the utter disbelief that the worm had finally turned. Then she picked up my new kitchen knife and pointed it at herself. "I'm sorry Libs, you've got to forgive me, I hate myself," she bleated. But I knew it was all for show. Like her pathetic suicide attempt years before – everyone knows you have to cut upwards but she'd cut along, just to manipulate Phil, to get out of childcare and get back to her frivolous life without losing him. And now she was trying to manipulate me. Me! Her familiar. I knew her better than she knew herself. She thought she could manipulate me like she did every man in her life.'

She is rhythmically banging the knife at her thigh and the bleeding is getting worse.

'Please put the knife down, Mrs Roberts,' I beg.

She doesn't seem to hear me.

'Then she took off through the kitchen door and through the garden gate – and ran into these woods saying she was going to kill herself if I wouldn't forgive her. I should have let her. But I was so entrenched in my role of faithful servant, the gibbering, limping lackey, picking up after her, solving her problems. So, I followed her. It was dark, but it was easy to keep up with her because she kept tripping on her silly fuck-me-shoes. She kept hobbling on – to this tree. I come here sometimes, to talk to her.'

She runs her free hand up the smooth bark of the tall twin.

'Jen had that big oriental knife in both hands, pointing it at her chest. "Is this what you want?" she bleated at me. And in that moment, I knew that our special relationship was nothing to her. All of us were just toys. Not precious family to be nurtured and cared for. I wanted to get back to my home, to my family, Frank, Marcus, Reece – and you. I was walking past her without looking at her, and she bleated, "I'll kill myself, if you leave me, I'll do it". So, I turned and shoved her in the back.'

Mrs Roberts' eyes are wide but she's not seeing me. 'And she gave a little scream and fell forward.'

Of course – that's how the high angle and force happened. Not a tall man stabbing from a height, but a small, bitter woman pushing out all her rage and impotence at her best friend – and gravity.

'I thought she was faking,' she says, with childlike wonder, 'told her to stop it. But she stayed so still. I used my foot to roll her over and could see immediately that she was dead. She'd been holding the knife to her chest when she fell. She looked like a doll, her eyes so wide, her long blonde hair spread out around her. I didn't mean it. I would never have hurt her on purpose. She was the other half of me.'

I'm nodding at her while very slowly using my right foot to sweep the gritty soil and sticks at my feet into a little pile, never looking down as she goes on.

'I waited for ages, willing her to breathe on me, staring into her beautiful eyes for the merest fleck of life. But she was gone. So finally, I left her there, staring blankly up at the forest.'

Mrs Roberts looks up at the trees above us. I look up too, but when I lower my gaze, she's looking directly at me. She's back here with me now, totally focused.

'It was a moment of madness, understandable madness,' I say gently.

She frowns. 'You're trying to be her, aren't you, the hair, the clothes – and I saw you sneaking off this afternoon with Marcus and Frank – trying to take them too.'

'No, we were just talking. I'm not like her,' I say desperately.

Mrs Roberts gives a strangled yelp. 'Of course you're not! You're a pale imitation. It's been agony these last few weeks watching you trying to transform into her. Jen died that night – in a terrible accident. I've been trying so hard to do the least harm and protect everyone. But now you've given me no choice. I have to kill you too. Like I had to kill Philip. Finally.'

'Finally?' I whisper.

'I pushed him down the stairs two weeks ago, thought I'd killed him.'

'You?'

'After that, I was going to let nature take its course, but you wouldn't stop trawling his memories – so I had to try again.'

'That was you in the dark.'

She nods sadly. 'It was really unnerving when you thought I was Jen. You shouldn't have been awake at all, my dear. I'd crushed up sleeping tablets in the hot milk and the cookies. Your dad wouldn't eat much – but you always loved my biscuits, so I thought you'd eat enough to knock you out all night. You gave me such a shock when I saw you coming down the stairs. It was almost like Jen had come back to life.'

I had eaten half a biscuit. So that's why I felt so strange and other-worldly.

'You were there in the house the whole time?'

'Yes, I checked you were OK and then I waited in the kitchen to check you were fully out, but as the kitchen door clicked open, you woke up again. Thankfully you were pretty groggy, didn't recognise me, and once you'd finally passed out next to him, I forced the tablets into his mouth.'

'But how did you know where the key for the pill safe was?'

'Your parents always kept important stuff behind that clock. You're your mother's daughter.' She falters and stares at me with wild eyes. 'I had no choice. Don't you see? I went over and over it all, and in the end I decided the only and kindest way I could shut everything down for good was to ease Philip's passing and leave evidence that would get you prosecuted – only prosecuted, and I would have visited you in prison. But even with all the evidence – the laced cookies, the empty pill packets, and your dad's high level of morphine – there was no investigation and some lazy coroner just let it slide. I thought maybe it was for the best then, and was going to leave you be, but when you sent that silly little text to Frank you gave me no choice.'

'But I hadn't worked out the truth – not about you.'

I fake a slight trip and push myself back up, after my left hand has closed over the little pile of dirt, which I hold tightly in my fist.

'You had all the pieces – you would have put them together eventually.'

'I promise I won't tell.'

'I brought you up, Hannah dear – I know you inside out – you think in black and white, in patterns and systems. Everything has to be neat and sorted. Your favourite game was always an organising game. And you were always the squealer. You'll crack.'

'But your DNA will be all over me.'

'So? This is a knife I took from your kitchen on the way here. I'll say that you confessed to your father's murder because he admitted killing Jen, and I was trying to stop you killing yourself but you were too strong for me. Everyone's seen how confused you've been over these last months. Your brother told me how worried he is about you at the wake. It'll all make sense.'

'Please, Libbie.'

'Finally! Now you call me that without hesitation? Oh this is unbearable,' she cries, tears cascading down her cheeks. 'But I have no choice – Frank, Marcus and Reece would be destroyed by my conviction, and they need me.'

'What about me?'

She takes a breath and settles into an eerie calm. 'I have to protect the greatest number. I'm so sorry.'

Like a starting pistol's been fired, she races round the tree and straight at me, knife raised.

CHAPTER THIRTY-FIVE

This is the standing-start jump of my life. I rock fractionally back, filling my lungs, bend my knees and engage every muscle to propel myself upwards. I'm swivelling mid-air as she circles the reclining tree and I land on it, dead centre, facing her as she's barrelling towards me, her knife just inches away. I kick out violently at her chest and chuck the gravel I've collected. Before she hits the ground, I'm off, sprinting straight into the darkest part of the woods, where there's no pathway, but which I know inside out from childhood. I run for thirty seconds, swerving and stumbling, my face thwacked by branches, my bare feet stubbed by roots, appalled by the cacophony I'm making thundering through the undergrowth. Then I launch myself directly into a patch of thick foliage, grazing my palms and slicing my face – and freeze.

My lungs beg to suck in air, but I seize like I trained myself to do all those years ago in the feet-tickling game. I separate my brain from the excruciating sensation. I watch my body's needs, but I am not them. I can hear her trudging to my right, breathing heavily. A grid of the wood and all its undulations and obstacles kicks into my consciousness from all our old racing and hide-and-seek. I tune in to her breath and calculate her position, her distance from me, and what's between us. She's too close. Her pleated skirts and M&S cardigans have lulled me into underestimating her fitness. Arcs of torchlight get closer and closer.

'Hannah,' she calls.

I'm letting out little puffs of breath as I pad my hands along the ground. It's all bracken, brambles and dirt. I ignore the sharp stings of a patch of nettles across my forearms. This husk is not me. I notice the pain, but I am not it. Then my right hand closes over a rock. I rotate my palm and weigh it silently. As the beam of light circles its furthest away from me, I throw the rock in the diametrically opposite direction to which I need to travel. It lands with a heavy thud, and the nanosecond I hear her dart, I lever myself up and scurry back onto the path, where I'll be faster. I feel the shift of the ground beneath me from uneven undergrowth to gritty pathway. But the regular beat of my bare shredded feet is syncopated with other footsteps. I daren't look back, but she isn't far behind. No point in silence now. I keep pounding along, screaming as loudly as I can.

'Help! I'm in the woods. Help!'

As the silhouette of the houses overlooking the outer path rises into view, I veer off the pathway and cut direct through the undergrowth again. I'm so close to where I could be heard, could be saved, when I'm smacked in the back with incredible force and fall headlong onto prickly ground. I roll onto my back and see her dark form towering over me, her face contorted, her knife raised.

'I'm so sorry,' she murmurs then launches herself onto me, her knife stabbing down at my chest. And it's like she's one of Mum's falling photos: she's in the air, her knife gripped in both fists, her hair flying out. But she isn't free in the air, she's the prisoner of it – she can't change direction, as she has no leverage. Falling isn't always freedom. I'm below her, earthbound, vulnerable – but I have the ground to push off. I lever myself with my right hand, so I manage to half turn to the left, out of her path. But I leave my right arm outstretched and twist my hand to raise my little knife, so it's pointing straight up at her.

Her knife slices down, straight through my forearm, skewering my arm to the ground. My mind blanks against the pain as my little knife punctures her chest. She gives a small cry, her body jerking taut – and then she deflates. My arm is impaled on the ground beneath her body. She is impaled on my knife.

Then she slowly turns her face towards me, her nose scraping the dirt. Her eyes are startled, like a wary deer. She takes a little breath, and quietly whispers to me.

'I'm so proud of you.'

I maintain eye contact, as I watch the life drain out of her and then her eyes become glassy and fixed.

I am alone, in the dark, trapped. The wood rustles around me. Her knife has stabbed straight through my forearm and is secured there by the weight of her body. I try to use my other arm to push at her. But moving my good arm makes my pierced arm flame in agony. I lurch into fainting and roll back, till the dizziness passes. She's far too heavy to shift. I am pinned here like a butterfly in a case. My phone is dead. Even if Mrs Roberts has one, I can't reach under her for it.

'Help,' I shout weakly, but it's hopeless. I know exactly how far sound travels in these woods and I'm a good five feet off hope. As my breathing quietens, I realise that Mrs Roberts' face is glowing. Except it's not, it's lit by something. I register her torch on the ground above my head. Just out of reach. I slowly inch my left arm out, crying as the knife pulls at the flesh in my right arm and a fresh wave of nausea hits me. I will have to rip open my right arm to reach the torch, I have no choice. Die here slowly for definite or risk dying fast, to try to live.

I think of Reece, Dad, Marcus, Mr Roberts, even Mrs Roberts, all of them in their own way trying to protect each other, too scared to ever take action. I think of Dad and his beloved Spurs motto, 'To Dare is to Do'; of Reece's stupid TV catchphrase 'Nothing ventured'; and of Boadicea's 'Win or perish'. I plant my feet in the dirt and push off them, lurching my body up, and feel the flesh and muscle of my right arm ripping apart.

I come round after blacking out for a moment and close my left hand on the torch. My right hand is still skewered, trapped under Mrs Roberts, but the discrete puncture is now torn open right along the length of my forearm and I must be bleeding copiously. I will lose consciousness for good soon. I swing the torch beam towards the rear windows of the distant houses and balance the torch firmly on the ground. I cover the beam with my hand and then release rhythmically. *Tee-hee-hee, Oh my God, Tee-hee-hee.* Short, short, short, long, long, long, short,

short, short. SOS. Over and over, time stretching and folding like gooey marshmallow.

My stabbed right arm is numbing, marinating in the thick soup of Mrs Roberts' and my blood draining and mingling into the forest floor. My left hand tingles and feels oddly bloated as my fingers cease to function for good. Of course, my silly little SOS message didn't reach anyone.

But it doesn't matter.

I've thought of myself as the victim in all this, all along: poor me, poor little sad girl scarred by tragedy and loss, so shocked to find that in adulthood, I resembled my awful mum. I've been justifying dyeing my hair, donning her clothes, dabbing on her Chanel, to fully embody her, distasteful though I told myself it was. Because I had to do it, to find out what happened – didn't I?

Stop lying, Hannah. One moment of truth before you die. I grin up at the tall trees moving above me in the breeze, beckoning.

I've loved being Mum. That shivering thrill of stepping into her legs and body like a wetsuit, the surge of excitement as I've rolled her body up over my arms and shoulders, the thrill of stretching my fingertips deep into her gloves and the explosion of pleasure as I finally pulled on her hood, slid down her mask and saw everyone's reaction to me through her eyes. She was a liar, a cheat, and a bitch – and I don't care. I've finally killed off my stupid, lumpen, worthless self. I've been admired like her, desired like her, and have experienced her power over men, over women . . . and over the old me.

I am Jen.

My body's limp and weightless. My breathing's short.

My eyelids flutter. Now that I'm whole, I can give in, take a final breath and let the dark woods claim their prize.

But as I feel the world receding, I take a sudden sharp breath as my back arches, my head jerks back and my eyes splay wide. Of course. Now I get it.

My body jerks in a violent spasm and I let out a howl – as I feel Mum leaving me for good.

My twisted, straining frame shudders at the height of its arch, then as though a pin is pulled, my bones cascade back to the ground.

I've had to fully become Mum . . . to let her go.

My head lands on its side, my cheek smearing the dusty ground, my vision fading. I stare in the direction of the discarded torch beam: towards the silhouette of our family home – and remember when we were a family. I feel rocks and twigs poking into my back, like Reece prodding at me in one of our games. I smell the fusty bracken and moist bark of this glorious forest all around me. I think of Mum's falling photos – of her telling me of the moment in between – 'Nothing above, nothing below, free.'

And as I take a final breath of cool night air, in this last moment, I am wholly me.

I am Hannah.

I hiccup a tiny snort of laughter, as blackness overtakes me.

CHAPTER THIRTY-SIX

My eyes flicker open to a blinding brightness. Stuccoed white tiles and long strip lights come into focus above me. I'm back at the hospital with Dad again, for another day of Feynman and badminton racquets.

But with the fingertips of my left hand I feel the stiff weave of clean, starchy sheets. My right hand feels oddly disconnected from me – and when I twist my head painfully, I see that it's bandaged into a massive white club and I'm attached to a snaking IV drip.

I'm in hospital, but I'm not the visitor – I'm the patient.

As I try to move my club hand, a jagged pain engulfs me.

'Agh.'

'Hannah?' says Chris's voice.

'Oww,' I say, rolling my head towards him.

'It lives,' he says, peering at me with a nervous half-smile, 'better warn the villagers.'

We lock eyes and I smile back.

'I'm not dead then,' I croak.

'Jeez, if this is the afterlife, what a swizz.'

I start to laugh, then wince in pain.

'Take it easy,' he says, pulling in his chair so that his face is close to mine. 'You gave us a scare,' he adds hoarsely.

We stare at each other and he leans further in so our foreheads touch.

'Thank God you're OK,' he whispers.

We stay like that in silence for a moment and then he straightens up.

'That promise you made me not to do anything risky was worth shit,' he says.

I grin. 'What time is it?'

'Ten past eleven,' he says, glancing at his watch. 'They operated on you early this morning and you've been asleep since.'

'How – did I get here?'

'Ah well, that's a right old story, that I wouldn't have believed if I hadn't heard it from the horse's mouth. And by horse, I mean Reece. He said that he got a bizarre message from you, came to your dad's house and through the landing window, saw some Boy Scout Morse code in the woods.'

'Tee-hee-hee, Oh my God, Tee-hee-hee,' I whisper, my eyes filling with tears.

'Yes, you should cry – it's so Netflix Original,' he says, wiping my eyes with a tissue. 'It's lucky he knew those woods so well. He found you passed out under Mrs Roberts, skewered to the ground. She'd stabbed near a major artery, and your arm was horribly ripped open. You'd lost lots of blood. The doctors say he got to you just in the nick of time.'

'And her?'

'Dead,' he says matter-of-factly. 'The police have questions for you, when you're able.'

I nod. 'How are you here?'

'You said you'd ring me this morning and when you didn't, I knew that the only possible logical explanation was that you were near death.'

I smile.

'So I rang Reece and discovered I was in fact, correct.'

'Where is Reece?'

'In the cafe with his girlfriend.'

'Girlfriend?'

'Some scary ice-queen woman.'

'Now is that a compliment or an insult,' says Anastasia, with a raised eyebrow as she walks over, next to an exhausted-looking Reece, both of them carrying styrofoam cups.

'Barbed compliment?' suggests Chris, grinning.

Anastasia play-punches his shoulder.

'God, Hannah, bloody Morse code,' says Reece. 'It was like I was actually in an episode of my stupid TV show!'

'I gather you saved me,' I say quietly.

'Yeah, well, you know,' he replies. 'I got that weird message from you and knew you were up to something. The house was empty – but then I saw this blinking light in the woods – and blow me if it wasn't that old SOS that Dad taught us.'

I nod.

'What did the knife comment mean?' he asks.

'Mrs Roberts killed Mum with a knife from a kitchen

set she still had hidden away. And Marcus unwittingly put another from the set out at the wake.'

'Ha,' he says darkly, '"it's always the little things" – as my character Detective Pennington said in Episode 1 of the very first series of *Muerte*,' he adds triumphantly to Anastasia. 'Yet according to the *Guardian* reviewer, that was: "clichéd dialogue".'

'She intercepted the message meant for Mr Roberts and knew I was getting close, so she came to silence me.'

'You still thought it could have been me?' he says, tersely.

'You, Marcus or Mr Roberts.'

He nods and swallows.

'Of course she did,' intervenes Anastasia in an upbeat tone, 'it was a logical possibility. Sensible girl – covering all the bases.'

She smiles at me and I smile back.

'Sorry, I have to get back to the office. You'll be all right?' she asks Reece, putting a hand on his shoulder, and he nods. 'I'm glad you're OK,' she says to me gently.

As she walks away, I raise my eyebrows at Reece who blinks back at me.

'You and her?'

He nods, looking like the teenager I remember.

'How long?'

'Couple of years.'

'But all those girls you're posed with in the papers?'

'Just for show.'

'We don't really know that much about each other any more, do we,' I say.

He swallows and our eyes click. I see him in shorts on a school sports day, his face smeared with mud in our woodland hideaway, and in the shadows as we munched Curly Wurlys.

'We know some,' he says quietly. 'Sorry to spring her on you – I was a bit in shock after last night and she came to help.'

'I'm still in shock that you came to see if I was OK,' I say. He gives me an odd look.

'What?' I ask.

'I was fast asleep when you messaged me. Heard nothing. But I was having this dream – about Mum running through the woods. It woke me up – without it I wouldn't have seen your message.'

'Or it was merely that the synapses in your brain were firing as you tried to resolve your rational sense of uneasiness?' says Chris.

'You were unnerved enough to check on her this morning,' says Reece.

'Yes – deductive reasoning,' says Chris, 'not spirits beckoning!'

'Mrs Roberts said that it was an angry push, she didn't kill Mum on purpose,' I say.

'But she was trying to kill you on purpose,' says Chris.

'Yeah.' I belch out a big sob and my body undulates with the waves of pain.

Chris puts his hand on my shoulder and holds it there till my crying subsides.

'You can tell us all the details later,' he says gently. 'Come on now. You've been some kind of Sherlock Holmes/Bear Grylls combo so far. Keep it together for the credits.'

Two months later, Reece flies back from filming in Spain, for dinner on my final night in the house. He arrives with the hood of a massive parka pulled low over his face, even though the press stopped camping outside ages ago. I've had my hair cut into a short, messy pixie bob and dyed it back to my natural brown. I'm still in jeans, but new ones that stay up without a belt, topped with a white embroidered peasant shirt with trailing red tassels that wild horses couldn't have dragged Mum into.

We're eating at the kitchen table with the doors to the garden closed on this cold December evening. The trees behind the garden wall have entirely shed their thick foliage. They leer less confidently at us than in the full throttle of their summer malevolence. I won't miss them.

'Thanks for coming back for this, brother dear.'

'Half-brother,' Reece reminds me.

'Yes, sadly I do still share some of your genetics. Still can't have everything.'

He makes a face.

We are awkward together, but he's here.

'Have you spoken to – your real dad,' he asks tentatively.

I shake my head. 'Maybe one day. But while I've been sorting the house, I've only wanted to think about Philip. Will you try to find out yours?'

'Philip was my true father, in all but biology – I don't need another one,' he says quietly.

'The press certainly love our convoluted little family,' I say, referring to the multi-page coverage that Mrs Roberts' death received, as all our sordid family laundry was aired. Dad was finally exonerated, though without any apology for the previous accusations. And Reece is a swashbuckling national hero. The newspaper headline read *Detective Pennington Saves the Day*, and he's had a huge advance for an updated warts-and-all autobiography.

'Stasia called today to say that *Muerte* has already been commissioned for two more bloody series after the one we're filming, now I'm so box office. Still, at least it'll keep me out of the country for a couple of years. I'm buying a villa out in Torremolinos. Though I'm not sure why anyone chooses to live there, given the stratospherically high incidence of murder that I have to solve on a weekly basis.'

I laugh.

'You could come out for Christmas,' he adds.

I shake my head. 'I'll be spending it with Chris,' I say, trying not to blush, and failing.

'Oh, right, as in—?'

I nod.

'Wow, good for you. How—'

'I took one look at his squirrelly face and I knew.'

He smiles, recognising the line from his show.

'How does he feel about dating a criminal?' he asks with a smirk.

'He has impressively poor morals.'

'Excellent. You could both come?'

'Yeah, once we've got ourselves properly settled in Brighton.'

I touch my neck and feel the outline of my stone hanging on my Dolores necklace, the one I took from Brighton beach after the fire. I've kept it over my heart through these awful few months, but soon I can return it. I'm going back to a place, but forwards in life.

'We've found a little house that looks out over the sea, so I can swim every day. Not a wood in sight.'

'You should meet Stasia properly soon – she's a good

person, you know. She was just protecting me.'

'I know. I'm glad you've got her.'

He nods. 'You managed to clear everything then,' he says, looking back into the empty house.

'I didn't use your clearing company in the end. I've spent the last two months sending everything off to charity shops and using charity take-away services and Freecycle. And all the photography equipment went to a local youth scheme.'

'Good.' He looks to the ground. 'And the photos?' he asks, quietly.

'Destroyed some of them.'

He gives a tiny nod.

'But I've kept some family ones for us both.'

'Thanks.'

'And some of her.'

He swallows.

'She wasn't who I thought she was, not at all,' I say. 'She had a whole life separate from being our mother and she let us down. But – there are buts. But – parents are allowed to have separate lives to their children. But – Mr Roberts and Marcus were equally to blame in the affairs. And – she didn't deserve what happened.'

'But – do you hate her?' asks Reece.

'I don't. She was the ultimate girl with the little curl.'

He raises his eyebrows, remembering the rhyme Mum used to repeat to us in her sing-song voice, on the occasional time she tucked us in when we were little.

'There was a little girl, who had a little curl, right in the middle of her forehead,' he says, but falters, so I finish it for him.

'When she was good, she was very very good, but when

she was bad she was – horrid.'

'I'm sorry – about everything,' he says.

I smile.

The corner of his mouth twists too, but the smile doesn't light up his face.

'How do you do that, just smile with your mouth and so asymmetrically? I know your fans love the whole moody thing, but you never used to do that?'

'Botox.'

'Nooo.'

'Yep. Slightly more on this side – it was a mistake the first time, but it got so many positive comments I kept it up. Rest of my face is dead from here up,' he says, gesturing.

A laugh burbles up out of me and we snigger together, my face creasing much more than his.

The air is full of the aromatic smell of simmering quince. The day after I got back from the hospital, I harvested the quince crop in Mum's old basket, stacked it in the kitchen cupboard in ordered yellow rows, and the whole house hummed with the citric milky aroma it used to have when Mum did this. Then I started cooking with them, taking time to be in the process, experimenting with Mum's old jam recipe and finding all sorts of new uses. And I stewed and bottled all the remaining quince fruit before they rotted.

Now it's December, the quince tree is a mere bundle of sticks, waiting for spring. One solitary blackened, shrivelled quince had clung to one of the top branches till today. But this morning I watched an acrobatic squirrel balancing at the top and pulling it off. Even masochistic me might have balked at eating that rotted lump.

Reece and I have just enjoyed a dinner of pork and

Marsala, topped with baked quince which had been basted with butter, lemon and sugar, the sweet slow-roasted pork perfectly complimented by the velvety-soft stewed quince slick with its sweet, aromatic syrup. Now I serve a moist granular cake of quince, almond and orange, with a bowl of pink quince-infused cream, alongside a plate of strong cheeses with tart, sticky quince pickle.

'That bloody tree sat in our garden all these years and we never knew that boring old quince could be so fantastic,' says Reece, eating a huge bite of the sticky, satisfying cake and licking the scented cream from his lips. 'That was an amazing meal, thanks. I'll have to run for miles to work it off.'

'Quince ginger and bay cordial now,' I announce as I pour a cloudy pink liquid into two champagne flutes. 'To toast – Feynman and Schro.'

'You're totally quince mad. When you do something, you're so obsessive,' he says as I pass him a glass of the pink opaque liquid. 'Which is just as well,' he adds. 'To Feynman and Schro.'

We clink the tall glasses.

'Nothing ventured,' he laughs and we sip.

Simultaneously we widen our eyes at each other, then he reaches for the door, falls out into the garden and violently spits the contents out onto the patio. I spit mine into the sink. I hadn't tested it in my flurry of quince cooking.

'That is truly foul,' laughs Reece as I join him outside.

'Like watered-down, off perfume,' I say as I chuck the whole jug into the bushes.

'Like that awful perfume you used to make from pulverising rose petals. You were always trying it on me.

How old were you? Six? Seven?'

'Something like that,' I say, transported back to a vivid recollection of me trying to wipe my brown, cloudy rose petal mixture onto the arched neck of my fast-growing brother, on a lazy family afternoon here in this garden. I would never have thought about that but for this sensory key to the memory.

I watch my famous brother as he lollops back into the kitchen to bring us big glasses of water, to wash away the fetid taste of the cordial.

My eyes settle on the pets' graves.

'The vet said that Dad murdered Feynman?' I call back to him.

'Mum said that?' he calls back.

'Yep.'

'No,' he says as he returns with the water. 'I was there. Feynman was dying, straining in agony, Dad couldn't bear it, so he held his favourite blanket over him for a couple of seconds to put him out of his misery. Mum exaggerated for an audience as usual. Ooh it's cold out here, let's go in.'

'No, let's stay a little longer. Say a last goodbye to the garden.'

'All right, I'll get our coats,' he says, darting back in.

I choose to believe Reece's version, not the vet's skewed one from Mum. I can never know the complete 'truth' of the past, but I've learnt from Dad that memory isn't linear and passive – it jumps about, it remembers and forgets, it rewrites. I can't relax with the Reece of my linear memories, can't trust him, or imagine any future relationship with him. But this Reece is a shifting thing, an amalgam of my disparate memories, new versions of old memories, absences, miscommunications, withholdings, revelations and new tentative connections. Like Dad grasping for safety with all his repetitions, I will keep trying to coalesce my incomplete, one-sided, rewritten and re-interpreted memories of Reece with the new memories I will hopefully add – and see if a new relationship is possible.

I've watched lots of Reece on screen while I've been recuperating: as a serial killer, as a foppish Regency love interest and as the leader of a mutant alien race intent on overthrowing the planet. He slips into all these different roles with ease but I realise that's only partly his skill; the role succeeds to the extent to which the audience chooses to find him credible, how much imagination they apply. So, for me, accepting Reece as a caring brother is partly about what he portrays to me, but also what I let myself believe of him.

There is no going back with us. But there may be a going forward.

'Well, no more quince from tomorrow,' Reece says, as he brings out coats.

'Na-aa. I've taken a quince cutting, to plant in our Brighton garden,' I say, as we pull on our coats. 'I've realised quince has its uses.'

He shrugs and sprawls back in one of the rusty green garden chairs. I sit down beside him, my right arm on the armrest, lying alongside his left arm. He unfurls his index finger and taps four short dots onto my hand. I smile and tap dot-dash-dot on his. I pull up my sleeve and motion for him to do the same. We both look down at our arms. The vivid red of my puckered scar running down my forearm lies parallel with the thinner, longer ridge on his.

'Hey look,' I say, 'matching scars.'

He snorts.

I close my eyes and my eyelids glow red under the light spilling from the kitchen. We loll peacefully side by side. Just like we used to do here many years ago, under the flickering sunlight on lazy afternoons, when we were kids.

ACKNOWLEDGEMENTS

Huge thanks to my wonderful agent Madeleine Milburn for her belief in me and my book. Also thanks to agent Liv Maidment for all her support and to everyone at the Madeleine Milburn Literary, TV & Film Agency, especially to Liane-Louise Smith, Georgina Simmonds, and Valentina Paulmichl in international rights and to in-house editor Georgia McVeigh and to Rachel Yeoh.

Thanks to everyone at my UK publishers Allison & Busby – especially my publisher Susie Dunlop, my editor Lesley Crooks, and to Claire Browne and Sara Magness.

Thanks for the marvellous artwork by Christina Griffiths, to my publicist Helen Richardson, and thanks to Christina Storey and Daniel Scott.

Thanks also to my website designers, Naomi Adams and Faith Tilleray, and photographer Ben Wilkin.

Massive thanks to Jon Appleton, Kay Holmes, Wendy

Lee and Anna Jean Hughes – who all gave me invaluable notes and encouragement with earlier drafts.

Huge thanks to my Fab writing group from my Faber Novel Writing Course: Jo McGrath, Katherine Tansley, Marija Maher-Diffenthal and Sarah Lawton – all very gifted writers – who gave me such brilliant advice and suggestions throughout the whole process of writing this book. And our weekly zooms throughout lockdown helped me in so many ways.

Thanks to all the other writers I've met along the way on the various writing courses I've done, and especially to the wonderful tutors: Martina Evans and Neil Fergusson whose writing courses I did many years ago at The City Lit; Joanna Briscoe at the Faber Six Month Writing Course 2019; the organisers of NaNoWriMo 2019 where I wrote most of the book; Anna Davis and Erin Kelly (and Anna Freeman's report) from the various excellent short online courses I did with Curtis Brown; Kirsten Martin's inspiring videos; and the wonderful Sophie Hannah's Dream Author Course.

Thanks to Alex Olive for his stories of childhood in Highgate Woods during our walk there; to Rebecca Harrison for her fascinating City of London organised tour of Highgate Woods; to my uplifting Lithuanian friend Loreta Bugiene; to Dr Berry Beaumont for her advice; to playwright Charlotte Jones who told me about sea swimming in Brighton; to Camilla Sacre-Dallerup for her inspirational book launch at Foyles; to the Estate Agent from Prickett and Ellis who showed me round a house backing on to Highgate Woods; to Martine Paulmier for the lovely meals in her breathtaking lounge; to Scott Newman for his bright handyman cards and vans; to my old voice agent Sue Terry for the inspiration of her old office building; to Sue Cowan-Jenssen for all her kindness; to poet and playwright Claudine Toutoungi for her friendship and inspiration; to my brother and sister who are nothing like the characters in this book but who I loved growing up with; to all the staff and writers I worked with at BBC Radio Drama, from whom I've learnt so much, and to all the tireless wonderful staff at UCH hospital I met when visiting.

And finally, thanks to my husband Andy and son Archie, for all their love, unstinting support and endless encouragement.

Liz Webb originally trained as a classical dancer, but after a back injury worked as a cocktail waitress and art model and then in a stationery shop before becoming a stand-up comic and voice-over artist. After ten years on the UK comedy circuit, she became a script editor and then producer in BBC Radio Drama. This is her first novel. She lives in London with her husband, son and serial-killer cat.

lizwebb.co.uk
@LizzWebbAuthor